THE
MERCHANT
PRINCE

THE
MERCHANT
PRINCE

ARMIN SHIMERMAN
AND
MICHAEL SCOTT

POCKET BOOKS
New York   London   Toronto   Sydney   Singapore

POCKET BOOKS, a division of Simon & Schuster Inc.
1230 Avenue of the Americas, New York, NY 10020

ISBN: 0-671-03592-4

First Pocket Books hardcover printing June 2000

10 9 8 7 6 5 4 3 2 1

Printed in the U.S.A.

To Kitty, my inspiration and Saviour
                                    —A.S.

For Courtney and Piers
                                    —M.S.

I'd very much like to thank the band of brothers who helped make this journey with Dr. John Dee possible.

To the prime movers of the project, Michael P. Scott and Bill Fawcett, I owe everything. Michael's writing talent, hard work, and wicked wit inspired me during the course of our collaboration. He spurred me on to do better and think deeper. He discovered Dee in the history books and presented him to me. I am creatively forever in his debt. Bill, the godfather of this project, matched Michael and me perfectly and allowed me to fulfill a lifelong dream. He is the alpha and omega of the project. It was his decision to make a literary figure out of a Ferengi bartender.

I want to extend thanks to our secondaries as well. To my good friend Peter Jurasik, God bless you. To Craig Shapiro, my agent at Innovative Artists, who looked after the details. He did a great job. And to America Online, who dutifully delivered most of the pages.

To all, heartfelt thanks—take a bow.

—Armin Shimerman

In my long and often colorful life, I have been many things: magus and mathematician, alchemist and spymaster, a reluctant warrior, a competent assassin. I have been often a rogue and always a villain.

I am all of these...and none of them. They are a part of my character, but they are not the whole of it. In my heart, I am a merchant, a dealer in whatever makes a profit.

I am Dr. John Dee....

—*Mysteriorum liber primus, 1582*
Extract from the Day Booke of John Dee, Doctor

PROLOGUE

SKIN, DRIED TO BRITTLE hardness in the artificial atmosphere of the tiny craft, cracked and wept thin ichor as the creature unfolded itself from the protective webbing. There was a single instant of disorientation as its squat limbs adjusted to the gravity of the larger ship; then it straightened and stepped out into the perpetual crimson gloom that approximated the light of its homeworld. Slit-pupiled eyes flared. Nostrils opened to breathe in the rich lush soup of its homeland. Then it seemed to remember that although the dripping hallways looked empty, its every movement was under observation. It straightened and hurried down the corridor.

Rahu paused outside the circular door, waiting while the scanners ensured that he carried no weapons or explosives, and that he carried no filthy bacteria from the vile world he had just left behind. A tracery of blue lights danced over his body, then strobed through a score of colors while the examination continued for what seemed like an unusually long time. Almost unconsciously the creature's eyes sought out the tiny scar on the floor where the last ill-fated messenger had stood. There were rumors that it had been infected by something from the planet below, other rumors that it had carried an Earth weapon in an attempt to assassinate the Overlord. Whatever the truth, the messenger hadn't got past the door: the ragged remains of its hoof hooked between the floor plates were the only evidence that it had ever existed.

The dancing lights changed to a warm crimson and the doors hissed open. Masking his relief, Rahu stepped through into the dank twilight of the Overlord's quarters. Folding into the Posture of Obeisance, forehead to the wet floor, tail curled tightly around his legs, elbows tucked in against his chest, no talons or spurs showing, he waited.

Cloth hissed as the Xifo, Overlord of the Clan, approached.

Rahu's nostrils flared, reading the bittersweet odors of power, sensing his master's impatience and arrogance. Aware that the Xifo was standing directly over him, Rahu remained still and unmoving. A single twitch could be interpreted as a threat.

"I called you here because I did not want to entrust your report to the comms," the Xifo said abruptly, then turned and moved away, leaving Rahu crouched on the floor. "How goes our progress?"

Rahu remained motionless.

"You may speak," the Xifo added.

"I have followed your instructions, Overlord. I have chosen a human agent." Rahu concentrated on breathing evenly, but every breath was now an effort, as the Posture of Obeisance constricted his chest and closed off his gills. Even thinking was difficult.

"And you have contacted him?" As the Xifo approached the wall, the circular port irised open. Beyond the protective screen of asteroids that concealed the enormous ship, the planets were brilliant points of color strung out across the perpetual night. Try as he might, he could not pick out the planet he meant to conquer.

"Not directly, Overlord."

"Not directly . . ." There was a dangerous edge to the Xifo's voice.

"I have control of the communications and computer terminals of his servants and chattels. I have *allowed* them to discover certain pieces of information which will bring the project to a more speedy fruition."

"But you have not contacted the principal. Why?"

"This is a creature of arrogance and ignorance: he has little enough dealings with his own kind. He would not deal with us."

"Why feed the data in pieces to a servant? Why not simply give the master all that he needs?" the Xifo demanded.

"I gave the servants enough to get started," Rahu gasped, breathless. "The rest will be provided in time. My observations indicate that the humans feel more strongly about something they create themselves, rather than something they have been given. However, the Overlord is indeed wise. Of late, the master has become impatient with the slow progress; I have considered approaching him anonymously, presenting him with information which he can disseminate to his servants. If I judge his character correctly, it will appeal to his arrogance."

"But you said he would not deal with us . . ."

"He would not know we were his benefactors," Rahu hissed. "With your permission, I will contact him."

"Do it!" the Xifo snapped, turning away. "You are to be commended."

"My lord is generous in his praise." The Posture of Obeisance was killing him and Rahu knew he had less than eight hundred heartbeats of life left before the pressure of his ribs on his small lungs crushed them.

"So, how much longer will it take him to create the device?"

"As the humans measure time, two years, perhaps three."

"So fast?" The Xifo sounded genuinely surprised. "By the Gods, the Collegium should fall on their knees and thank us for what we are about to do. If we do not intervene now and stop them, then one day soon, these barbaric creatures will rise up and destroy us."

CHAPTER

1

VENICE, 1575

"I SAW THE WAY she measured you, Master." Fear stripped away the carefully cultivated French accent that years of travel had perfected, revealing the Irish brogue. "You have made a bitter enemy."

Dr. John Dee touched the edge of the quill to the ink block, then deliberately etched a graceful looping curl to the end of the paragraph. "I am well used to women taking my measure," he said absently. He dotted an *i* with a flourish, then dropped the pen to the table. Rubbing his hands briskly together, the spymaster broke off a piece of Venetian cheese from the wedge on the table before him. Its milky aroma filled his nostrils with delight, and he devoted his entire concentration to it as he savored the first bite. Then he sipped from the goblet of young Venetian wine. It was sour and tart, but once it was laid down for a couple of years, it would be very passable indeed. Dee nibbled some more cheese. It was said that the Old Ones, who had walked this world in the days following the Creation, dined only on cheese and wine. At that moment, he believed it was true.

"Master," Edward Kelly said evenly, "this be not some kitchen wench making eyes at you. This be one of the great Medici women."

"Be she the pretty one with the copper tresses?" Dee asked, his voice muffled and full of the soft runny cheese.

"No, Master," Kelly sighed, "the ember-haired one was her maid. The hook-nosed one was Marie, niece of the Grand Duke of Venice. His favorite niece," Edward Kelly added significantly.

The English ambassador licked the last vestiges of his lunch from his ink-stained fingers and returned to his writing table to finish his writing, then tapped his teeth with the end of the quill. "Ugly girl with unfortunate eyes?"

"I didn't notice her eyes," the big Irishman said. "I was too busy watching the way the Medici kept fingering her dago dagger. But I grant you, she was ugly," he added with a toothy grin. "God's blood, but was she ugly! What did you say to her to put her so out of her humor?"

John Dee carefully penned his signature mark and then rolled his governmental report into a hollow wooden tube whistle and tossed it to Kelly. Within the week it would reach the court at London, where it would no doubt be read and discussed by no less a personage than the Queen herself. Unfortunately he had little to add to his earlier reports, or at least nothing he wished his monarch to know about. Dee might be doing his duty by Her Majesty, but that did not prevent him from turning a small profit for himself. Business should never get in the way of trade. Dee folded away his writing box and began to clean his quill; then he suddenly smiled, his dark eyes dancing with amusement. Kelly caught the look and groaned. The last time he had seen that expression, they had barely escaped a French mob outside of Chenonceaux in the Val-de-Loire while attending one of Catherine the Florentine's grand *fetes champetres*.

"You remember now," Kelly demanded of the small man.

"She may have proffered an offer," Dee said mildly, "that I was unwilling to accept." He blew on the nib of the pen. The sound was a low lewd whistle.

Edward Kelly immediately turned away and began to pack a few items into a leather satchel, mumbling that if they left now, they might be out of Venice before the vengeance of the Medici descended on them. "Did she, or didn't she, make you an offer?" he demanded.

Dee came to his feet, pressing his hands into the small of his back, arching his spine, and stretched toward a low-hung ceiling he could never expect to reach. Kelly's orange-red hair brushed the filthy rafters, but even with the oversized heels of his boots, Dee barely stood five feet. Lifting a candle from the bedside table, he held it high and turned to examine his distorted reflection in the clumsy mirror. He was proud of what he saw there. At eight and forty—a respectable, even a venerable age—he still had a full head of hair. It was iron-gray now, of course, but he felt it lent his rather sharp features a measure of distinction, and emphasized his bright blue eyes.

"Master?" Kelly persisted. "What did that witch ask of you?"

"She made me an offer." The small man shrugged. "She was intrigued by my size. She added that she had never been serviced by a man so small and mayhap it might make a merry *divertissement.*"

"And your reply?"

"I pointed out that I had eyed many a midget at court and that it was unlikely that they were all eunuchs."

Kelly groaned aloud.

"I protested her flouting my size. Though I am slight of stature, I am perfectly formed. Wouldn't you say so?" he asked Kelly.

"Yea, verily," Kelly muttered.

"I moreover cited that I was an alchemist and a mathematician, and as such, almost priestlike in my celibacy."

"And she believed you?" Kelly asked in astonishment.

"Nay," Dee sighed. "She had heard rumor out of London."

"Which rumor?" Dee was the subject of many of the most bizarre rumors that circulated in London society. Dee suspected that Kelly knew the good doctor was himself the source of many of the stories. Only last season, an extraordinary tale had gone the rounds of society that he was more than friendly with the Virgin Queen.

"Tittle-tattle about me and the Queen," Dee muttered. "Utter madness."

"Oh. That rumor," the big man whispered, and crossed himself quickly. That rumor had almost had them killed, first by Elizabeth's supporters, then later by those friendly to the dead Scottish queen. Lifting the bag off the bed, he turned to the shuttered window, unlatched it, and eased it open. Venice, washed bloodred in the late-evening twilight, spread about before them, slender towers silhouetted against the sky. The effect was marred by the pall of gritty smoke that blanketed the city and obscured the top floors of some of the taller residences, and the silence was disturbed by the shrieks of pigeons soaring in and out of St. Mark's Square. Leaning out, he looked down. Ten feet below, filthy, foul-smelling, begrimed canal water lapped directly beneath their window.

Dee joined him and peered down, wrinkling his nose, nauseated at the stench. "The rankest compound of villainous smell that ever offended nostril," he muttered. "Can you swim?"

"Why?" Kelly asked.

"Because I cannot. So you will have to jump in, swim to yonder boat, row it back here, then keep it steady while I descend."

Kelly shook his head quickly. "That's a foolish waste of time. It would be more provident if we both jumped in and swam to the next walkway. I could keep you afloat." An enormous black rat crawled across a clotted mess of refuse and dropped into the oily water.

"I would rather bed Marie de' Medici," Dr. John Dee said simply. "Now, mind your master and fetch that boat. I shall scribble de' Medici a note of gramercy."

"As you wish, Master." Handing the leather satchel to Dee, Kelly tugged off his worn boots and climbed onto the window frame, turned so that he was facing into the room, and lowered himself into the water. He sank beneath the surface, the coagulated water barely registering a ripple. When his head broke the surface it was streaked with filth, his red hair and beard plastered to his skull and matted with rotten fruit and bird droppings.

Dee jerked his head back so that Kelly would not see the look of disgust and amusement on his face. He held him in too much esteem. He laid the satchel on the open window ledge and was reaching for a poncet of civet to take the stench of the water from his nostrils when the door cracked and splintered inward, and a score of guardsmen, wearing the distinctive blue livery of the Medici, burst into the room.

Instantly, Dee caught the worried eye of his manservant, Kelly, and then swiftly turned to face his intruders. As the soldiers advanced into the chamber facing the blinding sunset, they could not see what was directly behind the man at the window. Dee deftly elbowed the out-of-sight satchel over the window's ledge and out into the water. Although he was listening for a splash, he heard nothing and could only hope that Kelly had caught it. Folding his arms across his chest, he faced the soldiers with an arrogance that belied his height. Behind a barrier of lowered spears, he watched two of the guards professionally rip apart his room, scattering Dee's personal items and heaving Kelly's boots into a corner alongside the stinking chamber pot. There was a shout outside the door and the soldiers straightened imperceptibly as a very theatrical Marie de' Medici strode into the room, light running silver and rose-red off the naked blade of the assassin dagger in her hands. Elbowing past the soldiers, she stopped before Dee.

"Spy," she spat in his face. Lifting the knife, the buxom wall-eyed woman placed it against Dee's cheek. The point almost touched his left eye. He felt its heavy coldness, knew from its feather-light touch against his skin that it was razor sharp. When he had occasion to do bloody-handed work himself, he favored the Medici-style dagger, though he had never once considered that it would be used on him. The irony amused him and he was unable to prevent his lips from twitching in a smile. "You stand accused of spying for the Virgin Queen of England, of plotting against the Medici and Venice. What say you?"

Before he could respond, one of the soldiers brought over the wooden flute Kelly had left on the bed and handed it to the big woman. Smiling as she slowly withdrew her dagger's threat from Dee's face and sheathed it, Marie de' Medici snapped the instrument in half and pulled out the thin small sheet of parchment. She stared at it for a moment and frowned, bushy eyebrows meeting above her nose in a straight line as she scanned the lines of meaningless symbols inked onto the thin paper. Her unmasked anger was palpable.

Majesty, your humble servant begs to bring you the latest news from Italy. The line was in Enochian script.

"This is in code!"

"Is it?" Dee asked mildly.

"But this name here is clear enough, Dr. John Dee. What do you have to say, spy?" she hissed. "What do you have to say to me now?"

"Alas, make assay, my lady Urinal. Someday you will meet a midget without a sense of smell."

CHAPTER

2

"WE HAVE A PROBLEM."

"I don't want to hear about it." Dyckon ab-ack na Khar touched the screen, freezing the image. Was the character wearing the costume of the Second Dynasty, second period, or Second Dynasty, third period?

"A serious problem."

"I don't want to hear about it," Dyckon hissed. Second Dynasty, second period.

"You will want to hear about this."

"I doubt it." Without moving his body, the Roc swiveled his head to look at his fellow student. And, although they had spent four full cycles aboard the survey ship, Dyckon still hadn't bothered to remember the other's name. Fawg set-ut, perhaps? Set-set? He deliberately allowed his lips to peel back from his fangs in a calculated insult of the third degree. Tiny spots of purple appeared on the smaller Roc's bald skull, and the sacs beneath the red eyes darkened and filled with liquid. "What could be so important that it would drag me away from my work?"

Now it was Fawg set-ut's teeth that appeared, the insult even more deliberate and calculated. "Your pet is in trouble."

11

Dyckon looked at him blankly.

"Your Humani. He transgressed some incomprehensible rule and was instantly placed in a sealed cage without sustenance. Remarkably quick creatures," Fawg continued, turning away. "Everything they do is done at such speed. Decisions, birth, growth, achievement, punishment, and then they die. Do you know," he added, "that my studies have shown that these Humani have no resistance, no reserves? They can expire in a matter of their days if deprived of sustenance and liquid."

"Your studies!" Dyckon snarled. "You mean you snatched some and conducted experiments. Forbidden experiments."

"In the name of science," Fawg said insolently.

"I've spoken to you before about using them like this." Catching the smaller Roc, Dyckon spun him around, slamming him against the curving walls of the survey ship. Fawg's leathery hide slit, leaking yellow viscous fluid against the smooth metal. "Enough riddles. Tell me what you're talking about."

"Your pet Humani, Dee, will die. That is all there is to say."

Contact with the human race was strictly prohibited. But not unknown. Theirs was an extraordinary culture. Their development progressed at such a highly accelerated rate as to be almost incomprehensible to the older races that dominated the Core Worlds that made up the Collegium. They had been discovered very early on in their evolution by a lost Roc trading ship. The humans then had been little more than thoughtless apes, and the tall, attenuated Roc, with their vestigial horns, serpentine tails, and retractable wings, had entered the locals' primitive mythology, as had some of the other races who had scouted the newly discovered planet at the edge of the galaxy. Once it had been logged and mapped, the area had then been sealed and the primitives allowed the necessary time to begin their growth and development. However, because of the extraordinary nature and progress of the primitives, the scholarly Roc had been granted the privilege of studying them. Generations of the long-lived Roc who had established their academic reputations based upon their studies of primitive races now turned their attention to the

Humani. Much could be learned from these primitive races, data which the older races had long since forgotten. The prime tenet of the Roc was to observe, but never interfere. Interference with the species of an experiment invalidated the results.

It had been a tenet Dyckon chose to ignore.

Despite the swiftness of the Humani's lives, the Roc was impatient. Whereas he was fully conscious of the honor of being one of the six chosen to lead the ongoing observation of the Humani, he chafed at the restrictions of life aboard the modified shuttlecar, which had been embedded into a crater on the moon overlooking the planet. The shuttlecar observatory was now several Roc generations old, made when the primitives were still climbing down from the trees. Facilities were basic and, because the Humani were beginning to develop rudimentary lenses capable of looking at their nearest heavenly neighbor, the Collegium had banned all unnecessary traffic on and around the planet. Only essential supplies of food and equipment were permitted. In the last few decades conditions had deteriorated aboard the craft. Determined to make his report as quickly as possible and thereby get home all the sooner, Dyckon decided on an audacious plan: he would make contact with one of the Humani, observe him at very close hand, manipulate and maneuver him and note his reactions. The Roc would then be able to accomplish within the dazzlingly short lifetime of a single primitive what would normally take four or five generations of careful observation. The acclamation he would receive when he returned home with his results would be well worth the risk he took in defying the interference tenet. But for the experiment to succeed, Dyckon needed an extraordinary subject.

And, in an age of extraordinary Humani, Dyckon chose one of the most extraordinary, Dr. John Dee, alchemist and astrologer, mathematician and magician to the court of Elizabeth, the Virgin Queen of England. The man was a genius—a rogue and a villain too—and he was the key to Dyckon's advancement. If he allowed his pet to die, he would have to start all over again.

CHAPTER

3

OFTEN, WHILE EXPERIMENTING with the age-old mystery of raising the dead, Dee contemplated what his own death might be. Elizabeth might arbitrarily find fault with him, as had been her wont with others, and he might feel the dull, cold steel of the axman. But somehow he thought it unlikely; Elizabeth needed him, or at least he liked to think that she needed him. Why, had he not prepared her horoscope on three separate occasions, and been spectacularly correct each time? Had he not chosen the most auspicious day of her coronation? No, Good Queen Bess, despite her learning—or perhaps because of it—held him and his arcane arts in respect. The manner of his death would most likely be poison or treachery, though he had always secretly harbored the fantasy of dying as an old man surrounded by children, grandchildren, and his dogs. The servants would be hushed and somewhere an old woman would be keening. Then, from without, there would be the jingle of harness, and the assembled family would part to reveal the august presence of Her Majesty, who would have made the supreme effort of traveling from London to Mortlake to pay her last respects to one of the grand old men of England. It would be a grand death, worthy of a masque, or an epic poem perhaps. Once on a blissful occasion the fantasy had so overpowered him that he had spent the entire month of April composing an elegy in iambic pentameter to be read over his grave. He had committed it to the fire when he realized that he did not want to be remembered as a maudlin second-class poet, but rather as a first-class mathematician and magician.

But he had never imagined himself walled up in a damp, black reeking tower, starving to death in godforsaken Venice. It was numbingly cold. His tattered raiment provided no respite for the arthritic iciness that lapped his curled body. He needed to move or he would cramp. The small man moved stiffly. Every bone, every sinew, every muscle was aflame with pain, but he welcomed the pain: it meant he still lived. He mentally tested each fragment of himself as it came into play as he forced himself to stand erect. Pressing his hands flat against his rib cage, he traced the curl and line of each bone with sensitive fingers, checking for broken bones or cracked ribs. Every breath was a gasp and a groan of effort, but when he achieved his full height, he found he could breathe deeply. He was bruised, but his ribs were mercifully unbroken.

Even in pain, he chortled, "These Medici torturers are amateurs," and then the smile faded. Or perhaps they were under instructions not to seriously injure him. No doubt Elizabeth would have his bones returned to England; she would want to see that each was intact and unbroken. Perhaps these Medici were not amateurs after all. Damn their eyes! Pressing the palm of his hand against the rough stones, he scraped off the moisture and pressed it to his cracked and chapped lips. In the pitch black of the sealed room, a creature skittered across the straw and Dee felt his stomach rumble. It burned with enforced abstinence. Yet, strangely, he had no desire for food. He had been here three days—or was it four? Moving as a blind man, hands stretched before him, he felt around the wall until he touched the fresh stone and damp mortar where the Medici artisans had walled up the portal. To the left of the door, his long, narrow fingers traced four vertical lines. Four days then. Four tollings of

St. Mark's announcing Matins prayers. He wondered how many Matins he could survive.

In the shabby attic room at the southern edge of St. Mark's Square, Edward Kelly carefully worked a mixture of soot and ink into a paste and applied it to his bright red hair and beard. The authorities were on the lookout for the red-haired Irishman, and his coloring was unusual enough to make him stand out among these swarthy Mediterraneans. Through the tiny slit window he could see the smoke from the fires of the dungeon where his master, John Dee, had been originally taken. Venice was agog with the story, and tales of Dee's torture were growing with every telling. It was said that first the branding irons had been unable to mar his skin, and subsequently that his bones hadn't broken on the rack, but rather that the rack itself had been torn apart. All they could do was to wall him up in the Western Tower and wait for his magic to diminish, for everyone knew that if the demons did not practice their evil art, then they became less powerful and vulnerable to human weapons. It was whispered that all Angleterres were in league with Beelzebub, that their queen was the Witch of Endor, that Dee was a magician, a sorcerer, a devil, or worse.

Kelly knew that Dee was nothing more than a man, a brilliant man, an extraordinary man, but a man nonetheless, human and all too frail, with an inordinate fondness for honey and fresh milk, and who lavished more love on his dogs than on any human. The big Irishman had seen his master weep publicly at the death of Hector, one of his favorite hounds—and had seen him order an assassination without a second thought. The very idea of John Dee broken on the rack angered and sickened Kelly. He itched for vengeance, but he was also a practical man. There was nothing he could do alone without risking himself. His duty now was to carry out Dee's last orders. He would return to the court of the Virgin Queen, deliver the coded message, and report to her what had happened. Perhaps she would declare war on Venice—but somehow Kelly doubted it. She wouldn't risk losing a frigate from her expensive navy. She would need it to fight the growing Spanish Armada if it ever came to that. No, Elizabeth was far too practical. She would probably order the assassination of a handful of the Medici and seize some of their holdings in London. It seemed a small enough price for the life of such an extraordinary man. Perhaps the Queen would instruct him to assassinate one of the Medici, but even if she didn't, then in a year or two, Kelly would return to Venice and exact a fitting price for his master's death. He would start with that ugly Medici bitch! Revenge should be cold and unexpected, Dee had been fond of saying. Curiosity had got him into this situation. Prayer and remorse would have to get him out.

Dee carefully etched another notch in the door, scraping the line with a sliver of stone. He had always been curious. In a lesser man the curiosity would have led to trouble, but Dee had been able to temper it with education, and had then used that education to direct his curiosity into areas that were dangerous and prohibited. Mathematics and astrology had always interested him, the extraordinary power of numbers and the obvious influence of the stars on the lives of humans. It was only logical that he would be drawn to the related arts of magic and alchemy—and the rather more practical world of espionage. He had successfully served both Mary Tudor and Elizabeth—one of the few men to survive the bloody transition with head and reputation intact—and had nominated the most propitious day for the Virgin Queen's coronation. He stood high in her esteem for that, and as long as she and her land were prosperous, she considered him her lucky charm. Sometimes, when she was maudlin, she called him her Merlin. Dee was unsure whether to be pleased or not.

Another rat squeaked in the corner and for an instant Dee thought he saw red eyes gleaming in the absolute blackness. He knew the creatures were getting bolder, and he wondered how long it would be before they swarmed over him while he slept. How often in Mortlake, where he lived, had he attended to villagers who had been attacked by rats while they slept, and lost fingers or toes or portions of their ears to the starving rodents. Sinking slowly to the damp, befouled, straw-covered ground, he rested his head against the cold stone wall. He felt moisture on his cheek and brushed angrily at it—then brought his fingertips to his lips, tasting the salt. 'Sblood! This was not how a man should die. Not in some foul hellhole, eaten alive by Medici rats. "Probably the best meal they'll ever have," he said aloud, startled by the cracked sound of his own voice. Then he laughed, the sound high-pitched and cackling.

The Medici guards standing on the outside of the sealed room crossed themselves at the sound and moved a little farther from the door.

CHAPTER

4

WHEN HE'D BEEN LITTLE more than a hatchling, Dyckon had found a talon lizard. It had lost a wing and a hind leg and was unable to fly or crawl, and though he knew it was cruel, he had kept the tiny iridescent creature, nurturing it with fresh fruit and flesh and tiny droplets of his own pale ichor.

When it had grown to the length of his arm, he had lost interest in the creature. It was too big now to keep in a cage, and too dangerous to allow to run about the den loose, so Dyckon had brought it out to the sand pits that bordered the Roc warrens and released it to its destiny. He had taken perhaps a dozen steps when he heard its high-pitched, anguished whining. The lizard had slid between two very tall and deep slabs of solidified salt and become lodged in the middle. Missing its powerful hind leg, it couldn't push its way out, and the gap was too narrow for Dyckon to reach in and dislodge it. And to Dyckon's great surprise, he hadn't the stomach to kill it or, worse, to forget it. What happened next both amazed and shamed him. It was a basic tenet of the Roc faith to accept the whims of fate that occurred to lesser creatures . . . which effectively meant all those creatures that had not been blessed by being born Roc.

19

Rocs were not to interfere with the mystery of Life; merely to observe and record and remember. To change the direction of a single creature in a microcosm was sure to destroy the direction of the Way of the macrocosm. It would have been merciful to kill the creature. But his upbringing and religion forbade that. He was forced to remember. So every day he returned to the warren's edge and attempted to feed the lizard. But to no avail; it was too far out of reach, and every day its cries of entrapment and hunger grew weaker and weaker, until the morning of the fourth day he had returned to find the talon lizard still and unmoving in the crevice. Only its eyes were bright with the last remnant of its life—and tiny fire spiders were already feasting off its still-living flesh. The lizard's half-dead lidless eyes held Dyckon accountable. Never to be forgiven.

He'd taken an oath then never to keep pets. Hunched in a scarred chair in his quarters, Dyckon sat silent and brooding as he watched the solid-seeming holo image of Dee curled in a position of huddled repose in his living tomb. How much longer had he left? Dyckon knew that there was research to be done, that he should ignore the petty creature and move on about his business, but he could not take his thoughts away from the tableau that was being staged before him. The emotions that twisted within him were strange, bittersweet; looking at the Humani, he kept seeing the accusing gaze of the long-dead but never forgotten talon lizard. There was no doubt about it—he felt sympathy for the man. But how was that possible?

The Humani was nothing, a worm, a fly, an amoeba. How was it possible to have feelings for an amoeba? With a sudden slash, his deeply curved talons passed through the shivering figure of Dr. John Dee that sat so lifelike on the small circular table before him. Dyckon cursed himself for the feelings he had. These feelings were unworthy of him, unworthy of any Roc.

When had his relationship with the Humani changed? Dee was a primitive, as far below the Roc as the Humani was above the Earth ape of the trees, but there was something about John, something wild and delightful and worthy of respect. He was intelligent, quick and curious—insatiably curious. He was vain

20

about his studies and boasted to the Roc of his pitifully small powers of observation. He was ridiculous in his appreciation of himself.

Dyckon's mouth gaped, showing his teeth in a gesture he had learned from the Humani. Maybe that was what had attracted him to the Humani: Dee possessed all the qualities of a good Roc. And whereas, without exception, the other Humani had run screaming from any appearance by the Roc, Dee had accepted Dyckon's first appearance—a misty shape in a fly-spotted mirror—with a barely surprised gasp and a thousand questions.

However, Dyckon had taken the precaution of projecting the image of a white-haired androgynous Humani onto the mirror's surface; on the rare occasions when the Roc came down to Earth, their physical appearance had reduced the Humani observers to gibbering fools. And every race, in every time, had a name for what they had seen; they called them demons. The good doctor had been hunting after gods and devils, angels and demons all his life; why then should he be surprised when the image of an angel suddenly manifested itself in his shaving mirror one cold December morning?

Without blinking, his razor poised over his cheek, Dee had bowed slightly, said, "I welcome you, Spirit of the Air," and then asked, "Why me?"

The angel in the mirror smiled, its eyes golden, its face serene. "Because you are an exceptional man, Dr. John Dee. You are a man of learning, of knowledge, and position. You have access to the great and the lowly and are accepted by both. And you are a man of infinite curiosity. That curiosity has led you down many paths, places your fellow Humani have not traveled, but it has taught you much about the nature of the Humani. And that is something I wish to learn. I have many questions about your people, and you may ask of me what you will. We will trade, you and I, story for story, tale for tale. You will satisfy my curiosity, and I will satisfy yours. But, be aware, Dr. John Dee, that what I tell you no one will believe!"

Dyckon was constantly surprised by the small man. They had been communicating for less than half a solar year, when the magician mastered a smattering of *rhe'enoch*, the official language of the Roc, and, quaintly, had attempted to present his reports to Dyckon in the Roc's own language.

"Mathematics," Dee had explained, when Dyckon had complimented him upon the achievement. "I have spent my life designing codes and ciphers; I found your language to be no different."

Perhaps it was then that Dyckon's own feelings had gotten the better of him. This Humani so desperately wanted to learn, to understand, to partake in the mysteries of the unknown. His thirst for knowledge was incredible, insatiable. There was an ancient Roc song cycle, sung by the Mothers to all fledglings, entitled "The Fledgling of Ten Thousand Questions." Listening to Dee make his report in halting *rhe'enoch*, and then follow it with question tumbled upon question, Dyckon was reminded of the lilting songs, and of his birth mother. He had not thought of her for millennia. The memory was pleasant.

The relationship changed as time went by. They became—Dyckon's mouth shaped the alien word—friends. Soon, Dyckon was telling Dee far more than the doctor was reporting back, and in order to facilitate communication, he had presented the Humani with a primitive communication device: a T-class flat screen, whose liquid technology had faded almost to the point of invisibility. Dee out of his ignorance had simply christened this Roc communicator an enchanted mirror, and had immediately constructed an elaborate series of magical rituals around its use. The Roc had observed the ceremonies and noted in an official Collegium thesis how all Humani cloaked everything they did not yet understand with rites and called it religion. And while on an abstract level the Roc understood the Humani concept of gods and devils, he could not, at first, comprehend the Humani psychological need for them. Like most of the advanced civilizations, the Roc had long ago lost the fascination for gods.

And yet looking at the Humani, Dyckon began to understand that it was this very need to worship, to pay homage to a greater being, that enabled and allowed many of the Humani to achieve great things. "They drive themselves nearly to madness with striving to grasp the as yet unknown. They do it in order to pierce the veil of their God's domain. This they do in the name of their God, who ironically asks absolutely nothing of them but to love one another." It was obvious the Humani consciousness preferred stress over bliss.

When Dee was at home at Mortlake, on the island kingdom known as England, he would report every night at midnight, staring intently into the silvery black surface of the viewing screen of his magical mirror and starting their communications by mumbling non sequiturs from the moribund Latin. Dyckon had originally found himself openly laughing at the little man's mysticism but then found himself looking forward to the witty and insightful reports on the court of Elizabeth, her courtiers, and the common people.

Dyckon was particularly interested in this period of history; instinctively he knew that this was a tremendously exciting time for the Humani race. For the first time since the fall of the Ancient Civilizations of Hyborea, Greece, Atlantis, and Aegypt, the world was awakening again, stretching out, discovering and rediscovering new lands. New continents were being mapped, and almost every tide brought a ship laden with new fruits and vegetables, exotic animals, and even more exotic human races to England. For the first time in endless generations, the Humani saw their world as a wondrous place. Their imaginations took flight, and they felt nothing was beyond their aspirations.

When had he become fond of Dee? At what moment had he stopped thinking of him as a pet and started to think of him as a friend? What was the cause that had made him realize just how much he looked forward to communicating with the Humani? When he had begun to become bored with the rest of his work, perhaps?

There were times when his contact with Dee was the only thing that made this never-ending mission bearable. John Dee's wit, his cunning, his zest for life, had excited something in the Roc. And Dee made him laugh. It had been a long time since he had laughed. And now his friend was walled up alive, condemned to a maddening, wasting, and agonizing death. On the planet far below, the holo image looked up, seeming to stare straight into Dyckon's slit-pupiled eyes. Dee would surely be dead within a day, perhaps two. Already the Roc could see the deterioration of Dee's physical presence. John's flesh was a sickly yellowish blue hue, deep black rings encircled his rheum-encrusted eyes, and his mane of hair hung limp and sticky wet. His always neatly maintained beard was now a haven for spittle, grease, and secretions. In the last few hours, the prisoner had developed a constant habit of biting at it while he feverishly scratched at the vermin that now openly crawled through it. Tufts of it scattered on Dee's shoulders and about his feet. The wounds from the rack were filled with white pus and oozed, and soon maggots would hatch and crawl in the cuts.

Dyckon sat back into the chair, high shoulders digging deep into the faded metallic cloth, the worn material parting and hissing foul gases. The Roc brought his hooked talon to his mouth, needlelike teeth unconsciously nibbling on the hooked spurs. A nictitating white membrane slid across his eyes over and over again. He was a study in concentration. And once again he was a hatchling, listening to his pet lizard scream in agony. Dee hadn't cried out.

Not yet anyway.

He had all the pride of the Humani; he would not allow Catherine de' Medici that particular pleasure. But Dyckon knew that even if Dee denied her that wish, the Humani would still die in agony. Dyckon fought desperately to regain his equanimity. Regain his emotional control. He was Roc. A proud member of one of the oldest, most powerful races in the Collegium of Worlds. He must forget the amoeba and move on. Every tenet of his philosophy thundered that. But this was no longer philosophy. This was no longer theoretical. Dyckon watched the screen, which showed Dee in the Medici tower. Dyckon found himself staring into the doctor's gray eyes. The eyes. There was so much pain there. Dyckon had seen those gray eyes bright with curiosity, alive with humor. Now they burned with pain, and soon they would grow dull and glassy and the light would go out of them. Could he allow that? To make any contact with the Humani was strictly forbidden. The Roc's savage teeth bared in a smile. Hadn't he broken that rule already? The Roc High Council and the Collegium were a timeless vastness away. Who would ever know? Could he get away with it? The punishment for such disobedience was unthinkable. It would be the ruination not only of himself but of his family as well. The Roc sat forward and stared intently at the holo image of his friend on the planet far below. Dee was now slumped forward, panting from the wet cold, arms tightly wrapped around his shins trying to conserve body heat, a once proud head, weary of its own weight, resting on his withering knees. And in the corners of the room, the rats were gathering.

Dyckon remembered the fire spiders eating the still-living flesh of his trapped pet. He remembered the look of silent horror in its eyes.

In the walled-up chamber below, the rats crept closer.

CHAPTER

5

THE OLD VENETIAN STRODE down the shadowy corridor, arthritic hip snapping with every step he took, the iron ferrule of his thick walking stick beating a tattoo on the smooth pavement flags, which echoed back off the bare walls. His every gesture radiated rage, and a high color had flushed his normally pallid cheeks.

"You are a fool," Cosimo de' Medici spat without turning his head. "An unthinking fool."

Francesco de' Medici chewed on his bottom lip and said nothing. His father had just broken the first rule of the Medici hierarchy: never to speak ill of another family member in the presence of an outsider. The hatchet-faced man glanced sidelong at the Turkish guards who accompanied his aged father everywhere. He was sure he could see the contempt and amusement in their eyes. He knew they would never speak what they had just heard; neither possessed a tongue, but he knew that they would never forget—nor would he. Taking a deep breath, Francesco controlled his rage, comforting himself with the thought that his father was an old man and would not live to see another year. Neither would his infidel servants. He, personally, would reinstitute the Egyptian custom of burying the slaves with the master.

"This man Dee is a spy," he said evenly, "and he improperly propositioned Marie."

Cosimo's laugh was harsh, without humor. "Your daughter's reputation has reached me in Tuscany; even the muckrakers talk of her. It is said that she could put Messalina to shame."

"Dee is a spy of the English Queen," Francesco continued evenly, ignoring the barb. "He was caught, tried, and punished accordingly."

The old man paused before he began the long climb up the stairs, and rounded on his son. "I don't care if you caught him with the keys to the treasury, having just swived your daughter on the steps of the cathedral. Release him before it is too late. You jeopardize us all. This is no common man. This is Dr. John Dee; he is a respected man of learning, education, and science. Moreover, he is friend not only to the English Queen, but to half the monarchs in Europe." He started his climb up the stair by placing his stick on the next highest step and pulling himself up. The Turks, like obedient hounds, waited patiently, expecting a summons to assist the Patriarch. But it never came. They knew then that he was in foul humor indeed. Someone would suffer and die this day. The elder Medici whirled in place and, with a look of dread Francesco had never seen, added bitterly, "He is also a powerful alchemist and magician. My own sources tell me that he has raised the dead and that he talks to angels in his scrying mirror. This is not a man to have as an enemy."

This time Francesco allowed the sneer to show openly on his face. "He is nothing more than a charlatan."

Cosimo stopped. He was standing two steps above his son. Without looking at either of the guards, he said, "Walk away. Do not look back."

The Turks climbed three steps, then stood with their back to the old man, heads bent, hands on their curved scimitars.

Francesco watched them with alarm. He could feel the pressure of the dagger he wore strapped to his forearm, hidden by his long sleeve, but knew it would be little use against the two bodyguards.

Cosimo stared at his son. His lip twitched, peeling back to show rotten teeth, and then, without warning, he cracked his hand across his son's face, leaving the impression of his fingers clearly delineated against the dark skin. "Never question me," he hissed, "never doubt me." Turning away, he strode past the guards, who obediently fell into step behind him. "Your stupidity is intolerable. I fear for the survival of this family when I am gone."

Rubbing his face, Francesco mounted the stairs to follow. While the two guards had not witnessed his humiliation, they knew of it; he wondered if he could risk having them killed before they left with his father for Tuscany.

Cosimo tapped and wheezed his way up the stairs. "Whose idea was it to put him in the tower anyway?" he muttered. He glanced quickly over his shoulder. "We cannot afford a war with the English. We cannot afford to have them cannoning our fleet."

"We would crush them."

"Perhaps. But war with the English bitch would be costly in craft and men. Elizabeth has spent much to create a powerful fleet and she has gifted mariners to call upon. We can match her with neither." Cosimo's breath was beginning to come in great heaving gasps as he climbed the stairs.

"Would England risk it all for this one man?"

Francesco had heard the rumors, and while he personally doubted the stories about Dee, the Church preached the existence of demons and devils and angels, so there might be truth to the story.

"There was a princeling in the French court, a fop with the manners of a swine," Cosimo said. "He insulted this man Dee, called him, as you have, a charlatan, mocked him openly at court. Dee played the saint, smiled, and said nothing, but his right hand was said to have gesticulated as if with the palsy. The movement might have gone unnoticed, but this was Dr. John Dee, remember, and people remarked upon the sudden movement. The following day the princeling vanished. He had gone to his bedchamber and fastened the door as was his wont. On the morrow, when the servants eventually broke into his room, it was found to be empty except for a single heavenly white dove that fluttered wildly about the ceiling." Cosimo paused on the top step to glance over his shoulder at his son. "And, lest you doubt this tale, let me add that I was at the French court when this happened. I myself examined the room. It was locked from the inside, and there was a sheer drop to the courtyard below. There was no human way in or out of that room. This man is not to be trifled with."

Francesco coughed gently, pressing his left hand to his mouth, and surreptitiously pressing his lips to the ornate ring on his thumb. The ring contained a tiny fragment of the True Cross and was a powerful relic. "But if Dee be an intimate of Heaven," he said, as they came out onto the landing, "why then does he languish in his cell?"

"Why indeed?" Cosimo wheezed. He stood, leaning on his walking stick, staring at the new plaster and ornate brickwork that filled the doorway of the tower room where it had been walled up. He fixed the eldest of the four guards who were gathered in front of the door with his grim and baleful stare. "Report," he commanded.

The man hesitated. "There is naught to report, sir."

The youngest guard, who did not know how much danger he was putting himself into by speaking to the Grand Duke without first being addressed, pushed forward. "On the first day, we heard the Englishman talk and laugh and once he seemed to be praying. Twice we thought he was in conversation, but we could hear no replies to his questions. For the last two days we have heard nothing."

"No other noises? No sounds of demons, no smells?"

"No screams, no cries of Jesu, no pleadings at the door?" snickered Francesco.

"Nothing, sirs, perhaps he has . . ." the young man began, and then stopped, head tilted to one side, listening.

"What is it?" Cosimo snapped, tilting his head to listen, but his ears were not as keen as they had once been and he heard nothing.

Rock scraped, mortar trickled and ran.

"What . . . ?" Cosimo asked again, watching the guards press back from the door. He was aware that something was happening, that they could hear something from within. He was about to demand an explanation when he stopped.

Dust was spiraling down from above, drifting across his eyes, gathering on his long, infamous, and much-mocked nose. There was a crack—the sound of a stone being split in half—and suddenly the entire building shuddered. Spiderwebs of cracks raced across the ceiling, chunks of it snapping off to hail down into the corridor amid a fine powdery snow of plaster. The eldest guard squealed with terror and turned to run, brushing past Cosimo, who recoiled with disgust. He was immediately cut down by one of the Turks.

"Break it down," Cosimo croaked, white spittle gathered at the corners of his mouth. "Break it down. Break down the door." Stepping forward, he rammed the end of his walking stick against the new bricks, but the sound was lost in a terrible rending as if the entire city were being brought down.

CHAPTER

6

EXTRACT FROM A LETTER written in code from Edward Kelly to Sir Walter Raleigh at the Court of Elizabeth of England:

Sir,

Once again I must entrust you to pass on this message to her most gracious and reverend majesty's Privy Council. On this occasion I am unsure if the tidings I impart be good or ill. All of Venice is afire with rumour, and no doubt in the days and weeks hereafter you will hear much discrepancy of what I am to tell you. No doubt it will be curiously embellished and embroidered, for even now—and it not past one hour since the event—I have begun to hear new versions of the tale.

But what is writ here be true, so help me, Jesu.

In my last missive, I unfolded to you that my Master was taken by the Medici. Well, our John Dee is free. Though, where he is I cannot say, nor have I the wit to speculate. Suffice it that I pray for his soul. Even as I set these words down, it maddens my mind and makes me reach for the wine, though I swear to you, by my hope for God's mercy, that there is no wine talking in this tale. It is incredible and bizarre and harrowing to the ken of mankind and, yet, it is. My own eyes beheld the truth of it.

I do not know what magic he worked within his cell, nor am I privy to how he worked his conjurations for he was in want of the implements of his Art. Yet, wondrously, my master called upon his Spirits of the Air and they abetted him.

It was close to the time of midday when the miracle happed. I can call it nothing other. All of Venice knew that the elder Duke, Cosimo himself, father to the present Duke, had made the arduous trip from the North to order my master's release. These Medici are byzantine in their secrets, but this city is so internuncial that nothing can remain unspoken for long. Cosimo was out of all humour and mightily moved that Dee had been imprisoned; Francesco was in a rage that his father was about to countermand his effected edict. The blow to his pride and honour was unprecedented. I have it on good authority that the two were about the cell door when my Master swelled to his full glory and took his leave. I was watching the palazzo when first I was aware of the Leviathan in the sky.

Long, slender, like a poignard's blade, it manifested out of the sun, falling like God's own dagger to the earth. As it drew nigh the earth, it o'ershadowed the sun. As it closed upon the tower, I began to itemise as I had been taught by my master:

Item: This Angelic Boat was fashioned of a silver metal and was sans window nor door, nay nor any other opening.

Item: I beheld neither sails nor oars. It halted in the firmament above the tower, and rocked gently from side to side, as a boat riding out small waves

Item: There was a humming sound, though that was mayhap a trick of mine ears, for no-one else reported this sound and I may have confused it with the moans of fear and terror that cried throughout the city.

Item: A purple light, which I will wager was no thicker than my wrist, flew straight and narrow from the bow of this craft. It lighted on the statue of Saint Peter which commands the uppermost point of the palazzo's tower, and in less time than it takes to fashion these words, the saint's head was sliced off as neatly as if it had been cut with a knife. I heard tell a Moorish fish-monger was crushed by it on the street below. His family have adjudged it a sign and converted to the True Faith.

Item: The purple light touched the roof, and the tiles gave up their wonted shape and ran liquid. Sweet Jesu, it chills me to re-member it. The tiles poured in a crimson cascade down the side of the building, then, like wax spilled from a candle, solidified before it reached the ground. It remains still. I quaked with the fear of God and his final judgement and knew not why I could not run, but stood as if transfixed by the sight.

Item: There was steam everywhere, billowing up around the silvery craft, as roof tiles, stones and mortar, bubbled and boiled. Before the cloud of vapours swallowed the airy vision I could see that the monstrous purple light was eating away the roof of the tower.

My Lord, I swear upon what is most Holy, less than a dozen heartbeats later, the cloud was gone. And with it vanished too the craft, and the roof of my Master's captivity. The sun shone unpartnered in the sky. From afar, the tower looked for all the world like an old candle after hours of late study. Even before the wild reports raced through the city, I knew that my master, Doctor John Dee, would not be found. He had made his escape. I only wish I knew how and when we will see him again; in all the years I knew him, I never saw him demonstrate such power-ful magic, but I am mindful that there was much that he did not tell me.

I fear he is gone now, Sir. To Heaven or Hell, I know not; I can but hope for one and fear the other. I ask only that he be re-membered in your prayers, as he is in mine.

I remain, Sir, your most humble and obedient servant, Ed-ward Kelly, in the service of Doctor John Dee and Her Royal Majesty, Elizabeth, in the Year of Our Lord, Fifteen Hundred and Seventy-Five.

CHAPTER

7

THERE WAS ONE ADVANTAGE to this antiquated technology, Dyck-on decided, lifting off the front panel to expose the ship's in-nards. A long-taloned finger carefully probed through the arrangement of crystal geodes while he consulted an old schematic displayed on his handheld pad, looking for access to the memory banks. He would never be able to do this with one of the new Collegium ships, which were grown and harvested in single units. The extruded fluids and fats melded together around the power units and memory banks, creating something that the Roc thought had all the appearance and texture of a particularly disgusting internal organ.

Before they had begun to use organics, ships were still con-structed from crystal, metal, and lumolics by craftsmen who took pride in their work. Nowadays, engineers had been re-placed by surgeons who cut and grafted the soft flesh with white-light scalpels, fluids puddling around their feet. Dyckon often wondered if the ships felt pain as they were being cut open, but he'd been too embarrassed to ask, though he had fi-nally concluded that anything that bled felt pain.

The Roc poked each of the data-recording crystals in turn, eyes fixed on the screen before him, images flickering into existence as his talons moved over the pink geodes and angular facets. The day-to-day minutiae of the ship—times and dates, temperatures, gravity, air pressure, humidity—were superimposed over fuzzy holographic images. The crystals were glazed and needed cleaning, but clear enough to provide a record of everything that had happened to the station and the shuttlecraft. And there were some things he did not want to leave a record of.

There! His talon had scraped the last geode and the images had appeared, flickered, and vanished. Dyckon curled his claw around the pink crystal and immediately the log, as well as the visuals of the shuttle's recent movements, popped up on-screen. The Roc observed the images silently, no longer wondering whether he had done the right thing: he was regretting it already. Regretting it bitterly. On the screen, the exterior monitors showed the pod-bay door opening and one of the small circular runabouts appearing, engines on silent running.

The images diverged at this point, one continuing to monitor the ship, the second following the runabout. Dyckon ran his talon along the length of the crystal, seeking the data streams he needed. They were just there, close to the base. It was all here, enough to ruin him: the records of the shuttle's locking on to the planet below, the calculations and orders for sliding through the layers of atmosphere, the fuel allotment for angling toward a leg-shaped chunk of landmass, the approach and traversing across a red-roofed cityscape toward a single tower, the initiating codes and purple light of the mining scalpel dancing across the roof of the tower, boiling the tiles to mud, turning the stone liquid.

Dyckon watched himself standing at the door of the ship. This had been the toughest part. He knew from his studies that the appearance of the spacecraft would cause terror in the city below. The people would panic and scamper, but would also keep their eyes averted Earthward away from the heavenly body, afraid to look upward lest they be blinded. More important, since this age predated sophisticated imaging techniques, there would be no visual record, other than perhaps a drawing or sketch by some artist—if he dared!

However, Dyckon was reasonably certain that should there be a Collegium investigation in the future, the authorities could never be absolutely sure that it had been a Roc ship. No way to lay the blame at his perch. The thorny part was that he'd needed to personally fly to the tower below, to save his friend. There was no other way; he could not remotely control the craft through the atmosphere, and the mining scalpel needed a precise touch. One false move and he could have carved Dee into neatly cauterized pieces. But coming to the Earth personally had been a terrible risk. If enough Humani saw him, it could create disastrous mythological and religious complications. His appearance would generate proof positive for their devils. They would cower for aeons. And he would be responsible for altering the development and direction of a sentient race.

And all for one man. Was he worth it? No, not for one man: for a friend.

And yes, he was worth it. Friendship was the one peculiar, ephemeral link that bound individuals and races within the Collegium of Worlds. It was friendship that kept the Collegium intact.

Dyckon had deliberately come out of the direction of the sun to blind those who might be brave enough to stare at the disturbance in the sky. He reduced power to the shields and deflectors, so that the craft heated up and steamed in the cool air, then cut the engines to impulse power. But he knew that, despite his best precautions, there was no disguising the fact that he was going to melt a stone tower in the middle of one of the most densely populated cities in Europe. Timing was also crucial; he knew he needed to get to Dee before Dee was beyond his help medically. Once he started burning in the slates and stones, the atmosphere in the cage would turn toxic, and there was bound to be some danger from splashes of liquid stone. This would all be for nothing if Dee expired.

Dyckon angled the sensors downward, checking to insure that none of the Humani were looking. They should be cowering in terror, their eyes covered, but far too many of the stupid man-apes kept looking up at the ship.

Who were these Venetians that they did not let their superstitions get the better of them? Most screamed and fled as they should. But he certainly saw those who cowered and studied. He knew they could not see him—he was in the darkness of the craft—but once he stepped out, what then?

Dyckon's bile rose and choked him as he thought of how stupid this rescue was. But it was too late now, he'd come this far and he was so very close; he could not abandon it now. Locking the craft into position, he stood and pressed open the door. His craft was hovering at the apex of the tower—or rather, where the apex had been. The scalpel had burned it away to bubbling froth. There was a gap three times his own height between the edge of his craft and the ruined roof, and although he could easily leap the distance, he would be exposed to the onlookers below while he was in the air. Far below him, another chunk of bubbling stone splashed into the canals and a plume of steam curled slowly upward, creeping along the tower. It was dark and gray, redolent of burnt stone and scorched tiles. There would be a moment when it would shield the top of the tower. It would sting and parboil him like a Decateurian rain, and if he fluttered too much going down or coming back, he might dispel it. But it was the only option he had. Dee would surely die if he waited any longer.

When he started feeling the pinpricks of heat on his claws and on his chest scales, Dyckon knew the steam was close. With a curse, he spread his taloned wings and leapt for where the top of the tower had been. His eyes burned with the heat and he licked them with his elongated tongue to clear his vision. He glided with a buoyancy he had not expected. Earth's lesser gravity gave him a strength five times that of what he was accustomed to. Out of a smeared wet vision, Dyckon saw that the tower wall directly below him was still bubbling from the mining scalpel. It would be best not to land on that. He maneuvered his huge wings, folding them back against his spine at the last moment to allow him to drop through the now gaping ceiling. The flagstones cracked and shattered beneath his feet when he landed.

The smoke and stench within the shattered room were stifling and the prickly heat was now unbearable. Dyckon unfolded his wings and flapped them to clear the air, and as the smoke curled and spiraled away, he discovered Dee coiled on the floor, in the same configuration all Humani adopted while they were in the womb. The man was unconscious and most of his bare flesh was scalded and raw, but his chest was moving and he was twitching uncontrollably, so at least he was alive. The Roc wrapped his talons around the Humani on the floor, spread his wings, then bent his knees and powered himself upward. His leathery wings crackled in the dank air. Dyckon paused for a moment to alight on the fused edge of the wall, gathered a breath of air and steam, and leapt from the edge of the tower back into the open door of the craft, the tiny form of the Humani clutched close to his body. The Roc smiled, showing savage teeth. He had done it; he had rescued his friend. And the punishment would be incalculable.

Dyckon's talons closed over the pink crystal, squeezing and then, with hardly an effort, cracking the recording crystal. The images faded. Dyckon bent his long head to look into the memory bank; some of the crystals were already black and dead. He scratched a talon through a few at random; when memory crystals overheated they often cracked, their crystalline web of memories shattering.

Now, there was no record of his rescue of the Humani.

It had never happened.

CHAPTER

8

2,678,840,456,355

Faintly, the sound barely audible above the constant susurration of the air-recycling ducts, a violin murmured. The big man sitting in the overstuffed leather chair frowned his annoyance and shifted forward, sharp profile haloed by the glowing computer screens. "Sound up two," he said. The volume came up, violins and piano andante con moto, the sound lost and plaintive in the enormous glass-walled room.

"Grieg," he said aloud, identifying the composer and the piece. "*Sonata for Violin and Piano in C Minor*, opus 45—second movement. Confirm?" he asked, glancing sidelong at the music bank, idly amused and irritated at himself for doing so.

2,679,346,589,249

"Confirm." The digital voice had been processed to imitate the voice of his late mother, and it gave him extraordinary pleasure simply to have her voice agree with him on occasion. He had instructed the music bank to play random pieces for exactly forty-five minutes every day for the past six years; it had now become something of a game to identify the pieces the music bank dredged from its comprehensive database. To date it had played over two thousand pieces; he had been incorrect on three occasions. Long, delicate-fingered hands moved in the air in time to the music, pressing down on imaginary keys of instruments he had never learned to play. He swiveled around in the chair and the nearest proximity sensitive speakers abated their volume as he approached, the haunting sound of Smetana's *Two Pieces for Violin and Piano* fading, while those at the other end of the room and on either side increased their output to keep the sound level constant.

2,680,132,211,105

Royal Newton glanced sidelong at the screen that took up much of the southern wall of his glass-enclosed office, and obscured a spectacular view of the blue-white Earth rising over the moon's ancient mountains. Eighteen inches tall, red against black, the digits ticked inexorably upward, providing a second-by-second record of the growth of his financial kingdom.

2,680,786,258,111

He had read recently—the November 2098 issue of *Time-Digest*—that his personal fortune was greater than the total wealth of any single continent. Newton smiled, showing perfect teeth; if only they knew. But *Time-Digest* had only printed what he wanted them to print—he did own the company—and he had insured that the article only reported what he wanted known; if the truth were known, his fortune could have bought most continents—and everyone and everything in them.

Straightening, the big man rose from the hissing leather chair, adjusting the cuffs of his tailored shirt, and moved slowly down the length of the office, head bent, hands locked behind his back in a posture that suggested gravitas and dignity; he had spent so many hours perfecting the pose that it was now second nature. He summed up his reflection in the glass walls, and liked what he saw there; he was fifty-two years of age, but looked ten years younger. He stood six foot two in his stocking feet, and a rigorous regime of diet, drugs, and exercises insured that his weight never varied by so much as a single pound. He was flat-stomached, broad-chested, handsome, with an easy, friendly smile topped by startling blue eyes . . . and bald.

Royal Newton could buy anything in the world he wanted—except hair. He had lost it all by the time he was twenty-five in a freak deep-sea-diving accident. The hair follicles the Swiss surgeons had grafted on—and guaranteed—had promptly fallen out, as had the next five attempts. He had only stopped when his skull had begun to resemble the surface of a pitted orange. His misery had been complete when he had discovered that he couldn't even wear a wig; the failed transplant treatment had tenderized his skin to such a degree that he could now wear nothing on his head—not even a hat—and wigs brought on the most incredible itching and burning. Newton rubbed his hand across his skull, hoping that the latest herbal remedy—a fulsome concoction of old fish and saw-palmetto extract—would work.

It was one of the great ironies of his life—and it gave him some bizarre pleasure—that while he could afford the most expensive hair treatments in the world, which would be administered in clinics of numbing sterility, he was reduced to slapping a rancid concoction onto his head which was prepared by a South American savage who brewed it in the gas tank of a 2002 Chevy. However, in his favor, the savage was incredibly hairy—even his wife had a beard.

Just went to prove that there were some things that money could not buy: it could buy you love, but not hair.

2,680,132,211,983

The Newton family fortune had been founded in the late sixties and early seventies of the twentieth century, by his grandfather, the enigmatic R. R. Newton. Born to abject poverty in a nameless town in Louisiana, R.R. had early on demonstrated an extraordinary aptitude for figures. Recognizing at a very early stage the incredible appetite the world would have for personal computers, he had invested every dollar he possessed—one thousand two hundred and twenty dollars—into an unknown fledgling company. He became a millionaire literally overnight when Apple Computers went public. By the time he was twenty-one, his personal worth was in excess of five million dollars. Using his gift for figures, he doubled his portfolio every year thereafter, weaving a spider's web of financial dealing that enveloped the globe.

When Royal inherited Minuteman Holdings from his father, R.R. Junior, in 2070, the wealth had already reached mythic proportions, and the family owned—either outright or in part—most of the major corporations in the Western Hemisphere and unabashedly several of the governments. The irony of it was that few of them even knew it.

2,680,134,872,007

But it wasn't enough.

The Newtons thrived on greed. "Too much is never enough" had been R. R. Newton's credo, and his son had shortened it to "There is never enough." Royal's version was even shorter: "More!" It was the first word he spoke every morning, and when he produced a son—which he kept promising to fit into his busy calendar—it would be the first word he would teach him.

The music faded, to be replaced by the dull chiming of a communicator. "On," Newton said wearily. The Minuteman Holdings logo faded off the screen to be replaced by the cautious face of a young woman wearing the corporate green-and-white uniform of his personal staff. She paused, eyes shifting nervously.

"Speak," Newton snapped.

"Data coming in on the Omni-Net, sir. We have confirmed UFO activity in the solar system." The voice trailed away. "You asked to be informed . . ." she added.

"Put the data on-screen." The woman's face was immediately replaced with a static three-dimensional representation of the solar system. Seconds later, the image was updated with the incoming data, and the planets began to rotate. The anomaly in the asteroid belt was a crimson dot, a tiny drop of blood against the blackness of space. "Full magnification."

The image blossomed as layer upon layer of information was fed in from the various orbital and ground-based telescopes. It remained nothing more than a microscopic fuzzy blob.

"Increase the resolution," he said, and stepped closer to the screen, as if that would make the image clearer.

"Image at maximum resolution."

"What is it?" he asked aloud.

"Insufficient data," his mother's voice informed him.

"Analysis?"

"Insufficient data. The object remains unidentified."

"But it is tangible, real?"

"Spectrographic analysis confirms that the object is alien to the asteroid belt. Insufficient data for further analysis."

Newton pressed his hands to either side of the screen and stared intently at the tiny object. Great wealth brought with it great privilege . . . and enormous tedium. There was nothing on the Earth that was beyond his control, there were no new fields to conquer, no new empires to forge. There was nothing new under the sun.

Except the endless reports of unidentified extraterrestrial objects.

Foreknowledge and information had built the Newton fortune; the same lust for knowledge had consolidated it. "Only fear what you do not know," his father had told him. Royal Newton's finger tapped the screen. "And this I do not know." An icy tingle of fear slid along his spine, and he smiled with the wonderful frisson of it.

CHAPTER

9

THE LAST TIME he'd felt this bad he had just spent a week with that wild Bathory woman.

Dr. John Dee groaned and decided that he was in pain. Not an individual pain or an ache or some dull gripe. Just a general all-over pain. He groaned again, trying to remember. . . .

He couldn't remember much of what had happened when he'd been with Elizabeth Bathory either; he vaguely recalled that he hadn't actually gotten out of bed the entire week, nor was he sure how he had acquired the countless scrapes, bruises, and bite marks on his body—though he had a very good idea—but his last clear memory was drinking that clear Magyar alcohol. It tasted like flavored water, a little brackish, a little bitter, and he'd had about a dozen glasses before it had magically transubstantiated itself and released a thousand demons into his body, which set his bowels afire and his head athrob, rendered every limb useless, and robbed him completely of any semblance of coherent speech. Only his loins seemed to have kept their vigor.

Later—when it was much too late—he'd learned that the grain was fermented by the old widow women of the village, who first chewed it into a paste and then spat the resultant mess into a communal bowl, where it was fed upon by crawling maggots. By the time Edward Kelly had gleefully aquainted him with this nauseating item of information, Dee had nothing left in his stomach to throw up. He had sworn off alcohol on that day, and had not touched a drop of hard liquor since . . . except wine, and wine was the nectar of the gods.

Memories—painful and bitter—began to return.

Though his body ached, he knew full well he hadn't been drinking any Magyar firewater. Gods, but he would have welcomed the taste of it, for at least that was sensation, and sensation proved that he lived. No, the last liquid to pass his lips had been the scummy brackish moisture he had lapped off the sweating stone-cold walls of the Medici tower.

It was obvious he'd died.

Died and gone to Hell.

Though every inch of his skin prickled with a burning sensation, the air around him wasn't hot—in fact it was rather refreshingly cool—but he had always known that Hell was not the Papists' brimstone and flames. Hell was a place where everyone's worst nightmares were played out—continually. Did that mean that he was condemned to an eternity of feeling like this—to having a tongue three times too big for his mouth, and a demon laboring in his skull, slowly excavating it with a hammer? Surely this was a drunkards' hell, and even in his rakehell days, he'd never been much of a drinker. Without opening his eyes, for he feared what he would see, the small man struggled to push himself into a sitting position. It would be just his luck to have his punishment confused with someone else's. If Hell's management was like that of the court of the Virgin Queen, overrun with petty scriveners and clerks, then he knew there was every chance that that was exactly what had happened. He was sitting up straight now, and the demon pounding in his head had moved down the back of his skull and was now chipping away at his teeth, causing him nothing but the most excruciating agony. What did the imp expect to find in there? Maybe this was the source of the legend of the tooth fairy?

There was a smooth metal wall behind his back and he

touched equally cool and polished metal below the palms of his hands. Hell was forged of metal? The thought intrigued him enough to overcome his anxiety and look. But as he attempted to open his eyes, he found that he was blind. Dee gasped in absolute terror; blindness had always been one of his greatest fears, especially because it was an occupational certainty for a man with his habits. He had spent his youth reading almost indecipherable manuscripts in poor light, while much of his adulthood had been spent copying and translating books and arcana in equally poor light. He was two score and eight now and although he had lost distance detail, his eyesight was still excellent. Moreover, he'd always been able to see in the dark, which had allowed him to move about secretly late at night in others' homes. It had been quite an asset in his trade. He'd go mad without his sight. A sudden thought made his stomach churn and twist: maybe his eyes, like Oedipus', had been torn out. 'Sblood! Maybe that was his destined punishment: to go through eternity blind and hungover. For a moment, he saw Divine Irony at work.

Raising a trembling finger to his face, Dee touched an unkempt beard.

The memories returned.

Sharp, indelible. Bitter and foul.

He touched his eyes, and dried tears and grime flaked off and fell away. He remembered that he had heard voices from without the corridor. An old basso, powerful and querulous; another, younger, a tenor, anger and spite in his words. He had recognized the tenor, Francesco de' Medici, and knew immediately that the only man the young nobleman feared was his father, the terrifying Cosimo. If he'd been strong enough he would have shouted aloud his joy. Either Elizabeth, blessed be her name, had ordered his release, or, more likely, Cosimo— fearing Elizabeth's retribution—was releasing him. Dee had been coming stiffly to his feet, sinews popping and cracking, eager to enjoy the look on Francesco's face, when the knifelike purple beam had pierced his darkness, followed by the explosion of light that had scorched his eyes. He'd lifted his hand to his brow to shield his face from the radiance only to have his arm and head scalded as the grim ceiling high above his head turned to liquid fire and rained molten droplets down atop him. The pain was unendurable and the scream that had bubbled and churned within him for days screeched high and free. Smoke welled up above him, wrapping him in its noxious cloud. And, though he sank to the ground to avoid it, it followed him, filling his lungs with bitter steam, doubling him over with racking coughs. He attempted to hold his breath, but, in a terrifyingly short space of time, his chest burst with the need to breathe. Black spots danced before his eyes. The gagging and the coughing became overpowering and eventually closed down all his senses.

And his last thought had been *So this is how it ends. . . .*

Except that it wasn't over. Not yet.

All that was before; this was now. Digging the heels of his hands into his eyes, he rubbed hard, cleaning them, then slowly opened his eyes and looked around.

Hell was very clean, he decided.

He must have slept, though he had no memory of doing so, but how else could the shining metal one-eared bowl, or rather one-eared ewer—and yet it was too shallow to be either a ewer or even a pitcher—have gotten on the ground directly in front of him? Someone—and then he corrected himself—something must have entered and placed it there. But when? And for what devilish purpose? He realized his mind was still too foggy to think on that and so he moved it onto those thoughts he could cope with.

With effort, Dr. John Dee pushed himself away from the metal wall and stood swaying in the center of the rectangular room. Except for the bowl-ewer, nothing else seemed to be different. He had explored his new domain earlier. Slightly larger than the Medici tower room, it seemed to have been shaped from a single block of metal, and there was no seam where the wall curved into the floor or ceiling. Nor was there any evidence of a portal of any kind—neither window nor door. Maybe this was his everlasting punishment: to be forever incarcerated in a small metal box with a fearsome headache. It hardly seemed fair; what had he done to deserve this?

The dark visions of Calvin and John Knox had been right, then. He had distrusted these men and others like them who preached the horrors of the afterlife. They had been a stumbling block in the way of the great adventures of learning and commerce and progress that had inspired the minds of the best and brightest of the European scientific arts. But now in anguish, Dee saw that those grim and bitter men in black had been right. Jehovah was indeed a vengeful and unjust God. Many of the crimes which he had been accused of in his life were simply untruths put about by himself to embroider his reputation, lies told by his enemies in an attempt to discredit him, or distorted fables of his more outlandish successes. He had lied and cheated and stolen, but that was part of life and living, and, of course, he had killed some people—though none who hadn't deserved it— so he felt it was a bit unjust of God to treat him thus. Whereto served Divine mercy but to forgive one's minor offenses? If he got a chance, he might put these points to God; there were few situations he had not been able to talk his way out of.

There was a substance in the bowl-ewer on the floor. Dee crouched over it for a closer look. His nostrils flared; his mouth suddenly flooded with saliva. Green, streaked with darkly crimson veins, it looked like something scraped off a midden wall, and yet it smelled delicious. Steam curled from the green paste, rich with the odors of exotic herbs and forbidden spices. The doctor tentatively probed the mess with his forefinger and quickly, eyes shut, slurped it into his mouth. Despite its wonderful odor, it tasted as revolting as it looked; but he swallowed. After the first few mouthfuls, he discovered that it wasn't as bad as he had first imagined. True, it was salty and overseasoned with what seemed like cayenne and had a brackish aftertaste that cleared his head and took his breath away. He could feel it burning its way down his throat into his empty, growling stomach and suddenly realized just how ravenous he was. He remembered that he had not eaten in the days preceding his death.

The doctor scooped up another handful of the green slime. Dee had often frequented the Pie Shoppe, which lay in the shadow of the tower, where he had tasted Mistress Kitty's Famous Meat Stew—famous for not having any meat in it—and he had to admit that this hellish green slime actually tasted better. But at least there they gave you a hunk of bread to go with it. He'd give his soul for some bread to go with this. He annulled that thought immediately; he wasn't sure he had any soul left to barter.

There were no eating utensils, so he continued to use his fingers, shoveling the disgusting mess into his mouth and all the while wondering why the body needed to be fed in Hell. How long had he been here? Not too long, judging by his growth of beard.

As he lifted the bowl to his lips to swallow the last of the green muck, he discovered the button in the bottom of the bowl. Licking his forefinger, he scraped the last tendrils of slime off the button and saw what appeared to be a series of curled hieroglyphs etched into the button.

PUSH. The word was in Enochian script.

Then he felt his heart leap in his breast and the green food churned and coiled in his stomach like a serpent. He took a deep breath, steadying himself. He recognized the writing. He knew the words.

John Dee carefully caressed the pattern of letters with his forefinger, and then abruptly realized that its presence shouldn't surprise him so. The language was Enoch, the language of the Angel who had contacted him, the same Angel who had spoken to him through the magical scrying mirror, who had taught him their wondrous and magical tongue. Sitting cross-legged on the floor, Dee stared into the bowl, looking at the simple button, lips moving as he redeciphered the text. Mouthing the word with quiet delight, savoring it like a fine, full-bodied wine.

PUSH.

Push. He had never questioned why he had been chosen to be contacted by Angels. Such occurrences were not uncommon according to his studies. Both Angels and Demons had much congress with mankind in the past, and there was plenty of evidence to suggest that such contact still went on. He knew the stories of

St. Paul, of Jerome, even of that peasant girl in France, Jeanne d'Arc. However, it was manifestly obvious that Demonkind paid far more attention to humans than the Angels did.

Everyone knew the story of Faust, which had occurred but recently. He'd sometimes wondered if the old wives' tales of Demonkind being paid by the soul and being forced to go out every day in search of a soul to bring back to their Infernal Master were true. But then, surely, God would have sent Angels out into the world on a similar mission, and surely He would have paid better prices for the souls of His beloved mankind? As he turned the bowl in his hands, the thought dawned on him that he might get an authenticated answer to this unanswered question soon.

He had been communicating with the Angels now for five years. The first few times had been startling—a blinding white light shining out of the bedchamber mirror, bathing the room in a cold white light that seemed to freeze the room. His reputation as a magician—and a counselor to the Queen—kept the locals away, and in any case, his household was well used to strange lights and sounds and odors lingering around Mortlake. Lying in his bed, trapped by the light, he had vaguely made out a celestial being in the heart of the mirror, the face of an Angel, the hint of wings, and then the divinity had vanished, leaving only burning afterimages and uncertainties in its wake. Subsequently he had only occasionally glimpsed the face and always only fleetingly. But he had no need to see it again; that first glimpse had been enough to convince him that he was looking at an Angel.

He had been bathed in the light at that same appointed hour for three nights in succession before the voice had spoken to him. He remembered being disappointed because there was neither angelic music nor the music of the spheres, nor indeed did the voice sound angelic. It echoed slightly and was cold, clipped, some of the words incomprehensible—and almost inarticulate—and he had often wondered about that. It had been marked by clicks and slurps and a tooth-sucking sound. Surely Angels would be able to speak the Queen's English and speak it well?

In the days and months that followed, he came to accept the

visitations as a normal part of his life. Every night, at midnight, the Witching Hour, the mirror would glow and he would report to the Angel, detailing all that had occurred that day. And then he would spend the remainder of the night answering the Angel's questions, and there were always questions, endless questions, most of them trivial and inconsequential. Dee had often privately worked at the reasoning for the questions, but who was he to question the Almighty? But there were times when he thought that perhaps the Angel was bored, just curious, or testing him.

PUSH.

He mouthed it again. Push.

And because Dee was as bold as he was curious, he began to question his Angelic visitor—simple questions at first, then more and more. He was always careful never to ask a question where the answer might bring him material gain, though he was sorely tempted—but he didn't think Heaven would approve of that. The Angelic language came next. A curious mixture of almost familiar letters, its very familiarity intrigued him. Until he reasoned that all languages had come from the one spoken in Babel and that this original language had been created by God—so naturally the Angel's language would be God's own language. *Rhe'enoch*, the Angel had called it, a peculiar guttural click before the word itself. Though he was a master of many of the Romantic dialects, and he could manage the barbaric Celtic brogues as well as the more liquid Yiddish and Arabic tongues, Dee's throat could barely manage Enoch, though he was more comfortable with the written form of the language.

Soon he began preparing the Angel's reports in their own language; it pleased him to think that perhaps the reports were going directly to the Archangel Michael, Gabriel, or Uriel. Where it went from there boggled the man's imagination.

Which immediately begged the question: what was the Angelic language doing on a bowl in Hell?

Unless, of course . . . Dee blinked, gray eyes widening in surprise . . . unless, of course, he had confounded his critics and gone to the other place.

PUSH.

Push. He pushed the button at the bottom of the bowl. And the bowl-ewer cleaned itself, tendrils of hardening green slime disappearing in a fine mist. Feeling vaguely disappointed—he had been expecting something more dramatic—he let loose the bowl and stood up. He was surprisingly stronger for the nourishment, his thoughts clearer, sharper. He began to pace the room like a caged animal, hands locked behind him, head bent.

He felt the air pressure change behind him and whirled around just as a portal appeared in the wall, tearing apart like a wound in flesh. White light flowed through the opening; then a shape appeared, vague and ominous against the light. Dee sank to his knees, eyes fixed on the shape, blinking furiously to clear his vision.

The creature that stepped into the opening was leathery, reptilian, slit-pupiled, and taloned, a rasping tail coiling behind it. The creature fixed its baleful glaze on the man and opened its mouth. A thin tendril of spittle drooled from between razor-sharp teeth.

Dee screamed in utter horror. Barely hanging on to his sanity, he knew then that he had not confounded his critics, he had gone where he had always expected to go.

Straight to Hell.

CHAPTER

10

"YOU IMPRESS ME, HUMANI." Dyckon eased his angular form into a narrow high-backed chair. "But then, you have always impressed me." The Roc brought his claws together before his face, long yellowish talons rhythmically overlapping one another, clicking softly. "I know my appearance is startling, unusual, and certainly still terrifying to you, and yet now you seem to have mastered your earlier terrors and stand before me without fear. I have never before observed such massive control of the human id in such a short time." A forked tongue flickered across ragged teeth. "Though I must admit that your collapse at our initial meeting gave me much pause. It had not occurred to me that your psyche would not be able to bear the shock. I've read the old reports, of course, of those early encounters between my people and yours. There is some mention of Humani expiring on the spot, or rendered insane." He sighed. "It somehow never occurred to me that my very appearance could render you insensible, but I suppose you have been under a great deal of strain recently and this must be a great shock to your system." Dyckon's mouth gaped in what he hoped was a friendly smile. For his first attempt at Humani banter and humor, he thought he'd done rather well.

Dr. John Dee adjusted the thin metal collar the demon had attached over his head, his fingers investigating and sliding across the flesh-warm metal harness as he listened to what for the most part sounded like a bastard version of English. Yet there were words and even phrases that were utterly meaningless to him. With the collar in place he could understand the demon's words; without it, the creature emitted harsh hissing, clicking snaps.

So, the collar was a magical device that translated the words, but not the sense of what the creature was saying. It was intriguing, and somewhat puzzling. Surely the demons of Hell spoke human languages: how else would they be able to tempt and lie to achieve their quota of souls?

The demon's mouth worked. "You have mastered yourself well. You have recovered from your earlier faint?"

"I am recovered; thank you for your concern. I had not eaten for several days; I believe I must have been faint from lack of food."

The demon nodded. "Just so." A razor-tipped claw waved toward the doctor. "Please sit."

Dee attempted to sit in a chair to face the demon, but it had been designed for a different arrangement of muscles and bones and his body kept sliding out of it. His vanity would not allow him to be so easily mocked, so he swaggeringly propped himself against a metal wall covered with small glass windows. The anger from his wounded pride gave him strength. Folding his arms across his chest, he stared at the demon, wondering which of the earls of Hell this was. The creature fitted the classical description of Demonkind: serpentine and lizardlike, leather wings, tail, claws and teeth, but there was an absence of horns. Dee frowned; there should be horns. And fire. The demon should be breathing fire.

"I know what you see when you look at me, Dr. John Dee. You have flirted with demons all your life, Dee, and yet, when you are presented with one, you show no signs of fear? Tell me, Humani, do you not fear me?"

"What do I have to fear from you now?" Dee said stoically. "If I were alive and I encountered you, I should fear for my immortal soul, but since I am dead and damned, and my soul claimed by your Infernal Master, I have nothing to fear from you or your kind."

The demon threw back its narrow head and began whistling, short, sharp blasts of notes so high that they hurt Dee's ears. It was not a torment, Dee concluded, merely a discomfort. They must apply torture by degree, he thought. In an attempt to ward off the attack on his hearing Dee lifted the metal collar away from his flesh, but the whistles continued. They did not emanate from the harness, but from the creature itself. The demon made no attempt to restrain Dee's actions to unfetter himself and it took the man a few moments before he realized to his astonishment that the creature was laughing. Though the sound was completely foreign, the delight in the creature's eyes was as obvious as it was familiar. Dee shook his head; this was far too strange. None of his researches indicated that the Hell-spawned had a sense of humor. Humor was the solace of mortals. Dyckon straightened and leaned forward, bony elbows balanced on jutting scaly knees. For a single instant a forked tongue flickered as it reined in its breath and stared at the Humani with slit-pupiled eyes. "You are not dead."

The doctor nodded firmly. "I am!"

"Then you are remarkably animate and imaginative for a dead man."

"I am dead and this is purgatory or one of Hell's antechambers."

"You are not dead, and I am no demon."

Dee shrugged. "I do not see the point in this game. The truth is self-evident." He spread his arms wide. "If you are not a demon and this is not Hell—well then what are you? You are no mortal creature, and where in the world am I?" Dee settled back into his position, proud of having scored a rhetorical point against his captor.

"What is your last memory?"

"Starving to death in a Medici tower," he stated flatly.

"And beyond that?"

He stopped suddenly. "Nothing but dreams." For a brief moment his mind's eye glimpsed the ceiling melting, and a vague shape in the billowing steam, a demon shape. Dee brushed it away; it was nothing more than a dream, a hallucination brought on by hunger and thirst. These were mad images.

The demon's mouth opened, revealing rows of triangular teeth. "Tell me what you think happened."

"This is a test, is it not? As St. Peter questions the souls entering Heaven, so you question the damned who enter Hell? Tell me your name, demon, that I may know what to call you."

"I am no demon. I am Dyckon ab-ack na Khar. Now, tell me what you think happened to you."

Dee, who thought he knew the names of most of the infernal host, shook his head. The name was unfamiliar to him, but there were obviously many demons, and this was probably just a minor official. Dee shrugged his narrow shoulders; what matter now that he spoke to this creature? Things could not get any worse. "My earthly body died in the Medici tower and my eternal soul was sent to Hell for my sins and blasphemies."

There was another high-pitched whistle. "Now, let me tell you what happened—or better still, let me show you what has happened. Turn around, Humani, and look at the screens." Again, as if the translating machine had stumbled, there was an English-sounding word that held no meaning. "Look into the glass windows," the demon amended when Dee continued to look at him blankly. "I knew I was keeping a copy of this for some reason," it added enigmatically.

This was the punishment then, Dee decided as he turned to look at the wall of twelve glass windows. He had spent his entire life questioning, had spent a fortune and more in search of demons and angels, had traveled across most of Europe in search of variety and sensation and answers. Now that he was dead, he had obviously been appointed a personal demon who would, no doubt, torture him throughout eternity by asking endlessly stupid and pointless questions. God's will be done. What fitter judgment for one who had been damned for the worst of the seven deadly sins—the pride of his mind? But perhaps his fate could be changed. He wondered who he could complain to. There was always a hierarchy. Maybe it would be possible to be appointed to another demon. . . .

Dee jumped. The windows on the wall before him flickered with dancing lines and then the same image appeared in each of the twelve. The room was filled with the sound of a great rushing of wind, hissing and crackling with suppressed violence. It was the sound of a storm brewing. The doctor stepped away from the windows, his recent green meal churning and bubbling in his stomach as the images through the windows suddenly made sense.

He was looking down over a city.

He was in the clouds.

Dee's knees buckled beneath him and he dropped to the floor, pressing his suddenly sweating hands flat onto the metal surface, swallowing deeply, sour bile at the back of his throat. He heard Dyckon's hissing laughter and abruptly resolved not to disgrace himself before the demon.

Then he realized that this was how angels and demons saw the world. His vertigo and fear were replaced by a growing sense of wonder and exhilaration. Dee came slowly to his feet, eyes and mouth wide as he looked through the windows.

This was what it was like to fly. This was the joy of Icarus.

He had once come into possession of an old diary of a brilliant man, da Vinci, who had once been employed by the Medici. He had dreamt of an apparatus that could make men fly like eagles, of wings that could be attached to a man's back and flapped by means of struts and levers. The diary had been in code, but that had been easy enough to crack—a crude cipher and mirror writing; it had taken Dee less than a day to decipher. Some of da Vinci's observations were mathematically brilliant, others less so. But the dream of flying had fascinated Dee and he had even gone so far as to forgo his reservations and have one of his craftsman fashion a set of da Vinci's wood and leather wings. As soon as he had slipped his arms into the harness, he had known that the device would never work. The disappointment had been great.

But now, looking at these images, his dreams were being fulfilled. He was soaring effortlessly through the clouds. He suddenly wondered if da Vinci had actually flown. And then he remembered that there were rumors that da Vinci had been in league with the Devil.

Now he knew it was true.

He could see a city through the windows, red roofs and deep shadows creating a patchwork across the earth. It took him a few moment to decipher the lines and circles etched into the pattern until he realized that he was looking at greenish blue streets and maroon plazas. From the color of the stone and earth, he knew he was not looking at any English city. The view lurched sickeningly, and Dee grabbed the edge of the angular chair that was near him and held on with white knuckles while his mind reassured him that the view without the windows was moving, but the floor he was standing on was perfectly still. The image grew clearer and suddenly Dee could see individual buildings, spires, piers, and palazzos, and then the images abruptly made sense.

"I know this place," he breathed. "This is Venice."

Dee watched as a tower appeared, growing out of the city, tall, slender, windowless. Even before the demon spoke he knew what he was looking at.

"This is where you were held."

Dee watched the hated building approach. The individual stones were clearly delineated, and he could see the green moss nestled in the roof tiles. He jumped as a narrow purple light flowed over the roof, boiling away the stones, like a needle into candle wax. Smoke coiled around the windows, obscuring his view, and he instinctively drew back, and when the smoke cleared he found he could see into the interior of the tower. There was a shape on the floor, half covered in tumbled bricks, white with dust and mortar. Patches of raw and livid flesh showed through the white dust.

Dee pressed both hands to his mouth, swallowing again and again as his heart hammered in his chest.

A shadow appeared over the fallen man, huge and monstrous; it blotted out the sun and then descended to cover him. He glanced over his shoulder at the Demonkind. "You . . .?"

"You did not die in the Medici tower," Dyckon said patiently.

"I rescued you. You are not dead, Humani, though I fear your world—the world of your Virgin Queen—has long since ceased to be." The images in the window flickered briefly. "This was the Venice of your day, 1575. Now look upon the Venice of today."

Dee's head snapped back to the windows, and he leaned forward, nose almost touching the glass as the images once more flickered and reassembled themselves. Although he had heard what the Demonkind had said, the words themselves made little sense.

The glass windows showed only an expanse of water, scattered with tiny islands. Each isle bristled with houses piled atop houses. Some lay in tumbled ruins, the red tiles like a bloody, bruised stain against the greenery that was struggling to claim the patches of earth. "Where is this place?" he whispered hoarsely.

"This is Venice. The city was finally lost in the Mediterranean Floods of 2026, along with most of the low-lying coastal towns and villages."

"Twenty twenty-six." Dee's mouth was suddenly dry, his tongue large and thick against his teeth. "What does that mean?"

"It is a date as you Humani measure time. That is the year this destruction happened. Dr. Dee, you have been gone from your world a long time."

"In God's name, what conjurer's trick is this!" He whirled around to face the demon and signed the Cross in the air between them. "Begone foul demon. Back to the pit that spawned you! There is no truth in this vision."

"This is no trick, Dr. John Dee. As you humans count years, this is 2099. You have slept for five hundred and twenty-four years. But now, I am afraid, it is time to die."

CHAPTER

11

SIR WILLIAM CECIL WAS one of the most dangerous men John Dee knew.

As Elizabeth's chief minister and closest advisor, he had survived the butcheries of her tyrannical father, Henry VIII, the twelve wild days of Lady Jane Grey's rule, and although brought up a Protestant, had managed to survive—and thrive—in Queen Mary's Catholic court. When Elizabeth took the throne in 1558 she immediately appointed Cecil as her Principal Secretary of State. Charming, witty, urbane, and one of the foremost antiquarians of his day, his first loyalty was to England and its Queen, and he was determined to protect the monarch and the land by any means possible. When recruiting Dee for the spy ring he was organizing with Sir Francis Walshingham, Cecil had given him a piece of advice that had stood the doctor in good stead on more than one occasion.

"When they talk and elaborate, they're looking for an excuse not to kill you. Those who stare and don't talk are the ones who will plunge the knife. Beware the daggers in men's silent smiles."

In his escapades across Europe, spying for Queen and country—and lining his own pocket—Dee had been threatened by everyone from vagabonds to royalty, and found Cecil's advice almost always to have held true. A minor lordling at the Flemish court had accosted him in a dark alleyway one noxious evening and accused him of witchcraft, of casting an evil spell and thereby seducing his wife. Dee hadn't bothered to tell him that the woman's reputation—and exquisite erotic skill—was the whispered talk of most of the European courts. While the lordling had misused the time to describe in detail the tortures he would work on Dee, the doctor had quickly killed him. In a tavern in Dublin he had been trapped between two burly footpads. They both had held massive blades, but only one insisted on talking. On the pretext of reaching for his purse, Dee had whipped out his throwing knife and driven it home into the throat of the silent footpad. The talker had turned and fled.

If this demon was determined to kill him, then why had he not already done so? Why feed him and chat with him? Suddenly— and for reasons which even Dee didn't fully understand—he felt more confident, almost happier, if that were possible.

The demon had said that it was time to die, but Dee didn't believe him. In his long life he had almost always managed to talk his way out of the deadliest of situations, and if he ignored the terrifying appearance and size of the creature, and concentrated only on the doubts he was hearing in the creature's voice, then this demon could be persuaded. Nevertheless, there had been that one occasion where he hadn't managed to talk his way out of trouble, and then, of course, he had ended up starving to death in Venice. But then since he'd already died once—what had he to lose?

Dyckon eased his form out of the chair. He towered above Dee, long arms dangling by his side, razor-tipped claws tapping against bony thighs. "Five hundred years ago, I made a mistake, Dr. Dee. I was younger then—young, arrogant, and foolish; I ignored centuries of law and allowed my heart and emotions to lead me. I did a stupid thing, and I have paid for it every day since then."

"Which law?" Dee asked, calmly, folding his arms across his chest, tilting his head back to look up into the demon's face, staring hard into his slit-pupiled eyes.

The demon was the first to look away.

"Despite what you may think of my appearance, we—the Roc—are not your demons. We are a race of scholars." Dyckon's mouth opened wide, a gaping maw of pointed teeth glistening like polished needles in the diffused light. A long strand of saliva dribbled from the corner of his mouth as the large tongue flicked. "We are observers, scientists, mathematicians, students of history—much like you were in your day. We are long-lived, so we can observe the sweep of history and report our analysis of it. We report history so that all may learn from it. It was my assignment to watch your world."

"You were the voice in the mirror. I thought . . ." Dee stopped abruptly.

Dyckon nodded. "You assumed I was what you call an Angel, and I chose not to disabuse you of that opinion. I used it to my advantage. I was young and still little more than a student then and you were one of the most brilliant humans of your time. They rightly called you 'the Philosopher of Albion.' I thought I would shorten what then appeared to have been an incredibly tedious investigation of your entire culture's methodology by dealing solely with a single Humani—you! By asking you questions and rewording your highly observant perceptions, I accomplished more in a single year than I would have in five years of the prescribed manner. It led to many of my advancements."

"I take it this behavior is forbidden." Dee chuckled, clasping his hands behind his back and strutting past Dyckon: A cocky gait at this moment was an incredibly risky maneuver, yet he did it, and it took an enormous effort of will to keep his shoulders relaxed. But he knew that if the gargoyle did not strike him down for his arrogance, then he would be relatively safe. Without moving its body, the Roc swiveled his head around to follow the human.

"We swear a sacred oath to observe only; we are bound never to interfere."

"But you did interfere," Dee observed icily. He realized that he had encountered creatures like Dyckon before, only in his world, they wore human bodies. The Virgin Queen's court was full of men like Dyckon, fawning, sycophantic, full of talk and threats, but lacking the nerve to carry them out. "Talkers are no good doers," Cecil had once said. Dee fixed Dyckon with a baleful glare. "You cheated by having me answer your questions for you. If you had been caught, my presence and my participation would have been a shameful reproach of your honor and perhaps all your years of work."

The Roc's narrow head shifted at an awkward angle, and the sadness in the beast's eyes told Dee this was an admitted nod of regret. "And of course, you would have been put to death because of your contact with me."

"And yet, when I was near death, you came to my rescue. Why?" Dee discovered that he was genuinely curious.

"Because . . . because I had grown fond of you, Humani. I could not allow you to die in such a barbaric manner." The Roc's shoulders moved up, flat-folded wings appearing briefly. "I enjoyed your humor, your thirst for knowledge, your joy of life. I allowed myself to think of you as my friend." He said the word cautiously. "I foolishly thought you were worth the rescue, but as I have said I was young. I carried you off in my craft, healed your burns and bruises, then set you into a deep sleep which prolonged your life. It was unwise."

Dee moved around Dyckon's chair and perched gingerly on the edge. With the gargoyle's admitting his mistake Dee knew the balance of power in the room was shifting. The Roc's resolve—which had obviously never been strong—was visibly ebbing away. All Dee had to do was to remind him of a few things and let guilt do the rest. Of course, that is, if demons or gargoyles or Rocs or whatever this monstrosity was called experienced guilt. Time would tell him soon enough.

"So you took pity on me and rescued me from the tower where I had prepared my soul for death, then kept me in this airship of yours for . . ." He paused.

"Five hundred and twenty-four years."

Dee's mouth went suddenly dry as the number of years began to sink in.

"For five hundred and twenty-four years. And now you have

reared me, nourished me, and offered to kill me again when I am unprepared. Why? You are crueler by far than the Medici."

The Roc turned and stepped up to the chair. Resting long-taloned hands on either arm of the chair, he leaned forward, his snout inches away from Dee's nose. The doctor's nostrils instinctively flared, but the expected smell of sulfur was not there, only the vaguest hint of sweet spice mixed with warm breath.

"I do not want to kill you, believe me, Humani, but I have no choice."

"There are always choices." Dee settled back against the chair, and closed his eyes, hands pressed together in an attitude of prayer, fingertips against his lips, playing the martyred victim. "Why have you awoken me from this death-sleep and brought me back to life now, only to kill me? Why, now, at this time?" Dee asked. Then his cold gray eyes snapped open. "Of course! Because I am a threat to you. Because something is about to happen."

Dyckon jerked his head back, slit-pupiled eyes blinking furiously. "How did you know that?" he hissed. "Who could have told you?"

"No one needed to tell me. I know the way worlds work. You have decided to kill me now because I am a political loose end."

Dyckon whistled in laughter. "I was right to choose you. You are indeed a brilliant analyst. Yes, you are perfectly correct. You are a loose end, unfinished business, you represent an unacceptable risk. I am about to be appointed to a position of authority in the Collegium of Worlds, and I am quite sure my rivals will investigate my background thoroughly. If they find this ship— and I am sure they will—I do not want them stumbling across an obvious error in my judgment. Your presence here and this memory chip"—he held up a pink crystal—"are the only evidence of my disobedience." The Roc's claws closed on the crystal; it shattered to pink dust between them.

"Why not simply return me to Earth? I give my word as a gentleman and a scholar that no one will be the wiser."

"I thought of that," Dyckon admitted, "until I became aware that it would be more merciful to kill you now."

Dee sat forward. "More merciful?"

"I can offer you a swift and painless death now."

"I hear a choice in your voice," Dee said quickly. "What is the alternative?"

"Your world, the Earth, has two years of life remaining before it is destroyed. And those twenty-four months will be a Hell on Earth." Dyckon gestured toward what Dee was beginning to realize were not windows, but some sort of reflecting glass.

"Look, Dr. Dee, and learn what has been, and what very soon will be. Use that keen wit of yours. When you have seen and comprehended, I promise you will beg me for a swift death."

CHAPTER

12

"WELL?" Royal Newton swiveled his chair around and stared out at the barren moonscape.

The squat, hulking man standing in the center of the room facing the desk kept his face impassive. He knew that there was a security camera trained on him, relaying the image to the monitor set into the arm of Newton's chair. It was one of Newton's petty tricks to insult an employee and then turn his back on them, encouraging them to make a face behind his back.

"I have no information," James Zhu said patiently, his eyes fixed on the top of Newton's bald head. The last transplant treatment had left it scarred and scabrous, and for a single instant it blended almost perfectly with the gray moonscape beyond the window. Zhu took a certain pride in his own thick mop of straight night-black hair—testament to his Mongol genes—and knew it offended Newton every time he looked upon his security chief.

"You have no information," Royal Newton whispered, allowing the chair to spin him around to face Zhu. "What do I pay you for?" he snapped.

"To protect you personally and insure the security of Minuteman Holdings," Zhu said impassively. He had this conversation with Newton at least once a month.

"My security was breached!"

"You received an email," Zhu said simply, his cultured British accent vaguely hinting his disapproval.

"An anonymous email." Newton surged to his feet. "In this day and age, anonymous mail is illegal—and virtually impossible. And yet someone manages to bypass countless layers of security to leave a message on my personal comm monitor. And you don't know where it came from!" he accused.

"I have my best men working on it at the moment. We've managed to trace a portion of its route, but it was bounced from a score of locations, including two satellites, and its signature was encrypted at every stage. Whoever did this knew what they were doing," he added.

Newton slumped in the chair and gestured tiredly at the chair facing him.

Zhu relaxed enough to place his thick-knuckled hands on the back of the chair, but refused to sit in it. On one rare occasion when Newton had been out of the office, the security chief had taken the opportunity to go over the room with a battery of sophisticated sensors. He had noted the locations of the safes, the concealed weapons, cameras, and microphones, and the electric coil inside the chair.

"Our security is breached, isn't it?" Newton asked.

"Not necessarily. Whoever contacted you may only have heard rumors and is attempting to panic us into making a precipitous move." Zhu smiled, the merest twisting of his lips, but his black eyes remained expressionless.

Newton looked up quickly, eyes narrowing. "That's possible. More than possible. The email was vague enough; it hinted that it knew we were working on a top-secret project."

"We are always working on top-secret projects," Zhu observed. "There was no mention of the project by name, was there?"

"None," Newton admitted. "How many people are aware of the project?"

"Across the world, there are upward of twenty-five thousand

people at work on the plans. It is almost impossible to insure absolute security with that many people. However, because of the cell structure, no one group of people knows precisely what is going on."

Newton ran his hands across his bald skull, then pulled his hands away hurriedly. "Yes, yes, you're right. So, someone knows we're working on an ultrasecret project. But they don't know what exactly. Someone is attempting to flush us out. A government agency?" he asked.

"Most certainly. United States, European States, Soviet States—one or all of them. However, I can guarantee that they will not be contacting you again. We have rerouted the entire mailing system and installed another series of firewalls. Any attempts to contact your old address will be immediately traced." Zhu nodded toward the wall of monitors that slowly ticked away Newton's ever-increasing fortune. "You are completely uncontactable."

The screens flickered.

Blanked.

Flickered again.

And then, pixel by pixel, a single word appeared, dull red against the black background.

TIAMAT

TIAMAT

TIAMAT

CHAPTER

13

Twice in his long life, Dr. John Dee had thought he had seen Hell.

Once when he'd contracted the red murrain and the fool of a physic had almost bled him unto death. He'd lain in his sodden bed and watched images straight from the book of Revelation play nine men's Morris in his bed chamber. Beyond the cavorting beasts, where the wall should have been, he had been able to look down into a vast cavern filled with flames and writhing shadows. Even in the depths of his fever he'd known he should be afraid, but instead he had been fixedly curious.

Curiosity had always been his greatest vice.

On the other occasion, following an evening in which he had dined not wisely and too well on Mistress Kitty's blue cheese, he had spent a night racked with pain, clutching his guts. Just ere dawn he had descended into a nightmare realm where all the creatures of his arcane studies had come back to point and snarl at him. It would have been easy to dismiss these two incidents as mere fever dreams and a diseased stomach, but Dee had been a mystic for far too long. He knew that the spirits often communicated with man in oracle-like dreams, sending him visions and portents. Perhaps those images—those terrifying, terrible images—had been preparing him for what he saw now.

If that was indeed their intention, they had failed miserably.

Dee's imagined horrors didn't come close to the sights that moved within the glass windows.

Mayhem. Rape. Torture. These were countless visions of atrocity and destruction.

One of Dee's closest friends was the brilliant French healer and mystic Michel de Nostredame. Dee possessed an early manuscript version of Nostradamus' famous *Centuries*, which the common people were calling his Prophecies. Part of the success of *Centuries* was in its very ambiguity. The quatrains were open to a number of interpretations, and Dee himself had spent many a solitary winter's night translating and deciphering the verses, trying to winnow those which were a product of Michel's genuine prophetic gift from those which were the product of his black humor. But at the heart of *Centuries*, the very core of the Prophecies, was the terrible promise of war. War on a scale as to be almost incomprehensible, fought with machines that even da Vinci's inspired imagination could not comprehend.

Dee had always found these the most frightening. These were the quatrains which carried within them the seed of truth.

And now he knew that the Prophecies had been legitimate.

"You are a brutal race." Dyckon's voice was distant, the merest whisper at the back of Dee's head. "Incapable of learning the futility of war."

Armies clashed. Huge armies. The style of armor and weapons changed, but the look on the soldiers' faces remained the same: fear and terror, combined with a terrible lust.

Each of the twelve windows before Dee showed him a different image. He was aware that each picture represented a different age, a new era. Almost against his will, his eyes roved over the pictures, looked at the grim visage of war across the centuries.

Swords became shorter, pikes longer, bows were replaced by crossbows of various shapes and configurations, and then these in turn were replaced by another type of weapon, a long hollow tube that belched white smoke, like a miniature cannon.

In the bottom row of screens, men no longer rode horses into battle. Metal carriages, horseless, careered across the battlefields, while in their wake lumbered squat metal beasts, who belched flame from their rigid nostrils. Unconsciously, Dee fell to his knees, eyes locked on the images.

Here a single warrior, cradling a miniature cannon in his arms, cut down a dozen unarmed warriors in drab green uniforms.

In the next screen a mud-locked landscape, crossed with trenches, festooned with twisted coils of wire, and littered with more bodies than Dee had ever imagined, blossomed deadly blooms of fire and smoke.

The screens blanked; then an image appeared on all of them. Dee blinked in surprise. This last image—a darkly beautiful cloud rising slowly to the heavens, expanding to a broad mushroom shape—confused him. It seemed so out of place amid all the other images of death and destruction, unless this too was some terrible weapon. The image of the mushroom cloud froze on the screen.

"You have seen dead men, Doctor?" Dyckon leaned across Dee, enveloping him in a vaguely spicy odor, his demonic visage superimposed on the window.

"Yes, many."

"You are familiar with all the aftermath of battle?"

Dee nodded somberly. "I have seen hundreds dead."

The mushroom image reanimated on the screen, growing slowly, majestically in the sky before collapsing in upon itself.

"What is this cloud?" Dee wondered. The terrible beauty of it fascinated him.

The image froze again.

"Can you imagine a device that kills tens of hundreds, hundreds of hundreds, thousands of hundreds in an instant? Can you imagine such a device, Dr. Dee?"

"No, I thank my God, I cannot," Dee muttered.

"But you are a man of imagination, Dee."

"My imagination knows not such perversity. Show me no more. I want it not to infect my mind." Dee whirled away from the images he'd already seen, rubbing the heels of his hands into his eyes, as if to wipe away their memory, but they had been indelibly seared into the back of his skull. For all his rubbing, he would never forget what he had just seen; the images would haunt him for all eternity.

The gargoyle continued. "In your day, Dee, men still looked into the eyes of those they were about to kill. And when two men fought there was always the possibility that one would walk away. That quickly changed. Humani technology has been at its most inventive when it is creating weapons of destruction. Cannons which man could hold in his hands allowed him to kill from a great distance, and then these cannons were perfected until eventually one man—anonymously—could destroy many others from many miles away. Finally your race perfected this device, which allows them to slaughter tens of thousands of others."

"It looks like a cloud," Dee muttered, "an impressive thundercloud."

"This thundercloud was made by man."

"This is a Leviathan bolt?"

"You could call it that, Doctor. But this bolt will transform an area the size of a small duchy to hurricane wind and hellfire. Nothing stands against it." Talons clicked against the window. "When this device was first used, three hundred and seventy years from your time, in a place known as Hiroshima, almost one hundred and thirty thousand people were killed or injured in an instant. And those who survived died slow lingering deaths months later from poisons in the air. Three days later, another device was used and over sixty-six thousand people were killed or disfigured."

Dee shook his head. The casualties were inconceivable, incomprehensible, like boiling water poured on an active anthill. No one in his right mind would use such a weapon, but what prince would not want to possess such a weapon to hold and use as the ultimate threat?

"In your day," Dyckon continued, "the population of your island kingdom was just under four million. Conjure that in your mind, Doctor, all of those people dying in a day. Conjure the agony and the destruction. Consider what it would be like to wake and discover that every living creature, insect, bird, beast, and man had been wiped out, and that the countryside had been scoured of all growth and vegetation. And then add to this the knowledge that the land had been so poisoned that it would be uninhabitable for tens of generations."

"Why are you telling me this?" Dee asked. The images he had seen in the windows had sickened him, and if this demon was to be believed—and he was still unsure about that—then the future of mankind was shaped in chaos and death. But was it really any different from its murderous past? As a student of the past, Dee knew only too well that the history of the world was written in blood and illuminated with the grim portraits of the mangled dead left after battle. In his lifetime, he had hoped that the worst of man's excesses was over, and that a new Golden Age would begin. But in his heart he had always known that it was a false hope.

Men liked to fight. They gave it pretty names and honors and suggested that it was necessary in order to protect the sanctity and sovereignty of the monarch and the land from the avaricious desires of others. In truth, men were but hairless savages, and it mattered little in what time or place they lived or why they fought. And looking at these images of the future, Dee was saddened to realize that nothing changed. Man was still a savage territorial beast.

"You must know the worst so that you can see that your Earth holds no haven for you." The Roc gestured toward the screen.

There Dee watched again as the beautiful blinding mushroom blossomed over the dark landscape and he knew that beneath the light untold multitudes were dying. It beggared belief. It was a policy of horror and madness. He opened his mouth to speak, but found that he had no words. He sat numb.

"Remember, this event occurred over one hundred and fifty years ago before this day. The device that caused this destruction is as ancient to the people of today as the catapult would be to the people of your time."

Dee nodded. He had already understood that what he was seeing were images from the past; this window was obviously a scrying glass.

"You are implying that man has now invented a more ghastly weapon; one that could kill . . ." He shook his head, unwilling to even contemplate the number. "How many?"

"Everyone," Dyckon said simply. "Everyone in moments." He turned back to the screen and tapped it with his claw. "Look at the future of your world, Dr. John Dee."

The screens went dark, and then an image appeared in the middle window, a tiny red cinder glowing against the blackness. The cinder blossomed, grew, expanded; then suddenly it was a raging fireball. The flames rushed upward toward the screen, and Dee fell back with a cry, shielding his face, expecting it to burst through the glass and engulf him.

The Roc reached down and helped him to his feet.

"The Humani are even now developing the technology that will do this. Their tragedy is that they remain naively unaware of what they are creating; they believe this technology will benefit your race, provide a source of unquenchable energy. But on the day it is put into service, this," he tapped the screen, "is what will happen. Within an hour of its operation, your world will be a charred and smoldering ball of molten rock."

"How?" Dee whispered.

"Simply put, the device consumes the atmosphere of the planet, feeding off the gases that support life. It is as if a sun had begun to burn on the Earth. A rippling wall of fire eats through the sky, melts the polar ice caps, then vaporizes the seas. The end comes quickly."

"Do you show me Earth's future? This *will* happen?" Dee asked, pointing with a trembling finger.

"No," Dyckon said surprisingly, "it will not. I am merely showing you what will be if Earth continues to tread the path it has set out upon. These pictures are from a time past and of another world that took the same path Earth is now taking. That world destroyed itself but it was the last to suffer such a fate. The Collegium of Worlds found that it could not stand by and allow more planets to destroy themselves by developing this technology. For too long we stood by and watched younger races burn themselves in their eagerness for ever-powerful technology.

Once it has been demonstrated that the Humani are ready to begin testing this new technology, the planet will be given over to universal martial law and placed under the control of the Nephilim."

On the screen, the image of a hulking dragonlike creature appeared, long narrow snout opening to reveal a maw of pointed teeth, thickly muscled tail flickering behind it. "Your people will be enslaved by taskmasters whose very name is a byword for cruelty. For five generations the Nephilim will control your world; and in that time, they will relegate your people back into the Stone Age. And while they control your planet, they will strip it of its resources, of its mineral wealth, leave it in such a condition that the resources will no longer exist to sustain a metal technology. So you see, Doctor, I would be doing you nothing but a disservice if I were to send you back. You see your choices: immolation in a global fireball if the Humani fully develop their power device, or enslavement under the Nephilim if they even come close. Believe me when I say that killing you is the kindest gift I can give you."

CHAPTER

14

TIAMAT

Crimson letters on a black background. The single word blinked repeatedly on the oversized screen.

TIAMAT

Only two dozen people in the world knew the code name of Royal Newton's latest top-secret project—Tiamat, the Assyro-Babylonian goddess of the sea. Less than half that number had any idea of the scope of the project, and only Newton, Zhu, and two of his chief scientists knew that Tiamat was the quest for the ultimate power: the development of stable, inexpensive, reproducible antimatter technology.

Whoever controlled the patents to this technology controlled the twenty-first and probably most of the twenty-second century. It would be the energy source for centuries to come.

TIAMAT

Newton rested his hands lightly on the keyboard. He was vaguely aware that Zhu was talking urgently into the comm unit on his collar, ordering a trace on the call, but even as he was reaching for the Enter key, he knew that his security chief would fail to trace the source. Whoever had managed to breach the firewalls and evade the endless traps and dead ends written into the system would easily be able to evade a search-and-trace.

ENTER

The screen cleared. Normally, Newton would have expected to see the face of his correspondent on the screen, but he was startled to see his own face looking back at him. He was even more startled when the image spoke to him in his own voice.

"Have Mr. Zhu leave the room; this conversation is for your ears only."

Without looking up, Newton waved his hand toward the exit, then waited patiently until he heard the heavy door click shut and the sibilant hiss as the locks slipped into place, guaranteeing his privacy. The image on the screen was quite remarkable. The face was his own, and a recent image, too—it carried that morning's tiny shaving nick above his lip—and the lip-synching was perfect. The sound of his own voice perfectly reproduced speaking back to him was mesmerizing. This type of technology, a process known as Impressioning, had been proscribed in the early part of the century, following the infamous and prolonged Hollywood Scandal suits, and Newton was hypocrite enough to be genuinely shocked that someone was using his personal face and voice in this way, even though he had used the same techniques on rivals in the past.

"Tiamat, Mr. Newton. What an interesting project."

The voice was perfect, the tone and inflection, the soft crinkling around the eyes, the slight moistness at the corner of his mouth. Whoever had created this image had access to the latest technology. Royal Newton sat back in the leather chair and brought his hands together, fingers locked, before his smiling face. "I suppose it would be foolish of me to ask who you are or who you represent?" he asked mildly. On a deeper level he realized he should be upset, possibly even frightened by this intrusion, but he found the entire situation exciting, challenging. And it had been a long time since anything had challenged him.

"Come, come, Mr. Newton, we haven't gone to this much trouble to disguise our identity to simply reveal it to you. Not yet, in any case."

The image on the screen smiled a smile to match Newton's own. The impression was so mirrorlike that Newton almost felt the need to reach out and touch his own face just to see if his hand would appear in the image.

"Tiamat, Mr. Newton."

"You're bluffing. You know the name and that's all you know," Newton said shortly.

"Don't be insulting! We know all about Tiamat. We know that you have been working for the past four years developing anti-matter technology. We can list your factories, your suppliers, show how much you have bribed officials and agencies in the developing countries in order that your toxic factories be allowed to continue unchecked."

Although Newton's face remained impassive, he was aware that his head was beginning to throb; whoever these people were, they knew too much. He would make it a priority to discover their identity—and crush them ruthlessly. His smile broadened imperceptibly.

"But rest assured, Mr. Newton, we are not your enemy. Rather, you might consider us friends. We wish to assist you."

"Why?" Newton asked bluntly.

"We represent certain interests, individuals, corporations, governments who have become increasingly aware of the precarious state of this world. Its defenselessness. We know you have been monitoring for UFO activity in the solar system; we know also that you receive regular up-to-the-minute reports of any intrusions into our system."

"I believe such craft to be of terrestrial origin," Newton said, realizing that if they knew this much, they were also aware of his own beliefs. "I was merely curious as to their point of origin."

"Believe us, Mr. Newton, when we tell you that they are not terrestrial. This planet is under observation—has been for quite some time. We fear that the day will come soon when we will need your Tiamat technology to power our spacecraft and weapons systems if we are to protect our world. Time is short. Very rarely, Mr. Newton, has a single man had the opportunity to make a profound difference in the grand scheme of things.

But you are in a position to do so. We cannot move quickly enough to develop this technology—our hands are tied; but yours are not. But we are in a position to be of inestimable assistance to cut through the bottlenecks and supplement your research."

A light began to blink on the hard disk. "We are uploading data to your machine, Mr. Newton. It will allow you to take your Tiamat project a step closer to conclusion. No need to thank us. We will speak again." The screen faded, the image of Newton's face drifting away until only the smile on his thin lips remained. For some reason, Royal Newton was reminded of a children's story, though, try as he might, he couldn't remember the name, alas.

CHAPTER

15

SUDDENLY DEE REALIZED he was in familiar territory; threats he could deal with. True, he was aware that his heart was pounding, thumping painfully in his chest, but it proved that he was alive. The strength of that realization struck him like a blow. The joy of that outshone everything he'd just been told.

He was alive!

Dr. John Dee wrapped his arms across his chest and grinned. In what seemed like the span of a day, he had starved to death in a medieval tower, gone to Hell and bested the Devil in his own lair, and learned a new version of the Apocalypse. He had led an incredibly wondrous life, but his death was unquestionably more wondrous by far. But then he wasn't dead.

And therein lay the rub.

He was incredibly, impossibly alive, just as Dyckon had said, and if that were so, then his ever-analytical mind reminded him that possibly everything this demonlike creature, this Roc, had said to him could be true, including the terrible images he had just witnessed. The thought bathed him in seasickness of fear and euphoria, the elation of self-preservation tempered by a wrenching nausea. Beyond all rational belief he had been resurrected like Lazarus to awaken again in another age, but an age of horror. He had been reborn at the end of Time, at Armageddon. Earth's destiny was to become an inferno and then a nothingness or else enslaved like the Hebrews in Egypt robbed of their learning. Dee stopped pacing the metal-and-glass chamber, abruptly aware that his legs were tingling and black spots were hovering at the edge of his vision. He was about to swoon! But he revealed nothing of this to his captor. Years of diplomacy had taught him to be inscrutable if he needed to be. He barely made it to Dyckon's ill-shaped chair before his legs gave way, dropping him into the chair with a thump.

"No," he said firmly.

"No?" Dyckon repeated, tail twitching nervously. He had watched the Humani stride around the library and recording room, head bent, hands clasped behind his back, as if he had not a care in the world. Then the man had calmly commandeered his favorite chair.

"I will offer you a deal," Dee offered dispassionately.

"Deal?" The Roc shook his head. Perhaps he had been mistaken about Dee, perhaps the shock of reawakening and the data overload had driven the Humani mad. "Deal. There is nothing to deal with."

"When all else fails," Dee said patiently, "there remains the deal, the bargain. Even after death, a man's soul is bargained for by God and the Devil. You and I can deal."

"There can be no negotiations. We can only wait for the inevitable. I am a researcher; I have no say in this." Dyckon had expected many reactions from the man—fear, principally, perhaps horror—but the Humani's serenity and calm acceptance of his fate and the death of his world were astonishing. His studies had shown him that mankind was by nature a passionate race capable of raging furies and numbing despairs. Outlandish theatricality was what he expected, and that was what he had prepared for, not this rational detachment. It was very unsettling.

"I refuse to sanction the inevitability of this vision you lay before me," Dee said easily. "It is merely a poor excuse for doing away with me; a sop to your conscience. The situation is: You do not want to kill me and I certainly do not want to die—again. That would be cruelty in extremis."

"Neither of us have a choice."

On reflection, Dyckon realized that he should not have been surprised by Dee's reaction. Had he not initially chosen him because he was such a remarkable man? It was only to be expected that he would have reacted in this remarkable manner.

Dee abruptly surged out of the chair and launched himself at the Roc, eyes wild, teeth bared. Dyckon slithered backward with a yelp of surprise, claws rattling off the metal floor. He lost his balance and was already falling when Dee hit him in the chest, driving him to the ground with a thud that echoed through the room. Squatting on the Roc's chest, Dee locked his hands around the front of the creature's neck, pushing his thumbs into the lizard's throat, scaled skin harsh and cool, like fresh-cooked fish.

Dee's powerful fingers dug deep into the throat and felt scales crackling. Pale, colorless ichor leaked from them. He felt the larynx spasming beneath his fingers, fighting the brutal pressure. He watched intently as a pale yellowish membrane flickered across the Roc's eyes. John Dee gloried in his own physical power and lusted for the death of this thing that had so shattered his reality. It was an abhorrence to God himself. He had the strength and the will, and he would wreak his revenge. The revenge he lusted after. This creature should not have fed him so well. He'd miscalculated; feeding Dee, giving him the wherewithal to nourish his body, and the images to spur him to action. A sudden sweet odor filled the room. The tableau held for a moment; then, just as unexpectedly, Dee let go and climbed off the quivering Roc.

The doctor stood over the creature for a moment, panting hard with his spent exertion, then reached down to help his victim up. Dyckon's leathery arm brushed away the proffered hand. He leaned on his left side, staring murderously up at the unshaven milky white face. Neither Roc nor human moved or knew what to expect of the other. After a long awkward hesitation, the Elizabethan slowly reached down again to help the Roc up.

This time there was no resistance, only the unspoken awareness that the Roc had lost more than a fight. The balance of
power in the room had changed irrevocably.

As he hauled Dyckon to his feet, Dee discovered that the creature weighed hardly anything. Bird bones, he decided. At Mortlake, he had experimented with dissecting creatures, and had
discovered that the bones of birds were hollow. So, despite his
terrifying appearance, Dee realized that he could snap the creature's neck with ease.

"I believe that you cannot kill me," John Dee said simply. "If
you had wanted me dead, why waken me? Why not murder me
whilst I slept?" He gestured toward the screens. "By proffering
me these visions you had hoped that I would choose self-
slaughter. You would relieve yourself of the ethical burden. You
are . . ." He hesitated. "You are too kind to kill me, and there is
neither policy nor humanity in my killing you."

The Roc abruptly turned away and strode toward a wall,
which dilated open into a door. Dee darted after him and
leaped through the opening as the door began to iris shut.

"Wait!" he shouted. As he raced after the Roc, he realized that
he was in an almost circular corridor, which had been designed
for Roc claws. Dyckon moved swiftly, feet and hands scuttling
along the walls and floor, while his tail balanced him. Dee slithered along behind, bare feet pattering along the warm seamless
metal, trying not to get in the way of the whipsawing tail.

"Wait!" he demanded, putting as much authority into his
voice as he could.

Dyckon stopped, but did not turn around. Dee scrambled
over the tail, crawling up the sloping wall to come around in
front of the Roc, where he found a countenance of steely menace. But he'd taken the measure of the creature when they'd
grappled and knew his opponent. "Why do you flee from me?"

Dyckon's tongue flickered, but he said nothing. The menace
was now not directed at him at all, but rather focused inwardly;
the Roc was angry at himself.

"Are you ashamed because you cannot kill me? There is
naught to be ashamed of. Why, this to me reports you to be a

man, a Roc," he amended, "of honor. And there is never shame in that. When all else fails, honor remains."

"My race is old, Dr. Dee, older than you could imagine. We do not have your conveniently short sense of purpose. Our honor springs from our work, our investigations. To befoul that work, to deviate from an eternity of form and practice, is to desecrate everything our ancestors believed in and trained us to hold sacred. We are cursed with a very long conscience."

"Conscience doth make cowards of us all," Dee said softly.

"I woke you to kill you, it is true, to cover up an unforgivable error of pride which I made a long time ago. And now I find my mistakes are compounding themselves. Error begetting error. Those in the Collegium who opposed my election to the Council are right. I am ineffectual, incapable of meaningful action. I could not even muster enough will to fight forcefully for my own life. Humani, you have compelled me to face my own weaknesses. I am not fit to set foot in the Collegium. It has all been a mistake. And what have I accomplished here with you?" he added, looking over Dee's head. "Nothing," he said bitterly, "except to make things worse. Put you in more pain and reaffirm my dishonor."

"You have given me back my life," Dee reminded him.

"And when your existence is discovered, you will be disposed of quickly and casually and I will be ruined, my family name dishonored."

"But first must I be discovered," Dee interrupted. Hooking an arm through Dyckon's, he led him down the corridor toward another blank wall.

As they neared, it suddenly dilated. "I have a proposition to make which will be of profit to us both."

The ill-matched pair stepped through the doorway into a glass-walled room, and abruptly Dee was struck dumb by the vision he saw in the glass. The sight was completely meaningless to his mind and senses, but the enormity and grandeur of it inspired a Gothic awe. Hanging, jewel-like, directly before him was a blue-white sphere capped top and bottom with white. It was enormous in its beauty. And familiar, hauntingly familiar. Dee felt he should know the image.

"That is your world."

Walking numbly to the glass, Dee peered out across the vastness of space to the planet, his brain reeling. Pressing himself against the glass, feeling vertigo beginning to eat away at him, he stared at its imperial blueness in a tapestry of black. He watched wispy white webs—clouds, he realized abruptly—move with a solemn slowness around the orb. When he finally glanced over his shoulder at Dyckon, his smile was brilliant. " 'Sdeath, but I always knew it was round. Ptolemy was right!"

The liquid was the color of blood, but Dee had drunk worse and so long as he did not look at the fluid and concentrated on the Roc's face, all he could taste was cloves and spices. "Send me home," he said simply. "Deliver me out of your way."

"But my studies are undeniable. Your world cannot live."

"You've said mayhap two years."

"It will take at least that long to develop the technology, and then assuredly the Collegium of Worlds will send in the Nephilim."

"Two years," Dee mused. "Long enough."

"Long enough for what?"

"Long enough to insure that the 'technology' is never created. I will see to it that they change their policy."

Dyckon laughed, then swiveled his huge head to nod toward the Earth, blazing white and blue against the void. "The world has changed much since your time, Dr. Dee. It would take you a lifetime just to reorient yourself."

"Even in my day, the world was changing, every returning merchant ship bringing tales of wonder from the New World. We marveled and accepted. But this I do know: People do not change." He leaned across the table to grip Dyckon's arm. "Tutor me in what I need to know and send me home, and in return, I'll prepare you for your future governmental responsibilities. I'll teach you tricks that will confound these political opponents of yours, and you will reap the rewards of the lessons I learned in the most dangerous, political courts on Earth. I will make you a force to be reckoned with." Dee saw something like greed flicker in the Roc's eyes and pressed home his advantage. "My world must be given a chance! Do not let all your studies have been in vain."

Dyckon looked at the Earth again, the world he had studied for so long, then back to Dee's face. "I'm not sure you could do any good," he said hesitantly. "You would be so out of place, a man alone, unprepared to face all the extraordinary mutations and advancements that time has brought. You have no idea of the changes."

Dee smiled triumphantly, knowing he had won. "Are men not still men? Motivated by the vices of greed and power? Do they not still strive to outdo their neighbor? Do they not still thieve and kill, lie and grasp?"

"Yes."

"Of course! It could not be otherwise. I am many things, Dyckon—but first and foremost, I am a survivor."

CHAPTER

16

SUCCESS HAD COME EARLY to Jim Church.

Two days shy of his twenty-first birthday, he was plucked from obscurity to play the lead in a major television series inaugurating the then breakthrough technology of Virtual Vision. Church stepped—literally—into millions of homes once a week during prime time. The immediacy of Virtual Vision meant that his was a very real presence, and he became a superstar in a way that Hollywood had not seen since the grand old days of the studio system. Within six months of the show's first airing, Jim Church had the highest TVQ ratings ever recorded. Before his series' second season started, his agent, the legendary Bill McQuillan, renegotiated his contract to make him one of the highest-paid television stars of his generation. Realizing that Virtual Vision had made his reputation and fortune, Church convinced a clique of industry friends to invest heavily in Microvision, the company which had been developing the three-dimensional imaging system. In a widely publicized proxy battle followed by a leveraged buyout orchestrated by McQuillan, the actor became the chief shareholder and CEO of Microvision. With Church at the helm of a multimillion-dollar corporation—and his business background limited to serving fast-food California cuisine in drive-through restaurants—the financial pundits and Hollywood gossip columnists had estimated that Microvision's stock price would plummet within weeks. As usual they were wrong.

They hadn't bargained on Jim Church's tenacity, vision, and extraordinary arrogance. He saw himself as a major Hollywood player, and he was determined to do everything in his power to make that dream a reality. In 2036, he opened a production company, Reel People, a subsidiary of Microvision, which was solely dedicated to the development of the Virtual Vision product. Utilizing the latest advances in the software, which allowed the capture and reproduction of any moving object, in any light, rather than the static, studio-bound blue-screen images of the earliest versions of Virtual Vision, the new CEO managed to secure the international rights to broadcast soccer matches in Virtual Vision. The entire future of sports broadcasting changed overnight. Two-dimensional images on a flat screen were no longer enjoyable. Now every sport had to be broadcast in Virtual Vision, which brought the action straight into the viewers' home in three dimensions. Viewers could run with the ball dribbling at their feet, stand behind the goal and watch the ball come soaring in. Accounts of people leaping off their seats to catch the three-dimensional balls and injuring themselves became commonplace.

Hospital emergency rooms nicknamed the casualties "Church injuries."

And James Church became a multibillionaire virtually overnight while still retaining his day job on the series.

James Church was thirty-two in the year of the Crash, 2039. In his authorized biography, he claimed that he had been standing in the doorway of his studio's editing bay working late with his editor on a scene from a new science-fiction series when the Great Quake struck. When he'd opened his eyes five minutes later, the studio, his home, everything, had vanished into a pit. The biography, written by his fifth wife in an attempt to recoup some of the money he owed her, had reported that he'd said, "Even after you've achieved your dreams, nothing in life ever changes. Life sucks." Legend had it that he'd then shoved his hands in the back pockets of his jeans and walked away, without ever looking back.

The tell-all exposé—written by his seventh wife—told a slightly different story. Church had driven to the studio parking lot in the early hours of the morning. He'd been too loaded to climb out of the car, and had slept in it overnight. The rumble of the terrible earthquake had just barely roused him out of his opiate dreams, and he'd stared, bleary-eyed, through the windshield as his studio and home slid into an enormous fissure in the earth in front of him. When rescuers came an hour later, they found the front two wheels of Church's car dangling over the edge of the pit with Jim laughing hysterically inside. He was quite convinced it was one of his own Virtual Visions and he was loving it.

The Crash wiped out an entire way of life in Hollywood; during the cataclysm, homes, entire blocks of streets, whole communities disappeared and were never seen again. Hundreds of families in Brentwood and Bel Air, who, previous to the morning of October the 22nd, had never suffered a calamity worse than a canceled TV show or low grosses at the box office, were now faced with homelessness, hunger, and social anarchy. Utter despair ruled. In a city of billions where the dead far outnumbered the living, James Church became just another statistic: missing, presumed lost, assumed dead.

In years to come, his Virtual Vision programs would still air on late-night TV around the world. The images now looked crude and blurred when compared to the latest imaging technologies. They enjoyed a cult following among fans who considered black-and-white two-dimensional movies the height of culture.

After a legal wrangle that lasted years, the liability insurance was eventually shared among the estates of his seven wives and twenty-one children, and by that time no one gave a thought to the onetime superstar-CEO James Church. He had become just another statistic of the Crash.

"I have a right to drink," James Church said suddenly. "Every right to drink. At eight A.M., I was a multibillionaire; at five past eight, I was zilch."

"Yeah, so you've told us." A wild-eyed woman, wearing layer upon layer of filthy, mismatched clothing snatched the paper-wrapped carton of Old Defiant liquor from Church's hand, leaned back her head, and drank deeply.

He allowed her to swallow twice before he grabbed it back, being careful not to squeeze the carton and waste some of the precious liquor inside.

It had taken him four days to steal the money to buy it. Church raised the carton to his lips, but a twisting curl of flame distracted him and he paused, staring into the dancing flames of the fire he had lit earlier. Peering into the mesmerizing flame, Church reexperienced, once again, everything he owned slipping into the widening pit. The images were sharp and clear. He watched again as his home slowly crunched and disappeared in the wreathing dust and smoke.

And when the smoke had cleared there was nothing but a bottomless pit gaping before him. He should have jumped in; he knew that now. That pit had come to symbolize his future.

Church raised his head and looked out into the night, across the tiny winking fires that burned in the concrete and steel debris that dotted the blasted landscape, each one marking out a closely guarded and defended patch of turf. Beyond the fires, in the shadowed night, lay the honeycomb of craters that had swallowed most of Los Angeles.

In the years following the Great Quake, it had been a poisonous uninhabitable wasteland. Most of the ruptured gas lines from the upheaval had exploded within hours after the morning's devastation, creating megaton explosions, and the resulting inferno had transformed the seaside metropolis, the nation's largest city, into lavalike rivers of plastic, rubber, chemicals, and tar. There had been pockets of survival for those in the Hollywood Hills or in the beach areas where the ground had not liquefied. The aftershocks continued for years. The cost of salvaging the city had been hotly debated in Washington, but the price had been too high for a conservative Congress who had promised to lower taxes. So, they opted to send in the Marines to evacuate those who would go and establish law enforcement if it was needed. But the debates had taken too long and the evacuation turned into a political fiasco for all involved when the troops were attacked by the survivors of the Crash who had quickly discovered that there were advantages to living in a city without law, without taxes, without the religious and political censorship that had come to dominate the early years of the twenty-first century.

Jim Church had survived the endless small earthquakes and the poisonous air of the early days, and the disease, hunger, and muggings of the years that followed, though even he wasn't sure how. Those days had become as blurred as the Virtual Vision show he had once appeared in and in moments of lucidity he was unsure if this life—living like a savage in a devastated landscape—was the Virtual Vision show, or if his previous life, that of a successful actor, had been the dream. The line between actuality and reality had become even more blurred of late.

He had seen things that would make great special effects for his new show. Or was this the new show?

He had started to notice lights in the depths of the Pit, the crater at the heart of what had once been Los Angeles, which was now known as Angel City. There were stories of homeless people now living in the ruins of buildings swallowed deep in the craters, humans who had started to change. . . . Church wasn't surprised; he had seen things come up out of the Pit, rats as big as dogs, cockroaches as long as his arm, flies with a wingspan as wide as his head.

In recent years, vegetation had started to return to the blasted landscape, a pale leprous yellow coating the pockmarks in the earth. It was a mutated fungus that pulsed with a tawny glow late at night, and released poisonous spores when touched. He'd lost several companions—for no one had friends on the fringes of the Pit—to the fungus, men and women who had breathed the spores and wandered into the depths of the gelatinous mass, beatific smiles on their faces. Many had died on their feet, and the fungus had crawled up their bodies, turning them into obscene statues.

But they had died happy, which was about all a man could ask for in these terrible times, and when things got too bad, that's how Jim Church was going to go.

Tilting the paper jug back, Church squeezed the carton gently, forcing the scalding liquid to sear down his parched throat. Well, he was almost sure he'd seen things and he was pretty sure about the lights. He knew his mind had betrayed him many times since that terrible eight-o'clock wake-up call. But it didn't bother him. "Everything sucks."

Steadying the bottle between his feet, the ex-actor looked out at the Pit again. There were lights moving in its darkness again tonight. He had been right after all.

White lights, set close together, like eyes, moving too fast for walking, growing larger, coming closer.

He flapped his arm for attention. "Do you see that?" he asked.

Mad Sally R. turned and looked uncertainly into the void. She had once programmed Apple computers for a living, until the Mac-Worm Virus hit, and the most popular personal computer operating system in the world had shut itself down. Overnight, over fifty-five percent of the world's home computers ceased to work; Mac programmers and engineers suddenly found themselves unemployable.

"What am I looking for?" she asked.

"Lights."

"I see lights." She nodded vacantly.

Church came slowly to his feet. The lights had grown bright—bright enough to illuminate the earth beneath. A helicopter—possible, but unlikely. Why would the Marines bother to send in yet another helicopter? They just kept getting shot down.

This one was silent. Church tilted his head to the side, listening. In the distance a dog howled off-key, sounding lost and lonely in the night, and close by someone invisible cursed their coughing neighbor, but there was no sound from this thing with the lights. It was completely silent.

Was it a helicopter? The mysterious lights suddenly disappeared below and to the right. He had to be sure this time. Church darted forward, dropping on hands and knees to crawl to the edge of the Pit to peer down. He grabbed an exposed tree root and lowered the upper half of his body below the rim of the crater. He saw the lights. In the dull mustardy glow of the vegetation below, a circular craft hovered mutely.

"Dearest God." Church gulped deeply, squeezed his eyes shut, and then opened them again. But the craft remained. The Old Defiant soured in his stomach. Maybe it was time to think about quitting or having more.

A door opened, a long rectangle of light slicing out into the gloom, and then a figure appeared in the doorway casting a tall, batlike, demonic shadow across the ground.

Definitely time to think about quitting.

The shadow hissed and clicked in a speechlike pattern as it moved. And then from behind the demon appeared a man. Small, neatly dressed in conservative fashion, followed by a man-sized steamer chest that floated two feet behind. The small man's voice carried clearly on the evening air as he turned and raised his hand in farewell. "Trust me, I know what I'm doing."

The demon continued to click and hiss.

And James Church buried his head in his hands and vowed that he was done with drinking, not another drop would pass his lips.

Dr. John Dee climbed out of the Pit, taking care not to scuff his wonderful new shoes, trying to adjust his posture to the unusual clothing, which gripped where it should not and was loose where it should grip. The doctor knew he should feel fear, or even apprehension; he was out of place and time, a stranger in this land. But it was a land of opportunity for a man of his peculiar and varied skills. When he reached the top of the Pit, a wild-haired man reared up before him, arms waving, spilling toxic-smelling liquor from a plastic bottle on Dee's new shoes.

"You you and him that thing! Alien. Mutant. Devil," raved the wildman.

"Hence, avaunt, vanish like hailstones; go, trudge, plod away i' the hoof; seek shelter you banbary cheese! You've ruined my shoes!"

The vagrant turned and fled howling into the night. Dee had spent a lifetime dealing with such ravings. "Some things never change," he shouted after the retreating drunk.

In the distance, James Church finished the Old Defiant in a single swallow.

He would quit tomorrow.

CHAPTER

17

THE AIR WAS FOUL, bitter sulfur biting at the back of John Dee's throat, stinging his eyes, coating his tongue. Blackened cinders curled through the air, twisting on the fetid wind, and he could smell rain on moist air which was tart and heavy with the promise of thunder. Dee breathed deeply. It smelled just like home, London in the middle of the sixteenth century!

Actually, London hadn't been too bad, but Paris had been a reeking cesspool; the stench of the sewers and the old cemetery lent the atmosphere the consistency of fish broth.

Concentrate, Dee reminded himself, *concentrate on the details and be aware of your surroundings.*

He was in an alien city, in an even more alien land, and Sir William Cecil's advice, given more than five hundred years ago, would surely still hold true. This was not Edinburgh, Paris, or Rome, but it was just as dangerous, and to wander around, openmouthed and wide-eyed, was to court disaster. Look busy, Cecil—the consummate spymaster—had said. Look as if you belong, and you shall not be troubled.

Dee found himself walking down the middle of a tumbled, shattered street.

What it must have looked like when it stood—houses of polished stone, metal, and glass—he could barely imagine. He stopped before an enormous slab of stone that blocked the street and ran a callused hand across its surface—its smooth texture was like nothing he had ever experienced before and there were curled metal tentacles that protruded from it at regular intervals. He scraped at the metal with his overlong thumbnail. Like most alchemists he used his nail as a spoon to scoop and measure reactants. But he did not recognize the rusted metal; it was so light, yet he could not bend it. What he could have accomplished with such metal at his disposal in his own time, he thought. Glass crackled underfoot and he bent to inspect a piece as broad as his chest. Holding it up to the south, where a dull yellow-white light stained the horizon, he examined it closely. It was a wonder; perfectly transparent, yet as thin as a sheet of the finest Flemish parchment. He tapped it against the stone wall; it sang with a sweet high sound, but did not shatter. He knew jewelers who would kill for a piece of glass like this. Dee looked around him—why, there were *fortunes* waiting to be picked up off the ground.

Clambering up onto the slab of stone—it looked like a portion of a wall—he surveyed the destruction that surrounded him, trying to imagine what marvels this wall had once enclosed. Gutted shells lined both sides of the street, and in places the roadway was split in two, like a broken plate.

Dyckon said that a great earthquake had devastated this place in 2039.

"Twenty thirty-nine," Dee said aloud. "Fifteen seventy-five," he reminded himself under his breath, was the last time he had walked this planet, and the realization of just how much time had rushed past him left him breathless and dizzy.

He was as far in the future as the mythical Arthur had been in Dee's past.

Was Elizabeth as much a wonder-book story to these people? Did they even know who Elizabeth or Burghley were?

"Five hundred and twenty-four years."

Why, even the patriarchs of the Bible did not live so long. Dee scrambled off the stone and hurried down the street. For the first time in his long life, he suddenly felt lost and alone—so alone. Something like fear settled onto his shoulders. The emotion was not unknown to him—only a fool claimed not to know fear—but the key to controlling fear was to understand it. What frightened him now? It was not the danger.

Traveling the highways of England was not for the faint-hearted. There was risk beyond every turn in the road. Much as there was here.

No—it was the overwhelming solitude that had gripped him. When he'd tramped the capitals of Europe he had always had a companion, that wild Irish rogue Edward Kelly, but Kelly was long dead and dust now. And so was everyone Dee had ever known. He found himself eulogizing the dead, the Queen he had served; did Elizabeth's line survive and rule Britannia? Did the cursed Medicis still hold Europe's purse strings? Had any of the bloodlines held? Would anything be familiar?

Dyckon had told him much, but not enough of his aerie knowledge of how the world had progressed since his abduction. Dee had learned of great wars fought, of new discoveries, new lands, new continents, each populated by new races and exotic animals. He'd learned what Dyckon had meant by the foreign word "technology." Mankind could now fly like eagles in ships of metal, traversing great distances in a matter of hours. Enormous metal craft, artificial islands supplied with every creature comfort, floated on and below the surfaces of the seas. Why, even the moon had been colonized and the red planet, Mars, briefly settled. It was only a matter of time before mankind pressed on outward and began to explore the stars.

Dee stopped in the middle of the street and craned his head upward to look for his moon. He would find familiarity there—he hoped. However, although the sky overhead was shrouded in a twisting pall of green-tinged yellow smoke and the heavens were invisible, the small man's lips twisted in a wry smile. Just like the skies above London in his own time. "At least the heavens remain immutable," he reminded himself.

"What have we here?"

Dee schooled his face to an impassive mask as he turned his head toward the voice. There were three shapes lurking in the shadows, only the ferocity of their eyes visible in the gloom. Vaguely irritated by his own stupidity—having just recalled Cecil's sage advice, he had then chosen to ignore it—Dee turned and walked away. Now that he was listening for the sounds, he heard the vaguest click of metal off stone, the soft rasp of cloth, and then he caught a glimpse of another moving at the very edge of his vision.

"Don't go, little man."

The figure materialized out of the shell of a gutted building to his left. Another appeared almost directly in front of him, perched atop a slab of stone, and Dee's hearing detected a fifth stealthily approaching from behind.

"I have nothing to give you," Dee said, walking forward, fingers touching the collar Dyckon had given him. It had translated the Roc's words, making them comprehensible to Dee, and he had understood the wild-haired tramp, but would it also translate Dee's words for these creatures?

"Everyone has something to give," someone said, answering Dee's question.

A man walked slowly into the center of the street and stopped, hands on hips. Ignoring the outrageous costume, which seemed to consist entirely of leather and buckles, and the mane of ice-white hair, Dee concentrated on the man's face. A lifetime spent in European courts had taught him much about people. His studies had taught him that a person's character etched itself into the lines of the face, in squinting eyes and curling lips. He had observed fresh-faced young men and women come to court to strut and parade and pretend to be important, and he had watched the corrupting influences that surrounded royalty work their hard ministry on their faces, etching lines and furrows into foreheads and around nose and cheek, sinking their eyes deep into their skulls, narrowing their lips. Within six months of their arrival, their faces would betray a terrible world-weariness and cynicism. And, as they aged, their faces would betray their bitterness. Sir Francis Walsingham, Elizabeth's spymaster, though five years younger than Dee, had the face of a man fifteen years his senior. Evil—whether experienced first-hand or by association—left its mark. It had certainly ravaged Dee's own features, but not nearly so much as the face of the man blocking his way. Perhaps he had once been handsome, even beautiful, but the skin had pulled gaunt on his face, tight across his cheekbones, forehead, and chin, leaving it vaguely skull-like. His lips were almost invisible, the thinnest blue-white thread against his white flesh, and his eyes were feverish, glitter-ingly madly.

"You have chosen to walk down our street, for which we charge a toll."

"Of course you do," Dee said, forcing a smile as he stepped forward, moving closer to the young man. "I do understand about tolls."

Time changed, the world changed, but people did not change; Dee had told Dyckon this, and here it was being reaffirmed. Humanity, in all its various shades, remained unchanged. The youth smiled. His teeth were rotten and black in his head. They reminded Dee of Elizabeth's. People remarked that she rarely smiled and put it down to the worries of state. In truth, it was because she was ashamed of her teeth. Even Dee's finest poul-tices and simples had been unable to clean the stains, though he had managed to ease the pain.

"Don't you know it's very dangerous to come out here into the Valley? Didn't anyone tell you that there are dangerous peo-ple in the Valley?" The last word sounded singsong high and shrill. The youth laughed. His two companions dutifully joined in from the shadows. "Why, they'll steal everything you have in-cluding your floating suitcase, little man, and then probably kill you for the hell of it."

"No one told me," Dee said truthfully. He was now close enough to smell the strange aroma—stale sweat, badly cured leather, and the metallic copper stink of old blood—that exuded from the white-haired youth.

"Pity." Smiling widely, the youth stretched out a black-gloved hand. "Our toll is everything you have."

"Of course it is," Dee whispered. "It always is with people like you." He was close enough to see that the youth's face was covered with fine white powder, concealing scores of tiny suppurating blisters. Dee had seen such powder and those blisters before, but he had survived the plague. It held no terrors for him.

"You should count yourself lucky that you came across us first. By taking everything you have, none of the other gangs here in the Valley will be interested in you. Unless, of course, they're really hungry," he added with a grin, slowly and deliberately licking his lips. His raised his head and looked into the shadows. "What do you say boys—are we hungry?"

"Famished," someone called.

"Could eat the hind leg off a small man. He's got chicken legs." The laughter was high-pitched and wild, too close to madness.

"Ah, that's a pity," the white-haired youth said. "The boys are hungry. But don't worry, we'll give you a chance, midget, we'll let you run. We find the run is good for our appetite." His hand shot out, fingers opening and closing nervously. "But first, I'll have that fancy metal collar you're wearing."

"Of course you will," Dee said again, stepping up to the youth, and calmly sliding the Medici poignard Dyckon had given him into the man's heart, turning the triangular blade once before jerking it out, and allowing the body—the eyes locked wide in eternal surprise—to fall to the ground.

Standing over his victim, he turned to face the youth's two companions, who had remained lurking in the shadows, shocked into immobility by the abrupt and emotionless slaying.

"You killed him," someone called, the voice squeaking.

Dee said nothing.

There was a sudden clatter of stones and a second youth appeared, a virtual twin to the body on the ground with white hair and black, buckled leather. He charged at Dee with a long-bladed knife in his hand. "I'll cut you and kill you and eat you."

The man had obviously never fought with a knife before, Dee noted, easily avoiding the wild slashing swing, catching the man's arm, holding it straight as he drove the poignard into his armpit. The youth's howl was cut short as Dee's long fingers wrapped around his chin and jerked, snapping his neck. Blood spurted from the rogue's nose. Dee quickly pushed the body away from him as the dead man's bowels loosened; he didn't want his new shoes splashed.

The doctor turned, catching a glimpse of white hair bobbing through the shadows as footsteps clattered off into the distance. John Dee sighed; he'd been less than thirty minutes in this place and already he had killed two men. And he felt not the slightest twinge of remorse. He reckoned he had done the world a service.

Crouching over the two bodies, he examining the ill-cured leather clothing and the men's weapons—badly sharpened and rusted broad-bladed knives. Cannibal highwaymen. At least in his day the highwaymen mainly stole purses, they never had you for dinner. He wondered what other delights this brave new world had to offer. Dee glanced back over his shoulder as he walked away. Both men had white hair, as did the third who had lurked in the shadows. Did everyone in this modern world have white hair? He idly wondered if he'd have to color his hair white like an actor, or perhaps he should have brought his powdered wig.

CHAPTER

18

THE TRANSITION FROM BLASTED WASTELAND to city was dramatic. The quake had left a fissure in the earth—a ragged tear that sliced down the street. On one side lay the tumbled desolation of the ruined old city, while on the other a metropolis was emerging. Angel City, Dyckon had called it. The city had once worn a Spanish name, but it had been ironically redubbed following the Great Quake of 2039. Taking a deep breath, Dr. John Dee stepped out of the ruins of Los Angeles and into Angel City.

He was a creature of the city. He had spent his life working in and around London and the artificial city of the Court. He had traveled to many of the great and emerging cities of Europe. He loved the pulse of city life, the energy of massed humanity, the thrill that lurked in every darkened alleyway. He had once told Kelly that he only felt truly alive in a city and the dour Irishman had reminded that him cities could kill you as easily as any knife between the ribs.

And this city, Dr. Dee decided, was more deadly than most.

Walking its garishly lit streets after dusk, Dee felt the ground beneath his feet pulsating from the sounds of discordant music, the air rich with the odors of alien foods that masked the sour stench of unwashed humans.

Once he had moved away from the tumbled wasteland and began to move through the streets themselves, the sheer size of the place, the number of the people, began to overwhelm him. He had never seen so many people gathered in one place. They pushed and jostled him with no pretense at courtesy, and it took every effort of will to stop himself from lashing out at them, although the pickpocket who attempted to lift Dee's purse off its belt found himself driven to the ground by a savage blow to the side of his head. The doctor longed for his horse to put him over and above the teeming crowd . . . and a stout whip to keep the scurvy mob at bay. It was like the gadding at Bartholomew Fair. Just so much bustling.

Despite Cecil's advice, in spite of his own best intentions, Dee found himself gawking at the crowd. There were so many people of a myriad colors and types, shades of flesh and hair that he had never imagined possible. In his own age, there had been frequent visitors to the Virgin Queen's court—men and women of all hues from coal black to soft brown, sallow-skinned, narrow-eyed men from the lands far to the east, olive-skinned aesthetic Aegyptians, golden-tanned Easterners who wore their heads wrapped in cloth, and there were rumors of ocher-skinned peoples in the new lands to the west. These skin tones and many more fought for space in Angel City, though it took him minutes before he realized that the green and striped crimson flesh could not be natural.

Their costumes were outrageous—perhaps no more outrageous than those of his own time—but the fabrics were exotic and marvelously lightweight, the colors so vibrant they hurt his eyes. He had to remind himself not to reach out and finger the dress material of some passerby. He recognized buttons and buckles, hooks and eyes, but many clothes were held together with a gadget of strange interlocking metal teeth which he'd encountered only earlier that day—a plague on it. He'd almost castrated himself with the infernal device while climbing into the loose-fitting leggings Dyckon had given him. His shoes, now soiled, were remarkably comfortable, and having spent a lifetime with his tiny feet forced into ill-fitting boots, he appreciated the butter-soft leather. If he had any complaint about them it was that the heels were almost flat; but in time, he'd find himself a cobbler—if such craftsmen still existed—and have a pair made with lifts fitted in the heels. In his own time he'd maintained that wall-eyed German who always charged way beyond the going rate, but was at least very discreet. And while Dee was unashamed and unrepentant about most things, he was sensitive about his height. In his own time he had been shorter than most, but in this age he was bitterly aware that he was very short indeed. On average, the men were a foot taller than he, but to his delight, the women were just as tall. He had always had a fondness for taller women.

In his own time, his ego had been assuaged by being a man of importance, a confidant of the Queen, an alchemist and magician of renown, a friend to many royal courts—someone to respect. No one dared comment on his height.

His political and scientific attributes had made him a valued companion to men and an object of desire to women. Whereas here, he was a nobody, a small gray-haired, gray-bearded man of some eight and forty summers, with no patrons to befriend him. Dee realized even his alchemical skills were negligible in this place. He looked up at the long rectangular trays of orange fire that lit up the streets. Sulfur, he decided, walking slowly down the street, head back, examining the orange lights; perhaps a mixture of sulfur and mercury held in solution. But what fired them, what brought them to such a steady glow?

The small man stood in the middle of the bustling street and carefully reached out to touch the metal pole that held the trays. He pulled back in shock. He had expected to find it hot to his touch, but the metal was icy cool. This was obviously the work of a master alchemist. Why was not the heat conducted through the metal pole? Perhaps this world wasn't going to be so bad;

the art of Alchemy had obviously been perfected to a high degree. The thought of the knowledge he would soon command gave him some pleasure. There was so much to learn, but of course, he reminded himself, so little time to do it in. Every window blazed with multicolored lights, some of them tiny globes, others along strips of milk-white light.

Dee stopped before a tavern window and stared at the flashing red and blue and yellow lights until his eyes burned. After-images were seared onto his retinas. "A powerful magician indeed," he muttered, unaware that he had spoken aloud.

"You talking to me, shorty?"

Dee glanced sidelong at the belligerent speaker, affronted by some unknown gaffe on his part. It took him a long moment before he realized that the person dressed in the see-through fabric with the shaven head and ears and nose festooned with metal rings was a woman. What had the future done to femininity? Were women no longer creatures of mystery to be adored? Were men no longer to make fools of themselves in their adoration? The woman glared at him with fierce kohl-rimmed eyes.

"No, I was not speaking to you," Dee said softly, turning back to the window. "I was speaking to myself. An infirmity of the aged," he added quietly, resisting the temptation to turn and look at the woman again. Was her costume really transparent or had he imagined it? He wished to lecture her on her lost glories, but instead she grunted and walked away, oblivious of any effect she might have had on him. "Alas, so this is the way the world wags."

His stomach rumbled and he suddenly realized he was hungry; possibly hunger was making him hallucinate. Dee breathed deeply, then followed his nose toward the rich odor of baking bread. On a side street, a display of sweetmeats and small rolls was laid out in a blaze of light in an open window. Dee sidled up to the display, mouth flooding with salty saliva while he secretly searched for the shopkeeper. He could not believe his luck: neither the master nor his apprentice stood watch over the wares. It would be simplicity itself to snatch the nearest bread roll and bolt. But he knew there must be twenty-first-century magic at play here. This was too easy. Leaning forward to better espy a strawberry tart, Dee struck his forehead hard against the invisible glass window. Black spots danced before watering eyes, and he reached out with questioning fingers to touch what looked like air to him, but felt like glass. He couldn't believe that there was a sheet of completely transparent glass between him and the pastries. His heart sank.

"Hey you—take your filthy hands off my window. I've just installed that. It costs a fortune!"

A snake-eyed man in a white coat was gesturing to him from within the shop. Dee noticed that his fingertips had left greasy streaks hanging in the air. Catching hold of his right sleeve in the palm of his right hand, he ran his sleeve across the marks—and left bloody red smears in his wake.

The snake-eyed man appeared in the doorway. "What the hell do you think you're doing? Look at the mess you've made. Are you ZZZed or what?"

"I am most assuredly not ZZZed, nor drunk," Dee said, insulted. "I apologize for the mess—must be the blood of those highwaymen who accosted me earlier." He smiled easily at the man he assumed was a baker.

"Blood?" The baker swallowed hard, skin turning the same color as his coat. Dee lifted his sleeve for inspection.

"Will you look at this? The second fellow must have bled all over me." He shook his head in disgust. He was getting sloppy in his old age.

"Second fellow?"

Dee nodded. "Couldn't have been the first. I pushed him away before he spurted."

"Two fellows?" the baker repeated numbly.

"Well, there were five—but the others ran off." The doctor leaned forward and added conspiratorially, "I think he grew fearful when he saw how easily I dispatched his companions."

The baker nodded quickly, the tip of his tongue just visible between tightly clenched teeth. Dee brushed at the window again, this time carefully aware of its invisible presence. "I was just admiring your pastries. If I had some of your local coin I would partake of some. Mayhap I'll come back."

"No!"

"No?" Dee frowned. "I shall come back later."

"Later? No. Wait!" The man disappeared into the shop and Dee watched him shove a handful of pastries, cakes, and rolls into a brown bag. When he reappeared at the door, he shoved the bag in Dee's direction. "Here. Please." He attempted a smile, which failed. "See—there's no need to come back later."

"Such generosity," Dee murmured. "I am in your debt sir, gramercy, surely there is something which I can do?"

"Nothing. Nothing. Thank you." The man stepped into the shop and slammed the door shut.

"Must have been closing time," Dee said, holding the bag up to admire it.

Some sort of parchment, a cross between paper and vellum. What superb craftsmanship. Opening the bag, he lifted out a flaking cream-filled pastry and bit into it. It tasted like heaven.

Squatting in a door, enraptured with the marvelous pastries—the texture and the creme were so delicate—which compared with nothing he had ever tasted in any European court, except for the majesty of English honeycakes, which were his especial favorite, Dr. John Dee watched the wondrous new world pass by. That there was much that was strange about it was undeniable, more people than he had ever seen in his life—and such noise. It made the cacophony of his own age seem little more than a whisper. In this time, no one spoke; they shouted and roared as they had in his time, only now they did so in a multitude of languages. As he had become familiar with the magical collar Dyckon had given him, he realized that it translated all languages, with only the tiniest of fizzing sounds as it shifted from tongue to tongue.

Dee listened to the mechanical clamor of a city rebuilding itself. He saw the skyline made up of unbelievable towers that stabbed the sky. He heard the rat-a-tat kicks of pounding hammers, the rumbling passage of something large and swift below the surface of the ground racing hell-bent to some destination, and the bellows-like swoosh of doors sealing and unsealing themselves as people passed through. He stared hard at the magic, colored lightning trapped in coiled siphons that spelled names or garishly approximated blinking palm trees. Hundreds of strange, metal, self-propelled coaches—low-hung to the ground—hissed down the black uncobbled streets. Dee had almost cried aloud in terror when he'd first seen one. But he soon discovered they were as plentiful as pigeons and restrained by the thoroughfares. They moved at a terrible speed and challenged those who dared to traverse the road. Though there were neither mudholes nor stones in the roads to jostle the carriages, there seemed to be no patience in those who rode them. They leapt from the carriages without warning and jumped into them with equal abandon. He had watched other people riding metal water pipes, with dainty thin wheels front and rear rimmed in a flexible material. They were propelled by feet and chain.

Where were the horses, the cats, the dogs, and the goats? Had there been a plague and all the livestock eaten? The only animals he had seen in this place were rats. *The rat, like the cockroach, will be with us forever*, he thought.

And there was magic everywhere—in the globes of glowing lights, in the flickering images that appeared in windows similar to those he had seen in Dyckon's craft, in the tiny black wire harness many people wore on their heads and spoke into, then waiting impatiently for an inaudible reply. But a reply from where and from whom? For those in close proximity were not in conversation with one another. Who were they speaking to— their familiars, perhaps?

There was squalor here, too, and that also was familiar. Amid the magic and lights, there were people in rags crouching in doorways, arms outstretched in the universal and timeless silent appeal. He saw young men and women, some no older than children, scrounging amid the litter and rubbish that piled high in the side streets. He watched an old man pushed to the ground by two youths, and his purse stolen, while people with indifferent eyes walked around him as if nothing was happening. He saw young men and women, shameless in their nakedness or near-nakedness, prostituting themselves on street corners, soliciting passersby with gestures and salacious looks he'd seen used in every country.

As he finished the last of the pastries, Dee felt unaccountably sad. Smoothing the wonderfully wrought brown paper bag flat, he reflected that in five hundred years mankind might have advanced, but poverty hadn't changed one whit.

CHAPTER

19

Extract from the day book of John Dee, Doctor, in the Year of Our Lord 2099:

What strange Providence the Almighty has devised for me. When last I sat at Mortlake and put quill to parchment to make entry in my day books, 'twas early Summer of 1575, in the reign of Her Majesty, our beloved Elizabeth I, Queen of England and Wales. May God have mercy on her unimpeachable soul. 'Twas just ere I ventured in service for Her Royal Highness on an accursed journey to Venice, to that ill-smelling city of Mediterranean stench.

I can well summon up to my thoughts that moment of peace at home as 'twere but yesterday—which to be truthful, it very nearly was. The day was filled with the hot, moist air of thunderstorms that run in from the sea and rattle o'er the eaves; and mayhap I should have harkened to the dire portent, but a little ere dawn, I had drawn my astrological chart, and there was not a jot of ill in it. Indeed, the numbers foretold a long life, journey to a distant land and success in my ventures. Thus, I see that my conjurings at least partially told true. A long life indeed, and a *journey to a land more distant than even I, who am cursed with the most fevered imagination, could dream. And success, well, I survived and I am alive; I count that success.*

But, dear God, what of the rest?

Save for the sounds in the study at Mortlake of scratching of quill on Flemish parchment as I completed my diary and the distant ravens bathing in the rafters, my house stood still and silent after the storm. It was a glorious moment of my soul's rest and quietude. The pretty air smelled of scented roses and the clear sweet scents of June, and the day's rain which had churned the earth to mud. And, now I think on it, I am sure I remember the delicate drip of water from the gutter spouts. A sound absented from this Time.

Alas, the memory of that peace be green, though the day be ancient. That was the last day I wrote in my day book. Of Policy, I durst not have my book about me at Venice or during any of my sojourns, but kept it safe at home, sith were it to fall into unfriendly hands, it would surely have meant my doom and brought grievous dishonour to my Queen.

I have done all in all for England and spent a life in a state of marvellous dishonesty, telling people what mayhap they wanted to hear, permitting them to see what it serviced them to see, and made all shadow of my personage which was oft a series of interlocking lies. Within this seeming dishonour is where my English honour lies. I am proud to have been Good Queen Bess' man. This being so, I forced myself, when alone, to be honest upon the chaste pages of my day book wherein I might remedy any qualms of my conscience and bequeath to History the Truth of my deeds.

Yet, in so doing, I have done myself disservice.

A lifetime of observations, notes and asides, some of which were dangerous enough to have me at best titled the name "Rogue" at worst "heretic."

Verily my thoughts upon that caitiff catamite, Pope Julius, had I been Catholic, were certain to have had me excommunicated in Spain and Ireland.

Albeit sans ink or quill nor at my manor estate and after an unconscionable delay, yet I begin anew with my day book.

It is three months hence since the antiquarian monster, Dyck-on, set me in this place, this Angel City. To chronicle the deeds and mis-deeds of mine ninety days would need an eternity of weeks, and perhaps, if there be time in the months to come, I will set them down. In the vernacular of this place, it would make a good fillum scripture.

I have since twice spoken to Dyckon. He manifested himself on each occasion rather alarmingly out of the magical device known here as the TeeVee. Much of what I learned of this place, I gleaned from this device.

I am at odds to discover how this speculorum works—except that it needs to be co-joined sans spell or incantation in an arcane fashion with a hole in the base of the wall. Once they are properly mated, weird energies inhabit the TeeVee, bringing it to miraculous life. There are some five hundred Channelling accesses via the box and each access is gateway to a host of extraordinary images. Diminutive lifelike images, but of width and depth, hover in the air like bidden spirits. Most have parley 'mongst themselves though some do hold intercourse with the viewer. Indeed, when Dyckon first appeared, I thought for the while he was just such another image. He was in need to beckon me twice.

He desired me to counsel him on the manner of how to deal with a political rival, another monster of his race, who strived to discredit Dyckon and his researches. I ventured the surest way— have the villain assassinated—but my nice and precise friend stood mute at that, the aspect of horror on his gargoyle features most comical. I then advised that he give tit for tat and undermine the caitiff, set about discrediting the other man's—beg pardon, Roc's—researches, and this he seemed to find more to his liking.

It is a wonder to me whereby killing a man cleanly is beyond the scruples of most, yet, destroying their Life's work, and thereby their honour, is perfectly acceptable. A life is but a body, a thing of dirt, whereas a man's honour is his everlasting soul. Now that I have spent three months in the far future and seen how mankind has technologically progressed—though as I fore-

told not a whit emotionally—should I be surprised in discovering that other races, older, wiser than we, are in want of emotional progress as well? There is a lesson of Antisagoge from my Rhetoric lessons here but I know not what it is.

When again Dyckon spoke to me, he made me to understand that he had been bold with my advice and set in action a series of events that had commenced the downfall of his rival.

Dyckon 'gins to be in my debt where I mayhap have use of him later. He congratulated me upon my lore and Art, though, in truth, I cannot own the credit of it. Sir William Cecil had employed such a trick on several occasions 'gainst those who thought they were better than he. Moreover Cecil made point of being witness at their trials and executions, standing where the condemned might make good view of him, so that his face would be the last image they would take into the next world with them. I did not think my benefactor would relish the same dessert.

There is much to commend this new world—much to condemn it. The native people are of much suspicion—and because of that, they are unwilling to peruse too finely their neighbours. They are inclined not to ask questions. A humour for which they will eventually pay dearly. To whit, whilst I made good to assemble a monstrous sum of the local coin, I did so with remarkable ease. Not a man of them enquired of letters of credit, nor patron, nor purpose, nor proper contract. But I run before my horse to market, let me impart how it chanced I came to such good fortune.

When Dyckon left me on the outskirts of Angel City, he made me a behest of three especial pieces of equipment from his craft.

Item: The language collar, a thin strip of metal that fit 'round the neck with lock touching the spinal cord. This gave me leave to understand every spoken language I heard, and more, gave the listener to hear me give answer in their own language or dialect.

Item: Dyckon bequeathed me a holo comm, a holographic communicator. I am unsure which magical spell controls this square purse-shape package, but I am given to believe it is capable of sculpting an image of the wearer, cousin to those of the TeeVee, and at once posting it a distance away and relaying precise voice and gesture. It is also possible for the possessor of the package to behold images and impressions of the area circling the hologram, but only if they are reflected onto a shining surface.

Item: The gem maker. Dyckon bade me to understand how diamonds were formed—he spoke much about pressure and time and whatnot, but I as in my schooldays listened negligently. However, if I but place a piece of coal into the gem maker's metal mortise, seal the pyramid top above it, and speak the magical Roc phrases, when the top be removed, a diamond as perfect as an angel's tear will have appeared. Alchemy in the highest degree!

In the days when first I arrived in this place, I discovered a yard on the docks where there was piled coal. By interposing my fingers through the mesh fence, I extracted a handful of nuggets. The worth of two hundred thousand dollars if my sums thrive still. I discovered a street where none but diamond merchants and jewellers sold their wares. It was called Grand Street but was much too humble a market for that grand name. With no friend to guide me I made bold to enquire at three or four shops selling each a diamond or two. I would have naught but cash, though they talked much of the Laws of the Land, promissory notes and credit cyphers which appeareth to be the chief coin of their realm. But, truth be told, it says not much good of the place that despite my flaunting of their financial Law no-one had the scruples to say me "Nay." What good is Law and Policy if they are not attended to nor enforced? The cash became so plentiful that but midway down the street I had to stop and purchase a square leather tax-collector satchel to carry all the money. I slung it o'er my shoulder and practised a look surly and gruff to ward off all who might think to attack.

In this city, like all that I have visited, money was Almighty, and Francesco de' Medici's adage, that money bought money, still proved true.

Within the week I had discovered the wondrous joys of a

chateau known as the Hilton Angel City, and though it was
passing dear, I established my residence and an identity there as
a diamond merchant from Scotland. I had been mistaken for a
Highlander by those I first met sith to their untrained ear I
spake with a burr. I found a source for my coal where I might
buy it by the bag, and if the Hilton maids ever stood awonder of
the coal that lived in the bath, they never said tiddle about it.
For which they gained much by me. They proved untrue that
what Great Ones do, the lesser will prattle about. Nor did they
ever pinch the least of my possessions. Though I suffered that
they would not bide me pinching them!

By listening to the business channels on the TeeVee, and noting the names that were repeated there, I communicated with
that peculiarly modern class of tradesmen known as bankers
and stock-brokers. I'm at a loss to know what the latter would
have been called in my day—thieves or Jews no doubt—and set
about putting Francesco's adage to work—investing a portion
of the enormous hoard of money I had stuffed into a plastic
bag.

At each month's end, the stock-brokers and bankers made me
to know that my investments had littered and made more
money. I suggested that they re-invest my gotten gains. For I in
truth had naught to lose. What had I invested but coal? And all
the while I gathered what information I could—from the TeeVee
and the journals known commonly as magazines—of the man
Dyckon had tutored me was in secret charge of the development
of the doomsday technology that would ultimately deliver the
world to bondage.

Royal Newton. The more I learned of the man, the less I
liked him. He was a commoner of great family wealth who
knew not his place and acted like monarchy; an overreaching
villain who oft thumbed his nose at the law and was rewarded
for it, a man who had merited nothing other than have the
good fortune to be born to money. His merit is not worth the
cold fart the rude wind blows in his face. I had come across
his like before. They were arrogant whelps coming to court,
bullying others, infecting the minds of those who listened with

their selfish opinions. No man's pie was free from their ambitious fingers.

In my time, Cecil and I had brought them down. And I will bring this Royal Newton down. This before God I promise. Because no-one is invulnerable.

And the mighty fall hardest of all.

CHAPTER

20

DEE KNEW there would always be places like this. Dark homes for the unpenitent and explosive, where forgotten men went to try and escape from their own inner torments. These places had existed in the times of the Romans and Greeks, probably even in the Golden World on the fabled Isle of Atlantis. So long as there were men with unhappy lives, with sins to hide, who needed places of solitude, there would be taverns. And in the way of clubs and secret societies, each tavern attracted a particular clientele.

And Dr. John Dee was seeking a particular type of clientele. He had dealt with men like this before in another time and in another place and knew what risks he was taking. He had set about deliberately choosing those taverns that nestled close to the edge of the ruined city, deducing that they would be more likely to attract patrons from the abandoned Valley. From the little he knew of Angel City he guessed that the people he was looking for would probably find security in the lawless and deadly ruins. Keeping to himself and sticking to the shadows, Dee picked his way through the slum's taverns. They were always dark and uninviting and smelled of old peanuts and beer. He made sure that he always entered and left at the busiest times, bought a nonalcoholic synthibeer, and paid for it with exact change—no credit chit. Nothing asked, nothing given.

Tucking himself into a corner stool, he swirled his drink and did what Dr. John Dee had always done best—watched and waited.

Some of the taverns he could dismiss out of hand; the type of people he was looking for would not appreciate loud, brightly lit, overcrowded, and overly friendly clubs. In some the music played—though the term "music" was charitable in the extreme— was so loud that it pulsed like a physical banshee in the air. The music was ensorcelled into tiny silver disks; Dee wasn't entirely sure how, though he fancied it was similar to the Arab magic of entrapping the djinn in a bottle. Obviously the alchemists of this time had developed the technique of capturing living voices and musical instruments. Though it seemed more like Magic to him than Alchemy and yet, he knew it was their Science.

Some taverns were dedicated to a single theme. One was de-voted to what he assumed was an Arabian deity, El-Vis, a raven-haired god, who sang with the voice of an angel, but danced like a lascivious demon. It existed right next to another dedicated to his consort, the snow-haired, big-breasted goddess Mary Lynn. An enormous statue of the goddess dominated the tavern and at regular intervals, gusts of air would blow from the floor, lifting the idol's gossamer dress around her waist—obviously some sort of call to prayer. Dee was unsure whether to be shocked at the display . . . or simply enjoy it. He had to leave the Bulldog, the British pub, because it was completely incomprehensible to him. The barkeepers wore hideous red costumes that were vaguely familiar to him, but they spoke a peculiar dialect of En-glish that was almost beyond the translation capabilities of the collar. They served beer that looked and tasted like tub water, the pork scratchings weren't even pork, and he assumed the dish known as bangers and mash was some sort of obscene joke. Be-sides, the place served no sack or canary to wash it down.

However, the moment Dee stepped into Ruby's Left, which teetered precariously on a crevasse over the sulfurous Valley, he knew he had found what he was looking for. The music was a low female voice rasping about lost love, the sound, soft and distant, barely audible, just enough to cover a conversation but not enough to drown it. The air was fetid with alabaster-colored smoke, a choking odor from the sticks these men put in their mouths, that reminded him of the Virginia tobacco Raleigh had brought back from the New World. Tobacco had once been a novelty enjoyed only by the British aristocracy; now it seemed it was the last refuge of the scum of the Earth. Despite the heat of the day, there was a low fire burning in the grate, the remains of what might have been a brace of pigeons—but which could equally have been rat—turning slowly on a spit.

Dee allowed the door to close behind him and immediately stepped to one side, moisture beading up on his back and in his hair as he allowed his eyes adjust to the gloom. Two dozen wooden tables were scattered around the center of the room, but most of these were empty, the shadowy patrons clustered in the booths that lined the walls. Dee nodded in recognition and decided to stay. This was the place; it reminded him of the stews in Rome and Venice and Plymouth, where he'd sat dripping with sweat with his back against the wall, his hand on a knife strapped to his calf. Moving silently across the sawdust-covered floor, he ignored the center tables and chose a corner at the far end of the mahogany bar that was in deepest shadow, then waited patiently, one hand resting lightly on the scarred bar, the other out of sight, seemingly transfixed with the talents of the holographic chanteuse.

In his own good time, the barman with the silver metal patch over his left eye noticed him and approached. He was about forty and had the well-proportioned physique of a muleteer. He wore a thin sleeveless undergarment stained with a representative sample of the night's mixings. Despite the scars that hatched the left side of his face, his hair was white and sculpted with care, and his curling mustache was a testament to hours of preening. Dee surmised that the barman had spent the last years trying to hang on to his youth. He was wasting his time.

"I'll have a synthibeer," Dee said, unaware that he had spoken in German to the barman.

"Haven't seen you here before," the barman replied, answering in his native tongue.

"I've just 'Emed here."

"From the old country?"

"From England."

"Your German accent is excellent," the barman said, then paused, white eyebrows meeting in a straight line above his eyes. "How did you know I was German?" he asked softly.

Dee concentrated on the singer, irritated both that the collar sometimes worked too well and that he had been distracted from his observations. He was forced to converse with this one-eyed slopman. He did not want this man remembering him.

"A friend recommended that I come here. He told me to look out for you."

"Little man, I don't have any friends," the barman said belligerently.

"Neither do I," Dee said, showing his teeth. He hoped that would end the prattle, but the snow-haired German was on the scent now and would not be deterred.

"What brings you out here?" he insisted. "You're dressed way too City for the Valley."

Dee made a quick decision to risk a certain amount of truth. By half-truths set a gloss on thy bold intent. "I was told if I wanted to find some good men for a job, that this is the place to come." This took the German aback and seemed to settle some question on his mind.

"You were misinformed."

"Probably," Dee agreed, pushing three dirty unbused glasses of melting ice across the bar. The barman automatically reached for them, unsurprised by the presence of cash under one of the mugs, and deftly pocketed the two hundred dollars without changing expression. He turned away to serve a customer at the far end of the bar, and by the time the one-eyed man returned, Dee had settled himself into the deepest recess of the corner.

"I'm Otto, by the way." The barman scratched at his underarm and then picked up a chipped empty glass and began to fill it from a tap. Otto's back was toward Dee, but the doctor could see that the synthibeer had no head and he guessed that it was warm. It was a thin hay color. With a turn the barman delivered Dee's mug with a deft thrust across the bar born of years of showing off. "What sort of men you looking for?"

Dee lifted his drink and brought it to his lips, but did not drink. He was unwilling to dull his faculties with alcohol. The glass was filthier than anything he'd ever seen. "I'm looking for men with military experience. Preferably a team," he added, "or someone with the ability and wherewithal to put together a team. I'm willing to pay good money for the right expertise. And a handsome commission for the right introduction."

"Of course." Otto grinned, his yellowing teeth a sight to behold. "Right then. How illegal is this work?"

Dee turned distant and said nothing.

"Maybe 'illegal' wasn't the right word," the barman suggested.

Dee shrugged.

The barman smiled. "I've spent too long here, I've forgotten the subtleties of my own language." He nodded toward the smoky room. "I could recommend some of the men here, it all depends on what you want done and what peculiarities you can put up with. The big black guy in the corner, for example, will have nothing to do with drugs, and would probably cut your heart out if you even approached him with any kind of work like that. The small Spanish guy in the next booth specializes in assassinations—he works alone. The three good old boys next to him are a demolition team, ex-SEALs, but they're patriots and won't work in the States. So you see I need some information, if I'm to recommend the right men."

"And how do I know you won't report me to the authorities?" Dee wondered aloud.

Otto grinned again. "That's a fair question, and I might ask you the same. But I've run this bar close to twenty years. Do you think me and my place would've survived if word got out that I couldn't be trusted? I've spent a lifetime soldiering. First rule of soldiering—" he began.

"Keep your mouth shut," Dee finished.

"Aye, I thought you had the mark of a military man about

you. I lost this," he touched the metallic patch over his eye, "in that stupid Alaskan mess."

He lifted his left hand and peeled off a flesh-colored glove to reveal an intricate metal hand. Otto flexed his fingers, tiny pistons and cogs clicking softly. A green light winked softly in the metal hand's center, briefly illuminating a network of microthin wires and computer chips.

Dee bit down hard on the inside of his cheek to prevent himself from crying out in astonishment.

"When I lost this in the New Mexico riots, the United States Army in its infinite wisdom decided that it was time for me to call it quits."

"May I?" Dee asked softly, reaching out to run a finger down the oiled metal hand.

Otto smiled proudly, extending his hand for Dee to examine. "You don't see many like this anymore. It's a work of art. Ceramic and titanium battery recharges with the electrical impulses of my muscles. The new stuff is plastic and bullshit-dangerous too. You heard about that pitcher for the Angel City Dodgers who two years ago secretly had a prosthetic arm and hand redo in Rio de Janeiro?"

Dee shook his head.

"You must remember him; his arm caught fire during last season's playoffs? How could you have missed it?"

"I must have been asleep," Dee whispered.

"Well, you remember," Otto insisted, "he ran screaming into the bleachers; damn near burned the whole stadium down. Would never have happened with this little baby." He patted the prosthetic arm affectionately. "His new goddamn technology didn't mean squat. Just overpriced bells and whistles. Give me simple steel any day."

The hand was impressive. Obviously a mixture of magic and metallurgy. Dee could see how the metal had been shaped to mimic that of a hand, but obviously magic or alchemy of some sort was required to make the hand work.

What had he said about muscles and electrical impulses? So mankind ventured to imitate what God had done so well. *And to think*, thought Dee, *in my time, Pride was accounted a sin*. "It is wondrous," he said aloud.

"Boasting again, Otto."

Dee looked up to find that the big black man the barman had pointed out earlier had appeared; he'd moved so silently that Dee hadn't even heard him approach. He stood six foot three and his head was as bald as a cat's-eye marble. A fishhook hung from his ear. He was all sinew and menace.

A man like this made judgments easily, and there was not a dram of mercy in his eye.

"Our friend here was questioning my credentials," Otto said, pulling on the flesh-colored glove, smoothing it until it lay flat. "He was looking to hire a few good men. He's from England. He says he'll pay well."

"Did you question his credentials?" the cat's-eye demanded.

Despite the dim light, Dee saw the barman turn pale.

The big man turned to look at Dee; then, without a word, he reached out and lifted Dee's right hand, turning it to look at the flesh of his palm. He ran a blunt thumb across the calluses and ridges that lined Dee's flesh. He squeezed the meaty part of the palm between his thumb and forefinger with just enough pressure to make it throb. "Well now, you've certainly worked with your hands."

"All my life," Dee said. "Why would you check?"

"We had a guy in here a little while ago, looking to hire some men for a job. Claimed he'd seen military experience in Paraguay and Chile, but he had the soft hands of a paper pusher. I reoriented him."

"You broke his nose and his jaw," Otto added, but the black man just shrugged.

"You are cautious; I admire that." Dee nodded toward his glass. "Would you allow me to buy you a drink?"

"I'd allow that," the big man said. "You've seen covert service," he said, more a statement than a question.

"How can you tell?"

"Oh, snoops like us can always recognize a brother-in-arms. I was watching you when you came into the bar. You immediately stood away from the door and waited until you could see clearly. You've got yourself the darkest corner in the room with your back to the wall, and I cannot see your left hand but I'll bet Otto's weekly gross that it's holding some sort of weapon. You look like a knife man to me," he added.

Dee held on to the grip on his knife and slowly, very slowly, raised the blade, placing it flat on the bar.

The big man smiled. "What sort of job are you hiring for? That is," he stopped suddenly and added, "if you've no problem working with people like me?"

"Like you?" Dee asked, genuinely puzzled.

"You see, Otto, that's why I like these Brits. No race wars in England. Let me rephrase. Do you have any problems working with a black man?"

"None at all, why should I? I hadn't come across many Ethiopes until I came to Angel City," Dee said truthfully.

The big black man stuck out a hand. "Morgan d'Winter." He grinned. "And I've been called many things in my life, but never an Ethiope."

CHAPTER

21

"IT WOULD HELP, SIR, if you could tell us where you were getting this information."

Royal Newton hissed with annoyance and turned away from the screen, choosing to ignore the sweating white-suited man. Standing before the enormous plate-glass windows, Newton clasped his hands behind his back and spread his legs, adopting the new pose he'd been practicing. He'd taken the stiff-backed, strutting walk from old vids of an Italian leader from the early part of the last century. The Italian first caught his interest because of his misshapen bald head along with his overextended jaw, which Newton found grotesque. But despite his crude ugliness, the man's posturings and the force of his personality seduced a nation. He had made them respect and love him. There was something to be admired there.

"I mean, sir," the voice on the screen continued, "your information has enabled us to advance this project by leaps and bounds." The scientist swiped quickly at a hint of perspiration that appeared from beneath his white hat. "I would imagine, sir, that you have several groups of scientists working on it. It strikes me, reading the data you've supplied, that one or more of them has made some spectacular breakthrough. The cold-fusion process is brilliant."

Newton stared out across the New York skyline. He could remember it when it blazed with lights and life, the streets and avenues laid out in a tracery of colored fire. He vividly recalled standing by this window as a child alongside his late and unlamented father and looking down over their city. Seen in the day, through the miasma of pollution and garbage that shrouded the city streets, he'd thought it looked shabby and decayed; the holes in the skyline where the Citicorp and the Microsoft buildings had once rivaled each other were like missing teeth. But at night, one forgot the reality, and the city became a magical jewel. Then only the necklaces of light remained. Sitting here on the two hundred and first floor of Minuteman Tower, the boy had often thought he could discern patterns in the streets. Something arcane and mysterious.

Neighborhoods seemed to have had an ebb and flow that transmitted some undeciphered message of humanity as a whole. But to Royal Newton, the pattern had long since been lost. Now whole sections were dark and burnt to the ground. Grim turfs were controlled by gangs who ruled their few square blocks like miniature kingdoms. The Feds and the NYPD mounted occasional raids into the ganglands, but in the last couple of years, the policing role was more one of containment. So long as the gangs remained in their own hoods and waged their petty wars with one another, the city preferred not to notice. It was cheaper too.

"You won a Nobel Prize, didn't you?" Newton said, without turning around. It was too much trouble to go and look at the scientist's name on the screen.

"Yes, sir. Twice. Both times for my work at CERN in particle physics."

"Am I hearing a little hurt pride here, Doctor?" Newton snapped, glancing over his shoulder, even though he knew the man could not see him. "You couldn't advance the Tiamat proj-

126

ect, and you're annoyed—possibly even jealous—that someone else did. Someone smarter."

Newton turned back to the window. There was a fire burning in Central Park. He hoped it wouldn't drive the wild animals out into the streets again. They were bad for tourism. His subways and restaurants lost money. Who set these fires? Why was there such discontent all around?

When the Animal Liberation Front had burned the New York Zoo to the ground on New Year's Eve 1999, and released the animals into Central Park, the experts had predicted that none of the species would survive a month; they would die of hunger. The experts were wrong. The strongest and the wiliest survived. Now wolves, panthers, and tigers roamed the park, occasionally crossing over to attack in the posh neighborhoods of East and West End, while snakes and alligators swam in the sewers. His own two personal favorites, the lions and giraffes, had all been hunted to extinction, but there were rumors of a herd of elephants roaming in the depths of the park who had suffered some mutated skin disease, which gave their flesh the consistency of stone. One of these days, when he had the time, he would go and bag himself one of those stone elephants. He could put its head alongside the other trophies he had taken in the park.

"No sir," the scientist snapped, jerking him back to the present. Newton was turning as the man immediately softened his tone. "Sir, I was merely suggesting that a pooling of ideas might bring the project to a speedier conclusion. Even if you could set up a vid conference—" the scientist began, and then stopped suddenly, looking off the screen to the left. In the background a siren began wailing. "Excuse me, sir, something is wrong."

Newton wandered away from the window and sank into the hissing leather chair, annoyed that his time was being wasted. The scientist suddenly vanished off-screen without a word, and Newton leaned forward and adjusted a control on the desk-sending compu-camera mounted atop the screen half a world away, panning back and forth, looking along the length of the laboratory, attempting to see what was happening in the background. The scientists and their assistants were standing by their stations, more puzzled than frightened. Newton could hear a series of prattling thumps, then a chain-link rattle. Then the entire facility shook with a massive explosion. The lights dimmed, died; then the crimson emergency lights kicked in, bathing the scene in lurid blood-red. He was reaching for the call button when the door chirped and James Zhu's face appeared in the monitor. Before he could speak, Newton released the door lock.

"The facility in Puerto Rico is under attack." The security chief's clipped British accent was precise and restrained, his Oriental face impassive.

"I see that," Newton said. Resting both hands against the edge of the desk, he pushed himself away from the screen, as if to distance himself from the images. The white-suited scientists were racing around the room, moving from door to door, peering out, then darting back. Barely visible through the frosted glass walls behind them, black shadows moved, briefly illuminated by muzzle flashes. Zhu came around to stand behind the chair.

"Grenades and Uzi 401s," he said softly. A high-pitched whine buzzed through the speakers. "Turbo-cannon," he muttered, and a small wrinkle of concern appeared. "Our people are completely safe. Their security cannot be breached. The walls are bulletproof glass. They can stand up to the impact of any cannon, rocket launcher, or ground-to-air missile," he began.

"I thought you took care of the insurgent problem in Costa Rica," Newton said softly.

"I did. There isn't an insurgent problem," Zhu said.

An intense white light appeared in the center of the glass wall, and then the glass began to melt, running in sticky streams to puddle on the ground.

"Handheld-laser fire." Zhu leaned forward, pointed tongue flickering between his thin lips. "That's impossible. It's too expensive. These are no insurgents."

The glass wall suddenly shattered, exploding into thousands of tiny shards. Two of the scientists were cut down in the deadly hail, their white coats blossoming with innumerable red spots. In the instants before the screens went dead, Newton and Zhu watched in silence as half a dozen black-suited men moved slowly and steadily through the room, guns blazing, lasers destroying everything in their path.

"We have a problem, Mr. Zhu," Newton said icily. "Fix it."

CHAPTER

22

"MAIL CALL."

"If it's bad news, I don't want to know." The flame-haired young woman pushed aside the mountain of paper to peer at the monitor set into her desk at the incoming post. Bills, more bills, a final demand from the phone company, up-to-the-minute issues of *Time, Investment Daily,* and day-old editions of *Daily World News, Entertainment Today,* and *The Daily Variety.*

Kelly Edwards pushed hair out of her eyes and stared across the room to where her brother was studiously ignoring her. "I thought I told you to cancel the subscriptions to the pulps," she said accusingly.

"Must have forgotten," Robert muttered, cyber-gloved fingers moving swiftly in midair across a keyboard only he could see. "Besides," he added, "we get the out-of-date editions of the ezines at a reduced rate."

"Robert," Kelly said evenly, "we are exactly fourteen days from bankruptcy and you're wasting the last of our money on magazines." Anger shaved the educated edge off Kelly's voice, revealing her Irish origins.

"Essential research," Robert Edwards said quickly, then turned his attention to the data strings he was manipulating in their only client's offshore—and highly illegal—account. "You were the one who said we needed to keep up to date on the latest developments. Maybe you'll find some work for us in them," he muttered.

On the other side of the world, a series of accounts vanished, only to reappear an instant later in an innocuous account in a bank on the Isle of Man.

"Maybe I shouldn't have got involved in this in the first place." Kelly Edwards placed both hands palm down on the desk and concentrated on calming her shallow breathing. Getting angry with Robert would achieve nothing. It wasn't entirely his fault that everything had gone straight to hell in the four weeks since she had opened the office.

Four weeks. Kelly grimaced; in those twenty-eight days, she reckoned she had aged a year for every day, which would make her fifty-six. She peered at her reflection in the monitor. Well, at least she didn't *look* fifty-six . . . though she thought she looked every day of her twenty-eight years. But looks were nothing to go by. After the latest series of cosmetic operations, her mother looked younger than she did. The last time they had lunched together, they had been mistaken for sisters and the waiter had thought that Kelly was the older sister.

Across the room, Robert pulled away the headset and peeled off the gloves, allowing them to dangle at the end of his sleeves. Standing, he pressed his hands into the small of his back, glanced over at his sister, and seemed relieved to discover that she was smiling.

"What's so funny?"

"I was thinking about your mother."

Robert's eyes flared in alarm. "She's not coming here, is she?"

"Relax."

Kelly glanced at the calendar. "Right now she's having that polarizing epidermal treatment she was talking about."

"Repulsive. This is where her skin changes color according to the amount of sunlight?" Robert asked.

"That's it."

"Didn't you tell her about the woman in Philly who ended up bright red?"

"I did, but you know your mother." Kelly shrugged. "Stubborn. Pigheaded."

"Just like her daughter," Robert quipped, ducking behind the massed banks of the Cray servers.

"That's your boss you're talking about," Kelly reminded him. "Though not for very much longer," she added softly.

Kelly Edwards wondered where it had all gone wrong. Well, no clients for a start and no money and broken promises and naiveté. And stupidity. Vast amounts of stupidity. And every nanobit her own. Kelly Edwards had worked with the Carroll Complete Management Agency for four years, and had hated every moment of it. The work was supposed to be interesting and exciting; CCMA combined the services of literary and theatrical agents with those of accountancy and stockbrokers. "We handle all of you" was the corporate motto, though in-house it was usually taken to mean "We handle all of your money."

Graduating from Trinity College, Dublin, top of her year with degrees in Business & Entertainment Studies and Investment Protocols, Edwards had been approached by CCMA and lured to the States with the promises of representing big-name clients from the worlds of business and entertainment, negotiating multimillion-dollar book and vid deals, then investing the clients' earnings in a variety of innovative ways.

Along with her four-year initial contract came vague promises of a seat on the board, stronger suggestions that she would be given a portfolio of top clients to manage, assurances of bonuses and incentives. She had been with CCMA for a year before she realized it was all a lie. She had been headhunted simply to prevent her joining a rival agency. She had managed a mixed bag of unknown authors and forgettable actors, none of whom ever earned enough money to invest. And consequently, she never was able to earn the promised bonuses and incentives. When her contract came up for renewal, Kelly had looked around the office, seeing those who had worked with CCMA for decades, gray and ground-down, then looking at the newer recruits who had been lured with the same promises she had fallen for. Then and there she decided that she was not going to spend the rest of her life trapped in this job, and tore up the new four-year contract.

She reckoned that there was room in the market for a mid-size business-and-entertainment agency. The bigger agencies only catered to the major-name clients. There were many mid-level character actors, software creators, and writers on the verge of the big time, struggling to find themselves an agency. In her last few weeks with CCMA, Kelly had contacted as many of her clients as possible, simply to let them know that she was leaving to form her own agency and to drop a less than subtle hint that she would be willing to represent them—for less.

On the first of April—and she considered the date highly appropriate—Kelly had opened a tiny office in downtown LA, on the corner of Hope and Fifth streets, with her brother Robert as her sole employee. It had taken four weeks from opening the office to bringing it to the verge of bankruptcy. Kelly suspected that CCMA had blocked her. Few of the people she had spoken to had even returned her calls, and those who had made appointments had promptly canceled them or simply never turned up. Their sole client, a Canadian multimedia author, had come via her brother through his computer undergound connections. The Canadian had been forced to invest his Chinese earnings in a bank in Beijing and was looking for someone to shift the account to a country where he could at least access his money. Kelly had been reluctant to accept the client, but beggars couldn't be choosers, and the Canadian had paid up front.

"I tell you what," Robert said suddenly, appearing from behind the massed banks of the computers, "if we are going down, let's take CCMA with us."

Kelly began flicking through yesterday's *Time*, pages slowly turning on-screen. "Can't be done," she said absently. "You would not believe the security."

"Excuse me, big sister, I've just hacked a firewalled Chinese bank and accessed one seriously encrypted account. Taking down CCMA will be a snap."

"Don't be too sure." Kelly grinned. "A Chinese bank is one thing, but an American talent agency is another entirely. Besides," she added, "with your record, they'd be sure to come looking for you."

Robert Edwards had served a six-month sentence in a reeducation center for violation-of-electronic-privacy crimes. It was a record that rendered him virtually unemployable. Just before she deleted *Time* magazine, Kelly scanned it, ordering the machine to hunt for the personalities listed and then cross-list it with their agents. Maybe it was time to start applying for a job again.

The screen scrolled. Thirty-two names listed, twenty of them with CCMA, eight with William Morris, one of the oldest agencies in the city, three with Courtney & Piers, the British agents. One unrepresented.

"Robert," Kelly said, hunting for the article, "run someone for me."

Robert Edwards pushed his hands into the skintight cybergloves and pulled on his helmet. A virtual screen and keyboard appeared in the air before him. Through the shimmering screen, he could see the top of his sister's red hair.

"Ready."

"John Dee," Kelly said, looking up.

"Spell Dee," Robert asked, fingers moving, tapping out the letters. Clearly visible through the virtual screen, he could see the letters appear on Kelly's forehead.

"D-E-E. John Dee. Says here he's head of a multimillion-dollar corporation. But he's unrepresented."

"Must be a mistake." Robert's fingers danced across the keyboard. "No one that big is unrepresented these days."

Kelly nodded.

"Give me that name again," Robert said a moment later, fingers moving in the air. "D-E-E. This is a mistake," he said immediately. "There is no John Dee. No such person exists."

CHAPTER

23

IN HIS DAY it would have taken an artisan months to create a believable likeness; now a floating sculpture could be done in moments. Dr. John Dee sat at the unadorned antique wooden table and stared at the photograph of Royal Newton, long fingers framing the ten-by-eight holographic image.

The picture on the table was so perfect, so real, that Dee felt as if he could reach out and wrap his hands around Newton's scrawny neck and crush it as the patriarch Abraham had crushed false gods. The image was three years old, but it was the most current picture of Newton he had managed to acquire. Dee traced his fingers over the holograph, following the lines and curves of Royal Newton's face, etching them into his memory.

Three years could change a man, but Dee was confident that he would recognize this monster if he saw him. He tilted the picture slightly at an oblique angle. Perhaps, he mused, it would have been better if Newton had allowed an artist to paint his picture; at least an artist would have been kinder. Nicholas Hilliard, Queen Elizabeth's court painter, specialized in miniatures, tiny, delicate, incredibly ornate portraits of his patrons. He had painted Dee once, on a piece of stretched and dried chicken skin. The delineation had been no bigger than the ball of his thumb, and yet the artist had managed to capture that sense of wonder in Dee's eyes. It had been his favorite portrait. For an instant, he wondered what posterity had made of Hilliard, or indeed any of the other people he knew, and then he quickly shied away from those thoughts. He had decided, shortly after he had come to this bizarre world, where tomes of information were but a keystroke away, that he would not inquire. They were all dead and dust now. Each name brought forth a fresh memory and some of the memories were painfully intrusive. Better to believe that history had been kind to them. And him. He could not help but wonder what history had made of him.

Dee looked into Newton's bright blue eyes, startling and vivid against his hairless skull. The eyes in the holograph were flat and dead, hooded and secretive. And, although he had never seen Newton in the flesh, he knew that his eyes in life would be identical. A man could always change his appearance, change his hairstyle, and in this age, even change his facial features and his skin color, but he would not be able to change his soul.

The eyes were the mirror of the soul.

He had met Hans Holbein, the great German painter, at Westminster shortly before his death. Holbein had been Henry VIII's favorite. The stout, round-faced artist had immortalized most of Henry's family and almost all of his court—and had still managed to remain in favor, even though he did not shirk from showing the Tudors as they really were. The soul's truth lies in the eyes, he had told Dee that bitter winter's night so long ago when they had huddled together against the chill in Holbein's apartment and whispered secrets that could have condemned them both as heretics.

Show the humanity in their eyes, and they will forgive the blemishes of their flesh.

Dee found no humanity in Newton's eyes. It was a mask of death. Pushing aside the stiff sheet of glassine paper, Dee opened the dossier and carried it to the window, to allow the early-afternoon sunlight to illuminate the pages. He could have turned on the overhead lights, but he hadn't quite got over his distrust of the glowing globes and tubes. Their stark brightness hurt his eyes. More, he feared them. His knowledge of twenty-first-century science was growing, but he still questioned it. It defied all he believed in. These future-folk might put their trust in it, but he knew that whatever spell entrapped the fire elementals within the glass would one day fail and he didn't want to be sitting beneath the light when the demon came out.

Dee settled himself onto the window ledge and looked out across a barren landscape of twisted metal, rotting and tumbled huts, diseased foliage, and reeking cesspits. The skeletal remains of tracks covered the ground in a pattern that Dee thought he could make sense of. This area had formerly been part of the old city rail depot, Union Station. It had been the rail tracks that had first attracted Dee to the place; the intricate twisting curls and loops reminded him of some of the arcane sigils in his grimoires. Fate had drawn him to this place, he knew that; fate had brought him to the long empty container car set back on a siding. There was a sign in the window, hand-lettered and flyblown, FOR SALE. Dee hadn't been entirely sure if the occupants—a ragged collection of down-and-outs—were the owners, and the looks of shocked surprised on their faces testified to the fact that they never expected anyone to take them up on their offer. Dee had bought the boxcar for twice what it was worth but only on condition that it was completely emptied out when he returned in twenty-four hours. When Dee and a very mystified Morgan d'Winter, the Ethiope he had hired in Ruby's Left, had returned the following morning, the carriage had been stripped bare, and only the stench of years of urine and rot remained.

"Your first job for me," Dee had told the mercenary, "is to make my new home secure."

"How much do I have to spend?"

"As much as you need."

"You must have some serious enemies."

"Not yet," Dee had said enigmatically.

A pack of rats were being chased by an equally wild pack of street children across the tracks. More than half the children were carrying rat corpses on their belts, though City Hall had recently reduced the bounty to a nickel a body. The small man bared his teeth in a humorless smile; this was just like home. He was lifting the first glassine sheet to the afternoon light when the outer perimeter security monitor pinged to life. Dee didn't even glance up at the screen.

Following Dee's instructions, d'Winter had installed the car in the center of a spider's web of alarms and traps. And, supplementing the hidden technological sentries, the devastated rail yard had its own native defenses, most of them in the form of feral children constantly scavenger hunting. No one would approach the hub car unnoticed or unannounced. Though the railcar looked innocuous from the outside, windows cracked and filthy, metal blistered and diseased, wheels rusted solid, the inside of the car was a revelation. Within the rotting outer body, d'Winter had installed a ceramic and adamantine steel environment shell, similar to the shells used on the moonbase. Capable of withstanding anything short of a thermonuclear strike, the shell came equipped with its own air and water recycling system, powered by solar panels that doubled as an electrical defensive grid.

"For the sort of money you're paying," d'Winter had said, "you could buy yourself an army."

"Put not your trust in armies," Dee had said. "This place"—he looked around and spread his arms in a flamboyant dramatic gesture—"suits me. I sit here at the heart of a metal maze, in a house that is not a house, a carriage that is not a carriage, surrounded by invisible and deadly guardians. Not to mention the little goblins ferreting in my garden. No, this place reminds me of home."

"You lived in a railway meat wagon in England!"

"I lived in an enchanted place called Mortlake. There was a maze in my garden, similar to the pattern of these tracks, and there too my home was sentried by invisible and deadly guardians."

D'Winter folded his arms across his massive chest and said nothing.

"You think me mad, Mr. d'Winter?"

"I think you're the boss," the mercenary said.

"I can see that you and I are going to have a long and successful association together."

The information in the dossier had come from a variety of sources, and none of it was recent. Dee read through the pages quickly, years of interpreting court reports and coded missives enabling him to swiftly determine that the dossier told him absolutely nothing about Royal Newton that he didn't already know. Or at least, it told him only what Mr. Newton wanted the public to know. But Dee needed more. If Newton was the rock— Dee smiled at the pun—upon which the Nephilim were building their plans, then Dee had to crush that rock. He had hired d'Winter to stage a series of raids on Newton's plants; these were designed to inconvenience the man and slow down his researches. Eventually, Dee knew, he would need to strike at the man himself. He simply didn't know how. The man was a ghost! He was everywhere and nowhere. His financial empire influenced every aspect of life, but its CEO eschewed life and all its treasures.

Dee flung the papers across the room, plastic sheets seesawing on the still air. The man had houses in practically every city in the world, offices in most capitals, but he was private to the point of reclusive. His few public appearances were always via holography, his companies were run by a series of shadowy gray men, and no one knew where he resided or was even sure of what he currently looked like. There had been a report that Newton was dead. Was it true? Probably not. He was more protected than m'lady's nether regions.

Another security monitor blinked to life. Dee idly glanced up and saw a shadowy, hooded figure moving cautiously through the twisted metal.

Another thief perhaps, someone drawn by the rumors of the eccentric Englishman living in one of the cars. The last three would-be thieves hadn't made it past the outer perimeter: the hidden weapons scanners had picked up on the guns they carried and detonated the plasma ammunition charges. One unfortunate had been carrying three weapons; there had not been enough of him left to scrape into a bucket. And it had taken all of d'Winter's persuasive powers to stop Dee from planting the bloodied and burnt heads on spikes as a warning to others. This figure was obviously carrying no weapons, so it had bypassed the first layer of defenses. The small man settled into a chair and faced the wall of security monitors. All the screens had now come to life, infrared and night-sight enhancing the image, targeting circles from the dozen heavy-caliber weapons and flechette pips superimposed over the figure. Lights winked on as the automatic weapons powered up as the intruder approached the exclusion zone around the railcar, LEDs flickering from green to red.

Dee tapped in the key sequence d'Winter had taught him, bringing the highly illegal biochip monitors into play. Biochip monitors were the exclusive property of government and police departments. D'Winter had been astonished when he discovered that Dee had no biochip implanted in his left shoulder. "I heard there was an operation to remove them; where did you have yours done?"

"I never had one implanted," Dee had said truthfully.

"But you must have—everyone has. How else do they keep track of your medical records, your licenses and passport?"

"It's different in England," Dee had explained.

The biochip monitor's invisible laser light washed over the intruder, reading the data encoded into the chip, transferring the intruder's personal, professional, medical, and financial history into Dee's computers. The words flashed on-screen in the final seconds before the guns fired. But Dee only saw the first two.

EDWARDS KELLY.

CHAPTER

24

"'S DEATH, WOMAN! You could have been killed!"

"You're telling me! I was the one getting shot at!"

Dr. John Dee sucked in a deep shuddering breath and locked his hands together behind his back to keep them from shaking. The moment had been wrenchingly horrible when he had seen the name—Edwards Kelly—flash on the screen. In the immediate instant, he had rejoiced in the memory of his old friend, that wild rogue with his red hair and grass green eyes whose Irish wiles had gotten him access to the downy beds of many of the noblewomen of the European courts. Even Queen Bess had looked favorably on Kelly—until she realized that he was Irish, and most likely Catholic.

But in that moment when he had seen his man's name on the screen, Dee had hoped that Kelly had somehow miraculously survived, as he had survived. And then the turret guns had opened up, and he heard the heart-stopping rattle of gunfire. He stabbed frantically at the key that controlled the servoguns, but it had seemed like an eternity until the shooting had ended. Dee had visualized his old friend cut to bloody strips of meat. It had been a nasty vision of slaughter, but then he had always been blessed—or cursed—with a particularly vivid imagination.

Racing hell-bent out into the night, oblivious to his own safety, still terrified by his vision, he found the hooded figure crouched in a compacted red ball in the center of a circle of devastation. Heavy-caliber machine guns had punched into the earth in a tight circle around the figure; there were leaden pockmarks everywhere. It reminded him of the horror of the plague. It took Dee a moment before he realized that the ball had been miraculously untouched; obviously no weapons of any kind, or anything that could be interpreted as a weapon, had been registered on the intruder by the ordnance scanners. Kelly had not moved a scintilla and it had saved his life.

Dee automatically made the sign of the Cross and whispered gratefully, "Damn his eyes, luck of the Irish . . ." He thanked Divine Providence that d'Winter had insisted on this modification to the defense system for legal reasons. It was perfectly acceptable in the State of California to shoot down an armed trespasser—justifiable self-defense, the courts had ruled—though there still remained the potential for a hefty fine for littering or pollution, if proper biodegradable lead shot wasn't used. However, even in the twenty-first century, it was considered illegal and even reprehensible to shoot down an unarmed person. So the weapons systems had been modified only to stop an armed intruder in the secondary defense zone.

"Kelly, what are you doing here?" Dee demanded, picking his way through the rubbish.

"Getting shot at!"

Dee stopped in surprise. The voice was female. He lifted a palm-beacon and bathed the hooded figure in harsh white light. A gloved hand pushed back the hood, and there was bright, bloodred hair glistening in the light.

"You're a woman?" he asked softly.

"I'm a very pissed-off woman. Just what the hell is happening here?" There was a pause; then the redhead regrouped and asked, "And just how did you know my name?"

"I thought you were Edward Kelly," Dee said, flicking off the light and turning away. The threat was over. The little idiot had lost her way and nearly died for it. Let her thank God and find her own way out. He turned his back on her and started for the railcar.

"Who the hell is Edward Kelly?" she shouted at him. "You've got it backwards, butthead, I'm Kelly Edwards and I don't believe in coincidences and more to the point I want answers for what just happened. Let me reiterate: How did you know my name?" As she took a breath to wait for the answer, her brow furrowed. "Unless . . . unless you have a biochip monitor," the girl accused. "They're forbidden to private citizens, you know!" She took an accusatory step toward him and the evening silence was immediately broken by the whirr and click of the guns as they shifted and moved to keep her in their sights. Kelly stopped and stared at the back of the retreating figure, squinting to make out his shape in the gloom. "Wait," she called. "Wait, I just need to talk to you."

Dee ignored her as he padded his way back to his sanctuary. Disappointment had left a bitter taste in his mouth, and he once again realized just how alone he was in this place.

"Listen to me, I came to talk to John Dee!" she shouted. She saw the figure suddenly stop and balance his right foot on a train rail.

Dee stood dumbfounded that this stupid woman with the familiar name had breached his anonymity. Who was she?

Kelly knew she had struck a chord in him and had to follow up her advantage of surprise. "John Dee. I'm here to see Mr. Dee."

Dee glanced over his shoulder. "Is Dr. Dee expecting you?" he asked.

"Of course the doctor is," Kelly lied, "and let me tell you, he's going to be mightily pissed when he discovers what nearly happened here to me. I could have been killed. He wouldn't have liked that."

"You could have been killed," Dee agreed, turning to face her again, amused by the young woman's audacity. "But you weren't. What do you want to speak to Dr. Dee about?" he asked, walking back to the circle which had been traced by the gunfire.

"I'm afraid that's private." Kelly smiled, flaunting her new-found leverage.

"Must be very important if Dr. Dee is seeing you at this hour of the night."

Kelly glanced at her watch. It was not yet nine. "It's still early. Why don't you just get him and then toddle off to bed. We'll call you if we need you."

"The good doctor retires early." He turned his head and studied her, then said softly, "Defensive grid off," and the system powered down with a descending whine.

"Come," he said to the young woman, "we'll see what he wants done with you."

Kelly took a deep breath and followed the peculiar man through the piles of rubbish which, she began to realize, wove some sort of defensive maze around the converted railcar. He was dressed in the neorenaissance style that had gone out of fashion some ten years previously. He wore brown leather riding pants and a blowsy tawny silk linen shirt that tied up the front with lace bows. There was a multicolored handkerchief tied below his left knee and a broad black belt cinched around his waist. He was laughably anachronistic. Silver-gray hair was pulled back off his face and tied in a tight ponytail and his beard and mustache were carefully combed and coiffed. She thought that his accent was English. Maybe he was one of those pompous British butlers hired by American low-lifes who had to buy the elegance they themselves lacked.

"How did you find Dr. Dee's residence?" he asked.

"Trade secret." She grinned.

Two heavily armed guards loomed out of the shadows, guns leveled at Kelly, but Dee waved them back. "I thought you said that the doctor had invited you here?" he added.

"Ah, yes," she thought quickly, "he did."

"Then, he would have given you this address."

She knew she'd been caught but there was no turning back. "Yes."

* * *

144

Dee stopped on the bottom step that led up to the car and turned to face the young woman in the bleached moonlight. Their faces were on a level. For a moment he stared into her green eyes, noting the shape of her cheekbones, the jut of her chin—and for an instant, the face of the man he had known five hundred and twenty-four years ago appeared, superimposed over the young woman's. His mind wanted the image to remain, to linger, to fool him with familiarity, but it didn't. Instead, it faded, and he knew that this stranger was not related to the Kelly he had known. He reminded himself that all that he had once had was lost a long time ago; there was no reprieve.

"Let me give a piece of advice, young woman. Do not lie to Dr. Dee."

"I don't remember asking you for advice," Kelly said, brushing past Dee, storming through the entryway, leaving a trail of citrus perfume in her wake. It was the fragrance of Naples. Shaking his head slightly, he followed her into the railcar.

She stood there disbelieving. "This is unreal," Kelly whispered, as Dee stepped into the car and closed the door behind him. "From the outside, it looked like . . ."

"Illusion," Dee said softly, "all is illusion. Such things as dreams are made on."

The interior of the car resembled a medieval monastic library. Heavy oak bookshelves lined both walls and a long wooden table ran the length of the room. There were books everywhere, real books, with real paper and card covers. There was no trace of the shiny disks that now held all the world's literature and correspondence. Some of the books were obviously ancient, with dark polished leather bindings and thick, rough-edged, uneven paper; more were the rare ephemeral paper bindings of the twentieth century.

Music wailed discordantly, plinking madrigals, atonal voices. Something Elizabethan, Kelly thought. The young woman was unsure what the room told her about the mysterious Dr. Dee— except that this type of affectation and extravagance took money, a lot of money.

Dee moved around the table and opened a small minibar nestled in a corner of the shelves. Kelly felt the breath of cool air emanate from the metal cabinet.

"Where is Dr. Dee?" Kelly asked.

"Oh, about," he said vaguely. "Can I offer you some milk?"

"Milk! Haven't you anything stronger?"

"Milk is a sovereign remedy for the nerves. You've had quite a shock, young lady."

"I was doing fine until your defensive grid opened up on me. I thought heavy-caliber machine guns like that were outlawed in the cities."

Dee laughed softly. "My dear, since I have come to this land, I have observed that the laws are obeyed more in the breach than in the observance." Kelly felt his sidelong glance as she examined the bookshelves.

"How say you to milk?" Without waiting for an answer he poured her a mug.

"I've never seen so many books before in my life. They take up so much room. I said no to the milk," she added, turning back to him. "What else have you got to drink?"

"Just about everything," he observed, and carefully returned the beaded glass of milk to the refrigerator.

"Any nonalcoholic whiskey?"

"Some ten-year-old Japanese," Dee said, reading a label on a curiously misshapen bottle, unconsciously translating the Kanji script.

"That'll do." Kelly Edwards was annoyed to discover that her hands were trembling slightly as she reached for the heavy crystal goblet. The warm liquor quieted her misgivings. So did this man's quiet courtesy; these British butlers were very well bred. "Your employer is a man of taste," she remarked.

"Oh, yes. Exquisite good taste. Years of breeding." Dee lifted the glass he had poured for her out of the refrigerator and drank deeply before wiping away the milky mustache with a sign of satisfaction.

Kelly sank into a high-backed Queen Anne chair, stretched out her legs, and crossed them at the ankles. She stared over the rim of the glass at Dee, who returned her gaze, unblinkingly. She was at least a head taller than he, her red hair, held back off her face by a simple band, winking gold in the dim light. She was wearing what Dee had at first assumed was a uniform when he had come to Angel City: a blue denim shirt and short denim skirt over a pair of knee-high, expensive-looking reptile boots.

"Have you known Dr. Dee long?" she asked abruptly.

"All his life," he replied. "Before I announce you," he continued, "I will need to know your business; otherwise the good doctor may simply refuse to see you."

"Oh he'll see me. I can be very persistent," Kelly said, innocently crossing and uncrossing her legs.

"You can be as persistent as you like, but the defensive grid has your biochip details in its cache. It would be a matter of simplicity to instruct it to shoot you on sight. So once you leave, there will be no coming back. The doctor," he added, "values his privacy." He smiled again, but then turned away. "So I think you will need to give me a reason why I should present you to the doctor."

Kelly Edwards took a deep breath and launched into the carefully prepared speech she had worked and reworked on the way over. "Because I've been doing a little checking into your good doctor and, do you know, I can find no record of him, no mention—*nada*, nothing, *nani mo nai*. According to the Federal Bionet he didn't exist up to a couple of months ago."

"This is I'm sure fascinating to you, but ultimately boring for me. As I said before, the doctor is a very private man. And obviously wealthy. And wealth buys many things, including privacy from your Federal Bionet. He does not want to be seen by many people."

"Well then, why did you allow me in here?" Kelly said. Dee gave nothing away but looked at her almost with admiration. She congratulated herself. She played the game well.

There was no politic reason to bring her to the inner sanctum, but he had done so. First point to Miss Edwards.

"Your name intrigued the doctor. In his youth, he once knew someone—a dear friend—called Edward Kelly. When your name flashed up on the screen, I believe he thought it was his old friend reclaimed." An enormous white cat appeared out from beneath the table and nudged Dee's legs, then wandered over to investigate the girl. She reached down to scratch the cat under the chin, and then her gold hairband slipped, allowing her red mane of hair to cascade past her shoulder and swipe by her knee.

She flicked her head up and back, sending her tresses flying; deftly, in one simple motion, she caught and secured them with the band. Then she returned her attention to the cat, which immediately arched its back in pleasure and settled into a rumbling purr.

"Gull likes you," Dee observed. "I've always thought animals are such good judges of character. However, you still haven't given me a good reason why I should introduce you to the doctor and, let us be honest now, we both know he didn't invite you here tonight."

"I am in a position to do him a great service," she said.

"Is that all?" Dee sounded surprised. "Well, it is true the doctor has been serviced by the best. You would not be the first woman to make him that offer."

Kelly flushed at his remark. She'd heard much worse every day of her life, but she'd been seduced by all this man's previous gallantry. "This is a business proposition," she insisted.

Dee turned the glass of milk around between his palms. "Really? That's what they all say."

"I've been doing some checking on this doctor friend of yours. First off, I discovered that he has several million dollars in a hundred or so banks around the world in small, insignificant accounts. Accounts that have never been reported to the IRS."

Dee's smile faded. "The good doctor will take it amiss when he discovers that you have been spying on him. I do believe he thought those accounts were discreet."

"Oh, they were discreet, but not discreet enough. They were precautions taken by an amateur—and if I can find them, then so can other people. And I don't consider it spying; it was legitimate research. And I'm very good at my job."

*　*　*

"I'm not sure the doctor will see it that way." His precautions amateurish? That gave him pause; his high-priced solicitor had sworn the accounts were well hidden, concealed behind a series of false names and equally false addresses. Was his operation so easily uncovered as to be breached by a woman? Dee rose from his chair and walked toward the entranceway. He gestured to the door. "Perhaps it would be better if you were to forget all about this and walk away now. The doctor has work to do."

Kelly remained seated, intent on nursing her drink. "Don't be ridiculous. I haven't come this far simply to walk away."

"But why were you interested in him in the first place? Why are you here? I must insist on an answer."

"Because your Dr. Dee seems to have appeared on the data banks out of nowhere. And we all know that's not possible. No one can be totally invisible or unapproachable. Even the Valley gangs have some records. But your Dr. Dee is a wealthy man, who has spontaneously amassed a fortune, and no one knows anything about him. He's not even represented, for example."

"Represented?"

"Yes, represented. Look, this neurotic hiding may be how they do things in Europe, but it won't fly over here. You get nowhere in this country without personal representation. That's why I'm here. A good personal representative can open doors, arrange contacts, advise on investments. And I'm the best there is. I was able to find him and only I can make him invisible again. Whatever money Dee has, I can double it in a month."

The girl was audacious. He'd give her that. The claim was as ludicrous as spinning gold out of straw. But was she what she said she was? He wanted her to be. "I believe he has a lot of money."

"Well I can make it a lot more!"

"Why?" Dee wondered out loud.

Kelly scooped up Gull and leaned back in the chair, gently stroking the cat. "I think I'm done talking to an employee. I want to speak to the employer now." She smiled insolently.

Dee shook his head. "I don't think so. I think you should go." Kelly shook her head. She sat forward suddenly and Gull jumped off her lap, white fur bristling.

"Well, I do think so. Let the doctor be the judge." She waved her hand around the room. "Besides, you don't think I can walk away from all this, do you? I know people who would be very interested in a setup like this. Get Dee for me now!"

"Now, that sounds almost like a threat, and the doctor does not like to be threatened," Dee said sadly, turning away. It was too dangerous to let this game continue—pleasurable as it was. The woman knew too much and as such was a threat to him. And Dee knew the only sure way to deal with a threat was to remove it. He depressed the button set into the arm of his chair. A door recessed into the bookcase opened silently and an enormous shaven-headed black man appeared.

Kelly only saw the huge silver pistol in his hand, and did not hear the terrifying click as the hammer was thumbed back.

CHAPTER
25

"WHAT DO YOU WANT ME TO DO with her, Doctor?"

"Doctor? *Doctor? You're* the doctor!" Edwards gasped, ignoring the big man with the gun.

"Yes, in truth, I am Dr. John Dee, but not, I am afraid, at your service." Dee bowed slightly, ducking his head and extending his left leg.

Kelly Edwards, with ill-concealed distaste, forced a smile to her lips. This situation had obviously turned out to be more dangerous than she had bargained for. She had been taken in like a fool and she didn't like it. "Look, perhaps it would be better if we were to start again; we seem to have gotten off on the wrong foot."

Dee folded his arms across his chest and looked at the young woman, his face a blank.

"Perhaps I spoke out of turn," Kelly continued quickly. "I think I'm still in shock from the guns," she lied. "If I offended you, I apologize."

"You breach my security, invade my home, insult my intelligence, and threaten my person," Dee interrupted. "Verily, woman, you have offended me mightily."

"What do you want me to do with her, Doctor?" d'Winter

151

asked again, his coal-black eyes fixed on Kelly's face, the enormous silver gun in his hand never wavering. He knew her type, knew her for what she was: a sucking leech, a blackmailer. He had listened to her bluster and threaten and guessed that she would try tears next, or sex. She was a web-spinner—a black widow. D'Winter figured she must have stumbled onto Dee accidentally, then discovered just how much money he had, and decided that he would be ripe for whatever scam she was running. But she'd been mistaken. Badly mistaken. He wondered if Dee would order him to fade her himself or leave her for the Valley gangs. The boys loved chicken legs.

Her grass-green eyes flicked in his direction. "Put away the toy," she reprimanded. "You won't kill me." Kelly Edwards sat back in the oversized leather chair and patted her thighs, encouraging Gull back up onto her lap.

"What makes you so sure?" Dee smiled.

The cat's deep-throated purring filled the silence while Kelly formulated a reply.

"I believe I can rely on your graciousness, your business acumen, and," she smiled thinly, "that a man of your wealth, in your position, with no public persona, is obviously no fool, John."

Dee stiffened; he was startled by her familiar use of his Christian name.

This woman was a liability as well as a threat. Women's meddling in men's affairs had undone Man since time immemorial. This was damned inconvenient. He didn't need her unwanted intrusion now. His organization was still too fragile.

And yet . . . and yet he enjoyed her audacity, her cunning, her nerve, and a part of him toyed with the idea of somehow having her stay. A pretty woman had oft been his undoing in the past, he remembered, and obviously five hundred and more years asleep had not dampened his enthusiasm for the fairer sex. Thank God.

"If you think about it, you will realize that there is no way I would have come to see you without some form of insurance."

Dee nodded. If he'd been in her situation, he'd certainly have set up a backup plan; in his day it had been called Edward Kelly.

His lips twisted at the irony.

Kelly ran her fingers through Gull's luxurious coat, holding the cat tightly so that the two men wouldn't see the shaking of her hands.

"Believe me when I tell you that I am very good at what I do, John. Everything I know about you—and I know a lot more than you can imagine—is sitting in a series of flash-mails on my workstation. In precisely"—she glanced at her watch—"sixty-two minutes, those flashes will be automatically sent to various government departments and press desks. Unless, of course, I return in time to abort the messages." She shrugged elegantly. "I would imagine that the first government agency, probably the IRS, will be hammering on your door before dawn. I'm sure they'll want to talk to you about back taxes. Then there'll be the NCA, the National Census Authority, who'll want to know how you've evaded their identity protocols all these years. But you can bet on it that my contacts in the media will be here long before them. And then whatever you have to hide, Dr. Dee, whatever your lifetime of dirty secrets, believe me, they will not escape the searchlight that's about to be shone on you."

Dee glanced sidelong at d'Winter. Although he had grown accustomed to the message genie who instantaneously transported his coded instructions from one computer to another, he was unsure if what the lady was suggesting was credible.

"Is this possible?"

"More than possible," the big man said bitterly. "This bitch could bring us all down." He glanced at his watch. "We've got an hour. If the messages haven't been sent yet, all we have to do is to find out where she lives and where she works and power down her machines. You can hold her here till I get back. Preferably in a closet, out of earshot. Muzzled would be nice."

"If the power so much as flickers on my machine, the messages will be dumped onto the Omni-Net immediately." Kelly shrugged. "If the doors or windows are forced, the security system dumps the mails onto the Omni-Net and into the newsgroups. You should pray that no one attempts to break into my place tonight," she added humorously. "By the way, could I get another drink?"

Dee reached out and placed a small hand on d'Winter's gun, forcing it down. He was not unaware of the mercenary's anger. He came around the leather chair and sat down facing Kelly, elbows on his knees, fingertips touching his lips.

"You're quite clever," he conceded.

"It's a bluff," Morgan d'Winter said carefully, eyes still locked on the woman's face.

"It well might be," the doctor murmured. He kept trying to catch the young woman's eyes to read them, but she kept her head down, focusing on the cat, her eyes concealed by the cascade of red hair. "But are we prepared to hazard the risk?" he asked, thinking aloud. Dee picked up the girl's half-finished whiskey. He walked over to the wetbar, thinking, *Is the woman that good?*

"There's no risk at all if you let me go." Then, boldly, she added, "Of course, I did come hoping to get a job."

"How did you learn this information of me?" Dee asked as he rinsed the goblet and activated the sink attachment that blew it dry. He asked himself why he continued to play this game with her. Shouldn't he just give her to d'Winter?

"Once I discovered that you were not represented, I set about doing a little research on you. Only to discover that there was no personal data on you, that Dr. John Dee simply did not exist. So I set out this evening to find out if there really was a Dr. John Dee. 'Cause if there was, I wanted to meet him." Kelly smiled, showing perfect teeth.

Dee tilted the bottle of whiskey and poured.

"If you are who you say you are, let me congratulate you on succeeding in doing what no one has been able to do in the last seventy-five years—successfully hide from the NCA. Doctor, you're one hell of a hacker."

"Here's your drink."

"Just set it down, thanks." There again was that Irish smile. "But lately you've been indiscreet, maybe even lazy, John. You've allowed your people to leave little details uncovered. No one is completely invisible these days. It was difficult but I was able to track your investments in bits and pieces across the Omni-Net. Traced the development of a string of dummy corporations, shadow and shell accounts, and once I had even a few pieces, the rest began to fall into place. John, you really need someone like me who can keep you anonymous." She waited for an answer, but he gave her none, so she plunged on. "I wondered why on earth you would buy a solitary boxcar, and came here to check it out. I never expected to find you residing in it on the edge of old town. I mean who could . . ."

"I understood that much of the information about my business dealings was deeply encrypted," he interrupted.

Kelly snorted. "When I said I was good, Dr. Dee, I meant it. I am *very* good. I can sniff out anything on anyone."

Dee suddenly stood up, startling Kelly, sending Gull darting across the floor. Dee stepped back to where d'Winter was waiting. With his back to Kelly, he said, "Find out what you can about this cunning drab. Play the same game as she, search the Omni-Net. I desire everything you can get handed me within ten minutes."

He glanced back over his shoulder at Kelly. "I will pose you a question—and be very aware that your life hangs upon your honesty." He paused for emphasis. "Are you, in any way, connected with Royal Newton?"

The look in her eyes told him the truth even before she shook her head.

"I am not. He would have nothing to do with someone like me."

"Then you have nothing to fear from us. But if my friend here finds even the tiddle of a suggestion that you know or are employed even peripherally by that pernicious bloodsucker Newton, then I'm afraid he must kill you. And I rather think I would regret that. Though, I dare venture, not as much as you."

CHAPTER

26

"A<small>RE YOU THREATENING ME?</small>" Kelly Edwards demanded.

Dee roared with laughter. "Absolutely." The small man sat down facing the woman and produced an archaic-looking dagger, with an ornate bejeweled hilt and a triangular blade that came to a razor point. It was as beautiful and old as it was lethal. "Do not think that because you are a woman I would be loath to use this on you. I do not subscribe to the theory of the weaker sex. It is a pretty heresy preached by ballad-mongers and romantic poets. In my experience the most dangerous of people were always women." Dee's eyes went out of focus, remembering. "I can recall when Grace O'Malley sailed her pirate frigate up the Thames looking for a lost son. The multitude were terrified that she in her revenge would raze the city to the ground. She proved more than capable of it. Moreover, there was that Scottish trapnest who lured men to her room and clasped them to her ample bosom where hung a bodice studded all with spikes. Every man of her victims died most horribly with a disfigured leer on their faces," he added. "Believe me when I tell you: Women can outdo Cruelty itself."

Kelly Edwards remained silent, watching the man intently, trying to decide if he was insane or simply telling her these things to frighten her. He was certainly succeeding. There was no passion in his voice, no anger; he was merely reporting facts in stilted language and a thick burr. And he handled the knife with a casual assurance. She had never heard of any of the people he mentioned; it sounded like weird comic-book stuff. From the way he spoke about women, she was slowly coming to the conclusion that he was psychosexually aberrant. But was he crazy enough to let his obvious hatred of females drive him now to commit some brutal act of sexual violence against her?

"I am not mad," Dee said, as if reading her thoughts, "though I am very, very dangerous." Sitting back in the chair he crossed his legs at the ankles. "However, I am inclined to like you. You remind me of someone . . ."

"Yes, I know," she interjected with barely restrained exasperation, "someone you knew a long time ago. Edward Kelly, an Irishman."

Dee toyed with the dagger in his hand, idly flipping it up in the air, deftly catching it. "You said you could be of assistance to me. How?" He glanced at the clock high on the wall. "And be quick about it; my associate will be returning soon."

Kelly took a deep breath and sat forward, fingers locked together, wrists balanced on her knees. He had effectively called her bluff; there was no data on her computer waiting to be sent out, and she had come to the chilling conclusion that this man—this madman—would kill her without a qualm of conscience.

She had one chance left. She had to make her case, prove her worth to this crazy Dr. Dee—and do it in less than ten minutes.

"If you wish to achieve anything in this world, you need representation. Even the lowliest street trader now has an agent; agents open doors, arrange deals, formulate contracts. It is this tedious day-to-day stuff that a man like you should not have to be involved in."

"I already have a lawyer and an accountant . . ." Dee began.

"They're fine—but they cannot open doors for you that I can."

"What sort of doors?" Dee asked, vaguely interested.

"All sorts of doors; I specialize in contacts in the business and the arts world, but I have connections in other agencies that could arrange just about whatever you need. You want introductions. I can make those introductions. You want connections. I can guarantee whatever business or personal connections you would find useful. It is contacts like these which, in turn, will allow you to be a player in areas where you would otherwise be shut out. To achieve real success, it is essential that the big boys treat you as an equal. Also, because agents are not bound by the same code of ethics that lawyers and accountants are . . . we can facilitate arrangements. Further, I specialize in data access . . ."

"You doubt that I've achieved real financial success?" Dee interrupted, his voice colored in mock surprise.

"Well, I think . . ." she began, not sure how to continue. But her captor cut her off, enjoying her dilemma.

"Nor am I in the least interested in being recognized by anyone, least of all by your 'big boys.' Would I have adopted this reclusive lifestyle if I desired that sort of recognition? But do tell me about this data access. I am not familiar with that term. What does it mean?" The dagger danced in the light.

"Data access is—well, data access. We can access and tailor data." The tension showed in her voice, and she idly wondered if he was a functional illiterate. "We—that is, my agency—can acquire information that would normally be unobtainable." She looked at him blankly, wondering if he understood.

Dee returned her stare. He had spent a lifetime accessing data. In his day it had been called spying.

"We can steal information," she said desperately. With that, his head swiveled full face to her and the dagger no longer held his attention. "I see," she said, a little relieved, "that seems to have caught your interest."

"It has indeed. Tell me more of that."

"From the renegade firepower I should have known you would have no problem with respecting legal niceties," she said. Now that she saw what he wanted, she gave it to him. "We have access to information databases that the lawyers and accountants simply cannot use. We can advise our clients in ways of increasing their income outside normal financial intercourse—then hiding the result—in ways that accountants would find unethical. My company is particularly adept at that."

"I'm intrigued," Dee admitted.

Of course you are, you greedy little shit. "For example," Kelly continued quickly, "as I've told you I have managed to trace some of your investments. You thought they were completely hidden, didn't you?" She smiled her best public-relations smile. "But not hidden deep enough, John. I was able to bypass state banking regulations as well as decipher coded accounts. Now, for example, I could take some of those investments, double their value, and then legitimize them."

"Quite a claim. Do it," he said suddenly.

"Do it?" Kelly said abruptly.

Dee's smile was icy. "Do it. Take one of my investments, and double its value. Do that, prove to me that you are indeed what you say you are—and not just a bladder of hot air—and you have a job."

Kelly breathed deeply. "Fine. I'll start first thing in the morning."

"No. Do it now. No time like the present, is there?" Dee said softly.

"Now?"

"Now!"

Okay then, how hard could it be? She had watched her brother Robert do it often enough, standing staring over his shoulder as he had manipulated data strings, bypassed security traps and firewalls to access accounts. She had listened and learned, but had always let him do it.

She cursed herself for the missed opportunities.

"Please feel free to use my equipment," Dee continued, backing away from where she sat to give her room to stand. "It is, I am assured, the state of the art." He clapped his hands sharply and one wall of antique books revolved silently to reveal one of the largest comm setups Kelly had ever seen.

She rose slowly to her feet, and walked across to the matte-black computer banks, trailing painted blue fingernails across the gleaming surface. The viewing screen reminded her of the screens NASA used in mission control. It was a truly impressive bank of machinery.

"You can use this equipment?" Dee asked.

"This is rather newer than the equipment I work with," she said truthfully. The Cray servers she had scraped to buy were at least two years old—ancient in computing terms—but these featureless boxes looked like the secret stuff the government kept for itself. "It may take me a few minutes to familiarize myself with this instrumentation," she added.

"Don't take too long," Dee advised.

Kelly sat in the padded black leather chair and pulled on the gossamer-thin gloves and the tiny string goggles that linked to the computer's virtual imaging system. She was aware that Dee was watching her intently as he sat opposite her and ran his hand over the blank desk, bringing the screen to ghostly life. She found his blank stare unnerving. Moving her hand tentatively, she watched the image on the screen change, shifting with her perspective. What she saw through the goggles in three dimensions, Dee would see on the screen.

"I choose," Dee said suddenly.

"You choose . . . You choose what?"

"I choose the account I want doubled," he said. "After all, it *is* my money."

Behind her bug glasses, Kelly's eyes widened in alarm. She reassured herself with the thought that a man like this would not be overly familiar with this grade of technology. She had been hoping she'd be able to choose a relatively simple account and manipulate the figures. He had made the challenge harder, but not undoable. Any agent worth their commission should be able to manipulate figures to lie to clients. In third-year business school they taught you how to shadow-diagram for temporary cash-flow situations. The little man wouldn't know the difference.

What happened next froze her. Out of a drawer, Dee pulled on a pair of his own tiny wire-framed spectacles—Kelly stared at them in astonishment—and wrapped the ends around his eyes, and then squinted at the large screen.

"Initiate log-in sequence," he intoned, his voice sepulchral and grave.

INITIATING LOG-IN.

"Confirm retinal and voiceprint."

CONFIRMED.

"Lock down all secondary and primary caches. Divert tertiary cache to the virtual servers; unlock overseas accounts on my mark, deactivate encryption on my mark . . ."

CONFIRMED.

"Mark," Dee said.

TERTIARY CACHE AVAILABLE, OVERSEAS ACCOUNTS AVAILABLE ON THIS SERVER ONLY.

And Kelly Edwards suddenly realized she had badly underestimated the little runt; he probably knew more about the technology than she did.

It had taken Dee a while, but he had finally figured out how this airy artifice worked. Some form of minor spirit—an imp or sprite perhaps—was trapped within the glass screen. The sprite was obviously in thrall for a certain period of time. These sprites had power over money: Dee had an image of gold or the peculiar plastic chips of this time magically disappearing and reappearing elsewhere. Although he had not grasped the root magic, he had quickly come to read and understand the arcane symbols that indicated his wealth and holdings and their transactions. His instructor had praised him for his speed and aptness at learning the computer hieroglyphs, but in truth they were as child's play when compared to the Angelic alphabets and Demonic sigils he had spent years memorizing.

Peeling off his spectacles, Dee sat back in the chair and brought his hands to his face, fingertips touching, almost in an attitude of prayer.

"Some months ago, I sold a patent to a Mongolian company, Mon-Gal Industries, with registered offices in Ulan Bator and Thailand. Payment was in Thai baht. The deal was delayed for a week or ten days, and on the day it went through, the Thai government passed a law forbidding the movement of currency out of their country. I believe that the company I was dealing with deliberately delayed the closure of the deal until the act was passed. Effectively, it means that they do not have to pay me. I would like you to transfer the monies from that account into something I can access."

Kelly nodded. "I take it you have tried to access this account yourself?"

"I have tried—and failed," Dee admitted.

Kelly nodded again. "Okay then." Breathing deeply, she attempted to calm her jangling nerves and directed her attention to the virtual world all around.

If Dee had failed, then to prove her worth, the trick was to make it look effortless.

Then again, maybe his warped masculine ego might feel threatened by that. No time for psychology now, she prompted herself. She needed to concentrate on the task at hand. She had seen her brother do this time and again, she reminded herself; it was simply a matter of finding the bank codes, breaching the firewall security, disabling the alarms and tracking software . . . then transferring the money from the bank to another bank. Simple.

"Is there a problem, woman?" Dee wondered, a dangerous edge to his voice.

"None," Kelly said lightly. "I'm just wondering if there is an easier way of getting the money out, rather than cracking the bank's security, which could take some time." In the virtual schematics mapped out in front of her eyes, she started picking her way through the data streams toward one of the commercial directories, deftly fingering through menus like a harpist. Accessing the server's search engine, she began formulating a search, beginning with Mon-Gal Industries.

Watching her movements on the big screen, Dee frowned and said, "I have their address."

"I'm looking for the name of their bank."

Puzzled, Dee said, "I have that too. . . ."

Kelly shook her head almost imperceptibly. "You have the

name of the bank they paid the money to. I'm looking for the bank they took the money from."

Dee nodded slowly, unsure what Kelly was getting at. He watched the images on the screen, the world's banks appearing as featureless monoliths in the virtual landscape, each one ringed around with threads of different hues and thickness.

"What are those threads—there?" He pointed.

"Security," the young woman said distractedly.

"But you can bypass them?"

"Of course," Kelly lied. Carefully, cautiously, fingers barely touching only the thin threads, Kelly began to probe the bank's glittering defensive screen, like a fly walking carefully over the surface of a web. With each touch of her gloved fingertip, shivering colors ran along the threads, which immediately thickened. Suddenly, Kelly reacted with an exclamation of pained surprise. She shook it off and went back to work.

Dee, who had been watching Kelly's face reflected in the huge screen, had seen her mouth tighten with pain as tiny bioelectrical warning shocks had run back along the connection and then continued up Kelly's fingers and arm.

"If you cannot do it . . ." he suggested softly.

"Patience, Doctor, I can do it," she said through gritted teeth. Robert had described the neuro-tingling that a misstep would engender. But she had never felt one before. It wasn't pleasant. Time and again, Kelly circled the bank's defensive system web, probing for an opening. But mostly what she found were shocks. She desperately realized now that time was running out; the longer it took her to crack the system, the less confidence Dee would have in her, and the more certain it was that the bank's automated defenses would kick in.

Although highly illegal, many banks, especially in the Far East, had installed biofeedback monitors that were capable of delivering a lethal jolt to anyone who attempted to breach the system. Neuro-tingling was just the DO NOT DISTURB sign.

"If you're going to do this," Dee suggested derisively, "it would be better if you did it today."

"Today?" she repeated, her face flushed with frustration. She ached to tear his eyes out for all he'd put her through.

Kelly Edwards's fingers paused, hanging in midair, and then her head slowly turned to look at the doctor, her black-covered eyes giving her an insectile appearance.

"Today," she whispered. And then she smiled.

For most of his adult life Dee had watched that same slow smile creep across the face of his now long-dead companion, Edward Kelly.

The doctor knew that if he could see the woman's eyes, they would be sparking mischievously. Dee turned back to the screen, to watch an arpeggio performance of what the woman was doing in the virtual world.

She spun away from the Thai bank systems, and followed a winding golden thread that spun and spiraled across continents. Her fingers danced in midair, and now the smile had turned into beatific serenity. She looked radiant.

Unsure what was happening, Dee could only watch as she approached a new grid, a dark square monolith that radiated innumerable threads. Ducking and weaving through the threads, Kelly touched the grid and instantly it changed color, slate gray to bright red. The discoloration lasted less than a second, but in that moment, some visible glyphs multiplied. When the discoloration faded, Kelly pulled off the eyeglasses and sat back in the chair, forehead shiny with sweat in an afterglow of success.

"Done and done."

"Done?"

"Your monies have been transferred to one of my company's holding accounts in the Isle of Man. You can move them on at your leisure."

"But what did you do? The bank's defensive systems were impenetrable."

"They were. But if you cannot go through a problem, you go around it."

"What *did* you do?"

"I went to Greenwich, where Mean Time is set and where all the banks take their dates and timing. I reset the bank's clock to the day before the Thai government banned the removal of currency—then I legitimately transferred your monies, and reset the bank's clock. Simple." She grinned.

"Brilliant." He grinned.

The door behind them opened and Morgan d'Winter appeared, a thin sliver of plastic in one hand, the gun hanging limp in the other. "She's genuine," he said simply.

"I know," Dee said.

CHAPTER

27

THE PLASTIC CRAFT SCRAPED sand and stones; then a slight figure silently slipped over the side and waded out of the foaming surf onto the bone-white beach.

Dropping to one knee, Dee lifted the feather-light crossbow off his back and then powered up the outsized goggles as he'd been instructed. Immediately the world was lit in shimmering shades of ghostly yellow-green. It momentarily disoriented and disquieted him with dread. He breathed deeply to steady his nerves. Behind him a dozen creatures came ashore, moving silently on the sandy beach in black fatigues which blended them into the fabric of the night. Looking monstrous and insectile in their night-vision goggles, body armor, and weapons, the team scuttled up the beach and fell into position with a practiced ease.

Morgan d'Winter materialized beside Dee, and gestured northward with a long slender flechette rifle. Although the mercenary said nothing, Dee could feel the disapproval radiating off the big man; d'Winter was very unhappy that the doctor had ventured out from the intricate defensive web he had spun for himself in Angel City. Kelly Edwards too had argued volubly, pointing out the foolishness—the stupidity—of the move, but

Dee had simply slammed both hands on the table, and, in the thunderous silence that followed, had reminded them both who paid their salaries. He was not going to be left out of the fun.

But it was one thing to plan a raid on a factory in a protected boxcar, and quite another to stand on a beach half a world away in the dead of night, while armed and ruthless mercenaries moved at his back.

Nothing was recognizable. A threat lurked in every shadow. For the first time since he had landed in this future world, Dr. John Dee had realized just how vulnerable he was, how dependent he had become on Morgan d'Winter and, to a lesser extent, on Kelly Edwards. He idly wondered if either of them would miss him if anything happened here tonight—and finally decided, *Probably not.*

Why am I doing this? he wondered, tramping up the beach, the gritty sand hissing beneath his rubber soles. *Because if I do not stop this madman Newton, then in a year both d'Winter and Kelly and all the world will meet their Maker or end up servants to some foul Demonkind.*

Moving stealthily through the thick undergrowth that lined the beach, using techniques he'd thought forgotten, Dee recalled that he had convinced himself in Angel City that this field trip was essential research. He had financed a dozen assaults on Newton's factories; all had been successful—to a degree, inasmuch as the factories had been destroyed, machinery rendered inoperable, or scientists killed. Yet Newton's progress seemed unstoppable, marching on, switching tasks from one plant to another, bringing in more men to work on his Tiamat project.

This plant was different, though; Kelly's researches had revealed that it was this factory that supplied material to a score of other plants throughout the Far East, the Pacific Seaboard, and a vast factory complex set deep below the main island of Niihau, the Independent Kingdom of Hawaii.

If they could take down this factory, it might cripple Newton's operations sufficiently for Dee to consolidate his own growing operation against him.

At the very least it would close this theater of operations for a number of weeks.

Crackled static in his earpiece startled him, and he gasped. D'Winter's angry voice spoke deep in his skull. "Stay behind me, Doctor, always behind and to my left so that I know exactly where you are. I don't want to accidentally shoot you, especially since you have come so far."

"Farther than you might think," Dee muttered.

Morgan was in no mood for Dee's cryptic allusions. "And I wish you'd carry something a little more powerful than that toy."

"Fuss, fuss, fuss. You remind me of my mother."

"You must have loved your mother."

"I hated her, she was a mad old biddy, with a soul stonier than a Papist's heart." Dee smiled fondly, remembering the old hag. "She was a boil, a plague sore, an embossed carbuncle of humanity."

"Not to mention the mother of a fool," d'Winter hissed. "You should not be here!"

Dee couldn't help thinking the varlet was right. The world had changed; he had no business being there. He was out of his depth, in jeopardy, and his very presence might foul the rest of the mission. He would not make this mistake again. He crossed himself quickly, more out of habit than faith, and hoped that he survived the night to implement the decision.

Dee followed d'Winter into the impenetrable-looking sub-tropical forest that lined the beach. Dee and d'Winter fell into step behind the point men, twin brothers who bore not the slightest resemblance to each other.

Both men, tall, elegant, their ebony skins melding them into the night, wore additional lighting fixtures on their goggles, which emitted a complex mixture of infrareds and ultraviolets, bathing the track ahead in invisible light. Dee had seen what the resultant image looked like—the world washed in harsh primary colors flickering like the tongues of flame, stomach-churning and sickening in their intensity—but the interpretation of the images was a highly skilled task. Good tracers could pick out the outline of a fly by its body heat at a hundred paces.

The trackers stopped twice: once to point out a monofilament tripwire across the track, and then again a hundred paces later where they used water-atomizer sprays to illuminate a hitherto invisible crisscross pattern of laser beams across their way.

Dee shifted the crossbow from one arm to the other and wiped his hand on his night fatigues. The material was supposed to wick away sweat, but he was sweating like a stallion and was sure he was leaving damp footprints in his wake.

Each step was getting harder and harder to take. He recognized the feeling that had settled into the pit of his stomach and churned his bowels. He was afraid. There was no shame in fear. He had once spoken to the Queen herself about fear; Mary Queen of Scots had sought refuge in the court of her cousin Elizabeth. Dee had stood in the shadows behind the throne while Elizabeth greeted her cousin with the tight-lipped smile for which she was famous. "She knows you are not her friend, and yet she came to you," Dee had remarked later.

"Only the witless coxcomb knows not when to be frightened," Elizabeth had said, signing the incarceration order which would see Mary shuffled from prison to prison in the years Dee remained at court.

This uncharted new island with its demon technology and potent weaponry horrified him. In military prowess humanity had somehow successfully mimicked the power of the Almighty. Once engaged, Death could come from anywhere. The enemy watched from on high, from devices which orbited the Earth, metallic, celestial guardians. Assaults were made with the swiftness of tigers and the killing was done with pinpoint accuracy. Despite his learning—or perhaps because of it—he did not fathom any of it. And his inability left him feeling exposed and witless. A small child confronting a genie. Even now, on this stinking isle that could easily have passed for an outpost of Hades, one of the death angels could be lining him up in its sight. Would it not be the ultimate irony to be struck down from on high in this manner?

Try as he might, he could not force his will to concentrate. He was deafened by the sound of his own heart, and had an incredible urge to relieve himself. The last time he had sweated like this, he thought, he'd been entertained by that Russian princess, who subsequently turned out to be neither Russian nor royal. She did a marvelous trick with her ears. Dee got distracted, remembering, rubbing his own ears absently.

Wonderful girl, she'd eventually married the second cousin of the Queen, an old man fifty years her senior. So that by marriage, she became Russian and royal and could thumb her nose at all her old detractors. She was a widow a month later, and the mourners all reported that the old man had never looked happier.

D'Winter stopped so suddenly that Dee, his mind elsewhere, ran into his back. The big man turned and glared at Dee, the whites of his eyes clearly visible behind the goggles. "Doctor! Behind me and to the left," he hissed.

"Sorry," Dee muttered. "I'm not liking this," he admitted.

"I thought you told me you'd done this before," d'Winter demanded.

"I did. I've led raiding parties and been raided too," he added. "But the circumstances were somewhat different." The last raiding party he'd led had been to rescue a young women from a convent. That time he'd been lucky to escape with his life. He still bore the scars of the Mother Superior's teeth in his buttocks; best meal the Papist bitch ever had.

D'Winter pointed down a barely visible track, his voice cracking in Dee's ear. "The compound begins at the end of the track. There is a high-voltage fence that the twins are working on now. They'll bypass the current, then cut us an opening. There is a roving patrol that checks in with the base every fifteen minutes. Once we know it has checked in, we'll take it out." He sighed dramatically. "I wish I could leave you here. But I can't. It's too late for you to have second thoughts. Just try and not get either of us killed, eh?"

"I'll do my best." Dee grinned. D'Winter sounded just like Edward Kelly. In stressful situations, the big Irishman often forgot just who was master, and who was in service. Dee knew he should disapprove of d'Winter's tone. But he recognized the concern behind it.

The big mercenary lifted his wrist to examine his watch. "The patrol will check in in ninety seconds; then Salveson and Ann will take them out. Then we slip in. Once we're inside, the rest of the men will move through the compound making as much noise, causing as much devastation as possible. They should draw the security. You and I will work our way through the administration building as planned. It might get chewy in there. Be careful."

Dee nodded. "Kelly's researches reveal that this facility is run by Marconi Alimo, one of Zhu's most trusted lieutenants. There are bound to be papers, disks, information of some sort that might be useful."

"If he's got any sense, there'll be nothing here."

"He is human; there will be something here. People are lazy. Even the best security system can be foiled by carelessness."

D'Winter raised his finger. "The fence is down. Let's go."

Dee followed d'Winter down the winding track. He was aware that the rest of the raiding party was somewhere about, but there wasn't a sound to be heard, just the tropical warm breeze ministering to the trees. He smelled the tang of the sea, the lushness of the vegetation, the strange muskiness of unseen birds and animals. And his own sour sweat.

He had instructed d'Winter to hire only the best, and each man was handpicked for his particular skills and talents. Thus far, this night, they had proven their expertise. They had the advantage of surprise, but that would be short-lived. There were so few of them; maybe he should have bought more, but d'Winter had said that six was enough.

Once they were through the avenue of overhanging trees, the factory complex appeared, a series of long low buildings, each one dappled in camouflage, heavy neutral-metal netting strung overhead to render it invisible from the air.

The fence that surrounded the factory was twice the height of a tall man, a thick mesh of spiked wire, designed to dimple and then electrocute its victim. A wide triangular cut had been sliced through the wire and the wire peeled back into a broad opening, the edges of the cut still glowing slightly, the stink of burnt metal on the air.

Ducking his head, d'Winter slipped through. Dee followed more slowly, crossbow held at the ready, infrared laser sight activated, projecting a solid beam of red light in his night-vision goggles.

There was the merest whisper of movements, and the doctor was vaguely aware of his mercenaries slipping away on either side. He abruptly realized that from the moment they had left the submarine anchored off the island, only d'Winter had spoken, and only then to give him instructions. Why, with a dozen like these, he told himself, he could have stormed the world in his own time.

"Wait," d'Winter whispered. "Cover your ears, and close your eyes." He crouched down, hands pressed over his ears, eyes squeezed tightly shut.

Dee had barely time to crouch before the first of the rattling explosions rippled through the compound in a wave of fire and noise. Before the harsh lights blinded him, Dee caught a glimpse of his men crouched or lying on the ground, while all around them, deadly spinning tops leapt high into the air and exploded in horizontal splashes of flame. Some of the spinning tops shot up eight or ten feet before exploding. Their sticky flames washed over the upper floor and ceiling of the low building, where they stuck, dripping in long sticky strands, burning with phosphorescent intensity.

Heavy plastic glass bubbled and burst, and the extruded plastic walls immediately began to boil and melt with tiny blue-green flames. Dee stared at the melting walls and was immediately reminded of the images Dyckon had shown him of his rescue when the walls of the Medici tower had run like wax.

D'Winter caught Dee by the arm and pulled him to his feet. "This way." He led Dee through a series of alleyways between buildings, following the plan superimposed over his night-vision goggles. Behind them the night exploded into streamers of colored fire as another series of explosions cut through the compound. An alarm began to wail, but died in a long descending squawk as the speakers melted in the intense heat. D'Winter turned to Dee. "This is the door," he began, just as the door behind him opened, a long rectangle of butter-yellow light shafting out in the night. A shape moved in the light, a gun monstrous in its hands, a red dot of laser light blossoming on d'Winter's skull.

Dee's crossbow bolt took the figure through the center of the chest, pitching it out of the light.

There was a whirring sound as the barrel of the automatic weapon cycled, loading another bolt as the bow cocked itself.

"Very impressive," d'Winter said shakily.

"Not really," Dee said. He sounded disgusted with himself. "I was aiming for his throat."

"You're a regular Robin Hood. Where did you learn to shoot like that?"

"You wouldn't believe me if I told you." Dee grinned.

Dr. John Dee and Morgan d'Winter moved cautiously through the bare door-lined corridors. Although their highly paid snitch had suggested that this building was uninhabited at night, he had said that it was not unusual for some of Newton's employees to work on into the night, especially if a major operation was under way. However, the gunfire and explosions should have brought any occupants out into the corridor, and so far all the doors had remained closed.

"This is too easy," Dee muttered despite his fears.

D'Winter grunted. He had come to the same conclusion moments before. If this compound was so highly prized, why were there so few guards? And if this building was the nerve center, then where were the guards, the gun emplacements, the security bots?

"I think we should get out of here," Dee said softly.

D'Winter turned to look at him. "You want to abort? But we've come this far . . ."

"What are your instincts telling you?" Dee dropped to one knee and unclipped a package of explosive spheres from his belt. Peeling off the sticky backing, he began pressing the spheres to the wall at his left.

"They're telling me that something is very wrong," d'Winter admitted.

"Learn to trust your instincts," Dee said. "I did and I do."

"But we've come so far," the mercenary muttered.

"We can come back . . ." Dee began.

And then the doors opened. The six doors—three on either side of the corridor—slid back silently to reveal squat gun emplacements. The gun-bots whirred, laser lights tracing across the corridor, patterning the two crouching men. D'Winter caught Dee and pushed him down the corridor toward the unopened door as the guns opened up, the hissing chatter of flechettes ripping into the walls, the metal needles eating through the plastic bricks.

D'Winter's shoulder hit the door just as the flechettes cut through the plastic spheres Dee had pressed to the wall. The resultant explosion punched a hole clear through the wall and ripped out part of the ceiling, bringing it crashing down. Another explosion catapulted the two men airborne through the doorway into the control room at the end of the corridor and right into the midst of six heavily armed men wearing the gray and red of Newton's security forces, who had been standing facing the door with leveled weapons. Everyone went down in a tangle of shouts and curses.

Without thinking, Dee pressed the small crossbow against the nearest gray uniform and pulled the trigger. The body jerked and jolted away from him, but the crossbow's cycling mechanism jammed as it attempted to load another bolt. Releasing the useless whirring weapon, Dee slid his dagger from his boot and rammed it onto the groin of another man, who was desperately attempting to disentangle his long rifle to bring it to bear on d'Winter. The guard died wide-eyed.

Morgan d'Winter hit the ground hard and knew immediately from the sickening snap and the icy numbness that ran down the length of his left arm that he had dislocated his shoulder. He looked up and caught the eyes of a swarthy guard who was coolly taking aim. D'Winter released his grip on the rifle and with his right hand pulled the heavy-caliber pistol from his shoulder holster and fired blindly. The massive explosion lit up the room, drowning out the whispering chatter of flechettes that ripped apart the table behind him. The hollow-tipped bullet took the gunman high in the chest, punching through layers of gray and red body armor, propelling him through the open door, where the gun bots ripped him apart. Body parts and flu-ids splattered the cream-colored walls.

Now, *this* was familiar ground, Dee thought grimly. He had fought footpads in Paris, villains in London, brigands in Ger-many, and assassins in the Queen's own court, and it always came down to this: bloody-handed knife work. With clinical precision, using his razor-tipped dagger, he took down another security guard, a heavyset man who hesitated a moment too long at the sight of the antique dagger. It was the last thing he ever saw. D'Winter's gun boomed again, and a body fell across Dee, sending the doctor crashing to the ground under the weight of the man, trapping him.

As he attempted to heave the headless body off him, he felt icy fingers of fire bite deeply into his leg. Dee hissed with pain, realizing he'd been shot with metal flechettes. He glanced down at his leg and saw the red dot of a laser sight begin to creep up his body toward his head. He knew what the dot meant. It was as telling and as malignant as any red pustule of the Black Death. He screamed in horror and frustration.

The surviving security man had crawled behind a metal filing cabinet and was carefully drawing a bead on Dee's head when d'Winter fired at the cabinet. The bullet punched through the metal, sending shards whining through the room, and the cabi-net rocked wildly as the trapped shell ricocheted within it. The noise was unnerving. Instinctively, the guard jerked away from the noise and out of d'Winter's line of fire—and Dee's knife took him in the throat an instant before d'Winter's shot re-moved the top of his head.

The doctor shoved the inert body off him and clutched his leg. Supporting his shoulder, d'Winter knelt before his employer and carefully parted the torn cloth.

Dee's face was white with pain.

"You've taken three needles."

"Will I live?" Dee breathed.

"You'll live—provided they're not poisoned, of course," d'Winter said sourly.

Dee looked around the room, now streaked and speckled

with blood and sparking munitions. "They were ready for us. That little weasel who traded us the information sold us out. Make sure he knows how upset we were before you kill him."

"Oh, believe me, I will," d'Winter promised.

Dee pushed away from d'Winter and limped around the room, pulling open the filing cabinets, opening drawers. They were all empty. "Nothing; they cleared it out. All of this for nothing. We were nearly killed for nothing." He shook blood and gobbets of flesh from his hands. "Ah, but this is filthy work. There has to be a better way than this. This is barbaric."

"There is," d'Winter muttered. "You should have listened to Miss Edwards."

"Listen to a woman! Do you think you have a fool in hand?" Dee snapped, limping to the door and peering outside. The gun bots whirred and chittered, and Dee sprang back, his injured leg giving way beneath him, sending him crashing to the floor. "We're trapped in here. Those cursed things are still working," Dee moaned.

Morgan reached into the pockets of the headless guard, rummaged around, and then took out what looked to Dee like a small wallet-sized box. He clicked it in the direction of the hallway. Immediately, the whirring gun bots powered down and retracted behind the false doors. D'Winter helped Dee to his feet. "You know we were lucky here tonight?" he asked.

"I know that. I'm not prepared to do this again, nor risk you or your men. There has to be another way."

"Miss Edwards's advice is to wage an economic war against Newton, and I agree with her. She's smart."

"For a woman," Dee agreed.

D'Winter shook his head. "If you don't mind me saying so, Doctor, your attitudes are right out of the Middle Ages."

CHAPTER

28

"YOU HAVE ENEMIES, Mr. Newton."

"I have always had enemies," Royal Newton said dismissively to the blank screen.

"Not like these."

Newton sat back in the chair and steepled his fingers before his face, concentrating on the bank of tiny monitors that had been installed beneath his communications console. They were the best that money could buy, boasting a level of sophistication that would not be released onto the market for another eighteen months, and only then when Newton's scientists had discovered a way to crack the built-in encryption. It had the ability to identify and track an individual piece of email as it made its way from source to destination. So far it had failed to trace Newton's incoming calls.

"Whatever their technology . . . it is at least a decade ahead of ours," Newton's scientists had explained. "It's almost as if the message is being generated within your own console, since we have no trace of it coming in, no fingerprints, nothing. It doesn't breach the firewall protection; it treats it as if it isn't there."

"How many factories have you lost now . . . ?"

"Too many factories, too many scientists, and far too much time," Newton admitted. Leaning forward, he stared hard at the screen, convinced that whoever was on the other end could see him. "You have to help me. If you want things to happen, you have to help me. Give me the name of my enemies. I will travel to the end of the Earth to destroy them." The screen flickered gray and white.

"Why limit yourself? Perhaps your enemies are not human, Mr. Newton; have you considered that? Oh, they may have human allies, but surely you have suspected that they must be more than human to even contemplate moving against you."

Newton nodded. "The thought had crossed my mind." Sitting back in the chair, he resisted the temptation to rub his hand across his head. "But I had the same thought about you."

"All you need to know about us, Mr. Newton, is that we have the best interests of Earth at heart. Trust us."

"Oh I do," Newton lied, "I do."

Rahu watched the human, Newton, and could see the deceit written clearly on his face. In the time that he had worked with this human, he had come to detest him; his treachery was despicable even by Nephilim standards. When the Xifo claimed this planet, Rahu was going to rip Royal Newton's bald head clear off his shoulders.

Teeth bared at the pleasant thought, he depressed the switch that downloaded the latest information on the cold-fusion process to Newton's personal computer.

CHAPTER

29

TOMOYUKI TSURU HAD KILLED his first man when he was fifteen. No weapons had been used, and the slender young man had never even been suspected. After all, he was the deceased's best friend and it was exam time. He had killed again a year later, using the same technique, and twice more the following year, each time disposing of pivotal classmates and potential rivals.

He encouraged them to kill themselves.

Tomoyuki Tsuru killed with a softly spoken word, a gentle insinuation, accompanied with the intimation that he was in possession of private knowledge inimical to the listeners. They lived in an Age of Information, where no one wanted their ugliest secrets exposed to the world in a keystroke. And in polite society suicide was preferable to disgrace. Tsuru ascended the corporate ladder in the same way he had moved through school and college, working unnoticed in the shadows through character assassination and ruthless business acumen. In the interconnected Japanese society of friendship and obligation, he preferred to work alone. He adhered to the advice of long-dead swordmaster Miyamoto Musashi, whose work, *A Book of Five Rings*, had been his bible.

Before facing an enemy, know him. To know him is to defeat him.

By the age of twenty-five, Tomoyuki Tsuru had climbed faster and higher on the corporate ladder than anyone else of his generation. He was thirty when he amalgamated Sony-Mitsubishi with Microsoft-Japan, making it one of the biggest computer and entertainment corporations in the world, rivaling even the legendary Microsoft Corporation.

When the Japanese and Australians threatened to go to war in 2015 over the newly discovered mineral deposits beneath the ocean, Tsuru had masterminded the terror campaign that led many to believe that Japan would unleash biological weapons on Australia's northern seaboard. When the Australian government had fallen in the resultant crisis, Tsuru's financial people led the takeover and overran the Australian stock exchange. In less than twenty-four hours, much of the Australian economy was in Japanese hands, though there were few Japanese and even fewer Australians who knew it.

Tsuru's Miya-Tsuru was one of the most powerful corporations in the Pacific Rim, and now, at fifty, Tomoyuki Tsuru was counted as one of the most influential men in the world. He had the final say on the development and release of the latest video and VR technology, having personally overseen the production of the next generation of computer hardware, and had masterminded the production of the newest wave of VR subdermal implants; not bad for the illegitimate son of a Neo-Shinto priest and a good-time girl.

Miyamoto Musashi's student survived and thrived and profited on information. Tattooed in perfect Kanji script on the inside of his right wrist was the swordmaster's basic precept, *The Gaze in Strategy*, the twofold gaze, perception and sight.

Perception is stronger than sight.

Tsuru lived his life by this simple mantra, and many men had died because they failed to recognize this in him.

His shining, smooth-skinned face a calm mask, Tomoyuki Tsuru sat on one side of the solid block of anodized aluminum and stared intently at the Gaijin, the foreigner. Through the wall of glass behind him, New Tokyo's skyline shimmered behind the sulfurous clouds that never lifted far above street level. Today, they were especially thick, rising from the street to blanket the windows two hundred stories above, bathing the room in lambent yellow the color of old urine.

Tsuru moved his hand slightly and the room lights came up, washing the room in milky-white brightness that looked sour against the sulfur clouds. The man standing before him did not flinch as the carefully positioned spotlight shone directly into his eyes. Most men squinted or glanced up at the light, or stepped back out of its pool, but this man remained unmoving.

Tsuru knew everything about the man that was known—and yet he knew nothing. The man standing in front of his desk baffled him. He went by the name of Dr. John Dee, but of course, this could not be his real name; Dee had appeared out of nowhere some months ago, and despite in-depth researches, Tsuru's people had been unable to trace him prior to that. Even cross-referencing people who had died or disappeared had failed to reveal anyone who might have been the man called Dee.

The Gaijin was tiny by Western standards, below average height even for Asia. His gray hair was overlong, recently barbered and tied back in a short queue held with a particularly effeminate black velvet bow. His beard was square cut, curls of white streaking through the iron gray. Tsuru idly wondered why the man did not dye either hair or beard—indeed, why he even *wore* a beard. In this day and age it was unseemly. Dee's black suit, cut in a style that was vaguely archaic, was Kevlar-meshed silk, and cost more than most men earned in a year. His shirt was cream silk and beneath it, Tsuru's scanners had revealed, he was wearing a one-piece Kevlar bodysuit. Identical to the one Tsuru wore himself for protection. Did Dee distrust him?

The scanners had also revealed a recent wound on Dee's left leg—three separate dermal patches grouped close together. A flechette wound? The doctor wore genuine lizard-skin boots, with risers in the heels and steel toe caps. There was a heavy, antique-looking ring on the little finger of his left hand, and a thin fillet of metal, not quite a necklace, around his neck. He perceived the doctor's mien to be aristocratic and accustomed to giving orders; this was a man who did not like to be kept waiting, and in Tsuru's experience, people like this could be methodical but hasty. Such men were often prone to bluster and bluff.

Tsuru breathed deeply, satisfied that he had evaluated the situation correctly following the precepts of his master. The Englishman's business proposal was an obvious sham. His agents had contacted Tsuru's agents through respected intermediaries with the offer of a universal translating device—fully functional, discreet, marvelous in its capabilities. There could be no such translating device and his scanners had proved to his reassurance that no mechanical or neuron devices had been smuggled into his office. Tsuru pondered why the Englishman's people—if, indeed, he was English—had insisted that this face-to-face meeting be arranged so speedily. What was its purpose? What was his hurry?

Tsuru looked beyond Dee to his companion. Behind the man, wearing a Chanel suit two seasons out of date, sat a woman, Kelly Edwards, a hard-foil briefcase on her lap. Curiously, the scanners had revealed that the case was empty. Why was she needed, then? Tsuru knew all about the woman; her life was a tedious open book. She was of no consequence, a second-rate agent, whose agency teetered on the brink of collapse, her only client the mysterious doctor.

Yet this Dee had chosen to have her here with him, and this intrigued Tsuru. She was attractive by Western standards— though he had never cared for redheads. She was negligent of her appearance and wore no jewelry except for the twin of Dee's fillet of metal worn loosely around her neck. Her feigned nonchalance was almost laughable. Her face was impassive, yet her body language, her pounding heart rate and high respiration, could not conceal her excitement at being there. Every fool knew that excitement meant fear. Why had Dee brought a fearful woman to this meeting? Had she a hold on him? Were they lovers, perhaps? But a man of Dee's obvious wealth could afford many lovers. Tsuru resolved to find out and use it to his advantage.

Know your enemy by his companions.

In the corridor outside, another of Dee's companions waited. This was the mercenary, Morgan d'Winter. A soldier for hire, good at times, but cursed with a conscience, and therefore unreliable. Twice he had refused to follow orders. His disloyalty had made him an outcast. Tsuru had traced the man's life from the moment of his birth to his last bloody campaign in New Texas. Another nothing, a nobody.

But what did that make Dee? The man also was a nothing, but not in the same way as Edwards or d'Winter. Dee simply did not exist. There were no records, no traces of a previous existence, no appearances through the exotic cyber-jungle of records and receipts, where every transaction left a myriad telltale fingerprints. No DNA samples, no blood types, no dental records, no records of birth—nothing from the NCA. He did not exist anywhere until a mere few months previously. The man was an enigma. More than that, he was a formidable force. No one had the power or the money to completely expunge all their personal records—not even Newton himself. It was an impossibility, and yet this little man had done it.

Without a past, thought Tsuru, there is no past to exploit. Even his accent was an enigma, a peculiar—almost crude—English patois. But when he spoke Japanese, his accent was flawless. When it became apparent that despite his distaste Dee was quite prepared to stand there and say nothing, Tsuru broke the long silence. "We have considered your offer, Dr. Dee." No medical or academic institution in the world had a record of Dee as a student; there were no theses in his name. Where had he got the title? Could the man's vanity be his undoing? The small gray man inclined his head slightly, saying nothing. "It would be true to say that Miya-Tsuru is interested in the device you are offering. But we have failed to see any evidence of your device. To be frank, we have begun to doubt the existence of such a device."

Dee nodded again, words still unnecessary.

Tsuru's smile was threadlike. "You have patience, Doctor. An admirable quality."

Dee did not offer a direct "thank you," which was how most

Gaijin acknowledged compliments, seemingly unaware of their own boorishness. Instead he put forth an intricate and ultimately self-effacing reply. Most impressive.

Miss Edwards watched silently.

Tsuru had tried to switch to English, which he spoke fluently, but Dee insisted on keeping the meeting all in Japanese. Tsuru saw it as a ploy to show him respect. The English always preferred speaking in their own tongue. They assumed everyone did. "Your accent is flawless. Where did you learn our language?"

"I have never learned your language," Dee said mildly. "I am simply using the translation device I have offered you."

Tomoyuki Tsuru's pencil-thin eyebrows moved slightly. "You are using the device now?"

Wrinkles of satisfaction formed around Dee's eyes and mouth. "I was given to understand that you wanted a demonstration, sir."

Tsuru rose from his leather chair and moved around the desk. On either side of the room, two dark-suited bodyguards in wraparound mirrored shades moved away from the walls and bracketed their employer; one was watching Dee intently, the other concentrated on the girl. Neither man's hands were visible. Tsuru stopped in front of Dee and leaned forward, hands clasped at the small of his back, staring into his face. Behind tinted contact lenses his eyes were invisible. "Remarkable," he said finally. "You have no apparent communication device, nothing with obvious circuitry. It must be an implant and yet . . . ?"

"No implants," Dee said simply.

Tsuru brought his hands around and pressed the palms together, almost in an attitude of prayer. "No implants. And you claim you are using the device now. But then we have only your word on that. Is that not so?" He hunted for the next word as if he was unsure of the man's name. "Doctor?"

"Is my word not enough among men of honor?"

Tsuru chuckled softly. "Your cleverness is not in question. Honor, however, is another matter entirely. The fact is, you are a cipher—a zero with nothing to define you. Who is to say what you truly are? My instincts, my training, suggest that you are wearing an implant. May I examine your teeth?"

Dee blinked in surprise at the sudden change in the conversation and Tsuru pressed his advantage and turned coolly to Edwards. "Or perhaps it is your assistant who is wearing the implant; perhaps we should conduct a full body search."

Kelly swallowed her anger and kept her face impassive. She'd undergone sexual-harassment training for her degree in communications. Allowing her personal feelings to intrude on a client's negotiation was a sure way to lose a client. She would not be manipulated. She was better than that.

Dee had not had Kelly's schooling. "Forbear, sir. This lady is under my protection and your guest. Shall it for shame be spoken or fill up chronicles in time to come, that a man of your nobility and power did mock his honor by disparaging a lady? I will have your apology now, sir, or these negotiations are at an end!"

"Doctor, I took no offense," interjected Kelly quickly.

"But I did; he has shown you disrespect."

"I merely wish to discuss the location of the aforementioned translator," replied the even-toned Tsuru, "but it is interesting to hear that in my language you are as adept as he. But your employer is quite right. My remark was rude and uncalled-for. My apologies." Tsuru made the slight civil bow prescribed by etiquette, but it was more a bow of victory than of subservience. He had learned that the woman was a weak spot in the Gaijin's armor. The passion in the man's voice had been undeniable.

"Thank you." Dee gave Tsuru his full attention and then opened his mouth to reveal his small teeth. "You may, indeed, examine me. As you would a horse. However, I should say to you that the device you seek is in plain sight."

Tomoyuki was startled. Glancing quickly from Dee to Edwards, he wondered what they both had in common. "Of course, the neckbands. It must be the neckbands," he said finally. "But my scanners picked nothing up."

Dee smiled icily. "I thought scanning visitors was frowned upon in corporate society."

"Many things are frowned upon, and yet, do we still not do them?" Tsuru said, unperturbed. "We are men of the world, Dr. Dee. How often have we done things of which our governments or society disapprove?" He paused to reevaluate Dee, who had now risen in his estimation. Tsuru waggled a finger at Dee. "You should not lecture me on ethics when you yourself bring devices to my offices made from unsanctioned technology."

Dee inclined his head slightly. "But it is people like you who sanction the technology, is it not?"

"How many languages will this undetectable translator translate?"

"All of them."

"*All languages!* Please, Doctor." Tsuru's face lit up in rare amusement.

"Your people have developed single-language translators," Kelly interjected. "The ability to translate written and printed word has been with us for some time. The technology is not perfect and occasionally the translations are suspect, to say the least. But perfect simultaneous real-time translation of the spoken word has evaded even the most highly advanced companies. Your own company has been developing this technology for almost a decade, and how far have you advanced?"

While the woman had been speaking, Tsuru's eyes never left Dee's face. But it was true. Miya-Tsuru had accomplished nothing with their research. It had been an unacceptable waste of resources.

Kelly continued. "You have developed dedicated chips capable of translating—crudely—one language to another. The technology is still in development and the translation is far from ideal and there is often a lag of seconds, even up to a minute before the translation kicks in. In a year, perhaps two, that technology will move on, and you will come close to simultaneous translation, but you will still never be able to offer more than the major languages. What Dr. Dee has developed is a device that will enable all spoken language to be understood by any listener, no matter what their nationality."

"How?" Tsuru blurted.

Dee smiled enigmatically. "Trade secret."

"You are saying that four people, from four different countries, could listen to a speaker from a fifth country and hear them in their own language? An outrageous claim."

"That is exactly what the doctor is claiming," Kelly continued. "Simultaneous translation of any one language into another."

"Impossible." Tsuru suddenly bowed his apology to Dee and then to Kelly. "I did not mean to doubt the lady. It just seems so incredible."

With a gesture to Kelly, Dee continued with the negotiation. "And I am offering it to you today. Think of what you can do with this technology. Your profit would be enormous. And you do not need me to tell you how far ahead of your competitors this will put you."

"Why have you come to me, Dr. Dee?" Tsuru asked.

"Because only you have something I want," Dee acknowledged. "Is this not the way of business?"

"It cannot be money; any of my competitors would be only too willing to pay your asking price."

"I do not want money, not directly."

"What do you want?"

"You have a controlling interest in the kryptonium mine in northern Australia," Dee said flatly, making a statement that brooked no denial, though Tsuru's interest in the mine was a closely guarded secret, deeply buried in layers of holding companies and false names. "I want to lease that controlling interest for the next year."

"I don't understand," Tsuru said, genuinely puzzled.

"I will allow Ms. Edwards to explain it," Dee said, because he was not entirely sure of the deal himself.

"It is quite simple," Kelly Edwards said. "Section 1031 of the International Tax Code allows corporations to swap one property for another for a period of time without incurring a capital-gains tax. There is a minimum of red tape with this procedure. In return for this device you will surrender to Dr. Dee all the economic rewards and risks and rights to the output of that mine. Technically, you will still retain legal title to the shares of all Miya-Tsuru mines as well as the aforementioned one in northern Australia. Dr. Dee will get any dividends paid on the stock and reap any gains on the stock's price during the one-year swap as well as stewardship of the day-to-day mine operations. In return Dr. Dee promises you full rights of ownership to the manufacture and marketing of these translating devices for now and forever. However, all research and blueprints to these devices will remain in Dee's hands until the expiration of the first year."

Tomoyuki laughed derisively. "You must think me an idiot to let you have a full functioning mine for a device for which I have no plans and cannot test."

"We do not think you a fool. You may test it in your laboratories all you like. Uncover its secrets; it shouldn't be too hard for Miya-Tsuru. Even if you don't succeed, we know you would need a year to set up your marketing strategies before you could possibly begin manufacture. At which time, we will gladly give you all the data we have on this device. But your insisting on the device's blueprints now is a deal-breaker for us."

Kelly didn't have to look to Dee for approval. This had all been spelled out in their strategy sessions.

Dee took a step closer to Tsuru. The bodyguards moved in, but Tsuru gestured them away. "More importantly, my friend, think what a year's use of such a translator used personally and secretly during critical international trade deals would do for you. You could listen in to the other sides' strategies in their native tongues. There is no data anywhere on these translators' existence. No one has any idea that they even exist. We have only approached one company with our offer. Your rivals would be at your mercy. The gain of such insider information would more than make up for the year's loss of dividends on a mine which is costing too much to run." Dee knew he had caught Tomoyuki Tsuru's attention. "After all, are we not men of the world? Do we not do things that society frowns on?"

Tomoyuki Tsuru returned to his desk and placed his hands flat on the polished metal surface. Inset into the metal, a holographic screen winked into existence, and without changing expression, Tsuru ran his fingers over the smooth desk, the gentle pressure bringing the screen to scrolling life. "The mine earned this corporation somewhere in the region of twenty-two million yen last year."

"Closer to nineteen." Dee smiled.

"Closer to nineteen," Tsuru agreed, unsmiling. "And you want the mine for a year. That is a fortune." The ridicule had left his voice and been replaced by a feeling of genuine uncertainty. His instincts battled his avarice for possession of the translator. If the thing could really do what the two said, it could bring in billions. The mine had been a liability, but what did this white wraith want with it?

Kelly spoke up from behind Dee. "Our figures estimate that the translator, properly marketed, will net you somewhere in the region of thirty million new yen in the first year alone."

"Why are you not marketing this device yourself, Dr. Dee?" Tsuru asked curiously.

"Because I have no interest in it," Dee said truthfully. "My aspirations are higher."

"Why do you want the mine?"

"I believe we are at a critical turning point in the world's future," Dee continued truthfully. "I believe that kryptonium is the key to allowing us to colonize the Heavens. This is the fuel of the future."

So this was the doctor's secret, thought Tomoyuki. He was a New Worlder—one of those fanatics who thought life would be better on another planet. Probably belonged to one of the crazy religions that kept trying to send their believers out into space. The last rocket had exploded on the launchpad, rendering a huge chunk of Brazil uninhabitable for the next ten thousand years. Kryptonium had been hypothesized as the primary fuel element in the new and experimental research in the development of a faster-than-light drive. Tsuru's advisors were certain it was ludicrous and would come to nothing. These people had seen too many reruns of *Star Trek*.

"A moment," Tomoyuki Tsuru said, and then sat with his palms flat on his desk.

Moments later, behind Dee, the slab of ancient oak carved with the likeness of a dragon swallowing its own tail opened, and ten confused-looking people appeared. Though they were of different nationalities, they all wore the Tomoyuki Tsuru uniform of gray-black suit with muted red tie or scarf. None of them looked happy; a summons to Tsuru's office was inevitably bad news.

"Stand here," Tsuru snapped, pointing to a position to the left of Dee. If the misguided little New Worlder wanted to trade the invention of the century for a financial gamble based on foolishness, that was his business. But before Tomoyuki Tsuru would give his consent, he needed confirmation of what he was getting. He then turned back to the gaijin. "Say something to these people."

The doctor glanced over at them and inclined his head slightly. "Good afternoon, ladies and gentlemen, delighted to make your acquaintance."

Tsuru pointed to the first man. "What language did he speak?"

"German," the man said in surprise.

"No, French," the woman beside him said.

"Urdu."

"Spanish."

"Chinese."

"Flemish."

"Enough!" Tsuru snapped. "You are dismissed." When the people had trooped from the room and the door hissed shut, he turned back to Dee. "You have a deal. When do you wish to conclude the sale?"

Kelly Edwards stood and opened her empty briefcase. "If you have the documents drawn up, we can conclude our business now," she said in perfect Japanese.

CHAPTER

30

THE TRIO MOVED SWIFTLY down the window-lined corridor, Dee in the lead, Edwards behind and to his left, Morgan d'Winter taking up the rear. No one spoke. Beyond the heavy glass the uppermost floors of New Tokyo's highest building peeked through the swirling clouds, which occasionally burned with neon reflected up from the streets far below.

Although the air space above the city was supposed to be restricted, light transports in the latest designs hovered and buzzed from building to building. Dee looked at the pitted black spires of the buildings poking through the clouds. More glass than he had ever seen in his entire life, an inconceivable amount of metal, buildings rearing to impossible heights.

The builders of Babel hadn't reached so close to Heaven before the Almighty had thrown them down for their pride. But, thus far, He had refrained from destroying these ignorant, arrogant people. The doctor clasped his hands behind his back as he wondered, and not for the first time, if God still cared about this place, or if He had turned His face away from the world He created.

There had been a potion Dee had made up in his youth, a mixture of herbs and mushrooms, that when drunk was supposed to call forth visions of the Deity. Instead, the images had been nightmarish. But they had been as nothing compared to the hellish truth of this twenty-first century. In the days and weeks when he had first come to this place, he had studiously avoided learning the history of what had happened in his times and to his people; but from the little he unwittingly had managed to acquire, he knew it had been ugly, very ugly.

The images he glimpsed in Dyckon's ship had convinced him that war had ravaged his world time and again. There was little joy in this new world. No simple human pleasures. Though jaded comforts seemed everywhere, all of humanity had been seduced by the devils of Pride and Vanity. These Vices had set up their idolatries in these people's clothes, their architecture, their faces, their hearts. Looking at the offensive city, with its glass-faced monoliths swimming through a sulfurous sea, a remnant of the visible sky ocher and metal above, the Elizabethan could easily believe they'd all been banished to perdition.

Scriptures taught that Hell was the place of the damned. Well, he had never seen a place more damned than this.

Nor had the people changed. Plato's, Moore's, and Erasmus' future worlds had promised Utopia, with philosopher leaders and scholar citizens. Virtue was to be a universal accomplishment.

They had been wrong—so wrong. It saddened him to think that those skills of cheating and lying he had learned and honed half a millennium ago were still as useful as they ever were. Lust and Greed were still in vogue. This man, this Tomoyuki Tsuru, who he had initially been told was a man to rival the great Medici barons, had turned out to be nothing more than a grasping merchant, a stony adversary, an empty, inhuman wretch. The Medici had maintained more clever servants. Dee's thoughts suddenly turned backward; what would the Medici make of this place and time? There were such opportunities for profit. He grinned suddenly. The Medici merchant princes would ravage it in ways it could not even conceive of. They had had a flair, an appetite for life. Here, men traded in small increments of invisible money and Latinate promises. They employed the same ancient techniques that Cosimo de' Medici had used—fair faces and a villain's mind. But here they put their full faith in invisible bankers and wildly fluctuating currencies.

Elizabeth, his Queen, had once told him not to trust in bankers, for they but bought and sold in shadows. Her Royal Majesty had insisted that she control her country's coffers herself. She would have nothing to do with fee'd moneychangers. Dee had taken the advice to heart and kept his own gold in a hidden, demon-cursed vault buried deep beneath his house in Mortlake. He idly wondered if it was still there.

He had attended a play once at a beer garden outside the London walls—he couldn't remember the play or the player, but it was about Justice, and the chief actor, a handsome fop whom he half suspected was a quean, had said, "What you cannot feel you cannot use."

Dee had just sold Tomoyuki Tsuru a device neither man understood and which Tsuru's scientists would never be able to replicate.

From what he had gleaned of Dyckon, Dee believed that the device spoke directly from one mind to another. Kelly Edwards had suggested that it was some sort of telepathic enhancement device—whatever that was! Dee knew that both of them had overlooked the obvious: The device was magic. Simple as that.

But the translator was unimportant, Dee reminded himself. He had gotten the rights to the mine. It was a crucial step. He hadn't traded the device for money—just for the mine and the minerals it contained. He needed to control the minerals.

Before they left the protection of the sealed building, they changed into foil bodysuits and full-face helmets. At this time of day, the atmosphere was poisonous to non-natives within twenty minutes: the skin would blister and weep without protection.

As they left the building, a flame-colored transport hummed down out of the foul air and dropped lightly onto the roof before the trio. There was a roar of air. In the foil suits they were all indistinguishable, but the pilot, wearing a suit to match the paint job on his craft, pushed open the folding door and bowed to Dee. "I can take you anywhere you wish to go," he said.

Kelly and d'Winter started to move forward, but stopped when they saw that Dee hadn't moved.

"I said," the pilot began again, changing over to fluent English.

Dee didn't even register the change in language. "No, thank you," he shouted over the noise. The pilot looked confused.

"I can take you off this roof."

"No, thank you."

The flame-suited man looked from Dee to his two companions and began to spread his hands to show that he had plenty of room inside.

"We do not wish to travel with you."

"Why not?" the pilot demanded belligerently. He suddenly grunted as a heavy hand fell on his shoulder, fingers pressing dangerously close to the nerves in the side of his neck.

"Because we don't," d'Winter said icily.

Dee nodded in the direction of the cigar-shaped craft. "The color scheme offends me."

The pilot backed away, muttering curses in what he imagined was a muffled unintelligible dialect, but which were clearly translated to the trio. For which, d'Winter shoved him hard back in his seat with enough force to leave bruises.

Watching the craft lift off the roof, rocking slightly on the updraft before humming away, d'Winter returned to Dee and asked, "Do you want to tell me what that was all about?"

"He spoke directly to me," Dee said. "How did he pick me out as the leader? You are the tallest; he should have spoken to you first."

"And I thought I was your bodyguard," d'Winter said wryly.

"I am slightly more experienced in some things," Dee said softly. "We will take the third or fourth transport."

He remembered an inn in Paris, the Pomme d'Or, a foul disease-ridden pit with the filthy waters of the Seine lapping into its basement, a constant wetness that chilled the skin. Teeth would quiver in your mouth. There was only one thing to recommend it: It somehow managed to hire the prettiest ample-bosomed wenches in all France. There was always a lot of cuddling required to keep clientele warm. Edward Kelly chose to drink there for obvious reasons—Dee unconsciously glanced over at the Irishman's namesake, who still managed to look elegant in a shapeless foil suit. When Dee was in Paris, a city he detested, and which he had been inordinately pleased to discover no longer existed, he used the Pomme d'Or as a meeting place for his various spies and informants. He had been coming out on a very late night after a particularly difficult meeting and had accepted a ride from the first carriage that had just happened along. He had not hailed it. It had been a trap, sprung on him by the husband of a statuesque Dane, Liv, who had initially been intrigued by his height, and then impressed by his prowess and endurance.

Dee glanced sidelong at Kelly Edwards, thought for a moment, and then quickly looked away. Never with the staff and never with the daughter of your employer; that simple rule had kept him out of a lot of trouble in his life, though there had been that occasion when Her Highness had seemed to look on him with more than a disinterested eye. Now, that was a royal invitation he should have accepted. Perhaps he would have ended up King of England—or with his head on a pole on the London bridge. Either way, it would have been worth it.

"Give you a ducat for them?"

"Pardon? You will give me a ducat for what?" Dee looked around.

"A ducat? What's a ducat? I never mentioned a ducat." Kelly scowled at him, eyes bright and green behind the faceplate of her helmet.

"Yes you did—you said a ducat for them." Dee made sure to add, "Whatever they are."

Kelly sighed. "It's your translation gizmo. It must still be translating. You were looking so pensive, I was wondering what you were thinking."

"Oh, yes, a ducat for my thoughts. I'd almost forgotten. It's an old saying from where I come from." And it was, Dee thought. "I was thinking of old times," he said wistfully. "And of a woman who made me an offer I was too afraid to accept. Do you ever get offers like that?"

"All the time; men make me offers I'd be terrified to accept."

A transport painted with a featherlike pattern wheeled out of the sky and approached the roof. D'Winter waved it in; it banked sharply for their roof. The roar of the aggravated air made talking difficult.

"Is there no man in your life?" Dee queried, trying to be heard above the noise.

"Not at the moment," Kelly shouted.

"Is there a reason? You are celibate perhaps?"

"Celibate!" Kelly choked.

"Diseased then?" he yelled. "There is no shame in that. And I have a sovereign cure for the . . ."

"Don't even suggest it!" Edwards snapped, and stalked off for a seat in the air shuttle.

Dee looked blank. "What did I say?" he questioned d'Winter, as he stepped past him toward the transport. "What did I say? I was only trying to be helpful."

"There's some questions most people don't ask."

"I'm not most people," Dee said simply.

"You got that right."

CHAPTER

31

JAMES ZHU LIKED TO CLAIM descent from Mongol warlords who had once conquered half the known world, though in truth his claim was as spurious as his British accent, which he swore he had picked up at Oxford. The accent had been copied off a cache of antiquated British vids of the last century named in honor of a python, and although he had indeed been raised in Mongolia, Zhu could trace his ancestors back ten generations, and none of them had ever stormed the crumbling Great Wall. However, Zhu had read and studied everything he could find on the great Genghis Khan and Temujin, his general, and had based a career upon the same tactics they had used to conquer the world.

Destroy that which you cannot understand and never ever be the bearer of bad news.

And Zhu was determined not to bring any more bad news to Newton. In the darkened, monitor-filled room, the ice-eyed man watched the figures flit across the screen; they were reports from his agents in Newton's plants across the world. And none of the data was good. There had been another attack on a processing plant on the island of New Britain off the northern coast of Australia. Simple sabotage this time, an explosive device hidden within a new batch of computer terminals. The explosion had ripped apart a relatively unimportant storage area, but the surge had taken down the servo network, and the entire factory had been unproductive for eight hours.

The downtime would cost Minuteman Holdings somewhere in the region of two million dollars. And this was just the latest in a series of attacks over the past weeks. The bill was tipping the billion-dollar mark, and they were still no closer to discovering the truth of who was behind these extraordinary and unprovoked acts.

Newton was becoming more and more irritated. And while Zhu feared no one and nothing, he knew what happened to people who irritated the bald man.

The big man ran his thick-knuckled fingers over a keyboard, and a series of images flickered onto a screen recessed into the teak-paneled desk. The screen wavered and danced as the encryption devices monitored the signal, and then a face appeared. "Tomoyuki Tsuru." James Zhu bowed his head slightly, acknowledging the other's presence, but not bowing deeply enough to pay him much respect.

"Mr. Zhu," Tsuru said evenly.

Zhu blinked.

Tsuru was speaking the Mongolian tongue of Zhu's childhood with a flawless accent.

"There seems to be some sort of misunderstanding," Zhu said immediately. "A factory of yours has failed to make a delivery to one of our subsidiary companies."

"When did you begin to concern yourself with factory deliveries?" Tsuru said superciliously. Doubtless he had disdain for Mongolians. The Japanese were like that.

"When it began to irritate my employer," Zhu replied. "All Minuteman inquiries have been blocked, turned aside, or countered. So I decided to go to the source, as it were."

"Well, I do not concern myself with factory deliveries," Tsuru began, and reached for the button that would terminate the contact.

"A kryptonium mine in northern Australia," Zhu said softly.

Tsuru stopped and looked back at the screen. "What about it?"

"It has failed to make a series of scheduled deliveries to our factories in New Britain, New Ireland, and New Guinea. We have a series of projects which are beginning to fall behind schedule because of this failure. Mr. Newton is becoming very upset. . . ." Zhu allowed the sentence to trail.

The last person who had made Newton upset had died in a spectacular explosion that had wiped out his entire family, and most of the small city of Aspen with it.

"Miya-Tsuro no longer controls those mines," Tsuru said matter-of-factly.

Zhu straightened. "You sold them."

"Leased them actually."

"Leased them?"

"For one year. You will have to take up your problem with the lessee."

"And that is . . . ?"

"A man who calls himself Dr. John Dee."

Zhu's fingers danced over the keyboard. The new neurocomputers were trained to monitor and follow voice communications, and the files on Dee should have already popped up on the subsidiary monitors. The screens remained blank.

"I've never heard of him, and according to my files he doesn't exist."

"I don't believe that's his real name, but believe me, he does exist."

Six minutes later, Zhu was standing before Newton, brandishing a handful of glossy photographs that had been taken from Tomoyuki Tsuru's surveillance cameras. He pushed the photographs of Dee, Edwards, and d'Winter across the table. "I think I may have some good news."

"Who are these people?"

Newton blinked at the photographs. At least the black man was bald.

"We have complete files on the woman and the bodyguard." Zhu placed two sheaves of plastic printout alongside their respective photographs. "But these are inconsequential."

"And this one? The man with the beard?"

"According to the NCA protocols, the man with the beard doesn't exist. Furthermore, the man with the beard has just leased the kryptonium mines in Australia from Tsuru. The Japanese will not divulge details of the deal, but it must have been something spectacular."

Royal Newton straightened and snatched up the photograph of Dee. "What! That *fool* Tsuru! One of these days—and very soon too—you will have to treat Mr. Tsuru to a lesson."

"He claims Dee is a New Worlder and needed the kryptonium for some experiments in fuel."

"I don't care what this mysterious Dee needs it for. I need it. It is central to the Tiamat project. Why don't you go and get it back for me, Mr. Zhu?"

"And if Dr. Dee does not wish to sell?"

"Perhaps you should demonstrate the futility—the stupidity—of denying me what I want."

"Of course, it will be my pleasure."

CHAPTER

32

THERE WERE TIMES when Kelly Edwards detested Dr. Dee. His attitude toward women in general and her in particular was positively medieval, and while his manners could be charming and quaint, he was often surprisingly—appallingly—shocking and crude. On more than one occasion when he had called her into his inner office, she had found him sitting on the john, and he had proceeded to deal with her as if nothing was amiss, farting away with aplomb.

She avoided meals with him when she could. His table manners were barbaric; each meal was a cacophony of chomping, smacking, and belching. He insisted on eating real meat and fish and fowl; he had declared the fungi steaks, a nutritional staple in everyone's diet the world over, to be nothing more than a crusty botch of Nature. He drank wine as if it were water, though she had never seen him drunk, and he had a passion for fruit, especially Spanish oranges, and he adored milk, cheese, and honey.

One wall of his bizarre fort in Angel City was covered in hundreds of globes, glasses, and jars of honey of various golden hues, from soft amber to a rich red. But he paid well. Very well. That made up for all of his strangeness.

Well, most of it anyway.

Kelly Edwards swiped her card through the lock on the foyer to her apartment and stepped into the enclosed hallway, looking up to face the camera that recorded her entry and compared her image against the picture in its database. The security device was still relatively new and was not entirely bugproof; only last week, old Mr. McIntyre, who had lived in the apartment-block building for nearly fifteen years, had been refused entry because the camera hadn't recognized him. The first thing the old man did when he'd been released from the holding pen in the nearby police barracks was to file suit against the apartment owners. He had left video messages for every resident of the complex. There had even been an arranged info conference. But the attendance had been scant. Kelly hoped he would win, but she had an idea that there was small print in the contract which covered every eventuality. There was always small print. No doubt, some sharp-suited lawyer would point out that McIntyre had put on sixty pounds in the last year alone and that the image he had supplied did not match how he now looked, and that therefore it was his fault. They would probably file a countersuit against him.

Who needed to buck the establishment? Who had the time?

"Recognized. Welcome, Occupant Edwards."

Kelly sighed as she stepped through the door into the foyer. Nearly two hundred years of computers and the synthetic voices still sounded like something out of a century-old vid. The woman made her way to the elevator banks, nodding to the bored-looking security guard seated behind the desk, who didn't look up from the small microvision screen strapped to his left arm. She heard the latest World Series scores droning on—

"Three to nothing, Dublin still in the lead, Buenos Aires still to score. . . ."

As she stood waiting for the elevator, she turned back to the guard. She grew embarrassed and a little annoyed that she had acknowledged him and had gotten nothing in return.

She decided that the guard couldn't be more than twelve years old—which was the minimum legal age for the stunner he wore strapped to his chest. Maybe she was getting old, she fumed, as the elevator arrived and the doors shuddered open. In her day, you had to be fifteen before you could legally carry a weapon. At twelve, she knew, he was capable of killing, but was he capable of judgment? The owners probably paid him minimum wage. Rat bastards. She wondered if he was allowed to wear the stunner off the premises.

Wouldn't the residents be liable if the guard used it illegally? She really needed to move; Mr. McIntyre was right. The place was a shambles. But where would she find something as moderately priced as this? She suddenly grinned. She would move; she could afford to now.

Kelly stood with her back to the curved plate-glass elevator walls. She had long grown used to the depressing view as she was lifted over Angel City, and the distorted circular ripples surrounding bullet marks in the heavy bulletproof glass depressed her even more. They were the signs of the times. Kids in the devastated buildings a mile away, close to the edge of the Pit, liked to practice their marksmanship and take potshots at the illuminated elevators, scaring those within. Thus far they had been content to use handguns and rifles, but Kelly confidently expected to discover any day now that they had moved on to using shoulder-launched missiles.

Okay then, this week she would start looking for an apartment in a better neighborhood. What she needed now, Kelly decided, was a long hot bath—and damn the expense.

Dee paid very well—it was one of the few things in his favor—and at least now she could afford hot baths every day rather than once a week, which was all she'd been able to afford on her previous salary.

The elevator shuddered and stopped, and the door hissed open, only to immediately close again. Kelly swore and stabbed the button again. This was the third time this week; the goddamn thing was always breaking down.

The door opened a fraction,

And the corridor outside dissolved into a blinding ball of flame.

* * *

Morgan d'Winter lounged against the filthy wall and watched the deal going down in the alleyway ahead of him.

Standing framed in the open doors of a van, a young couple were buying what looked like a Mk III Steyer, with one of the big two-hundred-round clips. The big mercenary nodded approvingly; the Steyer was a good gun, except that the barrel had a tendency to overheat on full auto. He'd discovered that the hard way, in the sewers beneath Washington, facing a horde of albino mutants who called themselves the Senators and claimed descent from the last legally elected government of the United States. One of the damn Senators had nearly chewed his leg off when his gun barrel had melted.

D'Winter waited until the couple had completed their transaction and had walked away. Then he stepped out into the alleyway and waited until the invisible guards had him in their sights before moving forward slowly, hands in plain sight.

"Come forward, come forward. Show yourself," said a voice cloaked in threat. A solid red spot appeared on d'Winter's chest, the beam coming from the huge-mouthed pistol in the arms dealer's hand.

"Getting nervous in your old age?" Morgan said, stepping out into the light.

"D'Winter!" The laser light disappeared, as the dealer waddled forward to enfold the big man in an enormous bear hug. When d'Winter extricated himself, he stepped back and tapped the dealer's chest with his knuckle. The resulting sound was hollow and metallic.

"Now you should have some of this, maan. It's sweet. The latest in body armor, maan, designed to turn da new generation of flechettes. You know dey jus bout go right through you—and Kevlar ha' no effect, none." The resultant smile shone like snow on a bitter bright day.

"So I've heard." D'Winter looked at the dealer, his features illuminated by the light from the van.

The Preacher had left the islands sometime in his youth, and though d'Winter knew that when he was drunk his accent was pure Angel City, nevertheless he affected a Caribbean accent to go with the dreadlocks which the mercenary was convinced was a wig. Whether the disguise was out of a need for deception, or an affectation, or just a perverted desire to hoodwink the world was unimportant to Morgan. He never saw the need to find out why.

"I hain't seen you, where you bin?" the Preacher said quietly, turning back to the van and sorting through the weapons he'd been trying to sell the young couple. "Dey shoulda taken da Glock," he said absently, shaking his clicking dreadlocks in disapproval. "Dat gun got no recoil. The Steyer on full auto pull itself out of deir hands. Dey see da gun on some TV program, dey, and nothing else can do."

D'Winter settled himself with his back to the van, arms folded across his chest, within easy reach of the two machine pistols strapped beneath his arms. Although his head was bent, and a long-billed black baseball cap concealed his eyes, making it look as if he were dozing, he was scanning his surroundings, trying to pick out the Preacher's guards, and anyone else who might have an interest in him. For the past few hours he'd had the distinctly uncomfortable impression that he was being followed. He had learned to trust his instincts; they had kept him alive and relatively healthy in his particularly unhealthy profession.

"Maan, you looking for somethin'," the Preacher said, glancing sidelong at the big man, "and I doubt it be guns."

"Information."

"I no deal in information, me. That's da Tailor's job; watch out for him though." There again was the sunny smile. "Someone took a shot at him recently and he nervous as a cat."

"This is the sort of information you *would* deal in," d'Winter said. He had identified two of the Preacher's guards, young dreadheads with bone-white snakes tattooed on their cheeks and foreheads, in rooms that looked down into the alleyway. The mercenary thought there might be a third guard on the roof of the building opposite, but he couldn't be sure. "I need to know if someone has taken out a hit order on me."

The Preacher's head came out of the van, eyes wide in surprise, dreadlocks quivering. "On you? Not that I hear of. No way." He frowned. "But hey maan, why you t'ink I know?"

D'Winter smiled humorlessly. "Because you're one of the few men in this city who specializes in the supply of untraceable weapons. Anyone out there even asking any questions about me?"

The island man scrunched up his mouth in a half thought and then wagged his head in the negative. "Nobody care bout you, d'Winter. You worthless trash." He grinned. "Just like me. But you got to know, on Mamon's grave, Morgan, no way I supply weapons if I knew dey be used 'gainst you, maan."

"Your loyalty is touching." D'Winter smiled. "You'll have me in tears in a moment."

"Piss on loyalty, maan; I wouldn't want be around if dey missed and you be looking for me! Not me, maan."

The mercenary threw back his head and laughed, the alien sound bouncing off the tired alley walls. "Why should you worry? You have your boys up there to look after you." To make his point he glanced up at the windows, where he'd earlier spotted the two guards. Both windows were conspicuously empty. Morgan d'Winter was turning toward the roof of the building opposite when he saw the flash.

He was running even as the rocket streaked into the back of the armored van, the Preacher's body armor failing even to slow it down. The weapons and ammunition in the back of the van detonated and the explosion lifted the mercenary off the ground and threw him fifteen feet into a backed-up gutter.

CHAPTER

33

EXTRACT FROM THE DAY BOOK of John Dee, Doctor, in the Year of
Our Lord 2099:

*Countless are the beds I have stood watch over. Countless the
friends and foes, family and lovers have I, with mournful eye
and weighty soul, seen writhe their last in agony. Be they victims
of disease, poison or torture. All creatures whose lives I once
touched—(yea, loved)—ended their term upon this earth in
pain. Providence's will was it could not be but so. We are shown
God's mercy only after suffering the pangs of death.*

*In my own time—and it grieves me to pen this—(though in
truth, I do not pen this)—I was a doctor of philosophy. Not a
physick, my interests lay in what the greasy multitude called
magic, but what their betters hight Necromancy and Mathematics. I was familiar with the workings of the human body—all
those who followed my bent were such—but I was not a practi-
tioner of the Healing Arts. But because I bore the title Doctor,
on many an occasion was I summoned to view the plaintiff sick
and dying; then to pass judgement like St. Peter, yea or nay, to
hopes of recovery, and mutter knowledgeably.*

God forgive me, but I oft dispensed little more than sugared water—(it did naught for the patient but ease their fear, surely not their pain)—and gave the grieving families the honeyed conceit that "everything was being done." For want of knowledge and resolve, I pawned my honour by lying at Heaven's door, avowing that the living cadaver was "as comfortable as possible."

Those words, those easy meaningless phrases, "everything is being done" and "as comfortable as possible," have survived to this Godless day.

Centuries later, mankind is still giving the lie to itself about death. There are no easy deaths. I have seen men and women taken by the plague, riddled with pox, wasted with a score of scabrous diseases. I have seen soldiers with hacked-off limbs, their innards exposed to the rude elements, end their days on cold muddy fields. I myself have poisoned and attended to those who had been poisoned.

There are no easy deaths. But the burning of human flesh is perhaps the most horrible of all. It freezes the mind.

There is a peculiar stink to burning flesh—once smelled, never to be forgotten. I am loath to recall the time I stood in Good Queen Bess' Tower dungeon and heard that twin aria—the hiss of hot pokers on tender flesh and the accompanying scream that curdles the blood. The fulsome taint of scorched meat needs must follow, like a beggar at a feast. It is cruelty itself that this memory in me has not faded.

In this wondrous new world of the Future, medicine, like all else, has taken great strides. Here, they have dredged clear the dangers that would in my times have run aground the small boat of man's existence. Then, most things could kill. A rotted tooth might make a man mad; a simple cut finger could blacken and putrefy, leaving no way to save life but to cleave the hand whole, or worse, the arm. Men and women died with blood on their lips for no good reason. Many doubled as if folded after every meal, and retched blood and black bile till all was silence.

Congress twixt man and woman could engender pox in one or both—a lengthy price for such a short act. And childbirth was a tarocci game played with blood and pain; the loss of mother or babe, or both, a frequent endgame.

I cannot chronicle the torrent of despair that washed over me when I had knowledge that both Kelly and Morgan had been impugned, both on my account.

Farewell the tranquil mind. Farewell content!

True, they are but salaried employees—one keeps not servants in this age—and I have no further responsibility towards them other than to fulfill their wage. But I would be less than honest to divulge that I did not feel some sympathy towards them. Morgan d'Winter, an Ethiope with a watchdog's humour, had proven loyal and true, and Kelly Edwards, yet though a woman, had a quick and ready wit, and had established herself as an invaluable counsellor and a patient tutor. I must needs confess that—aye, but they had earned my love. *As the sun breaks through the darkest clouds, so honour peerest through the meanest habit.*

In Elizabeth's time, I would have counted myself Fortune's friend to have had her for my housekeeper, but now . . . Indeed, it was Edwards who showed me how to o'ermaster this cursed machine to keep my day book. Like St. Ambrose's angel in reverse, it miraculously illuminates my spoken words into text here on this screen for me to peruse. But weeks ago, I would not have ventured aught but there was a demon trapped inside and, although I haven't forsaken the idea, Kelly almost has me believing that it is naught else but a cunning machine, a child of man's imagination. If Truth be told, I do not miss my quill, but with all my heart miss her ministering kindness.

The attacks on Kelly and Morgan had been deliberate, and, doubtless, I knew who had ordered them. I was a cypher, an enigma to my enemies, but my companions were not.

Newton was an Argus, all eyes. My companions were vulnerable and visible and had paid for my haste and want of subtlety. I should never have brought them to Tsuru. . . . He obviously made known to Newton, that hairless bastard, my offer and the names of those that did my bidding. I cannot think it but a trick of Time that Minuteman Holding proffered me millions for Tsuru's

mine of kryptonium just seconds ere I was made aware of my peo-
ple's ambuscado. This was a message meant to cower me. . . .

It was an Act of Heaven that either survived. For my sake they
had received mortal hurts. Standing before my televid, I had
watched in ignorance the events at the hospital on the west side
of the city, as the doctors worked to assuage their wounds. All
the majesty of Kelly's radiant red hair was gone, as was much of
the skin of her face.

She was as raw as a pig's liver. Alone in my stronghold, my
grief was manifest for all to see. Her clothing had melted on her
body and I was unsure, as the surgeons worked, whether they cut
plastic or flesh. I beheld neither knives nor saws. Mercifully, she
slept through her ordeal; there was no need for attendants to
hold her down. I thanked the Virgin Mother she still lived, yet
prayed fervently for the passing of her immortal soul sith, in my
time, if she had suffered in such a deadly state, her fate was in-
evitable.

Elizabethan medicine would have eased her misery with fatal
belladonna and deemed it neither sin nor murder.

But these doctors were confident, indeed most casual about
the injuries. The surgeon, a beautifully handsome youth with
sculpted locks, swore unto me that they could match her skin
type and grow a new epidermis within thirty-six hours. Despite
my translator, his words were as a mystery to me but I doubted
not but that it was witchcraft; I cared not and gave my word to
pay the hefty sum he craved.

Sourly, I took note that he only commenced to work when the
fee had been transferred from my account.

Morgan d'Winter too was burned in an explosion, though not
so badly as Kelly, but he had snapped the limbs of his left leg
and right arm. He had been taken to another city hospital. I do
not believe I had ever beheld so many physicians in one place.

I followed Morgan's progress on my televid monitors from the
moment he had been given admittance. There was blood on his
lips and I guessed that broken ribs had torn his lungs. In my day
he would have died a death most agonizing. Even had he sur-
vived his internal injuries, he would never again have walked

whole like a man. Better to put such a daunting spirit out of his agony. A doctor had approached the monitor in the surgical theatre. He was speaking into a blank screen—my wealth brought me some privacy—and I could tell that my anonymity had incurred his spleen. Was it only yesterday that Kelly had made me to know that monitors had been installed in every Hospital in the past Century to protect physicians from something called insurance suits by disgruntled patients or their heirs? The niceties of these future legalities were not foreign to my English understanding.

I gleaned that the suits had once been numerous, but still there was a potent fear of an action being taken. The doctor who waited on Morgan was a man of some years, balding, with a tiredness about the eyes that I could well recognize. Oft had I seen that same look in myself as the dawn heralded the end of another sleepless night spent labouring in my studies.

He reached for the communications control, but I bespoke first. "I desire another physician."

The man was first surprised, then took offense.

"You are weary," I said. "This man before you is important to me. I desire another physician, one who is afresh and alert and will minister to him correctly."

"There really is no need," the disgruntled physician began.

"I'll brook no impertinence. Find me another," I snapped, and began to peruse a list of surgeons at the hospital on another screen. I sorted the list by salary and chose he that was highest paid. "Find me Dr. Eisner."

"He is the most expensive doctor in the hospital," the tiresome man began. "I can do the work far cheaper."

"Cheap me no cheap; this is not work I wish put out to tender. I would have the best."

When Eisner arrived, he too proved to be as handsome as the young Adonis who tended on Kelly—and they obviously attended the same barber.

Moreover, he was as fresh as he was handsome. Being dear, he was obviously not as hard worked. To my mind though he eyed Morgan most cursorily, asked for an exorbitant fee that made the purse to Kelly's doctor pale to insignificance, and when the funds had been transferred to his account, bade me to know that d'Winter would be discharged in a day or two, then would limp for but a few days ere the bones were made whole. I knew not why, but I trusted Eisner's brazen authority and bid him do all that was needed. His promised results gave me great hope for Morgan's full recovery.

Hope is what we seek from all medicos. Truly medicine must needs be miraculous in this age when the Physicians are paid so much, for so seemingly little effort. But I could not help but wonder what sort of treatment either would have received had I not been in a monied position to pay for it.

Would they both have been "comfortable" and "doing as well as expected"?

The world had not changed that much.

So here I sit a day later in my antique chair and watch my monitor as Kelly and Morgan sleep. Their recovering bodies undiscomfited by their wounds nor their minds muddied with thoughts of Earth's imminent doom, they are at peace in their world. Whereas I am nothing if not fixated that Newton shall pay tenfold for what he hath done to me.

What the dog for seducing gold will do to all humanity. Biblical justice prescribes an eye for an eye. And I go to blind Mr. Newton with all the vengeance that is mine. I think on naught else. The inaudible foot of Time runs apace. But my plans needs must wait a day or two till my friends are completely mended.

Friends? Why that word? It has been a long time since it has passed my lips. Be it so, then—friends. Greater than gold, more precious than pearls.

Friendship has tumbled monarchs and built empires. Once I sought to stop Newton to save this world with its teeming millions. Now I do it to protect my friends.

CHAPTER

34

"THANK YOU FOR COMING, ladies and gentlemen," Royal Newton said, striding confidently into the long, high-ceilinged
room. "I am delighted you could all make it," he added—not
that he had any doubts that his invitation would be accepted.
He owned these fifteen people; they were all Minuteman Holdings corporate managers. He owned their jobs, their homes, the
limos and the flyers they had come in. He owned the clothes
they wore on their backs. If he'd been a religious man, he would
have known that he owned their souls. If they'd had any.

He walked down the length of the room and took his position at the head of the conference table, settling himself into his
formfitting chair, which shifted slightly on its cushion of air.

James Zhu, the watchdog, stood erect behind his master.
His eyes were lost behind mirrored glasses, blinds to his
thoughts; the enormous silver pistol on his belt was a bright
and deadly threat. The security chief tucked his hands into the
oversized sleeves of this season's black Armani suit—a New
Year's gift from Newton—and everyone in the room undoubtedly suspected that there was a weapon concealed up his
sleeve.

Newton smiled. Today was going to be a good day. He had known it the moment he had awoken and run his hand over his bald head and felt the very faintest of fuzz on his skull. He had actually fallen out of bed in his haste to get to the bathroom, and had then stood for what must have been thirty minutes before the full-length mirror, tilting his head from side to side, trying to decide if there were actually beginnings of hair on his pitted skull, or whether it was just a shadow. But there were no shadows thrown by the lights in the antiseptic bathroom, so it had to be hair. He kept wanting to touch it, to brush it with the palm of his hand, but he was afraid of rubbing away the hair follicles.

Finally! After all these years.

He remembered an accountant—long since gone—trying to explain to him just how much he'd spent on hair transplants, restoratives, and growth hormones. Newton had not been in the slightest bit interested. He wanted hair, a full head of bushy white hair, just like his father and his grandfather.

Their holographic portraits with their sculpted locks and carefully coiffed hair had mocked him for many years until he'd had the offending images removed from every house he owned, every office he visited.

"I know it is rare that I ask you to forgo your busy lives and travel here to join me," Newton began.

The nine men and six women seated around the long antique table of lacquered wormwood shifted uneasily. The last time they all had been called together it was to witness the execution of one of their own. Zhu had discovered that one of Minuteman Holdings' most senior managers had been siphoning off a tiny percentage of the profits of one of Newton's Southeast Asian factories. The factory, which processed Round Eye cocaine—known locally as Bald Man—made billions of dollars, and the manager had believed that less than one-hundredth of one percent would go unnoticed.

It had been a fatal mistake. Although Newton had known about the theft for many months, he had waited until the manager had retired on the occasion of his fortieth birthday.

The Korean police had invaded the party and arrested him before he had blown out the candles on the cake.

When the cream-covered blonde had burst from the cake moments later, she found the place deserted.

Officially, the charges were plotting against the Unified government. He was detained in a maximum-security laser holding cell and not allowed access to visitors, video accounts, biomed attendants, or teleconferencing. He was not even allowed to touch a computer keyboard. Legal counsel communicated strictly through penciled notes forwarded by speechless prison guards. He was tried by a military court in absentia and found guilty on all counts.

Justice had been swift and was televidded a week after the gavel fell.

And all of these prominent Minuteman managers who had been invited to sit around this same table to watch the execution knew with certainty that the luckless man was innocent of any conspiracy. They knew the real reason might never be revealed, but Newton's meaning to them was clear. This was the payment for treachery.

"This is an auspicious day in the company," Newton said happily. "A very auspicious day." The managers relaxed, relieved for the moment that none of them was being accused of anything. "Some of you may have heard of the Tiamat project?"

With one exception the men and women remained impassive, knowing from experience that acknowledging awareness of a top-secret project was not a good idea. The single exception—a young Canadian, new to the board—nodded yes. It did not go unnoticed. Newton's Tiamat project was one of the hottest topics of discussion whenever any of the managers got together. They had ferreted out among themselves from monthly expense allocations that this was the biggest undertaking Minuteman Holdings had ever attempted, and there was the fear that if the project foundered, then the entire organization might go down with it. Newton continued to smile, and didn't even glance at the Canadian, but he, and everyone else around the table, knew that the young man would regret the telltale gaffe. He would spend the rest of the meeting and the trip home conjuring up

visions of Newton's displeasure. He could be posted to an obscure location before either disappearing or contracting a fatal
disease. Many employees contracted lingering or fatal diseases—
even Minuteman managers. In-house it was known as Newton's
Dropsy.

"Tiamat was a project which I conceived some time ago. It
was essentially the search for unlimited energy." He rested his
hands flat on the desk, his fingertips touching the pressure-
sensitive pads beneath the wooden veneer.

"This is what we have come up with so far." A rotating holographic representation of a complex chemical and mathematical
formula appeared in the center of the table. "Now, you ge-
niuses," he said with some gaiety, "tell me what you're looking
at. Show me that your exorbitant salaries are worth it."

Royal Newton sat back his chair and idly watched his managers attempt to make sense of the formula. Each was brilliant
in his or her own way, and he noted with satisfaction that none
of them had good hair. Even the women.

While the managers whispered and conferred among themselves, Zhu leaned forward across Newton's left shoulder and
covered his mouth with his hand so that no one could read his
lips. "That problem we discussed yesterday; it has been taken
care of."

"Good. And the principal?"

"Still no sign of the good doctor; nor has he responded to our
offer. However, we have enhanced the image off Tsuru's security
vids. It has been distributed to our various operatives. It is only
a matter of time before we find the man who calls himself Dr.
Dee. Possibly by the end of the day. More likely tomorrow. My
operatives are on top of it."

"This is good news, good news, indeed. . . . Remember, I want
him alive. I'll need to talk to him for a few minutes. After that,
he's yours." Newton rubbed his hands briskly and returned to
gaze at his managers. "Well, have you deciphered it yet? Do you
know what it is?"

"It is extraordinary," a pinch-faced young woman said haltingly, attempting to hide her ignorance. "The formula should

not make sense according to the laws of mathematics and yet there is an internal logic."

The young Canadian couldn't stop himself and agreed. Needing to prove his worth, he ventured an answer. "These equations are light-years ahead of anything I've ever seen before. This is antimatter. Massive amounts of antimatter."

"Antimatter?" Newton said with rising inflection. "Massive amounts? Are you sure? I thought it could only be found in atomic antiprotons."

"Yes sir or no sir. I mean yes, so far only positrons are doable, but I don't know sir. I mean . . . if there was a formula for creating large molecules of antimatter, I believe it would resemble this. It is a brilliant extension of Einstein's and Hawking's and Forward's finest work."

There was a long silence, in which the Canadian was sure his pounding heart could be heard through the entire room. His will was up to date, his insurance fully paid up. . . .

Then Newton smiled, like a proud father showing approval of a son's knowledge. "This is, indeed, the formula for molecular antimatter." He paused, relishing the looks of horror and amazement on the faces of the rest of his staff. "We—in Project Tiamat—have been putting together the equipment to create and manage limitless amounts of antimatter. This formula is the key to our success." Rising to his feet, he rested both fists on the table and leaned forward. "Think of it: clean unlimited power overnight. That is the beauty of this power; no waste products to harm the environment, no radioactive by-products. We'll never risk dumping oil again, or ship hazardous fuel rods, or breathe smog or sulfurous air. Our world will flourish again. What's more, we'll convert everyone's power industries to work with antimatter for free. We'll make it easy to replace those technologies with antimatter technology where all you do is combine one molecule of Tiamat antimatter with one molecule of hydrogen—or indeed any other molecule—and the resulting energy will run a city for a week. The nations of the world have been praying for this for generations. Of course, we'll keep a monopoly on the patents as well as corner the market on the trace element, kryptonium, which is essential for the process. Every other polluting fuel source then becomes obsolete. All the conventional vehicles, factories, machinery, everything becomes archaic and contaminating. No longer would economies need to mine and manufacture dwindling fuel sources. Sure, some of the economies of entire nations could be destroyed, plunging some of them from high-tech to primitive. But that's where some of them belong.

"And the stars—the stars are suddenly available to us. This is the most powerful energy source in the universe. And Minuteman Holdings will control it. We control all the patents, all the raw materials, all the equipment for producing it.

"Think of that. And while you're thinking of it," he added, his voice beginning to rise, "consider this. I am going to need my entire organization operating in the closest harmony for this to succeed. It will mean long hours, it will mean sacrifices. But I promise you it will be worth it. When this is finished and antimatter comes on-line, you will control the source of power that will fuel this planet. At the moment, you fifteen people manage factories; soon you will manage nations!"

Royal Newton stood and spread his arms, and it took a long time for the genuinely appreciative applause to die down.

CHAPTER

35

"KELLY. Kelly? Wake up, Kelly."

She couldn't tell whether she stirred and heard his voice, or it was his voice that woke her.

"Kelly, how do you feel?"

Kelly Edwards tried to open her eyes and focus on the small man near her. But her mind was caught up replaying her last conscious moments. They whirled and twisted with images of fire, lapping tongues of flame reaching for her, burning her. The memory of her own screaming catapulted her out of the semiconscious anesthetic sleep. She squinted at the hazy figure outlined against the light, and then cold drops touched her eyes and she blinked and the world swam into focus. The room was vaguely familiar, book-lined walls surrounding a canopied four-poster bed, hung with heavy drapes. She blinked her stinging eyes. "What was that?" she gulped in a pitiably weak voice.

"A little witch hazel—a sovereign remedy of my own for sore eyes," John Dee said reassuringly. "How do you feel?" he asked again.

"Numb." There was a pause as she tried to hydrate her mouth. "So numb." Another pause. "Where am I?"

"Back in my compound. In my room. I had you and d'Winter transported here yesterday. I felt you would both be safer here."

"What's wrong with Morgan? Was there an accident . . . ?"

There had been an accident, an explosion—but d'Winter hadn't been there, had he? She couldn't remember.

"There was no accident. Like you, he was attacked, an assassination attempt. Like you, he was extraordinarily lucky. A few broken bones to be sure, but mostly cuts, bruises, scrapes. He's well on the path to recovery." Dee sat down on the edge of Kelly's bed and took one of Kelly's hands in his. It was enclosed in a plastic bag that held a glutinous jellied substance. "But you, my dear—alas, you were rather more seriously assailed."

"I remember fire."

Dee nodded. "There was an inferno shaped to kill you. But it chanced to strike early whilst you were still within the protection of the elevator. That and Providence saved you. Unfortunately, flames shot through the opening portals and burned you."

"I remember flames everywhere," Kelly repeated. "I remember burning. The pain." She tried to move her hands to her face, but the bed restraints held them fast.

"You were badly burnt," Dee said softly. "You must not touch the nascent skin. But, by my immortal soul, you will be fine," he swore. "You have had the best of treatment, I swear it. God's own ministers. The very best."

"How do I look?" she whispered, and the doctor saw the fear of lost beauty in her eyes.

Dee folded his arms across his chest and tilted his head to one side. His lips were curled into a wry smile, but his cold gray eyes were distant and serious. The formfitting gelatinous mask that had enclosed her head and face had been removed just before she left the hospital. The new skin on her face and skull was pink and featureless, completely smooth, and without eyebrows or lashes. He thought she looked angelic, like a cherubim, or seraphim. "Do you want me to lie to you?" he asked.

Despite the fear, she never hesitated. "Tell me the truth, how do I look?"

The question went unanswered. The door behind Dee opened and both turned to look as d'Winter hobbled into the room. Beneath his ebony skin, the bruises and scrapes on his face were raw and angry and his left leg and right arm were encased in clear plastic molds. Dee hooked his foot into a chair and dragged it over to the bed and Morgan gratefully collapsed into it.

"Damn me, but everything hurts and I can't move. I feel like an old man," he muttered angrily.

"You look like an old man." Dee smiled.

D'Winter nodded toward Kelly. "How is she, Doc? Is she up yet?"

"She has even now returned to us. But ever the woman, she would have me report her looks." Dee turned back to Kelly. "You look like a plucked chicken, pink and ready for the oven."

D'Winter shook his head. "One of these days, Doc, you and me are going to have to have a talk about manners! Where's your subtlety? Where's that English chivalry?"

"Kelly did not want me to lie to her. And I have told her she shall mend completely."

"You could have put it differently," Kelly said. "I'm sure I look horrible, but I don't know that I want to be the butt of your jokes." She raised her head and torso to inspect her bagged hands and stared at them. The new skin had taken in patches and was growing over the damaged dermis like a fungus. All of her nails were gone. The sight did her in and she immediately lay back and closed her eyes.

"You will make a full recovery, the doctors have assured me," Dee said confidently. Having seen the miracles that modern medicine had already made in his friends' damaged bodies, he had little doubt that they would heal.

"Within the week, all your skin will have grown back; your

hair will take a while longer. But for the nonce we can make you a wig. I wonder where we can buy the hair?" he mused.

"Buy hair?" Kelly whispered horrified.

"Yes. How else do you make wigs? I know—I *knew*—several women who made a tidy living selling their hair for such. Regular income too."

"Disgusting," d'Winter muttered. "I've seen some things in my time, but you English have some gross habits. Wear someone else's hair. Who knows what crap they could have put in it, or on it." D'Winter shook his head, then grinned and said, "And the sweat, man, the sweat. Phewww."

Kelly offered a weak "Thank you for the offer, but I think I'll get a hat."

Dee nodded and came to his feet. "I'll get one for you. I'll get you two, no, seven, one for every day of the week. A lady should not wear the same hat twice. If there is anything you need, anything at all, you have but to ask, and by my honor, you shall have it." Dee took a deep breath. "This is my fault, my friends. I'm sorry I have gotten you into this."

"I knew what I was getting into . . ." d'Winter began. "This is an occupational hazard."

From some faraway place, Kelly whispered, "Dr. Dee, why are we doing this? What has Newton done to you? Maybe we all should just quit while we're still alive."

Dr. John Dee was struck hard by the unmasked fear in Kelly's plea. She looked so confused, so helpless. He gazed at her swollen face and felt more tired and spent than he had allowed himself to feel for weeks. It would be so easy to quit now. His own world had passed away centuries ago; why should he continue? If he had died in Venice as he should have, none of this would have mattered. He silently cursed his Fate that not only was he now responsible for the world's further existence, but that he must bear the knowledge of the Future alone. It was unthinkable to share Dyckon and his dire warnings with Kelly and Morgan. They would think him mad—a gargoyle in a spaceship on the dark side of the moon, indeed! But he had come to care for them too much to bear the mockery that that would engender. He could not tell them the truth, and yet the truth was what they deserved. He was so utterly alone and his loneliness weighed upon him. *Why me?* he thought. *Why me?* Was this how Christ felt when He pleaded to let the cup pass from Him? Dee realized now that the cup was knowledge. And knowledge could be a curse.

John Dee looked at the two of them. Like children at their father's chair, they waited patiently for an answer to the present situation. What could he tell them? His mind whirred, searching desperately for an answer that would satisfy them and his own sense of honor. But no solution was satisfactory. In the end, the lessons of his youth won out.

Early in his apprenticeship, Cecil, his spymaster, had tutored Dee in Machiavelli every day. Readings from *The Prince* became his morning prayers. They came back to him even now.

A prince should appear a man of compassion, a man of good faith, and a man of integrity. The common people are always impressed by appearances. Everyone knows how praiseworthy it is for a prince to honor his word and to be straightforward rather than crafty in his dealings. Nonetheless contemporary experience shows that princes who have achieved great things have been those who have given their word lightly, who have known how to trick men with their cunning, and who, in the end, have overcome those abiding by honest principles. Fear makes powerful allies. Further, fear is strengthened by dread of punishment which is always effective.

"I should have looked after you," he began, leaning back against a wall and looking down at the floor. "I should have anticipated that something like this would happen. God knows, if I were Newton, this is exactly what I would do—strike at his companions, those he cares about, provoke him to anger. Angry men make mistakes," he said softly.

Taking a deep breath, he looked up at each of them in turn, impressing on them his sincerity, while lying through his teeth. Cecil would have been proud. "Newton has made a grievous error with me. You must know that but a year since, I was Royal

Newton's good right arm, his chief confidant and counselor. I amassed a fortune through his advice. He lavished upon me praise and power; and to protect me cloaked my identity in recordless anonymity. But there came a time when his thirst for power outreached the very bounds of Nature. It sickened me. My friends, he intends world domination through doomsday devices which quickly will bring nations to their knees. His munition sites that we are attacking harbor the armament and research for this infernal war. I swore by all that is Holy that I would stop him. But in my fervor to do right, I have entwined you in his hatred for me. He knows you and now there is no place on Earth that you may call safe. He will murder you to have at me." He turned away in a gesture of remorse and a semblance of regret. "Please forgive me for the peril I have put you in." Then, he turned back to them and said, "I want you to heal now. And then you can go away, somewhere far from me until all this is over."

Both Kelly and Morgan started to shake their heads.

"This is not open to discussion," Dee said firmly, his hand on the door handle. "Now, is there anything I can get for either of you . . . besides a new hat?" The smile that started to form on his face froze when he was reminded that it was his fault she was mangled and weak in his bed.

"My brother," Kelly whispered. "Have you heard anything from my brother?"

Dee looked at d'Winter, who shook his head slightly. "I did not know you had a brother," he said, returning to stand alongside the bed. He put a reassuring hand on her shoulder.

"My younger brother, Robert." Kelly attempted to rise up in the bed, but Morgan gently eased her back onto the pillows.

The mercenary glanced up at Dee. "The boy is in danger. He must be protected. If Newton knows about us, then he will know about Robert."

"Agreed," Dee said grimly.

"What about Robert?" she whispered, her voice raw and harsh.

"I'll see to it, immediately," Dee said, striding to the door.

"Don't worry, and try not to frown; you'll give that wonderful new skin of yours wrinkles."

Morgan d'Winter stood at Dee's shoulder as he accessed Kelly Edwards's personal records, watching the data appear on the giant screen over the doctor's head.

" 'Sblood, but I must be getting careless in my old age; I never thought to ask her about family."

"Then I'm as guilty as you, Doctor, because neither did I. But lately events have been hectic."

"That's no excuse. None. 'Sblood! She has a brother and a mother!" Slipping his long fingers into the cyber-gloves, and pulling on a headset, settling the hollow cups over his eyes, Dee began to move his fingers, manipulating the data strings that appeared in glowing holographic form before him.

Deftly accessing the central data bank, he backtracked to Kelly, pulling out addresses with his little fingers, sliding them onto the printer icon. Across the room, the soft-laser printer hissed out flimsy sheets of recycled plastic.

"You play this like a pro," d'Winter said admiringly.

"This is technology I can understand," Dee muttered. When Kelly had first made him put on the graphite cyber-gloves and taken him into the abstract digital landscape, she had never expected him to grasp the concepts behind it. Dee was obviously a man who was a stranger to technology. She'd been shocked and frightened when she discovered that he urinated into the bath—because he simply did not know how to use the toilet.

It had taken d'Winter a whole day to demonstrate the various equipment in the enormous bathroom, and then Dee hadn't come out for nearly three days and the entire railcar stank of a particularly pungent eau de cologne.

But Dee had taken to the cyber-world with extraordinary ease. Within a matter of days, his facility in the abstract world was greater than hers; he did not tell her that he had been shaping incantations and spells in just this manner for decades. This astral world—what Kelly called a cyber-world—was a place he knew well; this was the place of magic and incantation, of spells and cantrips.

"Her mother is in hospital in Colorado," Dee said, accessing the hospital records, calling up an image of a woman with emerald green skin. He attempted to adjust the color gain on the holograph, but the skin color remained green.

"Oh, she's undergoing," and here he haltingly read, "pigmentation replacement therapy—whatever that is."

"She's done something which messed with her skin color—she's having it changed back to normal," d'Winter supplied. "Rarely works; she'll end up looking piebald, unless she opts for the basic black option."

"Here's the brother." A series of images began to scroll on before Dee. "Hmm, seems he has flouted the law. No wonder Kelly didn't want us aware of him." A three-dimensional representation of a street map appeared. "I've got an address."

"Not too far away," d'Winter muttered. "Check the utilities records for the apartment."

"Why?" Dee wondered, even as his fingers were pulling down the records; then he swore softly. "Now I understand why; no light, heat, or water has been in use for the past three days."

"That's when the hit went down on Kelly and myself."

Dee pulled off the gloves and headset. "Say nothing to Kelly. Not yet."

"Why? Where are you going?"

The doctor pulled two sheets from the printer; one was a copy of the police image of Robert Edwards, the second was the street grid. "I must go and know the truth. I have promised her."

"I'll come with you."

"You will do no such thing. Rest here, watch over Kelly. I will do this on my own." He squeezed d'Winter's arm gently. "I know you may think me foolish, naive, nay sometimes even manifestly stupid, but, believe me, I am older than I look, and age has taught me many things." A needle-pointed stiletto appeared in Dee's hands and then, magically, disappeared. "I know how to take care of myself in a strange city." He pulled on a knee-length black leather overcoat and turned up the collar and settled a broad-brimmed leather hat on his head. "How do I look?"

"You'll blend right in," d'Winter muttered. "I just wish you were carrying something more lethal than a knife."

Dee paused by the door and pulled back his coat to reveal the chrome-plated sawed-off shotgun dangling from its holster under the coat's left arm. "Believe me; I learn very quickly."

CHAPTER

36

Maybe the trip through time had made him groggy; maybe he had been so ensorcelled by the many wonders of this new place that he had ceased to think clearly; maybe he was just getting old; but overlooking the safety of Kelly's family was an amateurish mistake.

Hell and damnation; how could he have been so stupid? The brother was an easy target.

How could he have not double-checked that? Acid dread ate away at the pit of his stomach. How often had he taught and been taught in turn that victory lay in the details? Battles were won and lost not on the battlefield, but in the tiny minutiae of planning beforehand.

And Dr. John Dee knew in his heart and soul that he had lost this battle because of his stupidity. Three days with no power consumption did not bode well.

Dr. John Dee stood on the swaying, noisy monorail and grimaced. The carriage was full of people, all of them looking as if they had dressed for a fancy-dress ball, but it was, in reality, just another day in downtown Angel City.

These people made the peacock costumes of holiday Venice

look drab, though they were equally malodorous, a mixture of too many perfumes, too much sweat, cooking, and the ever-present odor of cabbage.

They swarmed like summer gnats. John Dee and his era had never dreamed of a future so debauched and so aimless. This was the humanity he was trying to save—and looking at them, he was beginning to wonder if they were worth it.

Dee shook his head. He was not God; this was not his decision to make. He simply had to do what fate had ordained for him. He had always been a great believer in fate and destiny. And obviously Destiny had wanted him to end up in this place, at this time, with the future of humanity in his hands. Well, his father had always said he would go far, that he had a great future ahead of him.

Neither of them had realized just how far, or how great.

But he was certainly too old for all these heroics. At his time of life, he should be married with children, or, at the very least, thinking about retiring, about settling down with a wife and a couple of serving wenches, some dogs, a brace of hawks, a couple of horses, a few acres, and the pension the Queen kept managing to forget to give him for his services. She had fobbed him off for years. He smiled at the memory; sometimes, when events threatened to overwhelm him, he would visualize himself living out a life of quiet retirement in some country hamlet.

Even then, he had always known that easy existence was not to be his lot in life. He would not end up that way. But never in his wildest dreams had he imagined that he would end up in this hellish nightmare vision of Earth.

"Last stop," he heard the metallic coachman announce, and the croaking omen did not go unnoticed.

"My stop," he thought, shouldering his way through the passengers to drop onto the cracked sidewalk. He had returned to the barbaric part of the city where he had first prowled. Here were the El-Vis, Ruby's Left, and Mary Lynn taverns; here were the Streets of Red Lanterns that would make Sodom seem tame by comparison; here were the professional fighting arenas, the gambling dens, the opium pits, the markets where every-thing—including the vendors—was for sale. He felt more at home here in this part of the city than in the artificial security of the railcar.

He was again within spitting distance of the mindless anarchy of the Valley and its cannibal footpads. He had forgotten how ugly it was.

Picking his way through the filth-strewn streets, avoiding the potholes, some of which were big enough to swallow a man whole, Dr. John Dee realized that since he'd been here he had stopped thinking like a sixteenth-century man; he had allowed himself to be seduced by the effete morals of this time and place.

Over the months, he had come to realize there were certain modes of behavior from his own time that were unacceptable in Angel City.

Women who bared their legs or bosoms in the streets were not necessarily harlots, and took serious objection to having portions of their anatomy fondled.

Urinating against a convenient wall was a criminal offense—though shooting down a thief was not—while spitting into the filthy, slime-filled gutters was a crime punishable by imprison-ment. And Dee, who had always succeeded as a spy because he had the talent to blend into the local society, had adopted their modes of thinking. In his own day, if a man offended you, you either slew him yourself, or employed a professional to do it. In this time, in the more civilized portions of the city, people em-ployed lawyers. And if they did perchance decide to take the law into their own hands and kill an enemy, they did it with a gun from a distance.

Dee had never been one of those people who believed that there was honor in killing face-to-face—though there was the satisfaction of watching your enemy falling at your feet. Killing was bloody, filthy work, best accomplished quickly and in one's oldest clothes, which needs must be burnt afterward, since blood and excreta were extremely difficult to shift even with salt and alum.

When he killed Newton, he wanted to be looking into the bald man's eyes as he twisted the knife.

The small man glanced at the address on the map grid as he exited the tram depot and turned left onto Blunte Street. There, nearly at the end of the block, was the bakery where he'd first eaten. He remembered he owed the buttery bar money. He reminded himself to attend to it, though there was no time now to redress old wrongs, only Kelly's brother to think of. He moved on, turning right onto Rum Street.

Kelly and Robert lived on the fringes of Angel City's Chinatown, and there were more Oriental faces on the streets now than Caucasian. Right again, onto Nog. The streets were cleaner here, old men and women sitting contentedly outside of shops, faces shaded from the lethal sun by broad straw hats. Their expressions did not change as Dee walked past, though he could hear them muttering among themselves; some of the names they called him were quite inventive. Here the graffiti on the walls were in neat vertical lines of Chinese characters. As Dee stared at the painted words, they shifted as the translator kicked in: they were shop names, advertisements, turf markings, warnings. He finally turned left onto Gay.

The address was 4N. There was a shop here too, but its name was in English, a gold cursive script against a purple background. Garrick & Sons, Bespoke Tailors. And to the left of the shop was the insignificant-looking door that led up to the Edwardses' apartment.

Glancing over his shoulder, Dee tapped in the key code and the door clicked open. The doctor stepped inside and pushed the door closed behind him. And immediately knew that something was wrong.

Terribly wrong.

The air was heavy with a familiar odor. It was the smell of meaty flesh and metallic blood, of strange liquids gone stale, of curious molds and noxious fungi. He knew then that his worst fears were now real.

Dee pulled the shotgun out from beneath his coat and

pressed the release that chambered a round. Holding the gun upright in his left hand, with his back to the wall, his knife in his right hand, he cautiously climbed the stairs. The smell grew stronger when he reached the first landing and what he had first taken for complete silence was disturbed by the faintest of buzzing and humming sounds. He remembered battlefields and fought off his nausea and terror. Walking with infinite care down the corridor, testing every step before he put his full weight on it, he stopped outside a door that had an enormous ragged hole where the handle used to be.

Digging the tip of his knife into the plastic wood, he pushed the door open, then quickly stepped in, shotgun leveled, and knew instantly that he was at least three days too late.

The smell was indescribable; it enveloped him in a frightening claustrophobia. He had to run from it and duck back into the hall. With his mind heaving, he retched. When he had regained control of his stomach, he took a deep breath and peered into the room again.

The place was a shambles. It had obviously once been filled to the ceiling with computer equipment; now that was so much metal and plastic. The floor was covered in power cords and silvery reflective disks, bits of plastic, and unnamable technological components that crunched and snapped underfoot with every step.

And in the center of the room, dangling from the ceiling in a noose fashioned out of a mass of computer wires and cables, were the remains of a young man.

As Dee approached, swarms of flies left the body, revealing for an instant that the boy had been stripped bare and had died hard. The brutality of his death had been meant as a message for Dee. The flies swarmed around the room and then settled onto the body again, undulating black creatures planting their larvae. Dr. John Dee stood for a long time, his hands covering his mouth and nose, looking at the boy, wondering what he was going to tell Kelly. How was he going to tell her that her brother was dead and had been brutally tortured?

How could he hide the obvious, that her brother was a victim of Dee's war on Newton? Hadn't she suffered enough because of him? He knew she would hate him. Despite the smell of the gore, he stood lost in the doorway, unable to turn away. His strength had gone out of him.

Finally Dee stepped out of the room and closed the remains of the door behind him, never once thinking of cutting Robert down. It was time he started acting like a sixteenth-century gentleman again. It was time to visit Newton. Personally.

CHAPTER
37

JAMES ZHU FOUND his master in the building Newton modestly and rather mockingly referred to as the Small Gallery.

The Small Gallery was a donut-shaped building slightly over three kilometers in circumference cut into the wall of a lunar crater. And on Moonbase, where cots measuring two by one meters—called coffins—were rented weekly to the maintenance workers for the equivalent of just under four days' wage, the rental cost of the enormous space to Minuteman Holdings was colossal. However, the value of the space on Moonbase was minute when compared with the value of the art treasures within the gallery.

Royal Newton's great-grandfather, Karl, had begun the Newton collection by the simple expedient of buying all that he could afford—and there was a lot he could afford—and stealing what he could not. Art, after all, was a great investment. The thefts were never blatant; when his offer to the Hofburg Museum in Vienna to purchase the Spear of Longenius—the spear that reputedly had pierced Christ's side on the Cross—was refused, Newton had simply bought the entire museum.

He then appropriated for his own personal collection those pieces which he coveted.

Like most people, the Newtons admired art that reflected their own aspirations. Their collection was a paean to success, whether it was the success of an artist conquering his medium or the success of the collector winning out over his competitors. The collection was eclectic. There was Charlie Chaplin's original Tramp costume, from *Kid Auto Races at Venice*, dating back to 1914, alongside the complete First Folio Collection of Shakespeare's plays as well as all of Jackie Onassis' jewelry and fine furnishings.

Zhu detested the place. He hated working on the moon, with its dry, slightly tainted air, the constant feeling of disorientation, and the extra spring to his walk that put him off balance. He particularly disliked the Small Gallery, though he was one of only two people who possessed the access codes to the building.

He hated its solitude.

Paradoxically, Zhu loved galleries and museums. Within their dusty, dry quiet he could relax, blend in with the other anonymous tourists, wander aimless from hall to hall. But at least those galleries were furnished with taste, whereas this . . .

Whatever Newton had, he lacked taste.

Disdaining schools of art, cultures, and periods, Royal arranged his art alphabetically. Zhu strode past one wall covered in some of the finest pieces of the world's art—the Nabi Painters, Nevelson, Newman, nymphets, Noh masks, and nudes. He followed the gentle curve that brought him past rows of books, leather, buckram, cloth, and paper bindings shoved in side by side.

There was an overflow section, where Zhu found an original signed *Rubaiyat* shoved in alongside a paperback of the lyric poems of Catullus, Gutenberg's Bible resting atop an original *Star Trek* script, the collected works of Higuchi Ichiyo alongside the diaries of Napoleon. Everything of monetary importance was there, the list of titles was as vast as the array of stars that shone through the Small Gallery's beveled windows, and none of it was ever read, ever looked at.

Zhu walked on and approached the figure standing before the single spotlight that highlighted the Great Seal of the United States, which Newton's father had purchased from the Lost President.

Royal Newton's contribution to the collection had been to fill in some of its blanks, the acquiring of the *Mona Lisa* had been a great coup, but he was particularly proud of his almost complete collection of fragments of the ceiling from the Sistine Chapel. One of these days he was going to re-create the devastated Vatican building here on the moon.

Newton glanced up as Zhu appeared. There was a flat black disk in the bald man's hands. "Do you know what this is?" he asked, tilting the disk slightly, allowing the overhead lights to pick out the circular grooves cut into the plastic.

Zhu shook his head, disinterested.

"This is what was called a record, a vinyl, the very distant forerunner of the sound slivers. On one side—and it only plays one side at a time before you have to manually flip it over—is no more than three to four minutes' worth of music played by the Beatles, a musical quartet who were deified by the youth of their day. The Lennon Sects worship one of their number, I believe. I've just acquired this," he added. "It is of incredible rarity and worth twice what you earn in a year."

"Fascinating, I'm sure," Zhu said, disinterested, reaching over to pass a gossamer-thin transparent sheet over the vinyl disk.

Newton tilted the disk and immediately the three-dimensional image of a face appeared on the sheet. "I presume this is important? Who is this man?"

"He visited the apartment of Robert Edwards less than two hours ago. The sensors picked him up the moment he entered the apartment and tracked him. He came armed; he examined the body and then left. He touched nothing, and the sight of the body which we had left as an example"—Zhu smiled thinly—"did not seem to unduly upset him, though the smell did seem to offend him."

"Yes, yes. But who is he? Anyone could have entered that building."

"He has no biochip."

There was an immediate change in the bald man's demeanor. He peered down at Zhu's sheet, suddenly cut off from his surroundings. "Another one?" he whispered. Newton's jaw was slightly agape, his brow furrowed, and one side of his mouth had turned upward.

Zhu would have thought it was comical if he hadn't been struck by his master's utter state of shock.

He stood that way for a full minute, rapt attention focused on the photo. Then he seemed to think of something, and the episode passed.

Royal Newton carefully returned the record to its sleeve and placed it on the satin pillow beneath the protective lights that would prevent further deterioration. Taking the tissue sheet between finger and thumb, he carried it over to the spotlight that picked out the Great Seal and held it up to better scrutinize the transparency. The face that sprang into view was sharp and clear, the eyes cold and gray, lips thin, cheekbones strong and clearly defined.

Curls of gray hair escaped from beneath his broad-brimmed hat, matching his full beard. Even in the better light, Newton could not recognize him. He shook his head in disbelief. There were fewer than thirty people in the known world who were without biochips. Newton was positive that he knew them all, and knew that they had all paid exorbitantly to have the chips removed—a supposedly impossible task.

This fellow in the shot was definitely not one of them. Aside from the thirty, no one else could possibly evade detection. . . . But realizing now that nothing was impossible—that someone could be beyond his control and awareness—had taken all the breath out of Newton. The feeling scared him.

Zhu passed over a second sheet. "This is the image we got from Tsuru."

Newton held up the two images. The similarities were remarkable.

"I asked the computers to do a match and prepare a composite." The third image was a three-dimensional rotating head, with the hat removed. "I believe that the two men must be one and the same."

This seemed to relieve Newton somewhat, and he took a long

breath. "This must be the man known as Dr. John Dee." He smiled humorlessly with the good news. "Four of my best men were watching the Edwardses' apartment. They are on to him now. I will have him for you within the hour."

"You've said that before," Newton said quietly. "If this is the man who has managed to trespass on my factories, destroy my property, and evade capture, he may evade you still. There is a lot more to this man than meets the eye. All I can say is, at least I know now what he looks like." He held the image up to the light again.

Superimposed against the Great Seal of the United States, Dee's head revolved silently. *He has very good hair,* Newton noted.

CHAPTER

38

"I WAS JUST ABOUT TO SEND out a search party for you," d'Winter said as Dee stepped into the railcar. "I thought you'd be back hours ago."

Dee pulled off his hat and spun it across the room onto the computer keyboard panel. It slid for a moment but held on to the edge. Without saying a word, he shrugged out of his long coat and, leaving it in a puddle of cloth on the floor, dropped the shotgun on top of it, crossed to the bar, pulled open the fridge, and poured himself a tall glass of ice-cold milk. "Believe me, I would have been, but I was visited with company on the trip back."

Morgan d'Winter's hands shoved Dee's hat to the floor and raced to punch keys on the panel, bringing all the monitors and sensors to life. "I've doubled the perimeter guards, all the monitors and panels are to full alert."

"Don't worry." Dee slumped into his favorite chair, which immediately adjusted and settled to accommodate him. Gull, the cat, appeared out of nowhere and leapt onto his lap, purring softly. "I took care of them," Dee said.

"Took care of them?" Dee's chief of security scanned for trespassers, not completely trusting his employer's assessment of the situation.

Dee closed his eyes and rolled the sweating glass of milk against his forehead. "They must have been watching the apartment. If truth be known, I had thought to face them in the building."

"I take it Kelly's brother . . ." d'Winter asked quietly.

"Died hard, my friend. Died hard. And was left there as an example for us, or as a lure." An observation furrowed Dee's brow. "Or both." He opened his eyes and glanced down the corridor. "Kelly?"

"Asleep. She got mad as all hell a while ago, spent the afternoon devising some interesting strategies to screw Newton. Later, she just sat there and then nodded off."

" 'Sblood. I'm not looking forward to telling her about her brother's end," Dee sighed. He sipped his milk. "When I left the apartment, the first tail picked me up almost immediately. He was good, but I've had a lifetime of being shadowed through some of the worst thoroughfares in Europe. I correctly guessed that if I saw one, there would be more. I returned via the long route through Chinatown, stopping at every disreputable tavern I could find, asking the Far Easterners for directions. I'm sure my trackers were convinced I was hugger-muggering with my spies. It certainly seemed that way. It's an old trick, but still useful. The world is still deceived with false seeming. My first tracker was joined by a second, a woman, and then later by two more, a man and a woman. They kept on me in turns, first one pair drawing near, then the second—as if this were a means to fool me.

"I boarded the monorail, and they followed in the car behind me. Once, whilst they feigned conviviality, I caught them eyeing me. But I stared on past them as if rapt in weighty thought. Truth is truth and falsehood falsehood cures. I got off at the last stop before the Valley and made for one of the derelict buildings, moving as if the place were indeed mine. They followed me in." Dee's cold gray eyes went to the shotgun lying on top of his discarded coat. "Very effective at close range."

"Very," d'Winter said softly.

"I searched their bodies," Dee continued. "They carried no identification, of course; they were armed and all carrying small communication devices. I thought of taking one, but was unschooled if they could be traced."

"You did right; it would have been possible to trace the signature of the device right back to here."

"Ah, I had a notion that something of that nature could be done. Amazing." He nodded, reaffirming his chosen actions, then continued. "If they reported their last position before I slew them, their friends will canvass that worthless vestige of the city; that should buy us some time." Dee finished the last of the milk in one long swallow.

Without a word, d'Winter took the glass from his hand and refilled it. He returned it to the reclining doctor and then rechecked the security protocols for intruders. The perimeter was still quiet, and the feral children—who were usually the first indicator of intruders—still ran wild through the abandoned railyard. "You constantly amaze me, Doctor," the mercenary said. "You think nothing of blowing away four people and searching their bodies, and yet Robert Edwards's death has obviously upset you."

"Because it was unnecessary. It was a foul and bloody act. Death, in itself, does not upset me," Dee said, accepting the drink. "We are men, it is God's will that we are fated to die. In my time . . ." He stopped and remembered to edit himself more carefully in future. "I have seen more death that you can imagine. Natural, accidental, by disease or murder. And within each of these there is degree: it is better to die by some diseases than by others, there are some accidents that are more merciful than others, and there are ways of murder which are more acceptable, shall we say."

Morgan d'Winter shifted uncomfortably. "I'm not sure there are any acceptable ways of murdering someone."

"Are there not people who deserve death?" Dee sat forward, fixing Morgan with his intense stare. "If there is a rabid dog in the streets do you not cut it down?"

"Men are not dogs."

"You are a mercenary; how can you say that?" Dee accused.

D'Winter shrugged. "I've seen men behave like animals, that's for sure."

"And will you sit here and tell me that you have never put one down?"

The mercenary sat back in his chair and stared at the small man for a long time. Finally, he said simply, "Yes." He blinked away images of a village in South America and a Bolivian mercenary who delighted in . . . "Yes," he repeated.

"Mankind is an inconsistent thing. It must be taught right from wrong. In my infancy, where I lived we were tutored in the necessity of fealty and obedience by watching public hangings. They were governmental holidays."

"Where was that done?" d'Winter said, taken aback.

"A little island nation. You wouldn't know it." Sitting up in his chair, Dee warmed to his subject. "If a man plotted to kill his . . ." Dee paused for a brief moment. ". . . his prince, it was fitting and right that he hang for his crimes. But if the man was but a worker bee in a larger hive of conspiracy, his crimes might be mitigated in the public's mind by the knowledge that he had no real part in the policymaking of that treachery."

Dr. Dee searched d'Winter's eyes to be sure his point was being understood. D'Winter gave him his full attention. "If that be true, then how much more severity must be shown those that are the queens and chief handiworkers of that hive's treachery? Should they not be quartered and disemboweled as well as hanged, since their crimes are that much more heinous than those of the drudge who but acts and knows not why he acts? We will tolerate punishment most cruel for those whose crimes most merit it, but not for the poor wretch whose degree of sin does not equal the larger degree of punishment. There is degree in all things which must be observed else justice devolves to beastliness.

"Robert Edwards died hard. And it took him a long time to die. I never met the boy, but the sole reason he perished is be-

242

cause his sister works for me, and the brutality of his death is as a warning to me—the prince of this undertaking, as it were.

"There have been times in the past when men have died, when I employed men and regrettably sent them to their Maker. Those deaths do not touch me. I knew what I was doing when I hired them; moreover, they certainly knew the dangers when they shouldered the task. They were aware of the risks and had choice to say yea or nay. But there have been times, also, when men and women have been innocently killed because of me. It is brutishness in the highest when there is no degree in the punishment." Dee shook his head, bloody faces and torn bodies flitting behind his eyes. "Those deaths always maddened me and it is a matter of my honor that they were always avenged." His expression turned grim.

"Always," d'Winter quietly repeated, and didn't doubt him.

"We know, you and I, that Newton is behind this atrocity. Oh, he had no hand in the killing; he was doubtless a far way off, but he commanded this poor boy's death, sanctioned it, condoned it, and, by my eternal soul, he shall pay for it." Dee stopped.

D'Winter's expression had changed, tightened, and his eyes were looking over the doctor's shoulder. Even before Dee turned, he knew what he would find.

"I think you should tell me how my brother died," Kelly Edwards said before she collapsed into the room.

They rushed to her side and moved her to the couch that faced them, careful of her hands in their plastic bags, her hairless head damp with sweat. Dee spoke softly to her and massaged her temples. Morgan went for water.

She revived with a breath that filled her lungs with air and immediately reminded her of her loss.

Kelly Edwards listened numbly as Dee did his best to answer her initial question. With Gull cradled in his arms, the doctor told her simply, without embellishment, how her brother had died. She asked no questions; the doctor's carefully chosen words had drawn vivid, disturbing images. Nor was she suitably ready to probe between the lines and learn more. She only knew that she wanted her brother back and she wanted to cry, but her tear ducts were still damaged, and the tears could not come. It frustrated and maddened her. But later, later she would determine just exactly what had happened, and then she would weep for Robert.

Dee looked woefully impotent. He must be paralyzed with guilt, Kelly thought, as she watched him stand mutely staring at his hands, awaiting the questions and the recriminations that never came. There was so much to say, but neither of them could break the silence that both joined and separated them. And, so, they remained almost touching, yet each alone, suffering in their own hells.

When the door opened and d'Winter reappeared, Dee smiled silently in thanks for the momentary reprieve. Morgan precariously balanced a tray which held two bottles of pure unrecycled water and a tall glass of milk.

He passed the milk to Dee, who took it, apparently happy to have something to hold.

Carefully maneuvering the green glass bottle into Kelly's bagged hands, the soldier of fortune slipped a striped straw into the bottle and bent it. He looked up and caught her eye. In his presence, her stoicism crumbled and grief racked her body. But his eye was locked on hers and his look communicated to her his understanding and his empathy with her loss. It said, "I know. I understand. You'll get through this. Hold on." In their few months together, a palpable bond had taken hold between them. Kelly sucked in a painful column of air and then nodded understanding. She had control again.

With his help, she sipped the cool water.

After two more sips, Kelly turned to her employer and said simply, "You never adequately explained why you wanted Newton stopped. You suggested that he was developing some destructive machines that sounded like hydrogen bombs, though you called them doomsday devices, that would devastate the Earth. Why should the richest man on this Earth blow up the world? It doesn't make sense."

244

"The lady's right. I think it's time for answers," Morgan d'Winter agreed.

"I am not in the habit of answering questions," Dee said simply.

"Well, maybe you'd better kick that habit. We both work for you. You employed me to carry out attacks on Newton's factories. You employed Kelly to represent you and gain you entry into the marketplace. We were nearly killed. We know absolutely nothing about you—you don't even have a biochip. Technically, you don't exist. Which boggles the mind, man. No one—but no one—ain't got a biochip. You tell us Newton is developing a terrible weapon and that you're trying to stop him. I got no reason to doubt that *he* is trying to stop *you* about something. People like him are always up to something. I think his attacks on us, and Kelly's brother, only confirm that. But whether it's about this world-domination thing, whether it's just to stop our raids, or whether it's something else entirely is yet to be sussed out." The mercenary's voice had dropped to a low thunder, vaguely threatening. "You owe us some answers. Who sent you to settle the score with Newton? Who are you working for? Who *are* you, Dr. John Dee?"

"If I told you the whole truth, you wouldn't believe me," Dee said with a shrug, "so it is best I not burden you with that."

D'Winter looked away in exasperation.

"You owe us answers," Kelly said softly. "We have bought some answers with the danger you've put us in. With my brother's . . ." Her voice trailed off.

For a moment it looked as if Dee was about to walk out of the room. Then he stooped and placed Gull on the floor before leaning on the end of Kelly's couch. "Believe me when I tell you that it is better that you do not know who sent me, except that my mission is for the greater good of all mankind."

D'Winter exploded, "This is bullshit!"

Kelly was kinder. She desperately wanted to have everything that had happened make sense, and she believed in Dee. She didn't want to hate him. "You're some sort of government agent?"

"I have worked for governments," Dee acknowledged. "I was

chosen for my personal connections and, of course, my wealth. I'm with the English government now." He did not mention which English government. "I was recruited while I was still in Newton's employ. It was their agents who rooted out Newton's efforts. I am sworn to the utmost secrecy and cannot reveal aught."

"You can tell us nothing?" Kelly pleaded.

"On my honor, I may not," Dee avowed.

Morgan d'Winter grunted disbelievingly.

Dee knew Kelly needed something if she was to believe. D'Winter might later be swayed by her belief. The lies would come easily; it was a skill he had honed as Elizabeth's diplomat. "If I tell you some of what I know, you must give your word you will never reveal it."

D'Winter was not going to be easily led, but Kelly implored him for his promise of silence, "Please, Morgan, how else will we ever know?"

"All right," d'Winter reluctantly agreed, and planted himself next to Kelly on the couch. Gull rubbed his back against d'Winter's leg and purred. "Let's hear it."

Dr. Dee, with some show of uncertainty about breaking English security, then began to weave truth and untruth. The best lie is based upon the truth. "Newton is developing antimatter technology. However, our researches have revealed that when he detonates his devices he will have effectively signed the death warrant of the entire human race. It will set off a series of events that will end the world as we know it."

"It will cause climatic change?" d'Winter said.

Although Dee did not understand the terminology, he nodded, happy that the disbeliever had accepted the scenario.

Kelly asked, "Why not just tell Newton what his bombs will do? Surely, his engineers should come up with the same results as the English."

"We have tried. I have tried. These are among the arguments that rived our friendship. He is willing to risk all for the enormous wealth that this monopoly of power would amass if it succeeded."

"Doesn't he have enough?" asked Morgan bitterly.

"I know these kinds of men; they never have enough," responded Kelly.

"Lust for wealth is their God, and their God will confound them." Dee saw that they were coming around, so he continued. "Newton is very close to completion now. I have tried destroying his factories, I have attempted to cut off his source of essential minerals. But our incursions have only slowed him down. We have but scotched the snake, not killed it. But there is a great weakness in Newton's organization—and that is Newton. If he is removed from the picture, then the project will fall apart."

"That's what you intend to do, isn't it?" Kelly whispered. "You intend to kill him."

"Yes," Dee said simply. "I've rarely encountered a problem that a knife between the ribs didn't solve."

"Is it the 'degree' of punishment he deserves?" Morgan chuckled.

"There is an easier way," Kelly said slowly. "I suggested earlier that we buy up his essential supplies of minerals and metals. But now, why not go the whole hog and try to destroy his entire company?"

"Does this mean you will accompany me still, knowing the peril that might await?"

Kelly turned to Morgan. "There really is no choice."

Morgan shrugged. "I'll stick for a while. As long as the check don't bounce." He swiveled back to Dee. "Doctor, you better have been telling us straight." The threat was implicit in his voice.

"Friends, I am much relieved. Thank you, Kelly. Thank you, Morgan." There were no smiles—only grim determined faces.

They returned to the business at hand. "Kelly, how can we destroy his financial empire? Surely you would need vast wealth to even attempt such a feat?"

"I thought you had vast wealth? Are you willing to gamble it?"

Dee shrugged. "The money is a tool; use it whatever way you will. But while you're doing that, I'll be tackling the problem my way." The needle-pointed stiletto appeared in his hand, the blade flat against his cheek. "What do you intend to do?" he asked.

"I'm going to attempt a hostile takeover."

"Funny." Dee smiled. "That's just what I was going to do. And there is nothing more hostile than a knife between the ribs."

CHAPTER

39

A VELLUM ADDENDUM to the Day Book of John Dee, in the Year
of Our Lord 2099:

> *I have left off my machine that magically mutates my airy*
> *words unto things of text. In truth, there will be some documents*
> *that must be quilled with ink and parchment. The distribution*
> *of property and movable goods must be bequeathed in my own*
> *hand. It has ever been thus.*
>
> *I will preamble my preparations for I am loath to set about the*
> *appointed task at hand. The finding of virgin vellum in a time*
> *of paper and cyber-writings is nigh unto impossible. But for the*
> *tradesman Schenk of Amsterdam, a vendor of fetish undergar-*
> *ments and master of leather goods, which I procured via the*
> *Omni-Net, this Last Will and Testament would not have been*
> *written. But I was determined to have vellum of the finest qual-*
> *ity for my scriving; nothing less would do for what could well*
> *nigh be my final document.*
>
> *I sorely miss the services of Courtney & Piers, Her Majesty's*
> *royal quill-makers. There in Cheapside they fashion the finest*
> *pens of cygnus where they make use of only the five fashionable*

outer feathers. For my especial use, I fancied the second or third feather of the sinestre wing for that I am right-handed and the plume interfered not with my vision nor tickled my nose. Had they but lived to see this day as I have, they would have cried, alas, for the want of swan or goose. These creatures have scant scaped slaughter like the unicorn and are by proclamation kept in protected parks. Even the lowly crow, a multitudinous creature of pestilence, whose plumage might serve the pen-maker in a pinch, is scarce seen now. But I, being of a desperate mind to complete my testament in the manner I desired, prompted the feral children of my railyard with bounty if they could but bring me one. After many protestations of ignorance and stories of failure, they secured me three scrawny specimens—none of them crows. I culled from a monstrously mangled cardinal as big as a Canterbury pidgeon a workable quill and split the tip for my nib.

In times past, I was an adept at the grounding and preparing of inks. It was a necessary part of my avocation. I took delight in it. But now, there be so many choices of ink, I never took it into my head to do aught but buy. Moreover, I made purchase of a gold ink with much metal in it that put me in mind of my library of illuminated scripture. It is fitting and right that my last legal document be inscribed so. I fear that it may be the Omega of my work.

I cannot but think of my four wills that have come before this document. I disavow them now. For none of my heirs, yea, none of the great-grandchildren of those heirs, lives to inherit.

I, Johannes Dee, Magister, commonly known as Dr. John Dee, being of sound mind (that is to signify that I am not touched in the wits though sore pressed to explain my sanity in the face of these insane times) and body (more than sound body, for have not I withstood five hundred years? I have the soundest of bodies), do will and bequeath all my worldly goods to . . .?

To whom? I have no one. I am sore alone, more than any witness can comprehend. I am a man out of time, whose family and every friend are naught but dust, whose world survives but in the sere crumbling pages of History. As I think on it, there may be no reason in continuing this document nor the legal tradition that prompts it. For I see only failure before me which

means certain death of the world. If that be so then all is mean-
ingless. Wills and Testaments are but gifts to the succeeding gen-
eration. If all is lost then what purpose lies there in gifts? I
despair and my thoughts are black with thinking of nothing save
the horror—countless deaths. Nature blasted, History at an end.
I will write no further.

    I believe I slept in the moments twixt penning the above and
beginning again. Perhaps I dreamt. I do not know. I but know
this; let not my mind's eye forget God's great mercy. There is a
divine presence that shepherds us and keeps us safe. O lamb of
God, steel my heart and possess it not with fear. Take from me
now my foreboding sense of reckoning. Let me remember Your
hand in the world which vindicates good over wickedness. I will
trust in Heaven's theodicy and follow the hope You have seen fit
to sow in every breathing soul.
    I will press on.
    To wit: I leave my entire estate, all my goods and chattels, to
be equally divided by my two trusted servants, Morgan d'Winter
and Kelly Edwards. My fondest wish is that they forgive me for
what I brought upon them and that they live out the rest of their
days in comfort. In the event of one of their deaths, the survivor
is to inherit all with my blessings.

Johannes Dee

With a final flourish, Dr. John Dee dated the parchment, then
carefully poured a droplet of sealing wax onto the page and
pressed the hilt of his knife, bearing the Dee crest, into the wax.
Sitting back in the chair, the doctor looked beyond the document out the heavily barred windows into the gathering twilight
and darkening autumnal sky. The warm wind, which some wag
had christened St. Anne for reasons no one now remembered,
blew gustily, and delicate clouds of sand and silt skidded over
the rusted railroad track. He felt the familiar tug of dread. He
knew this feeling well. He had always found that waiting for
something to start was so much more draining than the exploit
itself. He longed for action. His thoughts were interrupted mo-

mentarily by a child's far-off cry of delight over some minor victory. Was it an omen for good or bad? The cry came again, and he saw the feral children race through the ruins, one of the monstrous rats hoisted high on a spear.

Anticipation had always eaten away at his confidence. He had never faced an enemy as potent as Royal Newton. Those he had gone up against in the past had oft been conscious of their crimes, or had been raised and bred to be ignorant of their crimes and simply acted according to a fault in their natures. He had once assassinated a heathen prince who delighted in cutting out the tongues of his wives. When Dee had asked him why, the man had simply said, "To shut them up, their endless prattling irritated me." Those Dee had spied upon or killed or had ordered slain in the past were capable of great evil, it was true, but in the end, their reign was always bridled by other monarchs around them. Even the greatest ruler of his age, his own Queen Bess, was conscious that if she were to act too aggressively, she would face the wrath of Spain and France and, probably, the Irish, Flemish, and Italian principalities as well. There was a balance of power that circumscribed everyone. From that political restraint came laws that protected the weak from villainous aggression. But Royal Newton had no one to naysay him. In the hierarchy of this world, he stood alone. Those who opposed him he either bought or killed, and now the world stood in awe of this man, fearing him, loathing him, mocking him, and some even respecting him. Mankind thought Newton's wealth genuinely put him above the law. No one was naive enough to admit otherwise. And now this single man, for no reason other than greed, had the power to destroy their mutual existence. Dee looked down at the dagger resting atop the cream-colored vellum etched with gold ink. Once he had questioned the morality of being a spy and assassin. Later, he had come to realize that his actions, though some might describe them as evil, could only be for the good.

Evil thrives while good men sleep. And the people of this time had slumbered deeply. Well now Dee had arrived to awaken them. He would teach the world that no man is above the law. He would remind them of the principles of the Old Testament. This future existence might condemn him, but his Elizabethan conscience would be clear. Dr. John Dee nodded and, pushing aside the dagger, appended a final line to his Will: "To thine own conscience be true."

He would have the words etched onto his tombstone.

CHAPTER

40

DYCKON AB-ACK NA KHAR sat forward in the contoured metal seat, large unblinking eyes staring fixedly at the image on the screen, hissing in annoyance as long rolling bands of interference distorted the picture.

"So now it ends," he whispered softly in a language that had become extinct long before his own race had swarmed up out of the primeval mud.

The image shifted, blurred, shifted again, and then steadied to startling brilliance for an instant—to show Dr. John Dee being shoved along the gangway of the incredibly primitive spacecraft, his arms locked behind his back in metal cuffs, an ugly squat projectile weapon pointed low near the base of his spine.

"So now it ends."

Every day, Dyckon had monitored the extraordinary Dee as he maneuvered about what was to the Humani an incredibly alien world. And each day, Dyckon had been reminded again and again of the small dark man's resilience and adaptability. Completely out of time, out of place, it would have been so easy for the Elizabethan to allow the newness, the alienness of the new world to overwhelm him. But Dee had refused to be intimidated. Like many of the other great men of his era who had gone adventuring into strange lands, Dee had simply blended his faith in his own ego and the divine rightness of his quest into an indomitability and set about to conquer this New World.

And for months Dyckon had actually believed that Dee could make a difference.

The doctor had even taught the Roc the most basic elements of diplomacy, simple subterfuges and ruses that were still remarkably effective. In his own quadrant of space, Dyckon had now been marked for advancement and there was talk in the Collegium of the possibility that the Chair of the Collegiate would one day be his—he would be the first Roc ever to hold the position and the first of his clan ever to achieve any notability.

And it was all due to one of most the remarkable lessons Dee had taught him: how to lie. You must say untruths and be ever double in both your words and meaning, Dee had instructed him. False face must hide what the true heart doth know. Dyckon had at first rankled at the deceit, but a simple bit of wisdom from the good doctor had changed his mind: Falsehood falsehood cures. To use an old Humani adage, one must fight fire with fire. There were lies and lies, the doctor had instructed him. Simple, foolish lies, immediately transparent and worth nothing. A lie should be worth something; it should also be unexpected. Dee had taught him the rules of lying: to lie about oneself, to lie about others, and to lie about circumstances.

"You play at a great advantage. No one will expect you to lie; therefore they will believe all you have to tell them. Tell them how good you are, lie to them about your achievements, tell them how bad your rivals are."

And, although he had been skeptical of the results, Dyckon had followed Dee's instructions, and the results had been some astonishing personal breakthroughs. Dyckon had come to believe that the doctor could do anything he set his remarkable mind to, including stopping an unstoppable Newton. But now, watching Dee being hauled away in chains, he was all too aware that the doctor was a Humani, nothing more, and therefore all too fragile.

The Roc recalled with sorrow the last time he had seen Dee hauled away in chains; then he had rescued him from certain death in the Medici tower. But that had been a gullible time and Dyckon had been enormously lucky. It had been a rash act of youth. But the times had changed and no one would rescue Dee from his present predicament.

"So now it ends," Dyckon ab-ack na Khar said softly, and powered off the screen. He remained seated before the black screen for a long time.

Xifo, Overlord of the Clan, waited, savoring the moment, before he pressed the tip of his tail into the slot and pressed. The scanner read the unique pattern of lines and ridges, the colored indentations and rippled scales, and acknowledged his authority by opening the blank wall before him, revealing the secure comm link. Twice before in his lifetime Xifo had used this device, and then, as now, he had been acutely conscious of the importance of his action. This comm had been used by his seed father, and his seed father before him, and two of his hatch siblings had also used it. On each occasion it had furthered the glorious Clan name.

Xifo pressed his claw to the blank plate, which immediately brightened in long slow pulses. He was aware that deep in the heart of the Collegium of Worlds, close to the Core, a sonorous bell was slowly tolling. Officers of the Law would even now be ushering the members of the Collegiate from their chambers and into the Great Hall. When everyone was assembled and the chamber had grown hushed, the ancient tapestry would slowly unroll from the high ceiling, and then his face would appear on the fabric that was older than most worlds. Then a series of tiny lights would appear in the top right-hand corner of the screen, indicating that his image was now visible to the Collegiate, the members of the Collegium who ruled the known worlds.

Or who thought they did.

Xifo knew in whose hands the power really rested. And one day he and his Clan would show the decadent Collegium just who was the real power in the galaxy. One by one, the lights blinked into existence.

"Grave news," Xifo hissed, using the time-honored speech. "A species, undeveloped and savage, has developed a threat to the order of things, and themselves, and us. Intrusion, for their own safety and security, is recommended."

"Define the source of the threat."

Xifo could not see who had put the question, though he suspected that it was one of the accursed Roc. The Roc for millennia had opposed the excesses of the Nephilim on the floor of the Collegium. They themselves were not a powerful group. But at times, their whisperings had swayed the powerful in the assembly and thwarted the Clan Nephilim.

"A fusion device which, when activated, will destroy all life on the planet. In addition, a by-product of this particular doomsday bomb will be massive amounts of antihydrogen atoms, which will shower the solar system, annihilating whatever matter comes in contact with it. There is the distinct possibility that the antimatter would ignite their sun into going supernova, resulting in lethal amounts of X-rays and possible time-space distortion."

"This device has not been tested?"

Xifo blinked, membranes flickering across wide eyes. A razor-sharp nail gouged a groove in the metal that housed the screen.

"No, it has not been tested. If it had," he added, though he knew it was a breach of protocol, "there would be no life left on the planet."

"And is this device close to completion?"

"Yes."

"So it is not as yet complete."

"No." Xifo strove to keep his face impassive, knowing it could be seen by a thousand sentient beings and only a deliberate effort of will kept his tail from rising above his head in the Aggressive Posture.

"And when will it be complete?"

It was the new Roc who was asking the questions, the one the pundits were guessing would be the next Chair.

"The creature promoting research into the development of

this doomsday device needs but one piece to complete the weapon."

"Then surely you must wait until that remaining piece is in his hands before you act. That is the Law. And the Law is clear upon this subject."

"The Law is very clear," Xifo acknowledged. "I will act when the creature is in possession of the final piece of the weapon." He terminated the contact with a casual movement that belied his rage. "Rahu," he asked, without turning around.

"Overlord?" Rahu hissed. The Posture of Obeisance had long since turned agonizing.

"Give the Humani the blueprints for the antihydrogen matrix. Give them the last piece of the puzzle."

CHAPTER

41

"WHAT SHALL WE SELL FIRST?" Kelly Edwards asked, bagged hands moving slowly across the keys, scrolling through the list of artifacts, holdings, titles, and deeds Dee had acquired in his short time in the twenty-first century.

"Make it something spectacular," d'Winter muttered, eyes fixed on the monitors. "Get their attention."

Alerted by the tone of his voice, Kelly turned stiffly to look at the big man. "What's wrong?"

"Dee hasn't disembarked from the shuttle."

"Impossible!"

A long list of names scrolled down the screen in front of Morgan d'Winter. "Look! All of these people got off. No doctor."

"Which means?" Kelly whispered.

"I don't know. Possibly he got sick on the shuttle. Maybe his heart gave out; you know that sometimes happens on the first trip into space. Maybe they rumbled him. . . ."

"Would they kill him?" she whispered.

D'Winter involuntarily shrugged. "Let us assume he has been taken prisoner. If Zhu discovered him, and who else could it be, he'll bring him to Newton before they kill him. Newton is the type who will want to gloat over his victory; and provided that the doctor didn't struggle, he should be uninjured. Perhaps an hour, maybe two. I don't know how long you have but whatever you have to do, do it now!"

Edwards turned back to her own bank of screens. "I was going to keep it until the end, but now I think we'll start with the diamond maker."

Kindersley Wiseman laid the note on his grandfather's deodar desk. "It is undoubtedly a fake," he muttered to himself as he opened the package. The great-great-great-grandson of the original Kindersley Wiseman who had founded the world-renowned diamond merchants, the House of Wiseman, on a single perfect emerald, the Teardrop, knew his precious stones and prided himself upon his ability to tell the real from the counterfeit with a single glance. The old man lifted the fist-sized diamond from the ornate wooden box and brought it up to the light, holding it between thumb and index finger. Refracted rainbows washed across his face and in that instant, with the hard icy feel of the diamond between his fingers and the bands of rainbow light upon his face, he knew the massive stone was genuine. His stomach twisted. This sudden mysterious business call would ruin him.

"And you have a device that makes diamonds like this?" he asked, turning to look at the blank screen. His technicians had tried to and were still trying to unscramble the picture, though Wiseman knew that anyone with the technology to develop a diamond maker would easily be able to conceal their identity if they so chose. He turned away from the screen and looked out across the veldt toward Table Mountain. The mud-cracked plain burned in the sun. A striped kudu leapt out of the tall grass and then settled down under a baobab tree to shade herself and leisurely flick her tail. She nibbled at her hind hoof.

"I have a device that will take any lump of coal and turn it into a perfect diamond. I have sent, by express courier to your Angel City office, a bag of coal that I have converted into diamonds. Please keep the diamonds as proof of my integrity and of their value to me. I am offering this device for sale. I will contact you shortly." The blank screen flickered and the spinning Wiseman Diamond logo reappeared. Though he knew it was a waste of time, the old man vidded down to his chief appraiser.

"Roberto, I have a rather large stone that I would like you to check the quality on. This is priority one. Come up and get it yourself, then report back only to me."

"Yes, Mr. Wiseman."

Seconds later, Flintoff, who ran the American office, appeared on the screen. The Englishman's normally placid expression had been replaced by one that was neither horror nor amazement, but something of both.

"I know, I know," Wiseman said softly before Flintoff had a chance to speak. "A bag of diamonds has just been delivered to you. Are they real?"

"There are so many we cannot count them all," Flintoff said quickly. "They arrived in a coal bag—hundreds, no thousands of diamonds of all shapes and sizes. We've examined about sixty, and they are all perfect. The bag is worth a fortune." He held up a scrap of paper. "It came with a note which said that you were expecting this."

"I was."

"Mr. Wiseman, what is this all about? Who would . . . ?"

Wiseman nodded, terminating the connection, and turned away from the screen. Standing up, he walked toward the glass wall, which obediently opened to allow the mild South African air into the antique office. Though she was too far away to have heard anything, instinct sent the kudu darting into the distance.

"A device that could turn coal into diamonds," he whispered.

His own father had begun the world diamond shortage about fifty years ago, acquiring—by fair means or foul—whatever stones came on the market and refusing to release them. In his own lifetime, Wiseman, Sr., had seen the price of the stones double, then double again, and Kindersley had carried on the tradition, driving the price of diamonds to astronomical heights. The artificial shortage the Wisemans had created had been exacerbated by a very real shortage of the stones. In the last twenty years, the number of diamonds that had been dug from the ground could be counted in the hundreds, and the number of fine diamonds was fewer than fifty. The gold standard had been replaced by the platinum standard, then the titanium standard, and finally the diamond standard. And now someone had given—given!—him a bag of pure diamonds.

A device like this would destroy the world's diamond market. A market which he controlled and manipulated.

Overnight, his fortune, built over generations, would be wiped out as the price of diamonds tumbled and they became as cheap as glass. The economies of many nations would be devastated; banks would close, the fortunes rendered as naught. This diamond maker must never be allowed to go on the open market. He would pay just about anything to secure it. Or destroy it in the process.

"Did you have to send him the whole bag?" d'Winter asked. "It must have been worth millions."

"Billions probably. But there's plenty more where that came from," Kelly said. "Besides, we had to make an impression on him."

"Oh, I think you've done that. But why are you targeting Wiseman?"

"Because he controls, through a subsidiary company, the SA Airlines and Spaceport. Much of Newton's airfleet and transportation, especially the big supertransports, is housed here, and South Africa is a major refueling depot. If we control the airport, we control the movement of all of Newton's goods. If we refuse to allow his transports to refuel, we cripple his movements even further."

"What do we do now?"

"While we're waiting for Wiseman to decide how much he

wants to pay for the diamond maker, we offer it to someone else. A bit of an auction is a wonderful way of driving up the price." Kelly grinned.

"Anyone in mind?"

"I was thinking perhaps of Mr. Newton himself. Do we have a particularly large piece of coal handy?"

CHAPTER

42

Patience, John Dee had long since learned, was a virtue which these modern people did not possess in spite their extended life spans. They lived their lives in a hurry and thus would they die. Dee grunted as the one called Zhu cracked a hand across his face, the heavy gold ring on his index finger catching the doctor's cheekbone, biting deeply and drawing blood. This one he would kill later, after he had disposed of the guards who had pummeled and thrashed him for no reason other than sport. This he swore to himself and to his Savior in Heaven. The lackeys knew no better, having been bred in the gutter, but their lieutenant, the wall-faced Oriental, watched the beating with a cold detachment, and when he participated, did so with a cold, calculating viciousness that suggested that the man took no pleasure from it, but rather did it because he thought it was expected of him. Patience, the doctor reminded himself, patience. Everything comes to he who waits.

Breathing deeply, Dee discovered that at least two ribs were cracked, certainly two of the fingers on his left hand were broken, and his teeth felt loose in his head. If he survived this ordeal, these injuries could be cured and repaired easily, he remembered; and if he failed, well, then it would not matter anymore, because they would all be dead. Either way he would have his revenge. He smiled at the irony.

Pain can be controlled. He had still been an apprentice when he had taken his first lessons in mastering that particular emotion. Those who studied the arts as he had knew that before they could master the exterior world, they must first take control of the world within. The pain of fasting and thirst was first overcome, then the purification of hot and cold; the ability to stand in a freezing cell or remain naked before a blazing fire was oft necessary to insure the success of a particular spell or cantrip. Physical pain was often mastered by simply divorcing the mind from the body. Dee had early observed that if a prisoner watched a whipping, the pain of his own beating was doubled; if a harlot smelled the stench of the gaoler's brand upon the bosom of others, then her own branding was an excruciating agony.

So, while Zhu and his guards had beaten him, Dr. John Dee had dwelt upon the wonders of his own remarkable life and divorced himself from the pain, using techniques that had been ancient in the Land of Aegypt before the pyramids had risen out of the desert.

"I think you must enjoy pain, Doctor," James Zhu said evenly, wiping blood from his knuckles and the bezel of his ring with a paper tissue.

The doctor breathed evenly, taking care not to stretch his injured ribs. His smile was bloody. "In my life ere this I have been beaten by louts aplenty. This cudgeling is not a novel experience. I have borne much and learnt a little from my beatings."

"What have you learned?"

"Every cudgeling seems monstrous until another cudgeling comes in to outmatch it. Pain is a thing forgotten."

For a moment it looked as if Zhu was about to strike him again, but then the big Oriental relaxed.

"Believe me," he said in his clipped British accent. "I do not do this out of malice, but rather necessity. You cost me some good men and embarrassed me before Mr. Newton."

"I quite understand," Dee said formally. "One has certain standards one must maintain. But, begging your indulgence, sirrah, I would suggest that if your men were as merited as you had hoped, they might still live today."

"An excellent point," Zhu agreed. "But it is so difficult to get good staff these days."

"Aye, but it was ever thus. Though," Dee added, "Fortune has smiled on me of late and I acquired some estimable people to assist me. I have always been a good judge of character. You, certes, are a better man than your master."

"All servants believe that they are better than their masters." Zhu reached forward, catching Dee by the lapels of his overall and pulling him to his feet.

"I counsel you to let me live and leave me my wits that your master may mock me and lord his will over me, like Pilate did to our Lord ere he washed his hands of him."

Zhu searched Dee's face, unsure of his next move. Then, with the edge of his tissue, he wiped blood from the corner of Dee's mouth and top lip.

"Going up against Mr. Newton was not a wise move," Zhu observed quietly.

The doctor looked deep into the Mongolian's eyes. "If the truth be known, I had no choice."

Zhu waved the guards away and moved around to stand behind the doctor, his hands on his shoulders. Dee instinctively flinched at the expected attack. Instead, Zhu massaged the tender areas of Dee's bruised back and then removed a vial from a pocket in his jacket and handed it to the doctor.

"Drink. It will lessen the pain. I don't want to have to carry you."

Dee did as he was told. He felt his blood surge to his ribs and his face and his fingers. There was a heat and a glow. It was as if he had a small sun radiating, healing within him. Dee straightened himself to his full height, testing the health of his no longer painful limbs and muscles. There was certainly a sensitive tenderness in his muscles and ribs and there was a numbed pain in his fingers and joints, yet all miraculously seemed well. Zhu pushed the small man forward resolutely toward doors that opened automatically.

"There are always choices," Zhu said, easing Dee out into the gently lighted corridor. A deep-throated hum seemed to vibrate the floor.

Despite the beatings he had taken, Dee's body felt lighter. "There be choices we make ourselves; some are thrust upon us. Deciding to kill Newton was perforce of the latter kind."

The corridor was filled with people; most in uniforms which indicated their rank and profession, all with pasty, unhealthy expressions. A few glanced cautiously at the big Asian, recognizing the man closest to Newton, watching him push the small manacled man forward. But when Dee met their faces, their eyes flickered away and they refused to hold his gaze.

"I suppose if I were to ask you why, you would not give me an answer?" Zhu wondered.

"Why not?" Dee said. "I care not, it is no secret. Your master is developing a device which, when activated, will utterly destroy our world. I seek to prevent him from doing so. There is no personal profit for me in killing him—why, I don't even know the man!"

Zhu nodded, disbelieving. "So that is why you targeted some of the Newton plants on Earth."

"Yes, I essayed to stop him from completing his doomsday device."

"I don't know who you are or how you accumulated so many resources so quickly and so clandestinely, or how you came to unearth Mr. Newton's most secret project, but I do know you're utterly mad. Mr. Newton is doing energy research. He wants to create unlimited energy—which, of course, he will control."

"The unlimited energy will consume this earth. No one on Earth can control it. He is being abused by outside forces. Of necessity, you must warn him."

Zhu stopped before a blank wall and pressed his hand against it. Almost immediately the wall split open and the security officer herded the doctor into an elevator. Zhu pressed his thumb against a smooth metal plate and although there was no outward sign of movement, Dee could feel the lift ascending, the movement evident in his still recovering limbs.

"Why should I believe you?" Zhu posed.

"If you do not believe me, in a few short hours you will know the truth of what I am saying."

"You don't seem particularly worried now?"

The lift stopped. Dee winced as his bruises protested. "Why should I worry? I am but the shadow of a man. I have done my best. My only concern should be that if I fail to convince your master, you grant me the boon of a clean and painless death."

Zhu placed his left hand on Dee's shoulder and pushed him forward. "I believe I can promise you that."

"Good. I credit you for a man of your word. For what value does a man have without his word?"

"Nothing."

"I wonder if Mr. Newton is a man of his word," Dee said, as the lift doors opened and he stepped out into Newton's opulent apartments.

Royal Newton strode forward, hand outstretched. "Dr. Dee, I presume."

CHAPTER

43

"Even were I not manacled, I should not shake your hand."

Royal Newton had been practicing the speech he was going to make to Dee before he would order Zhu to throw him out of an airlock. He had stood before the holomirror and watched himself mouth the words, derisive and triumphant, and he had imagined that the small man with the very good hair would plead and beg for his life. Newton thought that perhaps he would tease him a little, dangle a vague thread of hope, only to dash it again. But whatever he had been expecting, he was completely unprepared for Dr. John Dee's élan.

Royal Newton stopped as if struck, looked from the disheveled and bloodied captive to the immaculate Zhu who was struggling to keep his face impassive.

"You are extraordinarily arrogant for one in your position," Zhu snapped.

"Arrogance—aye, and pride—have always been my failings," Dee admitted, turning his head to look around the room. The entrance to Newton's private apartments was an almost perfect circle, with no obvious doors or windows. The walls were hung with paintings and tapestries, spinning holographic images and small stands holding a variety of artifacts. Arranged around the walls, lighted cabinets and ornate stands held an eclectic collection of objects, obviously from Newton's private museum. Purposefully, Dee stepped past a startled Newton to look at an arrangement of porcelain in the artfully arranged display cases. As he bent over one, tiny droplets of blood dripped from his nose onto the glass and he stepped back quickly, mindful not to stain the fragile delft.

"Magnificent," he praised.

He glanced over his shoulder at Newton and Zhu and continued on. "Quite magnificent. I am reminded of Marco Polo's description of the great porcelain works in Tinju. He told how the clay was dug from the ground and then piled in huge artificial mountains for some thirty or forty years, exposed to the elements, so that the clay could mature and transmogrify into that particular base from which porcelain was crafted."

Newton, fully aware that he had become a spectator in his own lair, finally managed to say, "Are you really a doctor? Are you an educated man?"

"More so than you would realize," Dee said, moving along the next cabinet, stopping before a particularly hideous example of the silversmith's art. "My title is not a medical one, though I have a smattering of that particular art too. But I must confess to lecturing in most of Europe's great universities and royal courts." He leaned his head close toward an enormous silver plate on display. "Mr. Newton, this is grotesque. This pretty nothing is as loathsome as a jeweled toad."

"My great-grandfather designed it."

"A man of flamboyant tastes, obviously," Dee said dryly.

Newton stared at Dee and looked at the plate. "You are quite right, I have always disliked it," he admitted, "but, unfortunately, Mother was particularly fond of it." He glanced over his shoulder at Zhu. "Release the manacles, but watch him!"

Zhu lifted Dee's arms and pressed his ring finger against the lock. The flat surface of his ring slid into the manacles and they clicked open.

Dee rubbed his chafed wrists. "I would beg a kerchief."

Zhu pulled a canary yellow silk handkerchief from his breast pocket, snapped it open, and handed it to Dee, who used it to dab at his bloody nose and split lips and then carefully wound it around his two broken fingers, binding them tightly together. "You will understand if I do not return it to you."

Zhu nodded and stepped back.

"You are an intriguing man, Dr. Dee," Royal Newton continued. "In fact, you are a total mystery. And more than likely, a sham. You say you have lectured in the universities of Europe, and yet there is not a scrap of evidence anywhere that vindicates your claim. In fact there is no record of anyone even vaguely matching your description anywhere. Which of course is an impossibility. You are an impossibility! Which leads me to the inevitable conclusion that you are a man with a past. A past you would like to forget. A past so notorious that you have broken all the rules of our society and changed your identity and erased all memory of it."

Dee grinned through bloodstained teeth. " 'Struth, my past is notorious. But you are in error. I am quite proud of it!" He stopped to look at another display. It contained a magnificent ruby resting on a tastefully tousled pillow of black satin. A single spotlight shone on the stone, and the tiny cabinet was ablaze with the resultant points of crimson light. Dee was riveted by its majesty.

Newton looked over his shoulder. "It once adorned the crown of the Queen of England."

"Indeed." Dee looked at the stone again, not recognizing it.

"No doubt you know that I bought the English Crown Jewels some years ago."

"No, I had not heard," Dee said truthfully, "though before your purchase, I oft handled the crown of the first Elizabeth of England. An ugly barbaric piece it was and unconscionably heavy too. I understand she complained of the neck pain and therefore avoided wearing it whenever possible."

"I brought you here to kill you, Dr. Dee," Newton said suddenly.

Dee shrugged. "And I came here to kill you. So, if truth be told, we are evenly matched."

Newton shoved his hands into his pockets. "Doctor, what have I ever done to you? To the best of my knowledge we have never met, though I am beginning to suspect that perhaps I might have crossed you in some deal or other, most assuredly when you bore another name. You do remind me of someone I knew when I was younger. Care to share?"

"No," Dee said simply. "We have never met previously." He added, "No, I came here to kill you because all my other efforts to stop your developing your accursed Tiamat project have failed. It is a perilous horror you follow. And I came here personally to kill you because you struck at those I care for. Your agents left me a bloody message; I thought I should reply in kind."

"You killed some of my men," Newton said reasonably. "Business is business."

"Butchering a boy in cold blood is not business." For a brief moment, there was a look of resolute venom in Dee's eye that made Newton flinch. He reconsidered having Zhu replace the manacles. But the little man moved on to another cabinet and then stopped in a state of awe. "One of da Vinci's notebooks!"

Newton, pleased that this trophy had impressed, risked coming close to the small man and peering over his captive's shoulder. "There is some doubt as to its authenticity," he said with mock humility.

"I have seen this book before." A statement that deflated some of Newton's pride of possession. "If there be a blot of ink on the last page, shaped like a man with a Roman nose, then it is the true genuine article."

Newton opened a drawer beneath the cabinet and pulled out a pair of white linen gloves. Moving slowly and with great delicacy he turned the thick yellowed pages of the ancient book. On the final page, which bore only two lines of da Vinci's reversed spider's scrawl, there was a smudge of ink turned purple and pale with age. It resembled a face in profile, the nose a hooked beak.

"So, this is the real thing!" Newton said proudly.

"I was once proffered a fake by a knavish Spaniard. It had the blot, but not the nose."

"I trust you dealt appropriately with the man."

"I had a colleague slit the rogue's nose," Dee said absently. He stopped suddenly, looking down at a thick vellum-bound book reposing on what Dee took for a music stand. There was something eerily familiar about the book. The title and crest on the stained white cover was lost beneath a layer of grime and curious fingerprints. "What is this?"

"Ah, but this will intrigue you. It is an original manuscript by your namesake, an Elizabethan magician and astrologer, Dr. John Dee."

"A mathematician and astronomer surely," Dee said softly. "Allow me a glance."

A peculiar feeling had washed over him, settling into the base of his stomach, souring his throat. He inadvertently sucked in air and what blood still ran in his nose. The object was out of place and time and its incongruity unnerved him. In all the time he had been in this future era, he had made no efforts to reclaim anything of his past, unwilling to know how the world thought he died or what his legacy was. But now, to be reunited with this object so familiar and in this place; surely he sensed the hand of Divine Providence in it. His own researches had taught him that accidents simply did not happen; the Lord swayed the currents of the Universe, it was simply beyond the ken of mere mortals. He knew the book; it was his notes for a manuscript he had once intended calling the *Mysteriorum liber primus*.

"I acquired it only recently. I gave a rather large bequest to the Oxford Library in England and, in return, I borrowed one or two of their more valuable pieces—purely for research purposes, of course. Your name being associated with it intrigued me as well." Newton laughed, the sound high and shrill. "I gave them some forty million and yet the books I took would have cost me much, much more. This one alone is valued at some twenty million."

Dee bent over the thick cover to open it, when Zhu, quick as a python, caught the doctor's hand. "Dr. Dee, or whatever your name is, we do not soil Mr. Newton's treasures by touching them."

"Here, you may borrow mine."

Newton handed Dee the gloves he was wearing. They were

273

slightly oversized and a wondrous white. Dee slipped them on and carefully opened the ancient vellum tome, cracking it softly. His own script leapt up to greet him and a sense of terrible longing washed over him. Here was proof indeed that his world was dead and done—an alien in an alien land, as much a stranger in this world as Dyckon would have been. He slowly turned the pages, remembering with a terrible clarity when and where he had written these words. With the smell of his world, sour and earthy, rich and redolent, in his nostrils, with the colors of his time bright and vivid in his eyes, and the sounds of birds and animals and blessed silence in his ears, he reread his thoughts. They were naive thoughts of a time now lost. Gone now, all gone, and replaced by this foul and bitter place which soon would also be lost. And not for the first time, Dee wondered if it might not be for the better.

"Very nice," he said softly. "This is, of course, a forgery."

"A forgery! No, no," Newton snapped. "Impossible!"

"I have seen this book before; indeed I have a very good idea who really wrote it." Dee traced a line of the text with his gloved finger. "Why, sirrah, just look at this script; look at the shape of the letters. Dee was one of the learned men of Elizabeth's court; his handwriting would have been elegant and cursive. Anyone could have copied this. Here, I will demonstrate. Why, give me a quill and parchment—that is a pen and page."

Zhu stepped forward and handed Dee his message pad, a gossamer-thin sheet of liquid crystal, and a stylus. Dee swiftly copied a line of text from the ancient book. "Now compare this to the original."

Newton placed the sheet down on top of the book, matching the writing.

"There are similarities," he admitted.

"More than similarities, I'll wager," Dee said, peering over Newton's shoulder. However, he was surprised to find that the two lines of text did not match exactly. This cursed world was ruining his once fine hand. Perhaps it was the gloves, he thought.

"However, I will take your word for it; I will have the book looked at again. And if I find I have been duped, I will burn the library to the ground. You are a truly remarkable man, Doctor. It will be a shame to kill you. Tell me why my Tiamat project offends you. Were you developing something similar? Now that we have met, I can see that there might be possibilities of joining our forces, perhaps forming a strategic alliance. It strikes me that we are much alike."

"We are nothing alike," Dee snapped. "You have no humanity." Clasping his hands behind his back he strode across the room. As he approached what looked like a blank wall, it shimmered, the matte cream color running like liquid to reveal the icily beautiful lunar landscape beyond. Low on the horizon, the Earth, blue and white and brilliant, was just beginning to rise. Dee stared at it, frozen in its grandeur.

"Your Tiamat project, when activated, will destroy the Earth."

"Nonsense. It will protect the Earth!"

Dee glanced over his shoulder in a rage. "Damn you, man. What reason have I to lie? Think! Where are you getting your information from? Shall I tell you?" He turned back to the panorama outside the window. "Out there, somewhere, a malevolent race watches this planet with eyes of lust. Our goodly haven, the Earth, despite its somewhat maimed state, still has much to offer them. They will strip the resources from the land, empty the oceans of their bounty, and use the human race as slaves and food. But for now, these monsters are held at bay from invasion by a series of checks and balances from above, for they too have their masters. However, if they can prove to their betters that the Earth is nigh unto destroying itself through the stupidity and the culpability of its own inhabitants, they shall"—Dee overaccentuated and repeated—"they *shall* be awarded the authority to come in amongst us and have dominion over us. They shall be our masters and we their lackeys. This world will be plunged downward into the darkest of Dark Ages. It will be Golgotha!"

Dee folded his arms across his heaving chest, fingers of his right hand touching the crucifix he still wore around his neck. He fought to control his anger and frustration.

Zhu moved closer to his master. "Mr. Newton, this man is just a paranoid religious fanatic. Shall I remove him?"

But before the bald man could answer, Dee pressed on. "Now, what would be serious enough to allow these creatures to invade our world? Only the threat of mass destruction. Mankind has, I am told, come perilous close on several occasions. But you, Mr. Newton, you are developing a device that, when activated, will burn off all of God's air on our planet in a matter of hours, then it will suck the energy from deep within the Earth's center in some sort of continuous apocalyptic reaction. Within the time of a single day our world will be a thing of naught, lifeless as this, the moon." He gestured toward the lunar landscape. "The remnants of humanity who survive the cataclysm will curse your name for all Eternity."

Newton smiled and shook his head, looking over to Zhu, who remained on alert. "I have never heard such arrant nonsense. Perhaps I was a little too hasty in my judgment. You may not be a fool, Dr. Dee, for a fool could not have gotten as far as you have, but I believe you have stumbled on some sensitive extraterrestrial information that has driven you insane. James, we thought we were in pursuit of a genius, it seems we were hunting a mad dog."

"You would not be the first to say so—though all who uttered those words now are long dead and gone. Yet I survive. Why do you not believe? I swear by all that is holy, I speak true!" Dee saw the mocking sniggery in their eyes. His instincts reined in his passion and he switched to Elizabethan diplomacy. "Tell me, Mr. Newton, where do you get your information from; where do your mysterious breakthroughs come from? You have confounded your own scientists with the mathematics you have supplied them with."

Dee wandered away from the window, moving toward a display of ancient weaponry alongside a full suit of armor. Some of the weapons were unfamiliar, but he recognized blade and shield, dirk and crossbow. Timing was of the essence; if he spoke for too much longer Newton would become irritated, and if he hurried, he would not be able to lull them into a sense of foolish superiority.

"I'll wager your information arrives hugger-mugger. In another age it would have come sealed in anonymous notes, but let me guess that your Tiamat begets itself on faceless blank screens. And let me further guess that you have failed to find the senders."

"Perhaps you are the sender," Newton said icily.

Dee shrugged. "The technology is beyond me. Beyond any human, even your own remarkable scientists. Is it not so?"

"It is advanced," Newton admitted.

A high-pitched chirrup startled the three men into shocked silence. As one they turned to the section of white wall that had flowed and altered into a huge screen. On the screen the single word TIAMAT pulsed in bloodred letters. The letters dissolved, and then Newton's own face appeared, smiling blandly. No one thought to usher Dee out of the room.

"Royal, we are disappointed in you." The voice was Newton's, the petulant tone and cadence a perfect match. "We have given you everything, brought you every step of the way to help you realize a dream, the dream of unlimited power, and, by extension, world domination. You know how important this technology is. You know it is crucial for the protection of the Earth. And yet we find that you have allowed yourself to be distracted by petty annoyances, you have claimed that you are under attack from an unknown source, you have claimed that your people were having difficulty completing the project, that they could not come up with a way of igniting the process. And we thought you employed only the best.

"No doubt if they were left to their own devices, they would discover it in a year or two or ten. But the world does not have that long. Even now there are alien forces beginning to gather at the edge of the solar system. We need Tiamat on-line immediately. The world needs Tiamat."

The image of Newton's face dissolved and a series of digits began to scroll down the screen at high speed. "The data is now being downloaded onto your machine, Royal Newton. The final piece of the puzzle is now yours. Take it. Complete Tiamat. The future of the Earth is in your hands."

The screen faded to black and Royal Newton turned to Dee in

triumph—and the doctor's thrown dagger caught him squarely in the heart.

Newton was still falling as the doctor ripped a massive two-handed sword from the wall. Expertly gripping the S-shaped jeweled hilt, he swung around to catch Zhu on the side of the head with the broad flat side of the steel blade, driving him to the ground. Blood streamed from the running wound. But it didn't dissuade Dee from landing two kicks to Zhu's rib cage for old times' sake.

White-hot fire seared across the swordsman's left shoulder and he spun in surprise, instinct throwing him to one side. He crashed into the weapons display, bringing the lot tumbling down atop him. Snatching up a small sixteenth-century light crossbow and a handful of small bolts, he half rose to his knees behind the display that held the da Vinci in order to load his weapon. He inserted both feet into the leather stirrup at the front of the bow to draw back and secure the string when another searing blast of heat struck the ground to his left, alchemizing an Italian poignard on the floor to a pool of metal.

Dr. John Dee launched himself toward the door, which obediently opened, just as Royal Newton, the dagger still embedded in his chest, fired again, igniting the da Vinci notebook and setting off the fire alarm, which immediately flooded the room with emerald green gas.

But by the time the gas cleared, Dr. John Dee was long gone.

CHAPTER

44

"THE MOONBASE HAS GONE ON HIGH ALERT," d'Winter said suddenly.

"What's happened?"

"The fire alarm has been tripped in Newton's private apartments and a medical team called." The mercenary was monitoring the news feed coming in on CNN and Reuters. The incoming reports were minor in themselves but, taken together, could only mean one thing.

Kelly Edwards smiled tightly, trying not to crack the new skin on her face.

"Then Dee was there!"

"Looks like it." D'Winter shifted his interest to the travel boards. "All traffic in and out of the moon has been canceled. Space debris is the excuse they are giving."

"What does that mean?"

"I don't know yet. We know Dee was taken off the shuttle, though there's no record of him on the prison manifests. I can only guess he was taken to Newton's private apartments and then, well, who knows, I guess he lit a fire under them."

"Is Newton still alive?"

"If he weren't, they wouldn't have sent in the medicos. So it looks like the doctor's assassination attempt failed. But it would also look like Dee's still free or they wouldn't have closed off the traffic." Morgan turned from the bank of glowing screens scrolling information. "How are you getting on?"

"I've traded the diamond maker and a lot of diamonds for a total of forty-eight percent of Minuteman Holdings. Wiseman couldn't close the deal fast enough. At present we own pieces of nearly one hundred different but highly significant companies. Right now we can control the movement of his aircraft, we control two of his major ports, and that limits access to his major ore-processing plant. Even as we speak, the shares are being processed through the system." She glanced up at the digital clock. "However, we need to have a controlling interest in the company by the time the Stock Exchange comes on-line. I think it's time to go back to Tomoyuki Tsuru and see how he's getting on with the translator. Maybe now he'll want to buy the holocomm that goes with it."

"Be careful of that snake."

"Oh I will. But we need his shares. He owns, through a series of subsidiaries, nearly twelve percent of Minuteman Holdings. If I can get that, I'll control sixty percent of the company."

"How long do you think you can keep this up until Newton becomes aware of it?"

"Until the Stock Exchange opens." She looked at the clock again. "About an hour."

"And if you fail?"

Edwards shrugged, then winced as her wounds protested. "It would be a matter of simplicity to backtrack the purchases. I haven't had time to hide us too deeply. I really didn't think it mattered."

"You're right. It doesn't. Is there anything I can do to help?"

"Nothing." Kelly smiled. "Just tell me that Dee is all right?"

"I can't tell you that."

Kelly Edwards nodded and her mangled hands began to move across the keyboard. "So he has an hour to destroy Newton. After that, it doesn't really matter much at all."

* * *

"I am sure you are pleased now that you allowed me to remove your heart," Dr. Snyder said unctuously, cleaning the inch-long gash in Newton's bronzed and hairless chest. "I always said that the heart was such an inefficient tool," added the middle-aged man with the plastic looks of a male model.

"Is there any damage done?"

"None at all. The chrome shell and valves weren't even scratched." Snyder lifted the needle-tipped blade Dee had flung at Newton and held it to the light. The tip was blunted and bent. "If we had left your heart where it was, it would have been ripped in two." Bending over Newton, the doctor carefully wove together the strands of the mesh cage that encased Newton's chest just beneath the surface of the skin. "The wiremail absorbed most of the blow. And you felt no pain?"

"A twinge, nothing more."

"Well, all the discomfort was obviously worth it." Dr. Snyder looked up as Zhu, head and rib cage swathed in a bandage, appeared in the doorway. "And how is your head?"

"Pounding."

"I am surprised that the assassin didn't kill you when he had the chance," the doctor remarked.

"He wasn't after me."

"Well, your boss has had a very lucky escape."

"Lucky," Newton snorted. "I spent six months in a hospital while you removed my heart and replaced it with a metal pump, and substituted self-healing lungs in place of my own pair. I spent nearly a year of agony while you buried this wiremail beneath my skin. So I don't call it luck. I call it planning." Newton pushed the doctor away and sat up, exposed strands of wiremail in his chest pinging and snapping. "So I take it you haven't got him?"

"Not yet," Zhu said. "I've pulled in extra officers, and we're conducting a corridor-by-corridor search. I've canceled all incoming and outgoing flights." He glanced at his watch. "It is only a matter of time. I should have him within the hour."

"Good." Newton leaned over and opened a line into the laboratory buried deep in the dead heart of the moon. "Update."

"The new calculations are phenomenal."

"I know that!" Newton snapped. "Tell me when Tiamat can go live."

"We are downloading the launch sequence to the Gobi site now. I've talked to Engineering and Mechanical, we hope to be able to test within the hour."

"So foolish, so predictable." Xifo, the Overlord of the Clan, watched the primitive data streams leave the moon and head toward the planet. Even now his translators would be working on them, pinpointing the exact stream that was the launch sequence for what the Humani, Newton, called the Tiamat project. Once he had the evidence in his claws, the Overlord could contact the Collegium and receive permission to invade. It had been a long wait, but it was going to be worth it.

The Earth was about to fall.

The Xifo's claws closed into a tight fist. A heartbeat later, thin green ichor seeped through his clenched fingers, where his talons had bitten deep into the flesh of his palm. But the Xifo didn't even feel the pain.

CHAPTER

45

FIVE HUNDRED AND MORE YEARS AGO, Dee recalled, he had been in a similar situation. History, as he had often observed, had a curious habit of repeating itself in the most bizarre way.

The small man ducked into a corridor to catch his breath and examine his wounds. His left shoulder was scorched as if a red-hot poker had been laid across it, and his earlier cuts and bruises now ached abominably. He carefully unwrapped Zhu's kerchief from around his hand. His broken fingers were a plum purple and beginning to swell and he knew it would not be long before he would be unable to hold a crossbow or swing a sword.

The last time he had been in a comparable situation, he had been trapped in a castle in the wilds of Scotland while a score of cannibal clansmen had rampaged around the filthy corridors, hunting for him, lured on by the promise of his Sassenach flesh and the hundred gold pieces that had been offered by the Black Laird for his head. Just his head. A bitter winter had locked the landscape in an icy and deadly grip, making travel impossible; however, he had managed to survive for ten days, living on his wits and rats. And at the end of the ten days, none of the clansmen still lived, and the Black Laird's head was impaled on a pike above the gates.

The doctor smiled at the similarities. In a fashion, this castle on the moon was also winter-locked—certainly travel without the walls into the freezing cold was impossible. And whereas before he had to survive for ten days until the weather broke, now he had less than an hour before Newton activated or attempted to activate the Tiamat device and the Earth fell to the demons. Then as now, he knew he hadn't the luxury of hope of an unlooked-for rescue. Then, as now, his death seemed as unavoidable as the sunrise or his next breath. The rational part of himself counseled him again and again to attend to his hurts, relax, and accept the inevitable. The various burns and bruises and fractures were beginning to deafen his thoughts to anything else. He had done all he could; it was time to think about prayer, his Eternal soul, and making peace with his Maker. The Latin homilies rose unbidden to his lips. But even as his mouth prayed for Salvation, his pride, the worst of the seven deadly sins, tempted him with the scenarios of his triumphs over his enemies.

Five hundred and more years ago, he had carried the fight to the Black Laird, the Chief of the Clan, taking him unawares, for they never realized that he would be foolish enough to return to the heart of the castle. The doctor smiled wryly as he maneuvered the crossbow back onto his shoulder. Yes, history did have a curious habit of repeating itself. Of course, that meant he was damned to Hell anyway. The pain still throbbed, but he had a mission and he was sworn to serve. He did not know what his Elizabethan reputation was, but he would not let his modern one be tarnished by the shame of not fighting to the bitter end. "Once more, once more," he coaxed himself, "onward, ever onward." His resolve, like his body, rose up slowly. There was work to do.

Dee stepped out of the corridor—directly into the path of two of Zhu's gray-suited guards. The two men stopped and stared at the small bloody man whom they had recently beaten and then went for their holstered weapons. Neither managed to draw his flechette gun before the sword claimed their heads with two quick flickering arm and wrist movements. Without a backward glance the doctor stepped over their twitching bodies, delighted that his ancient skills were still intact. But then, so was the pain in his hand.

Despite her care, Kelly Edwards's hands were bleeding, the bags encasing them beginning to fill with blood and fluid, as she pounded ever more furiously on the keys. Newton's web of companies was intricate and obscure, but Kelly was working by one of the oldest business principles in the world: follow the money. It was the golden thread that held all of the Minuteman's business empire together. A tiny publishing business in Chicago was owned by a Minuteman shareholder; Kelly traded a world-famous author's contract in return for a twelve-month lien on his two Minuteman shares. She then bought the contract from another publishing house in return for a variant of the same translation technology they had sold the Japanese. A bakery owner in Pittsburgh had been left a single Minuteman share in her grandmother's will. Kelly traded the use of the share for a twelve-month period in return for unlimited access to Pittsburgh International Airport, where she had just bought the Loaders Union two shares in return for the rights to import Guinness direct from the brewery in Ireland, one of the most sought-after contracts in the shipping world. The Free Hong Kong Bank was "rented" from its Yakuza masters for a three-hour period in return for a suitcase full of uncut diamonds and the guarantee that nothing would be taken. The Yakuza understood that the bank, with its outré and outrageous retroarchitecture, was being used for a movie set, since it had previously been featured in a score of feature films. When they returned to the bank, however, they discovered that every safe-deposit box in the strong room had been opened. Closer inspection revealed that nothing—as far as they could see—had been disturbed. Jewelry, bundles of currency of various denominations, incriminating photographs, documents, passports, all seemed untouched. No one knew that two Minuteman share certificates were missing.

Working behind her, eyes squinted closed as a pounding headache tightened across his skull, d'Winter worked his own hostile takeover of Newton's shares, using his own aggressive methods.

A Colombian drug dealer awoke to find himself dangling upside down over a vat of acid in his processing plant. He refused to give up the combination of the safe until he was actually lowered into the bubbling green slime and his thick black hair curled and twisted on his head.

The man known as the Tsar, who controlled the New Russian Mafia, was snatched while boating on the Volga. He later told a tale of being keelhauled along behind a boat, immersed to his neck in the icy water, until he revealed the location and combination of his personal strongbox. But when, with blue and swollen fingers, he investigated the strongbox, he found, amid the gemstones, hard currency, brick cocaine, and two Fabergé eggs, that the only thing missing was a single share certificate.

Madame Shern, the French assassin known as the Black Widow, surrendered her share certificate when she received a photograph of Cheesy, her poodle, peering out from a microwave.

Tomoyuki Tsuru climbed out of the deep sunken bath—an almost unimaginable luxury in Hong Kong—and was reaching for a towel when he got the distinct feeling he was not alone. He quickly fastened the soft plush white towel around his torso. The air directly in front of him began to shimmer and twist.

"Good evening, Tomoyuki Tsuru." The spoken Japanese was perfect, the voice female, with the slight flattened twang of the city dweller.

A face materialized out of the shimmering air, a vaguely familiar face, though at first Tsuru thought he was looking at a mask, before he realized that the woman had been burned. Behind her he could see the shaven head of a huge black man—and he recognized him first. The doctor's sidekicks: d'Winter and—what was the woman's name?

"Kelly Edwards. You may remember me, Mr. Tsuru, though I looked somewhat different the last time we spoke," she added wryly.

Tsuru reached forward, pressing his hand through the image to lift his silk robe off the wall, and pulled it on. He noted that the image didn't move or waver. The technology was incredible.

"I remember you, and the good doctor."

"You have found the translation device to be all we said it was?" Kelly continued.

Tsuru walked through the image into the indoor rock garden he rarely looked at.

"It is everything you said it would be," he agreed.

"I note you are bundling it with the new version of Windows."

"We have developed some software which will facilitate text to speech and the simultaneous translation of transmitted documents."

"The implications are staggering," Kelly said softly.

"They are."

"Think how much more staggering they could be if you controlled the device I'm using to talk to you with."

"What is it?"

"Another of Dr. Dee's inventions," Kelly lied. "A holographic projector, it transmits a three-dimensional image to anywhere in the world, using satellite positioning to fix its location to within a few millimeters. The image is then beamed to that spot and reconstituted by reflecting it off any nearby metal object. The carrier beam is encoded with full-motion video and digital audio." Kelly paused and added quietly, "Data is transmitted back along the carrier beam, too, so that only one device is needed for communication."

"So you can see me now!"

Kelly Edwards smiled again. "Yes, I have been watching you from the moment you stepped from the bath, though you could not see me until moments later."

Tsuru frowned as he tightened the robe around his waist.

"The doctor has also developed the technology to block the

signal. So privacy is possible. Of course, once the holocomm is introduced to the worldwide market, there is probably another fortune to be made installing the security barriers."

Tsuru sank to his knees at the edge of the swirling sand garden. "And you want to sell this device to me. How much will it cost me?"

"I will trade you this device for the use of your Minuteman shares for a specified period."

The Japanese looked up suddenly. "I had heard whispers that someone was acquiring all the outstanding shares of the company. Is it true?"

Kelly remained silent.

"I presume my twelve shares are important to what can only be a hostile takeover."

"Are you willing to trade?"

"If you are intent on bringing down Royal Newton, I will give you the shares for nothing!"

"We have seventy shares." Kelly Edwards turned to Morgan d'Winter. She turned to look at the digital clock. "Or at least, we will have in fifteen minutes."

"They have begun the launch sequence," Xifo snarled into the communicator. "Within a matter of heartbeats, this planet will have destroyed itself, and the death of the world will be on our conscience. I have to intervene! You have to allow me to act!"

Reluctantly, only too aware of the consequences of their action, the Collegium voted. With one exception, they voted to establish a Clan Xifo presence on the Earth for its own preservation.

Dyckon dissented. He realized that the Humani Dee had run out of time. So now the world would end. The Clan Xifo would turn it into a slave colony, wipe out its technological advances, and then keep it in a primitive Dark Age—*for its own good.* Or so they would claim. And in a thousand years, maybe longer, when the Nephilim had stripped the world of all that it possessed, they would move on, leaving it a devastated shell. Dyckon swallowed the bitter bile of disappointment: to have come so close . . . and failed.

Dr. John Dee rounded the corridor, brought the crossbow up, and fired in one smooth movement. The bolt caught the first security officer high in the throat, catapulting him off his feet and into the second security officer, who stood guard outside Newton's control center. Before the stunned man could rise to his feet, Dee impaled him on the ancient sword in a swift, savage movement. The doctor placed his foot on the corpse's chest, and struggled to unsheathe the sword from the man. With a painful last tug, the Elizabethan freed his weapon and retrieved the used bolt from the other corpse's esophagus. Amid the blood that was pooling on the carpeted floor, Dee placed the crossbow's leather strap on the ground to step into it and bend the bow and reengage the bowstring behind the protruding nut. His swollen hand stung from the exertion. With his weapons at the ready, he took a moment to look around and get his bearings, only to realize he now stood outside the doors to Newton's inner sanctum. This was the entranceway to the private part of the castle. *Providence has been kind,* he told himself. *It has gotten me this far. Still,* he thought, *I must best the jackal in his own lair. Come what may, there's hard work to be done and the devil take the hindmost.*

As the doctor approached the doors, they slid silently open. He quickly ducked inside and swiftly crouched down, balancing on fingertips and toes. He swiveled around quickly, seeking out potential enemies. At first he thought that the enormous screen-filled room was empty; then he spotted the two mute, white-coated technicians standing on either side of a third, seated figure, all of them staring fixedly at the screen. Directly above their heads, a clock counted down from twelve minutes toward zero. Dee let fly a bolt through the screen, exploding it into a shower of sparks and glass. Acrid black smoke leaked from the carcass. The three men turned, wide-eyed, to look at the bloody stranger who was marching toward them, archaic weapons in hand. "Tell me how to get to Newton," he demanded, brandishing the sword.

"Easy," James Zhu said, appearing from behind Dee, a huge-barreled pistol in his hand. "You want Mr. Newton, you just follow me."

On the screen the clock ticked toward eleven minutes.

Royal Newton was standing with his back against the huge screen that counted up his wealth as Zhu pushed Dee into the room.

8,680,134,872,007

A small screen set alongside showed the clock ticking toward zero.

"I should kill you now," Newton snarled, rubbing his face in his hands, then drawing his hands back over his face. "But I'm not going to. I'm going to keep you alive, so that you can see Tiamat go live in . . ." He turned to look at the screen. "In ten minutes."

8,980,134,872,007

"Well then, villain, the world as you know it will be worm's meat in ten minutes. For generations to come, men will learn to curse the name of Newton. It will become another word for greed and stupidity."

Newton shook his head, light running liquid off his bald skull. "You really do believe this stuff."

"I do."

8,990,234,872,007

"Look around you. What do you see?"

Dee kept his gaze fixed on Newton's face. "I see the spoils of a greedy and stupid man, who has purloined the world of its treasures. A man for whom money is everything. A man who believes that everything has a price, that everything that is most dear can be bought and sold."

9,000,100,123,012

Eight minutes.

"If he moves, shoot him in the leg," Newton said tiredly. "I will give you a few minutes to understand the great gift that I am giving to the world. Unlimited power and the ability to defend ourselves from alien invasion."

Dee folded his arms across his chest. "Now sir, that is a hateful error. For even now, a great invasion fleet is amassing, preparing to descend upon the Earth. Check your seers, your farseers."

"You are a deluded fool, Dr. Dee."

"It would not be the first time I have been called so. Though I may be a fool, I am not foolish. Cry halt to this insane countdown." The doctor glanced quickly over his shoulder at James Zhu. "And you, sirrah, have you nothing to say?"

"I am not qualified to give you any answer."

"Newton pays your salary and you are his obedient lapdog."

Zhu prodded Dee's skull with the pistol. "That's right."

"Bravo, Mr. Zhu!" Newton beamed. "You see, Doctor, everything can be bought—even loyalty. Mr. Zhu is well paid to see things my way. It's in his best interest to do so. He knows where his bread is buttered. His loyalty will always be with me and Minuteman Holdings." Newton returned his gaze to the Tiamat screen. He waved Dee toward an empty chair. "Now, why don't you just relax, and watch history in the making."

On the world below, the Stock Exchange opened for the morning.

9,000,100,123,012

8,999,157,457,202

7,207,322,287,159

6,000,000,000,000

Dr. Dee stared at the countdown clock. There was but six minutes left. "Newton, listen to me, sir. Postpone Tiamat. Seek out the source of your clandestine informers. By whatever is holy to you, sir, I swear you are being gulled. Can you not wait but a day to have your minions prove if what I say be aye or nay? 'Sdeath, man. It will be well worth your time."

"Dee, time is money. In five minutes, the introduction of Tiamat will make me the CEO of the greatest, most lucrative industry ever conceived. The world will be forced to come to me, and only me, for cheap, inexhaustible energy. It is the beginning of a massive fortune. Richer by far than Minuteman Holdings ever made me. Waiting a day would cost me millions. So you see, even if your alien theory were real," and here he turned back to Dee and smiled, "and we all know it's pure science fiction, waiting even a nanosecond beyond the countdown is definitely not worth my time."

He turned back to his screen secretly pleased at the little speech he had made. Surprised that it had come off so much better than anything that he had ever planned to say.

"Mr. Newton," Zhu said confusedly. He was watching the movement on the larger screen and he hesitated, not sure of his next move.

"What?" Newton whispered, genuinely confused. "What?" he demanded, still concentrating on the Tiamat screen.

Five minutes.

Dee swiveled back toward Zhu, and followed the direction of his eyes. He rose from the chair and moved forward toward Newton's bald head. Zhu followed closely, the gun now listlessly resting in his hand.

Dee spoke first. "I came here to kill you but it seems I have achieved more, much more. It seems I have destroyed you."

Tiamat was going perfectly. It would all be in running order in a matter of moments.

"Be quiet! You are mad. Mad and raving." Newton grimaced fiercely and shook his head in annoyance at the disorder in his office behind him. It was too much to bear.

159,758,789,752

"But that I hate you deadly, I should lament your miserable state. Cease this monstrosity. Stop your countdown."

Newton, fixated on the action televised on the screen in front of him, shouted in his exasperation, "I am tired of his lunatic ramblings. Kill him. Kill him now."

000,000,000,000,000

A shimmering image abruptly twisted and formed in the center of the floor. Kelly Edwards and Morgan d'Winter were staring wide-eyed and smiling at the doctor. Kelly was grinning so widely, her new skin was cracking. "We did it, Doctor! We did it! You've won. You are the controlling stockholder of Minuteman Holdings."

The girl's voice nearly spun Newton out of his chair. He saw them, their shimmering presence violating his privacy. Their audacity outraged him and he took out all his fury on his incompetent bodyguard. His voice screeched. "How'd they get here? Kill him!" Newton shouted. "Kill him now. Kill them all, you son of a bitch. What are you waiting for?"

Dee turned to Zhu and held out his hand. Zhu silently placed the pistol into it, butt first.

"What are you doing? What are you doing! You work for me. For me! Who pays your salary?"

Zhu pointed toward the screen, and Newton turned, staring incredulously at the zeros crawling across the screen.

"The loyal Mr. Zhu is now in my employ," Dr. John Dee said evenly. The doctor passed the pistol back to Zhu. "Please stop the countdown." It was unlikely Royal Newton heard any of this exchange; his mind was wrapped around his lost trillions; the enormity of what had just occurred, the impossibility of it, suddenly swept up the length of his body, stabbing pains in his fingertips, along his left arm. As he fell forward, arms outstretched to embrace the screen, he realized that he was too young for a heart attack . . . and besides, the artificial heart was guaranteed for life.

"Stop!" Dyckon ab-ack na Khar shouted. "The countdown has stopped. We must withdraw our ships. The Humani have obviously seen the error of their ways and realized their danger."

The Xifo chose to disobey the direct order of the Collegium and commanded his ships to press on to take the Earth. However, he was ritually torn apart by his crew and ceremoniously eaten to expunge the error.

Later, much later, Dyckon appeared before Dee, using a variant of the holocomm technology. "I never doubted you," the Roc said.

"Nor did I," Dee said truthfully.

"You are a remarkable man, Dr. John Dee. More remarkable than these people will ever know."

"I had help. Right now," Dee said with a yawn, "I am just exhausted. After all, it isn't every day one gets to save an entire world. Let us see what wonders the morrow brings, eh?" Dee continued, "But first I must sleep."

"And dream?" Dyckon asked.

"I have no need to dream. My life is now dream enough."